DOUBLE DELIGHT

DOUBLE DELIGHT

ROSAMOND SMITH

A WILLIAM ABRAHAMS BOOK

DUTTON

DUTTON
Published by the Penguin Group
Penguin Books USA Inc., 375 Hudson Street, New York, New York 10014, U.S.A.
Penguin Books Ltd, 27 Wrights Lane, London W8 5TZ, England
Penguin Books Australia Ltd, Ringwood, Victoria, Australia
Penguin Books Canada Ltd, 10 Alcorn Avenue, Toronto, Ontario, Canada M4V 3B2
Penguin Books (N.Z.) Ltd, 182–190 Wairau Road, Auckland 10, New Zealand

Penguin Books Ltd, Registered Offices:
Harmondsworth, Middlesex, England

First published by Dutton, an imprint of Dutton Signet,
a division of Penguin Books USA Inc.
Distributed in Canada by McClelland & Stewart Inc.

First Printing, June, 1997
1 3 5 7 9 10 8 6 4 2

 REGISTERED TRADEMARK—MARCA REGISTRADA

LIBRARY OF CONGRESS CATALOGING-IN-PUBLICATION DATA
Smith, Rosamond.
Double delight : a novel / by Rosamond Smith.
p.   cm.
"A William Abrahams book."
ISBN 0-525-94299-8 (acid-free paper)
I. Title.
PS3565.A8D68   1997
813'.54—dc21   96-29873
CIP

Printed in the United States of America
Set in New Baskerville
Designed by Jesse Cohen

PUBLISHER'S NOTE

This is a work of fiction. Names, characters, places, and incidents either are the product of the author's imagination or are used fictitiously, and any resemblance to actual persons, living or dead, events, or locales is entirely coincidental.

for Rosemary Ahern

God is indeed a jealous God—
He cannot bear to see
That we had rather not with Him
But with each other play.
                    —*Emily Dickinson*

All things are possible, because all
things are ordained.
                    —*The Book of the Millennium*

CONTENTS

And now it was too late to turn back and there was a comfort, a relief, in that, in the knowledge that it was too late to turn back, he'd come too far to turn back. The oily waves slapped, nudged, mauled. How like human fists. *Swimming for my life* through moonlight like broken pieces of crockery, swallowing water, choking, unable to breathe except through his mouth, his breath like torn strips of cloth, legs heavy and shoulder muscles cramping as if it was a stranger's body in which he was trapped, doomed. Yet his senses remained alert, sharpened. Seeing ahead the agile swimming figures in the treacherous water as they passed swiftly into the shadow of the bridge, their flashing white feet, legs easing from him—*Help me! Don't leave me! Wait!*

The Summons

*S*trange *that it would come to me by such commonplace means* not by special delivery, or registered mail, but with the regular mail delivery. A few first-class letters, the usual bills, printed matter, advertising flyers. In a grimly official-looking manila envelope with a translucent oval window through which

GREENE TERENCE C
7 Juniper Way
Queenston NJ 08540

glared up at him like an accusation.

The return address was SHERIFF'S OFFICE, COUNTY OF MERCER, TRENTON, N.J. 08650.

It was a Saturday in late March. Overcast, smelling of wet, rotted leaves, with a faint undertaste of spring. A day of no significance except (but this could only be coincidence) it was the day before Terence Greene's forty-fourth birthday.

An event which, but for the arrival of the summons, Terence Greene would not have recalled.

———

"Daddy, something for you!—looks like *trouble.*"

Eleven-year-old Cindy, the Greenes' youngest child, was the one to bring Terence the summons. She called down into the basement, her voice thrilled. But where was Daddy? Why wasn't he interested? Annoyed, she called again, "Dad-*dy*. Mail."

Below, in semi-darkness, because one of the overhead lightbulbs had burnt out, Terence was absorbed in repairing a loose rubber tread on the basement stairs. His wife Phyllis had complained she'd almost tripped, might have broken her neck, so Terence was making the repair, or about to. The problem was, when he'd switched on the light over the steps there was a dazzling flash, and darkness. So he'd gone to look for a flashlight in the utility room, which required some minutes of searching since the flashlight wasn't in its designated place, and when he found it, he discovered that the battery was dead; so he'd gone off to search for a new battery, for he was sure he'd purchased more than one at the hardware store; this search led him, whistling thinly through his teeth, upstairs into the kitchen, to search the closet, and at last into the garage, to his work bench which was cluttered with tools, where he located a battery for the flashlight but was distracted by the realization, as he glanced about the garage, that he had much to do here. *My house, my home. My responsibility. And I am equal to it.*

He was husband, father, homeowner. What pleasure he took in a morning of simple, manual, household chores.

He had a wife, Phyllis. A nineteen-year-old son Aaron, now at Dartmouth. A fifteen-year-old daughter Kim. And eleven-year-old Cindy, once the baby of the family, whom Daddy loved beyond his love for the older children. *Because she is closest yet to babyhood, innocence.*

Only Cindy and Terence were home, in the Greenes' large colonial house at 7 Juniper Way. And Terence was preoccupied, frowning and smiling to himself, whistling, now back downstairs in the basement, shining the flashlight about into the shadows, where, to his dismay, he discovered the rolled-up carpet remnant he'd intended to haul upstairs and out to the curb for the Saturday morning trash pickup. "Damn!"—this was the third time he'd forgotten. That week, his wife had said, "Terry, you won't forget the carpet again, will you?" and Terence had laughed and said, "Certainly not."

But there it was. A memento, layered with dust, of the beige wall-to-wall carpeting they'd had installed in the family room a decade ago, or more—Cindy just an infant, Kim in first grade, Aaron a slim sweet-faced child who had adored his father. But several months ago Phyllis had had a new carpet installed in the family room, so what need was there of the old? None, obviously.

Grimacing, Terence tugged and shoved at the remnant, pushing it into the shadows beneath the basement steps. Since the trash pickup wasn't for another week, there was no point in keeping the bulky thing in plain view, and upsetting Phyllis.

Like the garage, the basement needed to be cleaned, cleared. Terence took note of that shelf cluttered with rusted, long-unused gardening tools, from an era when Phyllis had had time for tending rosebushes. Another shelf, weighted with yellowed copies of *The Way, The Truth, and The Light*, a religious journal of conservative political opinions faithfully passed on, for years, to the Greenes from Phyllis's lately deceased father, a Presbyterian minister of New Bedford, Massachusetts. And cast-off sports equipment of Aaron's, devoutly requested and soon neglected: an absurdly expensive German-manufactured tennis racquet that, in Aaron's judgment, "wasn't worth shit," and twenty-pound dumbbells and other weightlifting equipment that within weeks had bored an impatient teenager. Seeing these things, and numerous others, Terence felt his throat constrict. For here was the shadowland of the household, the graveyard. He'd clear it out another time.

Shame. Hettie's boy, isn't he? But how much does he know?
But look where he lives! He's in charge.

Tuffi appeared suddenly underfoot, wanting affection, wanting to be fed. Terence said, exasperated, "But you were just fed, Tuffi, weren't you?" The terrier was quivering with emotion; since Aaron's departure the house was too large and too lonely; Terence could see the mute animal perplexity in Tuffi's liquidy amber eyes, but had no time for it now. Once a puppy, everybody's darling, Tuffi was now an aging thick-bodied dog with graying whiskers and an occasional odor as of decomposing organic matter. Terence sighed, and rubbed Tuffi's bony head, and accepted the eager silky-damp licking of Tuffi's tongue against his fingers. "Yes, yes, good dog, good Tuffi, of course you're loved, never doubt it!"— so Terence murmured, pouring dog chow into Tuffi's empty bowl. Though it was not a good idea, and how many times he'd instructed the children, to indulge an overweight dog.

Terence went to fetch his hammer, where had he left his hammer?—feeling a touch of panic, that Saturday morning was passing so swiftly. It was a time precious to him, hours of quiet, privacy, household chores. A day when he didn't have to commute to 81 Park Avenue, Manhattan, to the headquarters of the Nelson P. Feinemann Memorial Foundation where he was executive director, as he did five days a week; a day he could take a curious, stubborn pleasure in tending to the house in which he and his family lived. What anonymity in household tasks. For while *Terence C. Greene* was a name of distinction, authority, power in certain quarters, it was not a name that, murmured aloud, in the basement of his house, would seem to mean much at all.

Overhead, the sound of Cindy's footsteps. On Saturday mornings the child was lonely, restless. In imitation of her mother and her sister she ran and rushed about, breathless, yet with no evident objective, no clear purpose. Somehow she seemed not to have friends, or at any rate friends who lived near Juniper Place. Thinking of Cindy, hoping Cindy didn't know where he was, Terence felt a prick of tenderness, guilt.

He wondered if in all families there was one child about whom a parent felt somehow guilty *as if I can't protect her enough, shield her from hurt.* His older children Aaron and Kim he'd had to surrender, they weren't children any longer, not as they'd been; they hadn't need of Daddy's protection, and certainly didn't want it. But Cindy. Cindy was different. Too intelligent for her childish ways, too childish for her intelligence. *The one most like myself, that must be it.*

Terence gripped the twelve-inch claw hammer in his right hand, swinging it in a short arc. He wondered how many millenia had passed before the human hand had evolved such a tool. The ordinary household hammer was a model of efficiency and compression: the handle a marvel of simplicity and the head an ingenious combination of power (the power to pound nails *in*) and its reversal (the power to pull nails *out*). Since becoming a homeowner, Terence had come to love the feel of a tool in his hand: screwdriver, pliers, saw, hammer. In the local hardware store he admired those tools—power saws, axes—for which he had no use. He stocked up on nails, screws, bolts, washers. There was a pleasure in purchasing such things as if he were demonstrating to the hardware clerk and the other customers that he, Terence Greene, was certainly one of them. His name, his address, there on his credit card, stamped in raised plastic letters, like Braille.

Terence C. Greene.

Terence smiled. He'd created an identity for himself, and a personality to inhabit it, affable, reasonable, good-hearted and a good citizen, the way, as a shy but gifted child, he'd modeled clay figures in school.

No one in Queenston knew of his past. Not even that it was a shadowy, mysterious past, only haphazardly known to Terence Greene himself.

"Daddy?—mail's here!"

Cindy had discovered him after all, and was calling down the stairs excitedly.

"Something for you, Daddy—looks like *trouble.*"

So Terence came upstairs, not having nailed down the loose tread, annoyed at the interruption but determined not to seem so. He ran his fingers lightly through Cindy's wind-blown hair and said, "Yes, sweetie? What's up?" Tuffi, too, nudged at Terence's heels, aroused by Cindy's excitement.

"From the sheriff, it says. Oh, Daddy—I wonder what it *is.*"

Cindy handed Terence the official-looking manila envelope. Her eyes were widened, her voice thrilled.

Terence frowned at the envelope, the computer-printed name and address. He had no reason to fear the police, certainly no reason, yet the printed words SHERIFF'S OFFICE, COUNTY OF MERCER, TRENTON, N.J. 08650 made him flinch.

What do they want with me? They have no right.

Terence supposed the envelope contained nothing crucial, since it had come by first-class mail. Still he felt a moment's unease. Resentment.

He smiled, teasing Cindy. For the child was lonely, in one of her moods, melancholy tinged with grating exuberance. He made a gesture as if to tear the envelope in two, saying, "What do I care about the 'sheriff of Mercer County'?—what can he do to *me?*" and Cindy gave a startled little cry and stopped his hand. "Daddy, don't! You might be *arrested.*"

Clearly, Cindy was frightened for him. She was excitable, anxious. Terence supposed she must be dieting again, starving herself. She could not have been more than five pounds overweight, with the fair, rosy complexion and softly shaped body of a child in a Renoir painting; to his fatherly eye a beautiful child, if fidgety, and lacking grace; to Cindy herself, pitiless in judgment, fat, ugly. What was that terrible word children used repeatedly, curling their lips as they uttered it—"Gross."

Shrewdly Terrence said, holding the manila envelope at arm's length, "Let's make a deal, honey. I'll open the letter if you eat some breakfast."

Cindy's pale green eyes fluttered. She said evasively, weakly, "Daddy, I had breakfast."

"No, you didn't."

"Oh, how do *you* know?"

Terence didn't know; but saw by Cindy's expression of guilt and defiance that he was right. He felt a moment's annoyance at Phyllis, who'd gone off in her car on a round of Saturday errands without making sure that their daughter, who'd been eating erratically for weeks, had eaten a proper breakfast that morning. "Daddy, I can't. Don't make me, I *can't*," Cindy said, her lower lip trembling, and Terence said, smiling, "Just a bowl of cereal, sweetie? Why not? And I'll open my letter," and Cindy said, "If I start eating I'll just get hungry, it always happens that way, *I hate it*," and Terence said, touching the child's feverish cheek, "You're hungry because you haven't eaten, which is why you should eat. Isn't that reasonable?"

Cindy shrugged. "If you say so, Daddy."

Allowing herself to be led, sullen but unresisting, to the formica-topped breakfast nook where, whistling cheerfully, clowning as he'd always done, as Daddy, in the challenging role of Daddy, when trying to inveigle his children into behaving sensibly, Terence briskly set out breakfast foods: a box of raisin granola, a ripe banana, a quart of vitamin-enriched skim milk. Cindy sighed, and picked up a spoon, and, head bowed, out of daughterly duty it seemed, began to eat. Terence discreetly looked away, not wanting to discomfort her. She was a child of eleven with a hearty appetite, and clearly ravenous.

Terence understood his daughter's predicament. She was the younger sister of a very pretty, popular, self-absorbed teenaged girl. The daughter of an energetic, attractive, and frequently quite critical woman.

"Daddy, open your letter now," Cindy said, her mouth full.

Terence pretended he'd misplaced the letter, making Cindy laugh by discovering it, with a look of alarm, inside his shirt. He ripped it open ceremoniously and out fluttered a pink printed form—" 'Summons for jury service.' Well, at least I haven't been arrested."

" 'Jury service'? A trial? Oh Daddy, that's cool."

Terence scanned the document, which was the most perfunctory of forms; not only computer-generated but a poor carbon copy. In a mock-pompous voice he read, " 'You are hereby summoned to appear at the Mercer County Courthouse, 209 South Broad Street, Trenton, New Jersey, to serve as a petit juror commencing on the seventeenth day of June, at eight thirty A.M. By order of the court.' "

Odd how his hand, holding the summons, was trembling. He hoped Cindy didn't see.

Cindy said, disappointed, "Not until *June*? That's so far away. I wish the trial was *now*."

Terence said carefully, "The summons doesn't mean that I'll be chosen for a jury, Cindy. That I'll be judging an actual trial. It just means that I'll be considered."

The past year had been one of highly publicized and lurid trials across the country. Multiple murders, celebrity murders, rape, police brutality and corruption, terrorism. The idea of *the public trial* was in the air, like festive carnival music. Cindy said, "I hope it's a murder case, Daddy! First-degree! New Jersey has the death penalty and they're going to start it again, soon—'lethal injection.' We were discussing it in social studies."

"In sixth grade, discussing the death penalty?" Terence was startled.

Cindy laughed. She was always delighted, like the older children, when her father expressed surprise at the most obvious things; it restored her faith in the fallibility of adults. "Oh, Daddy," she said, clicking her teeth against the spoon, "—we discuss all sorts of things in school. Sex crimes, AIDS, capital punishment, *politics*."

"Do you! Well, I suppose, yes."

Feeling rebuked, Terence quickly folded the summons,

and stuffed it into a pocket, and returned to the basement, to continue his morning of tasks.

Phyllis said, concerned, "But, Terry, you can get out of jury duty: I did, everyone does. Don't worry."

Terence protested, "But why would I want to get out of jury duty, Phyllis? I think it might be interesting."

"It would be a terrible waste of time."

"Why not think of it as a privilege, really? I've never once been summoned—"

"Yes, you've been fortunate."

"It *is* a privilege. In a democracy—"

Phyllis stared at him, as if she believed he must be joking. She said, "Your work at the Foundation is much too important, and you're much too busy, to waste time sitting around that dreary courthouse, in dreary Trenton. Tonight, we can ask Matt Montgomery what the most practical excuse is for someone in your position. A judicious telephone call might get your name off the computer altogether."

"But—"

"Terry, everyone knows that jury duty is an absolute waste of time. Unless you're a person who doesn't have responsible work, and is expendable; or retired, with nothing better to do. Or you're investigating the system, writing a book—whatever. You wouldn't be chosen for a jury, probably, in any case. You'd simply be kept penned up in the assembly room for five days straight, as I was. You couldn't bear it."

Terence said, stubbornly, "How can you be certain, Phyllis, what I can bear? And why wouldn't I be chosen, as well as anyone?"

"Because prosecuting attorneys in Trenton think that Queenston residents are too 'liberal'—that is, intelligent and fair-minded; and defense attorneys think we're too 'conservative'—that is, too smart to be manipulated by their rhetoric and tricks." Phyllis smiled at Terence, with an air of knowing something about him unknown to Terence himself. "They want average Americans on juries, darling. Or sub-average. Not *you*."

Terence persisted, "But I am an average American. In my heart."

Phyllis frowned at him, as if his remarks were beginning to offend. "Don't be perverse, of course you're not."

"Tomorrow I'll be forty-four years old—"

"Now what has *that* got to do with it?" Phyllis was thirteen months older than Terence, and in recent years had become sensitive about remarks related to age.

"—and not once have I been called for jury duty. I happen to think it would be an interesting experience."

"No, it wouldn't," Phyllis said, as if she'd indulged Terence long enough. "Even if you were named a juror, which isn't likely, the trial would be dismal and depressing—probably drug-related. Trenton is such a depressed city, you'd come away miserable. You're so susceptible to—atmospheres, moods. Believe me, darling, I know you." Phyllis was trying to speak lightly, but her appeal was uncharacteristically urgent. She even leaned against him, and kissed his cheek. "Don't I?"

"I suppose so, yes."

Terence sighed, like a child cheated of an adventure.

And now, dusk. And now, the outer life.

Cocktails at the Hendries'?—dinner at the Montgomerys'? Unless it was the other way around.

In Queenston, all seasons were social seasons. Another sort of music, not a carnival music exactly but festive, distracting, continually played. You could not blame a woman like Phyllis for always listening for it, smiling in anticipation of a ringing telephone, an invitation. Yes, you see, we're loved, we exist! We've been *invited*.

In affluent Queenston, Terence C. Greene endured two overlapping identities. One was that of the husband of Phyllis Greene, whom everyone knew and liked, or in any case admired; the other was that of the executive director of the Feinemann Foundation, about which they read occasionally in *The New York Times*. It wasn't clear what Terence did, except oversee the granting of more than $8 million yearly to American museums, theaters, dance troupes, individual artists. The Greenes' friends and neighbors were lawyers, stockbrokers, bankers, business executives, developers, speculators, and here and there someone associated with the "arts"—all with comfortable incomes.

Hettie's boy, among them. As if he were one of them.

In fact, it was Phyllis's income from inherited investments and cash gifts from her parents that made the Greenes' social position in Queenston possible. It was the result of a generous cash wedding gift—"To help you young people get started"—that they'd been able to buy the six-bedroom Neo-Georgian colonial on Juniper Way, Timberlane Estates.

"—You really shouldn't have interfered, Terry. Of course I don't know what the circumstances were, but she says you forced food on her. And now—"

There was an air of hurt and accusation in Phyllis's voice which she tried to disguise with exasperated laughter. Terence, absentmindedly selecting a necktie from the many ties hanging in his closet, murmured a chastened assent.

"—one of her binges, the poor child. All she ate!—I stopped her from telling me, it was too sad. At least she doesn't make herself vomit, like these bulimic teenaged girls you hear about. If that comes next—!"

Terence frowned at himself in the bureau mirror. In certain lights, his face, his very head, looked *carved.* A wooden man, an upright animated doll. Inside the eyes, an unknowable life.

"Because," Phyllis was saying, angry, hurt, "—we have the same features, skin coloring, body type. She blames *me.*"

Without pausing in her monologue, Phyllis came to take away the gray-striped necktie Terence was holding, and handed him, in its place, a sleek navy blue silk tie, a recent purchase of hers. Unquestioning, Terence knotted it about his neck.

The tie was beautiful, and, oddly, he was a handsome man. The lean, angular face, the nostrils wide and dark like cavities, the pebbly-green eyes with their look of sweetly confused expectation—somehow, his unpromising features added up. And he smiled a good deal, even through a look of pain.

Phyllis murmured, "And Kim!—I swear, she's trying to break my heart. She used to be so sweet, she was my little girl, remember?—and now!—since that damned slumber party at Suzi Ryan's when I caught her in a lie I simply can't *trust* her."

Terence, searching for the mate of a cuff link he held in his hand, murmured a guarded acquiescence. He knew from past experience that it was unwise to agree too readily with Phyllis when she condemned their children.

"—So completely different, hair, skin coloring, body type, she might as well be adopted. And she behaves like it!"

Terence had put the summons to jury service on his desk, downstairs in his study. He would deal with it on Monday morning. Phyllis was right, of course: He would arrange to be exempted.

"—her friends, and not us. When did it happen, was it overnight? And boys. Boys! If her phone isn't ringing, it's because the pack of them is here." A pause. "Of course, she *is* pretty. Mother thinks she has *her* eyes."

In her stocking feet, graceful, but brisk, Phyllis came to Terence, again without pausing in her speech, and reached into the drawer in which Terence was searching, to withdraw a jeweler's box—which, opened, yielded, not the missing mate, but another pair of cuff links. These were splendid gold cuff links shaped in the initials *TG*, a birthday gift from Reverend and Mrs. Winston some years ago.

Terence murmured thanks, and bent to kiss Phyllis's cheek. But she was gone.

Holding a yellow dress up against herself, frowning into

the full-length mirror, "—And Aaron: Did you call him, as you promised? No? Tomorrow, then? I know he never returns calls, I must have left a dozen messages last time, but you should *try*. No matter what he says, I think he's troubled about something. It's that terrible pressure at Dartmouth, as bad as at Harvard, or Princeton—and of course they grow up so much faster than we did. He respects you, at least. You must *try*. He has accused me of—well, snooping! I just have to learn to remain calm. Matt Montgomery says it's all in the tone of voice—and eye contact. With children, as with voters. Terry, are you listening? Find out what Aaron did with that four hundred dollars we sent, but don't alienate him. It isn't the money—I mean, not simply the money—but reassurance he needs that he's *loved*."

At this, Terence, struggling with the cuff links, made a snorting sound. Not quite laughter, not quite derision. Phyllis cast him a swift sidelong look of reproach.

"It *is*. You judge your son too harshly. Just because he has that air of—well, he's combative, I know; but that doesn't mean he isn't sensitive, and doesn't need our love. Ever since the skiing equipment—"

Terence, not wanting to be drawn, as into a whirlpool, into this particular subject, hastily murmured agreement.

"—So, tomorrow? Terry? Just before noon, when he's likely to be still in bed?"

Terence murmured yes.

"—and I'll listen in on the extension. In absolute silence."

With a disappointed gesture, Phyllis had tossed aside the yellow dress, and was now slipping over her head a black dress that shimmered seductively over her hips, and curved out quite impressively at her breasts. Terence, watching his wife through not one but two mirrors, felt a remote stab of desire: How beautiful Phyllis was, when not looking directly at him.

"—And tonight, be sure to congratulate Matt on his speech to the Central Jersey Realtors. He really did get a standing ovation—almost! And that interview I arranged for him in the *Chronicle*—did you ever get around to reading it? No? Oh, Terry! Matt is a good friend, and my client, you should take some interest. I will admit his campaign got off to a rocky start, but—''

Phyllis was now speaking of her work as a publicist. (At the age of forty, she had decided to start a public relations business in Queenston—"Queenston Opportunities"—with some of the money left her by her late father.) As always when Phyllis spoke of her one-woman enterprise, her voice lifted with girlish excitement; her face seemed to lighten.

"—And mention it to Hedy too, will you?"—Hedy Montgomery was Matt Montgomery's wife—"I'm afraid she's becoming just a little—cool. Jealous. As if Matt and I—!''

Terence murmured yes, he certainly would.

The recession had hurt Phyllis's business, as it had hurt many small businesses of its type, but, supported by her investment income, Phyllis had kept it afloat; even, for two or three months, without clients. It would have broken her heart, she'd said, if she'd had to give up her newly furnished office in the Village. Terence sympathized with Phyllis's ambition to *do something*, to make a name for herself locally— he thought it ironic that his wife's ambition exceeded his own.

Currently, Phyllis had her most ambitious project to date. She was managing the campaign of their friend Matt Montgomery for Queenston Township supervisor. Montgomery was a private attorney actively involved in zoning and environmental issues, a prominent Queenston resident, and how well he did in the upcoming April election—how skillfully Phyllis Greene was judged to have guided his campaign—was certain to be a matter of common knowledge, and gossip, in the area.

With sudden vehemence, as if her thoughts exactly paralleled Terence's, Phyllis said, "I know that everyone—even my friends—even my family!—is waiting for me to fail. *But I won't give you the satisfaction.*"

Terence protested at once, surely this was untrue?—unjust?—but Phyllis waved him aside. "I say no: *I will not.*"

How severely she was eyeing her mirrored reflection, flat-footed, brooding, with a petulant twist of her mouth. Terence saw, not for the first time precisely, but for the first time with such poignancy, that his wife, attractive, self-assured, financially independent, was yet a mysteriously disappointed woman.

She was shapely and compact, in height about five feet three (in her stocking feet, as now); with blond-streaked hair that lifted from her forehead like a bird's crest, artfully waved and sculpted; her face was round, full, inclining to plumpness. During the day, no less than in the evening, she was elaborately made up; at night, she applied medicinal-smelling creams and oils to her face. (Had Terence ever seen his wife's face naked, exposed?—raw?) She was particularly conscious, and critical, of her eyes, which were too small, for her taste, and required eye shadow, eyeliner, mascaras—"A lifetime disappointment." Yet, for all this, Phyllis Greene was attractive; in fact, quite glamorous. If her moods at home with her family were mercurial ("There Mom goes again!" was a cheeky refrain of Aaron's, for years), her mood in public was unwavering: She'd become, with years of practice, one of those supremely confident affluent suburban American women in whom The Smile has become an art.

How such women smile, and smile!—it wearied Terence Greene, just to observe.

In Phyllis, it was indeed The Radiant Smile: Erupting with such force when she entered any social gathering or public place, such a beam of joy, bounty, magnanimity toward all, its effect was one of sudden music, or laughter; of a dazzling blinding spotlight shone into dark corners, banishing all shadows. Seeing Phyllis release The Radiant Smile as they entered a crowded, festive room, and seeing how other, kindred smiles were released, in their direction, Terence felt himself blessed. *I have married my salvation.*

For why otherwise do we fall in love, except to be saved. By another's love. Another's power.

Twenty-two years ago, Phyllis Winston had been a virginal young woman, a minister's daughter—very pretty, very assured, of that type of American girl defined as "popular" in high school—with whom penniless Terence Greene had fallen in love during the frantic summer after his graduation from college. He had been awarded a graduate fellowship to study for his Ph.D. in history, at Harvard; through his four years as an undergraduate he'd earned consistently high grades, and the admiration of his professors; but he was in debt for thousands of dollars, and desperate to repay his loans; he'd signed on to work an exhausting ten-hour shift at a "historic" resort hotel in Rockport, Massachusetts, where, that June, a gathering of Presbyterian clergymen had convened. (Rockport had been chosen because it was a dry town, and the hotel served no alcohol—as Terence belatedly discovered, nondrinkers are notoriously frugal tippers.) Among the clergymen was the kindly, avuncular Reverend Willard Winston, accompanied by his wife and daughter. How sweetly the daughter smiled at Terence Greene, the young waiter assigned to the Winstons' table in the vast hotel dining room: Terence who was tall, attractive, deferential, and self-conscious in his white linen uniform; how nice, how generous, and how Christian of this striking young woman to speak to him, in the dining room and elsewhere, as if they were equals; even, it seemed, to seek him out with a friendly smile. That smile!

Terence, a lonely young man beset by fears of inadequacy, which no amount of academic success could quite assuage, had been astonished that Phyllis Winston, Reverend Winston's daughter, should notice him at all. How wonderful the young woman was in her openness, her female *energy*. Phyllis was quick to assure Terence that, while she was a Christian of course, she wasn't at all pious or excessively devout: Religion was a part of her life but not her *life*. Avidly, they'd discussed social issues of the day, civil rights, the newest books, films, art; whether God exists or whether (Terence thought himself daring, to speak of such a possibility to a minister's daughter) we have created Him in our own image.

Phyllis's serene smiling attitude was most impressive: "Oh, well—*faith* takes care of that."

She'd been the one to initiate their kisses. And more.

"You seem so lonely, Terence. Your eyes—you look like an orphan."

Her words were not so blunt and condescending as they might seem but had been expressed with girlish sincerity, warmth. Terence, struck to the heart, had tried to laugh, and stammered a clumsy joke, "So that's what I look like—an orphan. I've always wondered."

In this way he fell in love. The waves of the wild Atlantic lapping, licking, crashing about his head.

If such a woman loves me, marries me—I must be worthy after all.

"—listening, Terry? Please remember."

Terence saw that Phyllis had changed her dress another time. She was now wearing cream-colored silky pleats, a shimmering skirt of pleats, he was himself zipping her up the back, with an air of finality. Husbandly, overcome by love, Terence bent to kiss his wife on the nape of her neck. She shivered, and laughed. As if the gesture was unexpected.

Terence saw that, somehow, he'd gotten dressed as well. How it happens, how our nakedness is covered, what a mystery! He smiled to see himself such a Queenston citizen, an imposter in a gray pin-striped flannel suit that gave his lanky body a distinguished look, a suit Phyllis had selected for him at the Queenston Esquire Shoppe; his dress shirt was of starched white cotton; the gold-gleaming *TG* cuff links were properly in place at his wrists. And the navy blue silk tie perfectly knotted. A wooden man, a sharp-carved face, and the eyes trapped inside, alert.

Terence, giving in to vanity, in a gesture that reminded him of Aaron, preening and primping at a mirror, turned just slightly sideways, to examine what he could see of his profile. Since he'd begun swimming in earnest at a local health club, rarely less than five mornings a week, his posture had decidedly improved.

Phyllis was switching off the light, Terence followed her from the room. "—doors and windows, Terry? And the basement. And, of course, the burglar alarm. Oh, I hate that alarm. I'm afraid of it—"

Terence was already moving off, briskly. He liked to prepare the house for his departure because it was a way of preparing the house for his return.

Part of his routine was to check even the windows on the second floor. Though knowing they were locked, or should have been. In theory, a canny burglar could climb up onto the garage, and make his way across the roof to the bedroom windows. Were Terence Greene a housebreaker, that was the route he would take.

But all the houses in Timberlane Estates, as generally in Queenston, were protected by burglar alarms. In theory, no house could be entered in such a way. Violated.

Terence knocked on Cindy's shut door. The father of daughters, he knew never to open such a door uninvited. The child, though inside, did not reply at first; there was a murmur of music, voices. "Cindy-honey, it's Daddy." He heard a reluctant *Okay, Daddy,* and opened the door to poke his head inside, playful-Daddy, clown-Daddy, appealing to his eleven-year-old as if he were of her generation, and no threat. He saw that she was alone—of course, Kim, though home, would not care to keep company with her younger sister; slumped in an oversized T-shirt in front of the television set where, yet again, *Dirty Dancing* was in rowdy noisy full-frontal force. (Cindy owned the video. Though she often expressed contempt for those girls in her class who watched such videos repeatedly.)

"Cindy, we're leaving now, and we should be back by midnight. Kim's staying in, you know. Try to get to bed at a reasonable hour, will you?"

"Sure, Daddy." Cindy barely moved her eyes from the

television screen. She was puffy-eyed and sullen from (Terence gathered) an afternoon of intermittent quarreling with her mother; whether about her compulsive eating habits, or other matters, Terence was excluded from knowing.

"Promise? And tomorrow we'll have an outing of our own. We'll—"

Terence's voice trailed off. He wasn't sure what they might do the next day, Sunday. His birthday? He was of the vague impression that Phyllis had planned something.

"Sure, Daddy."

Cindy shifted her shoulders in the slovenly T-shirt, in a negligent shrug very like an elegantly dismissive gesture of her mother's. As if she were embarrassed of her daddy's cheery manner, his phony smile. *She sees through me* Terence thought, alarmed. *But what does she see?*

On the television screen, the animated, antic figures of impossibly good-looking young people writhed, rocked, spun, stomped to a harsh percussive music, unmistakable as the rhythms of copulation.

Terence Greene, who was Daddy, gently shut the door of his daughter's room, as if erasing himself.

But where was Kim, Kim wasn't in her room?—downstairs somewhere, Terence supposed. Quickly he checked windows, yes all the windows were locked for he himself had locked them, and checked them, numerous times. The six-bedroom brick, stucco, and wood Neo-Georgian "Custom Colonial" on two and a half acres of prime land, three miles outside the village of Queenston, would not have been Terence's personal choice for a house, the first time he'd seen it, in the company of Phyllis's parents, he'd winced at its size and pretentiousness—the extended width of its facade, the portico and columns and prominent brick chimneys—and the grotesque, inflated price! Even the sign had offended him—LUXURY ELITE CUSTOM-BUILT HOME PRESTIGE SETTING. For what was the house but a disguised tract home, exactly like others in the Timberland Estates development in basic design and differing only in superficial details like the color of the many shutters and the positioning of the three-car garage. Terence had wanted an older, smaller house farther out in the country, or in the village, within walking distance of the train depot; but Phyllis, like Mr. and Mrs. Winston, had loved the house; and the house was to be a wedding gift from the elder Winstons, after all—"You young people must allow us to do *something* for you!"

A *something* that would be replicated, over the course of years, into numerous *things*. Terence, the son-in-law, had not felt, in the face of his young family's enthusiasm for gifts, any protestation of his would be welcome.

Outside, the rapidly waning March light had acquired a silvery cast. Rain splattered the windows like unwanted thoughts. Why did he and Phyllis go out so frequently, every weekend without fail? Why not stay home with the girls, for a change?

Something, well of course it must be the summons, the summons—

All that day, since morning, since he'd ripped open the manila envelope from the sheriff's office, he'd been feeling uneasy. Not himself. Why?

No right. What right have they.

Terence was thinking of his lost childhood, how he'd been sent about, sometimes by Greyhound bus, to live with relatives; and finally placed, aged ten, in a foster home. The first of several foster homes. By the time he'd been the age Cindy was now, he hadn't been what you would call a child any longer. Of Daddy's early life, his children knew nothing. Phyllis, though always sympathetic, knew little. For what point was there in revealing sad, sordid facts of personal history to one who loves you, and whom you love? And, truly, Terence had forgotten most of it. *Hettie's boy, that's his strength. Forgetting.* The only household of his distant past he could recall clearly was the ramshackle old stone farmhouse in Shaheen, New York, a rural community in the foothills of the Adirondack Mountains. He'd been taken in as a child of about five, to live there with an older half-sister of his mother and her family of four boisterous children and a truck-driver husband who'd tried, not very effectively, to teach Terence to box, to protect himself from the tough farm boys at the country school, and, more successfully, to swim. Aunt Megan had loved Terence, hadn't she? And Uncle Frank? But then, when Terence was nine, his aunt had died of pancreatic cancer, the fastest, most lethal cancer of all.

"Daddy!—*oh!*"

The outcry was indignant, furious. Terence had absent-mindedly opened the door to the family room, to glance inside; he found himself staring into the shadows where on a sofa his daughter Kim and another teenager—a boy?—long straggly hair, pasty face, skinny hips?—were squirming together like eels, or had been when he'd blundered into the room. Close by them, the gigantic television set, a new purchase, loomed above them: The screen was antic with flailing, gyrating adolescent bodies—MTV, the volume reduced to near-audible shrieks and thumps.

"Daddy, gee!—you could knock, at *least.*" Kim, quickly on her feet and pouting, brushed her long russet-red hair out of her overheated face, and tugged down her tiny pink sweater, so tight and fine-knit that it showed the imprints of her individual ribs, her friend, hurriedly on his feet, tugged too at his clothing, and wiped at his mouth, and gave Terence a wide, gleaming sort of smile. With startling composure, in the deep, gravelly voice of an adult man, he said, "Hiya! Mr. Greene, eh? I'm Studs Schrieber, gladtameetcha!" The boy was perhaps seventeen years old, with dark, sunken eyes, a pale grainy skin, puffy moist lips, a half-dozen earrings in each ear, and a tiny gold ring through his nostril. To Terence's astonishment, he shot out his hand to be shaken.

Terence had to check himself not to come forward to shake the boy's hand: The social gesture had lodged in him so deep, it had acquired the force of biological instinct.

He stammered, "What are you doing here? What is going on?"

The young people answered at once, as a duet, yet uncoordinated—Kim in childlike protest, Studs Schrieber with ease. *"Watching TV!"*

A rule had recently come into force in the Greenes' household: Kim, grown alarmingly popular this past year, was not to entertain any friends, girls or boys, without informing her parents; and never any boy in her room upstairs.

Terence strode to the television set and switched it off. Kim continued to protest, and Studs Schrieber continued to smile inanely at him, his hand extended to be shaken. "Mr. Greene, uh—? I'm Studs Schrieber, and—" The nose ring glittered, like the boy's small, crowded-together teeth.

Calmly Terence said, "Yes. Good. But you'd better leave, you. You'd better leave. Now. Right now."

"Ya, sure, Mr. Greene, I was just going, only—"

"Daddy, you are so *rude*! Studs and I were just—"

"I know, I know, and that's fine, that's fine, but—the visit is over now, you see."

"Gee, Mr. Greene, you mad or something? It's all cool, really—ya know?"

"I know! I know. But the visit is over for today."

Only reluctantly, as if he were slow to acknowledge Terence's poor manners, did Studs Schrieber withdraw his hand; and even then he continued to smile, though wanly, with an air of being hurt. He touched the nose ring lightly. He brushed his straggly hair out of his face. He winked at Kim —*was that what he did? winked?*—and, as if resigned, turned to stomp snakeskin boots on his feet. (He'd been in his stocking feet, on the sofa.) He was a sinewy boy, very thin, but probably strong, like a snake. He wore black—tight black T-shirt that showed his tiny nipples, black denim, black socks and black boots. The hairs on his forearms were starkly black and wavy and Terence had a swift shuddering vision of his hairy, monkeylike naked body—the thick tufts and swirls of black hair on the torso, the belly, the region of the genitals. *An animal, upright.*

Sharp-eyed Studs Schrieber saw the sick look in Terence's face but said, affably, "Hey Mr. G., sorry to getcha all upset or whatever," as if it were a joke between them, a masculine joke passing Kim's comprehension, "—like I said, I'm outta here. Right, Kim? Cool!" The boy laughed, snatching up a designer denim jacket with an obscene flapping red tongue stitched on its back; he dared to grin, nose ring twinkling, at Terence. His dark eyes shone with good humor.

Terence was trembling. But managed to maintain an air of polite calm. As, at the Feinemann Foundation, in the midst of heated, protracted arguments among fellowship judges, he was the model of reasonable behavior, dignity. He walked with the departing boy and his embarrassed daughter to the front door of the house and waited pointedly as they whispered good night; noting that they did not kiss; did not dare to kiss; and when Studs Schrieber trotted down the walk, the red tongue flapping goodbye, it was Terence who shut the door firmly after him, and bolted it.

"Jesus!" he whispered.

At once, Kim became hysterical. "Daddy, how could you! So *rude*! So low-*minded*! I'm so *ashamed*! We weren't doing any*thing*! You know we *weren't*! Studs will laugh at me, he'll tell everybody, oh Daddy I hate you, I want to *die*!" The tilting escalation of Kim's voice, the way in which her warm brown eyes brimmed with tears of indignation and loathing suggested how the girl had learned from her mother; Terence was stunned, seeing the mother in the daughter, and not knowing how, to whom, to respond. He tried to touch Kim but she shrank from him, exactly as Phyllis might have done at such a time, crying, "Don't you touch me, *I hate you I said!*" She pushed past her stricken father, and ran upstairs to her room. For a girl who probably weighed less than one hundred pounds, her fury had the power of making the entire house shake.

Terence took from his breast pocket the pristine white cotton handkerchief Phyllis had so carefully folded into it,

and wiped his face. He was shaking, his mouth was dry. Yet
he smiled. For it *was* funny, wasn't it? Normal, American?
Like something on TV?

The unfortunate incident in the family room had occurred shortly after six; the cocktail party at the Hendries'
was scheduled to begin at six; but it would not be until six-
forty that Phyllis emerged from Kim's room, and came downstairs to join Terence, after having comforted the girl. During
this time Terence, the loathed Daddy, paced about in the
foyer, in the dining room, in his study. His heart was still beating hard, his mouth was still dry. If it hadn't been for the nose
ring, he was thinking. Or the flapping red tongue. If—

Phyllis, in her cream-colored pleated dress, was still
lovely; and not nearly so angry as Terence expected. She'd
been crying, but the color was in her cheeks, and her gaze,
meeting Terence's, was sympathetic. They clutched hands,
like survivors. "Doesn't it always happen, Terry? Just as we're
going out?"

"Is Kim—all right? She seemed—"

"If it isn't one of the girls, it's the other. Cindy all day,
punishing me for mentioning so very discreetly that, yes, she
is a bit overweight—she *is*, why pretend otherwise?—and
now Kim, flaunting this boyfriend of hers. Do you think
it's Freudian?—unconscious? Adolescent girls and their
mother?" Phyllis laughed, wiping at an eye, carefully, not to
smudge her mascara. "It has nothing to do with you, Terry
—don't blame yourself. It's all between daughter and
mother, and mother happens to be *me*."

Phyllis was breathing hard, yet composed. Like an ac-
tress who has stormed through a difficult, demanding, brilliant scene.

Terence said, awkwardly, "This—'Studs Schrieber'—is
he—"

"Oh, isn't he something! The hair, the nose ring! The
voice!" Phyllis shuddered.

"You mean you know him?"

"Of course I know him, Terry—he's *always* here, lately."

"He *is?*"

"I've spoken with him, and he understands the rules. He understands *me.* He's rather sweet, actually. A senior at Q.D.S. One afternoon, when you weren't around, he fixed the garbage disposal for me."

"Him? That little bastard? 'Studs'? *Sweet?*"

"The Schriebers live in that big plantation-style brick house on Manor Drive, you know the one. The boy's real name is Edward, Jr. I call him 'Eddy.' And he's much nicer than some boys his age, believe me."

Phyllis was chattering as Terence, a bit dazed, helped her into her coat; an ankle-length golden-russet cashmere coat of surpassing beauty. A line of Heraclitus ran through Terence's brain like a needle—*A man cannot see that to which he is closest.* And it seemed suddenly to Terence that an actual needle had pierced his brain; he was blinded, paralyzed; his hands shot to his face, to shield his eyes, as Phyllis asked what was wrong? what on earth was wrong now with *him?*

Terence wanted to request of Phyllis that, for once, they stay home. With the girls, and with each other. Just that night.

"Terry, are you ill? Oh, Terry—"

"—not ill, I just think— If—"

"Please don't you disappoint me, too. It's been a hellish day, I'm so looking forward to enjoying myself."

So Terence recovered his composure, and smiled at his anxious, vexed wife; smiled to reassure her, he wasn't ill, only perhaps just a little shaken, but already it was past, overcome.

As they left the house by way of a kitchen door entering the garage, Terence carefully activated the burglar alarm system. At once a magical force-field of pulsating, highly potent energy leapt out, in a labyrinthine pattern through the house, upstairs and down, and in the basement. *Peace of Mind Guaranteed With Arcadia Burglar & Fire Alarm Systems. 24-Hour Central Station Monitoring. Fully Insured. Security Our Business.*

So Terence Greene knew, all would be safe in his absence.

The Trial

A sun-dazzled but cool, windy day: June 17.

The first time Terence Greene saw Ava-Rose Renfrew, several blocks south of the Mercer County Courthouse, Trenton, New Jersey, he had no idea who the striking young woman was, of course; nor even that, in the midst of rush-hour traffic, he'd slowed his car to stare fixedly at her. *A gypsy girl? Here? In Trenton?* He was lost in the unfamiliar city—if not exactly lost, he'd missed his exit off Route 1 and had had to take the next exit, hurriedly, fearing being shunted across the Delaware River into Pennsylvania; now he was winding his way back toward Broad Street, in a maze of narrow one-way streets, skirting the edge of what appeared to be an economically devastated neighborhood—weatherworn brick rowhouses, debris-littered sidewalks, abandoned hulks of cars at the curbs. Where *was* the courthouse? As in one of those panicky dreams of things falling, slipping, sliding, melting even as you reach out to grasp them, Terence envisioned circling the courthouse forever.

All weekend, Terence had been anticipating Monday morning with a thrill of expectation. Instead of commuting to New York by train, he would be driving to Trenton in his own car. Instead of disembarking at Penn Station and walking to the Feinemann Foundation offices on Park Avenue, where everyone deferred to him, he would be checking in at the Mercer County Courthouse, as an anonymous New Jersey citizen. His number, 551. How his heart lifted!

And then, suddenly, seemingly out of nowhere, as Terence turned a bit blindly onto a busy street, the young woman ran heedlessly, against the light, in front of his car. How curiously she was dressed! How splendid her waist-long mica-glinting hair, whipping in the wind! Terence smiled to see her. Other drivers sounded their horns, a truck driver whistled out his window in masculine derision, but Terence merely smiled. His impression of her was imprecise, but he guessed that she was in her mid-twenties; very pretty; snub-nosed, with a fair, healthy complexion. She wore an exotic silk jacket or smock, emerald-green, with a multicolored design on its back; her legs, slender and urgent in running as a dancer's, were a startling daffodil-yellow. Distracted from driving for a moment, Terence followed the running girl with his eyes. He saw her continuing without hesitation across a second street, this time with the light, and bound up the steps of a squat gray building—Trenton Police Headquarters.

Terence Greene would always remember: The morning of June 17 was raw, bright, and gusty, like flags flying.

There was no entry to the Mercer County Courthouse except by way of the front doors. Terence half-ran up the hill, and then up a flight of stone steps; he carried his attaché case, bulky with documents, and a copy of that morning's *New York Times*. How imposing the courthouse was, looming above him: a sepulchral public building, built in 1903, grim gray granite, stolid columns, a portico like a heavy brow. Terence felt the weight of it, the sinister dignity, as an indicted man might feel it being brought to his trial.

Why this urgency, this expectancy. Breathless from the steps.

Inside, though he was already late by five minutes, Terence had to wait in line to pass through a metal detector overseen by a sheriff's deputy. Hurrying then, with a pack of men and women who appeared as unfamiliar with their surroundings as he, down a long corridor and to a stairs, led by signs for the Jury Assembly Room. Inside, the courthouse was far less formidable than its exterior. It was an antiquated place, poorly lighted and poorly ventilated, smelling of disinfectant, backed-up drains, human perspiration. Terence passed the Mercer County Clerk's office, the Mercer County Family Services office, the offices of Juvenile Welfare, Adult Probation, Drug Counseling, Dependent Children. How somber the atmosphere, how subdued the men, women, and teenaged children, most of whom were black, who stood about waiting in the corridors! As soon as Terence saw the Jury Assembly Room—a long, cavernous, low-ceilinged and fluorescent-lit room in the basement, so crowded that a line backed out into the corridor—he began to wish that he was somewhere else.

But, politely good-natured as always, he smiled at the brisk female administrator who oversaw the line; he signed in, received his JUROR badge, threaded his way through the crowd until he found a seat as far away from the television set (which was on, and loud: a game show in frenetic progress) as possible. On all sides, people were chatting, laughing. Not one of them looked like a Queenston resident. Most were dressed very casually—sports clothes, work clothes, T-shirts, jeans, even, on one massive, muscular young man, brief runner's shorts. Terence in his navy blue gabardine suit felt uncomfortably out of place. At least he had brought a newspaper, and his work. The crowded atmosphere, the noise and bustle, agitated his nerves, but he would lose himself in the privacy of his own thoughts.

Pursuing Justice?—and why, and where.

Hettie's boy. Too late?

And so, with maddening slowness, the hours passed.

The hours passed, and, to Terence's disappointment, no panel of jurors was called to the courtrooms on the fifth floor. Had he come so far for nothing? He read the newspaper thoroughly, he took a sheath of grant applications out of the attaché case, read, made notes, tried not to be distracted by the damned television set. . . . One of the grant applications was from a woman poet now in her early eighties, who had had a distinguished career in the 1950s, as Terence recalled, but, in recent years, had been eclipsed by the virtual flood of younger poets, and nearly forgotten. Poor Myra Tannenbaum! Terence had assumed the woman was no longer living.

Each year, the Feinemann Foundation gave away hundreds of thousands of dollars to artists. Poets, prose writers, painters, sculptors, playwrights, composers . . . the only criterion, apart from excellence, being that the artist be an American citizen. Nelson P. Feinemann had been a controversial financier of the 1920s who had had a reputation for his ruthlessness with business rivals and associates alike; in some quarters, even at the present time, his name was synonymous with duplicity. (Had not one of his vice-presidents gone to prison in his stead? Had not one of his sons committed suicide?) Yet, like his predecessors Andrew Carnegie, John D. Rockefeller, J. Pierpont Morgan, and Andrew Mellon, among others, Feinemann had left a considerable fortune for philanthropic purposes, and so his reputation had wonderfully improved. Never in the eight decades of its operation had the Feinemann Foundation encountered an artist who refused its largess, whatever his or her publicly proclaimed standards of personal integrity. Quite the contrary! Thousands of applications flooded into the office, and it was the responsibility of Terence Greene, and carefully selected panels of judges, to decide among them. A task that seemed to grow more onerous each season . . .

Trapped. Am I trapped? They'd said that his mother had "gone away" but they had never said anything about his father and so for years, for more years than seems possible, Terence had believed that he was so special a boy, he had had no father. *Isn't he a sad case! Poor little bastard.*

Why had I wanted, what it was I'd wanted?

His handsome leather attaché case had been a gift from Phyllis for Terence's forty-fourth birthday. She had bought it as a substitute for Terence's old briefcase, battered and creased as an old shoe, which he'd owned as a young academic. The sleek new attaché case boasted the initials *TCG* in gold; it was made of Italian leather, with a Gucci label. Dreamily, Terence found himself thinking of the horse chestnut tree behind the sprawling farmhouse in Shaheen, for the smooth leather case, which smelled still of newness, was a deep russet-red, the hue and even the texture of horse chestnuts. He and his cousin Denton, who was two years older than Terence, had collected the most beautiful horse chestnuts and hidden them away in a drawer in the room they shared until, weeks later, forgotten by the boys, the chestnuts were discovered by their Aunt Megan, softened, rotting. *Boys, what is this? What a smell!*

By noon, Terence hadn't yet been called for a jury. He was feeling cheated, impatient, angry. No choice but to have lunch at Mill Hill Tavern across the street, amid a maze of tables, customers, cigarette smoke, an odor of grease. He ordered a glass of beer, a sandwich. Almost, now, he wished he were in New York, in his comfortable office where frequently he ate, excellent food delivered from a deli on the first floor. He opened his attaché case, determined not to waste time. Shuffled through papers. X was applying for a $40,000 grant for the purpose of. Y was applying for a $49,000 grant for the purpose of. Strange that Terence Greene should be determining people's lives when he'd had so little to do with determining his own.

Hettie's boy. What a laugh, see him now!

Terence smiled. For after all no one did see him now; no one from his old, lost life.

By degrees he'd become aware of customers at a table to his right, talking animatedly together, laughing frequently and loudly. There were three of them, seemingly related, grandparents and a teenaged grandson; they ate their lunches avidly, sharing portions. Bowls of steaming soup, enormous stuffed sandwiches. The man was perhaps seventy-five years old, snowy-haired and -bearded, with a heavy, flushed face and eyes crinkled at the corners: He talked the most, as if giving instructions, while the others nodded, or interrupted, or challenged him. He wore a nautical cap, a white dress shirt that strained against his hefty chest and stomach, and a black clip-on bowtie, slightly askew, that shone like dull leather. The woman was both grandmotherly and girlish, in her late sixties perhaps, and hefty too, with a moon-shaped, good-natured face, enormous bosom and hips that jiggled when she laughed, and crisp dyed brassy-blond curls atop which was perched, with quaint propriety, a black pillbox hat of the kind Jacqueline Kennedy had made fashionable in America, many years ago. And the boy—a tall hulking kid built like a linebacker, but with a droll baby face, and a giggle that erupted like firecrackers. He wore a cheaply cut sports coat in which he seemed to feel uncomfortable, and a Phillies baseball cap reversed on his head.

What were they talking about so intensely?—a trial? (Terence thought he heard the words "D.A."—"judge.") What was so urgent?—so funny?

Trying to be inconspicuous, Terence slipped his work back inside the attaché case, and set the case on the floor directly behind his chair, for safekeeping; his sandwich was brought him, and a second foamy glass of beer, and, feeling happy suddenly, Terence ate his lunch while eavesdropping on the diners beside him. He could not follow the thread of their remarks, nor could he decode them, but he was fascinated. From time to time the snowy-bearded patriarch would lean close to the others, tug at his beard, and murmur something severe, in a lowered voice. And the woman would giggle, and shiver. "Yes, *yes*! Amen to *that*!" And the boy would stretch his muscled shoulders suggestively, as if primed to fight. "Man, yeah! They *better*!"

Once, startled by the vehemence of the boy's response,

Terence involuntarily glanced over at him, and the others. He saw them, suddenly silent, looking at *him.*

The moment passed. Terence looked quickly away, to the food on his plate. He was embarrassed to think that the old couple and the boy might suspect him of eavesdropping.

His fleeting impression was that the elder pair frowned a bit at him, though more searchingly than critically; the boy, handsomely blond when seen full face, though with a mildly blemished skin, narrowed his eyes, then, unexpectedly, like a small child, smiled.

Friendly, good-natured people. Perhaps a little simple.

Terence, who'd been enjoying his lunch thoroughly, saw with regret that it was time to leave. He drank down the last of his beer, went to use the men's room, returned to his table, picked up his check and paid the waiter, and left a generous tip. Quite deliberately, he didn't glance at the party at the table beside his (though noting that the woman had left the table) but walked briskly out into the bright June day, which was warmer now, but breezy. How good he felt, and how simple life was!

It was five minutes to one. The Mercer County Courthouse, diagonally across the street from the Mill Hill Tavern, looked less forbidding now.

No sooner had Terence returned to the jury assembly room when he and approximately fifty other men and women were sent up to the fifth floor, herded into a courtroom of modest proportions, addressed by a woman judge of youthful middle age, in full judicial costume. The case to be tried was one in which the defendant was charged with "aggravated assault"—the *State of New Jersey v. T. W. Binder.* (To Terence's surprise, the defendant was in the courtroom already, seated beside his lawyer: a sullenly attractive young man in his early thirties with a thick neck, rounded shoulders, a recent haircut.) One by one, jurors' numbers were called, as in a lottery; as in a lottery, Terence was resigned to not being selected; yet, astonishingly, at the fifth draw, "Terence C. Greene" was called.

Conscious of the rather formal, stiff figure he made, in his expensive suit, Terence crossed the courtroom floor and took a seat in the jury box. Seeing the young man staring at him, only a few yards distant, he began to wonder whether he wanted to sit in judgment on a fellow human being after all.

It seemed to him, as the draw continued, and other jurors came forward to take their seats, that T. W. Binder was looking at *him*—or was he imagining it?

Yet, during the voir dire, when he was questioned by the judge, Terence was careful to give answers of a kind that would not disqualify him. Was he associated in any way with law enforcement officials, did he have any connection with the legal counsel for the defense? Had he ever been the victim of a crime or crimes? (Several of his fellow jurors, answering "Yes" to that question, were thanked and excused immediately.)

Had Terence Greene ever been the victim of a crime or crimes? He thought for a moment, and said, "No, Your Honor. I have not."

He believed that was a truthful answer. Really, he did not remember. As a child—well, all that was lost.

Next, the judge asked if Terence was familiar in any way with the case to be tried: Had he read about it, seen or heard news broadcasts, spoken with persons involved? (At this question too, obliged to answer "Yes," several jurors were excused.) Terence, who, like all Queenston residents, read *The New York Times*, and rarely any local newspaper, said, without hesitation, "No, Your Honor. I have not."

The judge's final question was baffling: Was Terence acquainted, in any way, with the "Ezra Wineapple" case?

Ezra Wineapple?—he'd never even heard the name.

"No, Your Honor. I am not."

Satisfied with these answers, the judge thanked Terence, and moved on to question the next juror, and the next. As the procedure continued, with the assistant prosecutor and the defense attorney requesting from time to time that jurors be excused, rejected jurors left the box, potential jurors took their places, but Terence Greene, and two or three others, remained where they were.

And so, for the first time in his life, Terence Greene was to be a juror in a criminal case.

The trial would begin the next morning. The fourteen jurors were excused early. Terence, buoyed by feelings of excitement and apprehension, was halfway to the parking garage when he realized—what? The attaché case Phyllis had given him was missing.

He'd forgotten it completely.

At first, he thought he must have left it in the jury assembly room; then he remembered placing it on the floor, behind his chair, at lunch. So it must be there, at the Mill Hill Tavern? Unless, seeing that it was an expensive case, someone had made off with it?

Terence half-ran back up the hill, to the tavern diagonally across the street from the courthouse. It was mid-afternoon now, and less crowded. Trying to keep the desperation out of his voice (Phyllis's beautiful gift! for his birthday! filled with documents from the Feincmann Foundation!), he asked the manager if anyone had found an attaché case with the initials *TCG* on it, but the manager said no, not that he knew. Terence searched about, on the floor beneath the table he'd had, and nearby; but found nothing. It must have been taken: stolen.

"God *damn*."

The amiable young waiter who'd waited on Terence, for whom Terence had left a generous tip, claimed not to know anything about the case either. "Where'd you set it?"

"Here. Right here." Terence felt a fool, pointing at a spot on the grimy floor. The memory of the corned beef sandwich he'd eaten so hungrily returned, as a garlicky-acidic belch. Yes, what a fool!

Bringing a luxury item like a leather Gucci case into a tavern in Trenton, absentminded as usual. As Phyllis would say, what could Terence expect?—*off in a world of his own.*

It occurred to him then that though the case had been taken, its contents would have been of no interest to any thief; so he went into the men's room, and, distasteful as the prospect was, sank his arm to the shoulder into the trash receptacle stuffed with used paper towels. He pawed about, grimacing. Recalling how (strange, he'd forgotten it during the judge's questioning) his wallet had been picked from his pocket a few years ago, in Penn Station: credit cards, insurance papers, driver's license, cash—gone.

Nothing in the receptacle but paper towels.

The manager was looking on, sympathetic, but guarded. "You want to try the women's room, too?"

But Terence Greene knew himself defeated. And his stomach was reacting, too. "No, thank you. I don't think there would be much point."

So strangely apprehensive, sleepless as if on the verge of a new life *as if I myself were on trial, the charge unknown.*

The *State of New Jersey v. T. W. Binder* was a distinctly minor case, involving only four witnesses for the prosecution and one (the defendant himself) for the defense. It would be completed within three days. It was presided over by a recently appointed woman judge, argued by a young and rather rawboned assistant prosecutor and a weathered-looking public defender with sideburns and old-fashioned horn-rimmed glasses that slid down his nose as he gestured. Its participants were Trenton residents of no unusual distinction. It would set no legal precedents, occupy no more than a column or two in the *Trenton Times.*

And yet: Are there "minor" cases?—do not all such cases lead to "major" consequences?

Thirty-two-year-old currently unemployed T. W. Binder (his first name was "T.W.") was charged with aggravated assault in an attack upon a young woman in her own home, the previous December; the young woman, Ava-Rose Renfrew, who had been "viciously beaten" and had "suffered permanent injury" as a consequence, was to testify, as were three witnesses, of whom two were members of her family. The State would prove, the young prosecutor asserted, in his reedy, nasal voice, that the defendant had *knowingly, purposefully, and recklessly intended to inflict serious physical injury or did inflict such injury*—in violation of the New Jersey statute against aggravated assault.

The defense counsel, in a more practiced, modulated, insinuating voice, scanning the faces of the jurors as if he, and they, had done this exercise many times before, emphatically denied the charge, asserting that the defendant Mr. Binder had at the most "pushed and pulled" and "attempted to restrain" the young woman in question. There was no proof—"I repeat, ladies and gentlemen of the jury, and will repeat: *absolutely no proof*"—that so serious a crime as aggravated assault had been committed or intended.

Terence Greene, with his fellow jurors, sat very still, listening intently to the opening arguments on the first morning of the trial. Though much was dryly formal and summary, and much was repetitious in a way worrisome to a person of Terence's intelligence, he found the proceedings riveting. The judge at her elevated desk, in her black judicial gown; the stiff young prosecutor who glanced frequently at his notes; the defense counsel who continually pushed at his glasses, and seemed perpetually on the brink of sarcasm; most of all, the husky young T. W. Binder in his cheaply cut brown suit, hair recently razor-shaved at the sides and back of his head, eyes hooded, sullen—how real and purposeful they all seemed, and, in Terence's imagination, how significantly they were linked! *And I, too. And I.*

Terence noted that the officers of the court employed simple, clear, formulaic phrases, much repeated. The assumption was (no doubt, it *was* true) that the men and women in the jury box were not very bright. The judge, in her opening instructions, had said several times, "Remember: I am the judge of the law, and you are the judge of the facts." The prosecuting attorney summarized the case he was to present, summarized the summary, and repeated it; the defense counsel did more or less the same thing, though with more animation in his tone. Terence, the lone juror from Queenston, and the only man of the seven men on the jury to be wearing a suit, had to resist his habit of nodding sympathetically when someone spoke to him. It was an old mannerism of his undergraduate days when he had not only nodded as his professors lectured, but squinted and worked his mouth, half-consciously, gripped by a terrible need to *know*—to know not only what was being said, but its secret, subtextual meaning. *For life is not ripples on the surface of a stream, it is not on the surface at all.*

He listened. Yet his mind drifted. He was in two places simultaneously—in the fifth seat in the jury box, but also in bed, a single lamp burning. *How could you, oh damn you!— that lovely Gucci case!* and he'd apologized another time, he *was* a fool, he *was* careless and absentminded and deeply, deeply regretful, would she forgive him?—another time? and almost shyly he'd touched her, her shoulder smooth and warm beneath the wide satin strap of her nightgown, and, after a moment, brushing away his hand as she might brush away a fly, she sighed audibly, and switched off the lamp. *Yes of course I forgive you, until next time.*

His little boy leaping up into his arms. A swift hug, a wet kiss. *Dad-dee!* and his heart was torn with love. And now, Aaron grown to his father's rangy height but with thicker, darker hair, darker eyes, that look of impatience slamming through the downstairs on his way to the garage to his gleaming white '91 Pontiac Firebird calling back over his shoulder words you didn't want to hear.

Terence repressed a shudder. Perhaps he was imagining it, but it seemed that T. W. Binder regarded him more fixedly than he regarded the other jurors. Was the man innocent, or guilty? He had a low forehead, a prematurely creased skin, steely eyes. That trapped expression Terence saw sometimes in Tuffi's eyes, when the dog hesitated before trying to descend a few steps; before slipping and falling with a startled yelp.

Everyone was waiting for the prosecution's main witness, Ava-Rose Renfrew, the alleged victim, to be summoned. Yet, expectations were balked, as in a deliberately teasing avant-garde play. For the defense counsel argued X, and the prosecutor argued Y, and both requested that the jury be sent out of the room, and so the jury was herded out by a young blank-faced sheriff's deputy to wait in the jury room adjacent to the court for two and a half hours.

Two and a half hours! Terence, pacing about, trying not to listen to the others jurors' chatter, could not believe it. He knew little of courtroom procedure, but he knew enough to fear that the trial might end abruptly, if the defendant decided after all to plead guilty; or if a plea-bargained deal was struck with the prosecutor. And then—what? Would he and his fellow jurors be sent back down to the jury room? *Then never, never would it have happened. Never would he have known.*

But the trial continued. The jurors were herded back into the jury box, and there was T. W. Binder, hunched as if reconciled to his fate, staring.

And, now—Ava-Rose Renfrew?

But, "Your Honor—!" the defense counsel said, and there was yet another interruption. For a document was mislaid, or missing.

So time passed, but slowly. The judge and the two attorneys conferred at the far corner of the judge's bench, out of the jury's earshot, and, again, fidgety now, Terence worried that the trial would end before it had begun.

Noting with sympathy how the courtroom stenographer typed, typed, typed, every word, every phrase, no matter how inconsequential or much repeated. Moving her keyboard to the corner of the judge's bench, brisk as an automaton, continuing with her typing, face blank and expressionless, eyes slightly upturned. Phyllis's age, solid-bodied, but with a faded cast to her skin. *Because you're selfish, off in a world of your own. No wonder the children don't respect you.*

The trial resumed. Terence, swallowing hard, sat straight and tall, listening to every word.

Now, at last—Ava-Rose Renfrew.

The young prosecutor stood irresolutely at the front of the room, waiting for his witness, whom one of the deputies had gone to bring into the courtroom. Everyone watched the opened doorway, which was at the very front of the room, just beyond the jurors' box: But no one appeared. As in a play in which actors seem to have stumbled over or forgotten their lines, there was a palpable air of embarrassment and tension. Terence could see the young prosecutor's Adam's apple shifting in his throat. Where was the witness?—what was wrong? After several minutes, the deputy returned, flush-faced, and spoke quietly with the judge; the judge signaled the prosecuting attorney to come forward to speak with her; clearly, the witness was not where she was expected to be.

There were comings and goings in the courtroom. Visibly nervous, the young prosecutor conferred with an assistant. At the defense table, T. W. Binder sat stiff and huddled, head slightly lowered, not knowing where to look. Annoyed, but speaking with magisterial calm, the judge apologized to the jury—"You see, it isn't quite like television. Things don't happen smoothly." The deputy left the room another time, by the same door, and everyone watched that door expectantly, even as, breathless as if borne by the wind, there appeared at the rear of the courtroom, unannounced, the young woman herself—"Oh! I'm so sorry! Are you-all looking for *me*?"

It was the gypsy-girl, the running girl, Terence had sighted the day before, on the street.

Still breathless, the color in her cheeks and her crinkly hair windblown, Ava-Rose Renfrew, the prosecution's main witness, stood pert and contrite as a little girl before the judge's bench. There was a moment's flurry, a nervous giggle, when, it seemed, she confused her right hand with her left as the bailiff held out a Bible to her for the swearing-in. Terence could see how her left hand, obediently raised, trembled.

"Do you swear to tell the truth, the whole truth, and nothing but the truth?"

"Oh, I do! Surely! That's why I'm here, isn't it?"

There were startled smiles throughout the courtroom. The pretty young woman's voice was low, hoarse, and crackly, as if she hadn't quite cleared her throat. But how pretty she was, with her heart-shaped, creamy-pale face, like a flower's petals!—and how strangely dressed!

Ava-Rose Renfrew was wearing a long, drooping skirt made of diaphanous layers of mauve, pale gold, and green; and a gorgeous purple silk jacket with flaring sleeves, chunky iridescent purple buttons, and embroidered or appliquéd designs—crimson roses, creamy gardenias, hummingbirds, butterflies, rainbows. The designs were made of metallic thread, velvet patches, sequins, colored beads. There was a small fan of feathers stitched to a pocket. Her slender legs were encased in gauzy tights and the skirt trailed over flat black "ballerina" slippers of the kind high school girls used to wear in the 1950s. And she wore a red satin rose in her hair, and turquoise feather earrings, and several bracelets on each arm, and several glittering rings. And there was a sweet fragrance in the air, in her wake, as of a flowery perfume.

Terence Greene breathed in this scent, enraptured.

Terence Greene stared, enraptured.

The exotic young woman, an incongruous sight in the witness chair, amid such somber surroundings, glanced nervously and eagerly about. Her eyes seemed to be tearing— she dabbed at them frequently with a tissue. She licked her lips, fingered one of the feather earrings. Yet when asked by the judge to identify herself to the court, she spoke readily, even buoyantly, in her odd throaty voice, as if in the presence of friends. "My name is Ava-Rose Renfrew, Your Honor. My place of residence is 33 Holyoak Street, Trenton—that's on the west side, by the river?—where I live with my family, my great-aunt and -uncle and my boy-cousin and my twin nieces and any other Renfrews coming through town. My sign is Pisces and my life's vocation is The Craft of Beauty." She paused, glancing at the jury, adding, "That is, The Craft of Beauty is my business, too. I am a businesswoman. I make my own special things and sell them in Tamar's Bazaar at the Chimney Point Shopping Center?" Her voice lifted, as if she expected nods of recognition.

The jurors, Terence Greene included, sat stony-still, resisting any sign of sympathy. Wasn't this their obligation, as jurors?

Now more composed, the young prosecutor led his witness through her testimony by asking a sequence of pointed questions. To each, the young woman answered thoughtfully; sometimes half shutting her eyes, with a look of pain. Terence, listening mesmerized, found that he was clenching his fists. What an outrage, what an obscenity!—that any man should beat so delicate-boned and lovely a woman!

When Ava-Rose Renfrew was asked by the prosecutor to point out her assailant, she did so, with the alacrity of a child, pointing her forefinger at T. W. Binder. "That's him, sir. There." The defendant had begun to huddle in upon himself as soon as Ava-Rose Renfrew appeared in the courtroom; now he lowered his head further, though stealing a cringing look at his accuser. His eyes moved jerkily in their sockets. His face had turned a dull brick red and was oily with sweat. Ava-Rose Renfrew cried sharply, as if in rebuke of something Binder had said, some urgent silent communication, "Yes! You! Wanted to kill me, at Christmastime! Didn't you! They've got you now! Aren't you *ashamed*!"

The defense counsel was on his feet, protesting; and the

judge instructed the prosecutor to restrain his witness. Ava-Rose Renfrew's eyes spilled tears glittering as gems which she wiped away quickly with a tissue.

She continued. "Yes, sir. A terrible beating with intent to kill. Because I wouldn't see him any longer, and he threatened me, telling people to tell me, he'd kill me and then himself—thinking I'd be scared, and marry him! Marry *him*, that wanted to kill me!—and talked of burning down our house, with all of us asleep some night! *As if I would do such a thing, a Pisces!* So he came over uninvited, he'd been drinking all day, this was December 27, yes sir, around dusk because the Christmas lights were all lit up—we make a big to-do about Christmas, strings of lights outside and in, on trees outside and on the fence and roof, and a big Christmas tree inside, that *he* knocked over out of meanness—and my cousin Chick tried to stop him but he pushed through the door, and there I was coming down the stairs, and he ran up the stairs to grab hold of me, and Darling was on my shoulder—he's our African gray parrot, he's thirty years old and losing some of his feathers out of nervousness, so we try to be nice to him, to talk to him so he doesn't feel trapped he's a parrot—because they're incredibly smart, African grays: They know they're parrots, not like other birds don't have a clue which end is up—so it was so specially nasty, so cruel, and he knew it, to grab me like that and terrify Darling so the poor fellow hardly leaves his cage now, doesn't trust anyone on two legs, who can blame him!—and most of his tail feathers, beautiful scarlet feathers, have fallen out! Well! That man sitting over there grabbed me on the stairs, and near-about tore my hair out of my head, and punched me in the face, and threw me down the stairs, hitting, and kicking, and there I was like a puddle on the floor begging him to stop but he wouldn't stop, kicking me in the head with his nasty leather boots! And my cousin Chick was trying to pull him away, and my Aunt Holly Loomis ran out of the kitchen to help me, but T.W. knocked them aside, imagine!—a boy, and an older woman of sixty-nine!—hitting *them*!—like a maniac crying, 'I'm gonna kill you all! I'm gonna kill you all!' My nose was bleeding, and my eyes, I couldn't believe how vicious he was, kicking me in the *eyes*!—and I lost consciousness right in the midst of him kicking me, and next thing I knew it was later, and I was in the hospital, in the emergency room. They put in stitches all over my face, and did some surgery on my left eye where they said the tear duct was torn, but it was lucky, they said, real lucky, that I hadn't lost my eyesight. So I believe the Almighty took pity on me, seeing that *he* had not."

The judge had several questions, intended to amplify the witness's testimony (one of them was Ava-Rose's weight: 105 pounds); then the prosecutor asked her to please approach the jury box, to show the jurors the "permanent facial injuries" she had suffered as a consequence of the "vicious and premeditated" assault. As the young woman obeyed, self-consciously, brushing her hair nervously out of her face, Terence Greene felt his pulse quicken; a mist came over his vision. He'd been clenching his fists so tightly, he realized that his nails had dug into the palms of his hands. *Not wanting to feel like this. Not wanting to feel anything at all.* But there, hardly more than twelve inches from Terence, the young woman stood, a faint blush heating her face but her head uplifted, eyes clear. As the prosecutor read from a medical report, in his flat, reedy voice, Ava-Rose Renfrew turned her head from side to side, like an obedient (but somewhat embarrassed) child, indicating tiny, near-invisible white scars on her face—at a corner of her mouth, at her chin, beside and above her left eye, trailing like a cobweb through her right eyebrow. How unnerving: The young woman *was* very pretty, yet, if you looked closely, the fine white scars were like cracks in porcelain. The prosecutor noted that she had had, as well, a concussion; three sprained ribs; a sprained finger; numerous cuts and bruises; and the tear duct in her left eye was permanently damaged, so that, at times, it watered uncontrollably and affected her vision.

Not wanting to feel. Not anything. Staring his eyes misting over at the young woman standing so awkwardly close, her head uplifted and her gaze (a shimmering amber-green) fixed resolutely to a point on the wall above the jurors' heads. Her hair!—longer and fuller and more beautiful even than his daughter Kim's!—it tumbled down her back and shoulders like a mane, crinkly as if with static electricity, many hues, streaks, silvery-brown, blond, ginger, with single hairs that glittered like metallic thread, cascading to her slender waist in tattery waves and curls.

Terence, with a gentleman's sense of propriety, cast his eyes down, as the prosecutor continued to speak. So far as Terence Greene, juror number five, was concerned, the trial was over: T. W. Binder, a brute who would attack a woman like Ava-Rose Renfrew so viciously, was clearly guilty as charged—if not guilty of more.

When the trial was recessed for the day, in late afternoon, the judge cautioned the jurors in what they must not do, under penalty of being expelled from the jury and perhaps causing a mistrial: They were not to discuss the trial with anyone—" 'Anyone' means just that: any member of your family, any fellow juror, any stranger"; they were not to read local newspapers, watch local television news programs, drive in the vicinity of Trenton in which the alleged crime occurred.

When Terence left the courthouse, he crossed the street to the Mill Hill Tavern, to make another inquiry about his lost attaché case. But it had not been found—"Sorry, mister! Guess it's gone." Terence sighed, though he wasn't surprised. *No wonder the children don't respect you.*

He glanced into the bar, where, amid a gauzy cloud of smoke, a few men stood, drinking. One of them was the tall, big-bodied old man Terence had seen at lunch, the white-bearded patriarch with the booming voice—now talking to the bartender, laughing and jabbing at the air with a forefinger. He was wearing the nautical cap as before, perched jaun-

tily atop his head. Terence, seeing him, was about to speak;
then halted. For what would he have said?

At dinner, Terence must have been lost in a dream,
scarcely tasting his food, for both his daughters teased him
at once—"Daddy, where *are* you?" And Phyllis, who had
been telling one of her lengthy, bemused anecdotes about a
Queenston friend, or a new client of hers, reacted sharply,
hurt. "Your father is in Trenton, in court—he's a juror. He
takes it all very seriously."

At once his daughters joined forces to tease and inter-
rogate, though Terence had explained his vow of confi-
dentiality.

"Daddy, what *is* the case? *Why* can't you say?"

"Nobody will know, Daddy! Come *on!*"

Terence said, patiently, "I gave my word, you know. I
would never violate it."

Cindy, the more aggressive, leaned forward, elbows on
the table. Her voice was high-pitched, aggrieved. "*Is* it a murder trial?"

"Honey, I just can't talk about it. When it's all over,
I—"

"But why can't you tell *us, we* don't have anything to do
with it, *we* wouldn't tell! I think you're silly, Daddy!"

Phyllis tapped Cindy's arm, gently. And gentle too was
her murmured admonition—"Cindy, not so *loud.*"

"Oh, damn! Always *me!* Always *I'm* to blame!" Cindy
cried, incensed. She was short-tempered these days because,
after weeks of dieting, she had lost only a few pounds; her
plain, pudgy face had not changed at all. "Daddy, *why* can't
you tell? Who would know?"

Kim said meanly, " 'Cause Daddy doesn't trust you,
that's why. He doesn't trust any of us."

Evening meals at the Greenes'!—even in Aaron's frequent absence (he was away that night, with friends), Terence felt the strain on his nerves. Kim was tense, giggly,
distracted; unpredictable. By a decree of Phyllis's, she was

forbidden to rush from the table to answer the telephone; she had to sit and listen to it ring, and ring and ring, until, in Terence's study, the answering service clicked on. Nor was Kim allowed to check the tape until the meal was formally concluded. Phyllis, who had grown up in a household of enforced good manners, felt strongly about this—"We are a family, after all," she said, "and we owe one another respect." (Terence wondered if any of the calls for Kim were from—what was his name?—that boy with the ring through his nose. In theory, the boy had been banished, by Phyllis, from the Greenes' household; but that did not mean that Kim did not see him elsewhere.)

Terence said quietly, "*I* would know."

Both the girls exploded into laughter as if they had never heard anything so hilarious.

"Oh, Daddy—who are *you!*"

"*You* won't tell on *you*—will *you?*"

The pretty, slender fifteen-year-old and the plain, pudgy eleven-year-old giggled, squeezing hands as if they were, not sisters who frequently quarreled bitterly, and could not bear each other, but sisters close as twins.

That night, as they undressed for bed, Phyllis said, impulsively, "Tell *me.*"

Terence glanced up at her, not knowing, for a moment, what she meant.

He'd been seeing, vivid in his mind's eye as a waking dream, a human face—pale, floating, fine-cracked, beautiful.

And that tattery glittering cascading hair all curls and waves.

He said, stammering, "I—I will, Phyllis. Of course. When the trial is over."

Phyllis, seeing a look of pain and guilt in his face, came to him unexpectedly, and kissed him lightly on the lips. "Poor Terry! You take everything so seriously, don't you! I *knew* you shouldn't have gotten involved."

———

Hettie's boy. You *won't tell on* you—*will* you?

Most of the following day in court was taken up with the continued testimony of the prosecution's main witness, Ava-Rose Renfrew. Today, the young woman was dressed more somberly: in a long-skirted black dress of some filmy Indian fabric, sheer as muslin, and many-layered; with a lavender knit shawl draped alluringly about her slender shoulders, and the brilliant red satin rose in her hair, and her flat black "ballerina" shoes Terence smiled to see. Her mica-glinting hair was brushed to a sheen, and she wore fewer items of jewelry—though her earrings, miniature peacocks' tails made of feathers and sequins, were certainly eye-catching. As she spoke, she glanced about the courtroom, and at the jurors, with a faint smile, as if seeking out friends.

Now it was the defense counsel's turn to question the witness. How many hours!—trying, by slow maddening repetition, to trip her up in petty inconsistencies, or to reduce her to tears. Several times, Ava-Rose's hoarse, cracked voice dipped near-inaudibly, and the judge had to ask her to please speak more clearly. "Oh, Your Honor, I try!" Ava-Rose said, pressing a tissue to her tearing left eye, "—but he's so *mean!*" A sympathetic murmur ran through the courtroom and the showy little attorney stepped back, as if he'd been slapped.

Still, he persisted. Questioning the witness, for instance, about her age. On one document, evidently, her age was given as twenty-nine; on another, thirty-one. When, in fact, *had* she been born? Ava-Rose hesitated, then said, "Why, I— I'm so embarrassed!—I don't rightly *know.* My momma died when I was a little girl, they say she'd just showed up in Trenton one day, with me, no wedding ring or anything, in 1958. Everybody in the family knows when my birthday is—March 12—but nobody knows the birth*date.* Why does it matter?— any age I am, that man hurt me just as bad, last Christmas; and meant to hurt me more." Ava-Rose fumbled for a fresh tissue, to dab against her eye.

Quickly, the attorney tried another tack: questioning the witness about her relationship with the defendant. How long, and how intimately, had they known each other, at the time of the alleged assault?

Ava-Rose said, quietly, her voice hoarser than ever, that she had known "T.W." for several years but in different ways—"friendly, real friendly, and not-so-friendly."

The attorney pushed his horn-rimmed glasses against the bridge of his nose, and asked, in an insinuating voice, "And how did you first meet Mr. Binder, Miss Renfrew?"

"Why, I—didn't meet him, exactly. I just looked up, and he was *there.*"

"Yes? And where was this?"

Ava-Rose took a deep breath, sitting very straight, and explained, in a halting, rushing, wondering way. "Why, I was leaving Tamar's Bazaar one night, where, as I said, I rent a little space to sell my things—The Craft of Beauty—and there was this *man*, this strange bald-headed *man*, following after me. Tamar told me he'd been hanging around peeking in at me, *I* never paid him any mind because that's the wisest strategy—a policeman once told me that, for my own good —pretend you don't notice, you aren't scared to death, so they can walk off and be gone. Well!—this ol' bald-headed man was hiding, waiting till the store closed, and I'd be coming out alone to my car, and I had a crawly feeling up the back of my neck like I knew somebody was following me but I didn't dare look around!—and next thing I knew, there was T.W. getting off his motorcycle, one of those Harley-Davidsons all shiny black and chrome, T.W. who I'd never laid eyes on in my life coming to my rescue, saying to this man who'd been following me, 'What d'you want with this lady, mister?' and I just stood there staring, so surprised I wasn't even scared! Naturally, the ol' bald-headed man told T.W. to mind his own business, nothing was going on, he tried to walk away but T.W. stopped him, and they had words, and T.W. punched him in the face, and went kind of wild the way he does when he gets started, so the bald-headed man got beaten pretty badly, on his knees, then on his back, and T.W. was kicking him, and nobody in the parking lot wanted to come near, nor even call the police!—that's how people are, these days. Oh!''—Ava-Rose was breathless, hiding her face in her hands and speaking haltingly through her fingers—"I knew T.W. was a dangerous man, but I was grateful to him, too, for saving me from that other man. And so—''

There was a tremulous pause. The defense counsel had removed his glasses, and was rubbing at his eyes.

What a blunder! Terence Greene, who profoundly disliked the defense counsel, felt a moment's sympathy for him. In the matter of cross-examination, wasn't it a rule of thumb that an attorney should never ask a witness a question the answer to which he didn't himself know? At the defense table, T. W. Binder sat slouched, his gaze downcast and his face heavy with blood. Exposed, now, as a dangerous man, he sat very still, in the midst of courtroom tittering, as if he hoped he might be invisible.

The remainder of the session passed, for Terence Greene, in a blur of frustration and gathering rage. He could look nowhere but at Ava-Rose Renfrew's tear-streaked face, he could hear nothing but her low, hoarse voice, though he did not always follow the logic of her words. He did not hear the defense counsel's words at all—he had blocked them from consciousness. *What I would have liked was both of them on trial, the defendant and his lawyer. What I would have liked was to find them both guilty, punish them both.*

That afternoon, when court adjourned, Terence Greene did not drive directly home to Queenston, but took a westward route through Trenton, with the intention, as he told himself, of driving along the Delaware River, north, and then east, in a roundabout way to his home. It was a June day of surpassing beauty: a fair, cloudless sky, a quickening in even the polluted urban air of hope, anticipation. How his blood pulsed! How he longed for—he did not know what! *To speak to her. To apologize. My shame as a man, among men.*

Yes, that was it: to apologize, simply. Terence shuddered

at the possibility, however remote, that *his* wife, *his* daughters, should ever suffer at the hands of a brute like Binder; or be so maliciously treated, in public, by a crass, unscrupulous mercenary like that damned public defender.

Terence did not know Trenton streets, but he knew the general direction he wanted, to the river. Once there, he would turn north on the River Road, and so swing up and around to Queenston. Not for years had he and Phyllis and the children visited the Delaware Valley, but Terence could recall, with pleasure, Sunday excursions to New Hope and Washington's Crossing State Park—where, literally, on Christmas eve of 1776, General George Washington had crossed the icy Delaware River from Pennsylvania into New Jersey. Aaron, as a boy, had been intrigued by historical sites; and Terence, even as an adult, found a true romance in them. Phyllis had loved the old riverside inns where, to celebrate special occasions like anniversaries, they'd gone for romantic luncheons. . . . Now their lives were so busy elsewhere, they had not been to the Delaware Valley, nor as much spoken of it, in years. And of course the children were hardly children any longer, to tolerate any family excursion.

Dad-dee!—get real!

Terence could envision, in his mind's eye, the broad, placid, yet swift-flowing river, shimmering like phosphorescence on the far side of the grubby city. His heart swelled with an emotion he did not understand.

He was driving on a street called Pennington Avenue, but there was a confusing divide, and, after several blocks, a street sign caught his eye: HOLYOAK.

Holyoak!—*forbidden territory.*

Quickly Terence reasoned that, so long as he was a considerable distance from the Renfrew residence, there was no danger. He was miles away, surely—in the 800-block.

This was a working-class neighborhood of rowhouses and small shops, on the edge of a slum. Blacks, Hispanics, a smaller number of whites on the street. The next block, and the next, brought him deeper into what appeared to be a black ghetto; then, abruptly, there was a railroad underpass, and, on the other side, an urban wasteland of warehouses, railroad yards, small factories, rubble-strewn vacant lots. Miles passed. What were the street numbers, here?—Terence could not see any. On his right was a grim little fortress of a building—the Chimney Point Youth Detention Home—but it seemed to have no number. On his left was a fire-damaged boarded-up Methodist church. Then came a stretch of weathered woodframe houses and bungalows set back in scrubby lots; then a fairly busy intersection, with an Abbott's Ice Cream, Ace's Tavern & Family Billiards, Hunan Take-Out, 24-Hour Laundromat. A semirural residential block, and, to the left, a vast weedy cemetery; atop a leafy wooded hill, a gaunt, aged building, apparently no longer in use, made of dirty buff-colored bricks, with several tall, blackened chimneys.

Chimney Point. Forbidden territory.

Now Terence was in the 100-block of Holyoak Street. He saw, ahead, that the street came to a dead-end: In the distance there was a vague liquidy glitter that could only be the Delaware River. So Holyoak wasn't a through street! He would have to turn around and go back the way he'd come.

He was excited, his breath quickened. A pressure like a band around his chest as if he were in the presence of danger. *Why have I done this?—why such a risk?*

Afterward Terence would recall how the car's momentum had borne him forward; as if, somehow, the car were his body, and *he*, behind the wheel, whoever *he* was, had surrendered all volition and all responsibility.

Rapidly the street numbers ran down. Terence's gaze was riveted to a barnlike woodframe-and-stucco house set back in a lot on the left. Even amid its rundown neighbors this house stood out: ramshackle and derelict, yet distinctive, the kind of house to make you smile, like an illustration in a child's story book. *Hers?*

Though he knew it was risky, Terence could not resist braking his car to a stop in front of the house. (Was he con-

spicuous, here?—in the new-model silver BMW that was Phyllis's choice?) The house was old, its original structure
probably built as long ago as the previous century; even the
additions were old, in need of repair. A badly weathered slate
roof upon which moss grew in patches; a crumbling redbrick
chimney; three windows on the first floor, and three windows
on the second—several panes repaired with plywood, and the
first-floor shutters painted a bright robin's-egg blue, while the
second-floor shutters remained a rotted-looking gray, unpainted for decades. On a sagging front veranda were household cast-offs, an old upholstered sofa, a small squat
refrigerator, a television set. Along the veranda's rain gutters
and coiled about its posts were strings of lights not yet taken
down from Christmas. Was that a number 33, in glow-in-the-
dark glitter, nailed beside the front door?

Close about the house, obscuring parts of the first-floor
windows, were overgrown trees, shrubs, flowers, weeds—a
garden behind a leaning picket fence, gone wild in the front
yard. Trumpet vine, sunflowers, blooming thistle, wild rose,
and domestic rose grew in lush profusion, with, here and
there, an unexpected lawn ornament of questionable taste—
a brilliant pink flamingo tilted on one stick leg, a bug-eyed
pickaninny eating a slice of watermelon, a miniature elk.
There was a badly rutted driveway curving about to the rear
of the house, and beside it, sunk in weeds, an ancient Stu-
debaker convertible coated in rust.

*And if someone sees me? If—somehow—I, the juror, am found
out?*

Terence was leaning out his car window, squinting in
the sunshine, his heart beating painfully hard. So this was 33
Holyoak, the home of Ava-Rose Renfrew, the place of the
"aggravated assault"! In the waning but still bright air it quiv-
ered with warmth, a pulsing secret life. Individual panes of
window glass winked. The robin's-egg blue shutters were defined with the hard-edged clarity of a child's crayon drawing.
Terence was thinking nervously that, if someone appeared,

if Ava-Rose Renfrew herself appeared, seeing him, he would press down hard on the gas pedal, drive into the turnaround at the end of the street, and escape.

It was then that he noticed a movement on the roof of the house, toward the rear. A human figure?—two figures? Two young girls in tiny bathing suits, sunbathing?

Terence did not mean to stare quite so openly, craning his neck. Perhaps he was thinking—he, the father of daughters, and in any case a person who never hesitated to offer his help if help seemed needed—that there might be danger; that the girls were younger than they were. They had not yet noticed him, lying on their backs on the sharp-peaked roof, with identical straw hats over their faces; their bodies were thin, flat-stomached, with tiny breasts and long lanky legs; both wore red bikinis the size of handkerchiefs. Terence blinked up at them, until a barking dog, close by, distracted him, and drew the girls' attention—one sat up, snatching her straw hat off her face, and the other sat up, snatching her straw hat off hers, and both, seeing Terence Greene, a stranger in a fancy silver car parked in front of their house, began to wave at him, giggling.

Were the girls twins?—perhaps thirteen years old? At this distance they looked identical, and each, with flyaway mica-glinting fair-brown hair to her shoulders, uncannily resembled Ava-Rose Renfrew.

Hastily, Terence started up his car. The girls called out to him in high-pitched teasing voices—or was it to the dog now lunging, as he barked, at the front left tire of the BMW? Terence heard a cry of "Mister!"—unless it was a cry of "Buster!"

The dog was a burly wooly-brown mongrel with a German shepherd's face and a husky's deep chest; its legs were stumpy for its body, and its tail, perhaps a foot long, was a wildly thumping rod. Its barks and yips were impassioned, whether in hostility or overwrought friendliness, with an oddly human-sounding quaver. Terence muttered, "Go away, damn you! Please!" as he started up his car. He propelled the car forward, to the abrupt end of Holyoak Street (beyond was a vacant lot, overgrown with weeds and littered with trash, including parts of cars and tires, through which a vague path led down to the river), made a sharp turn, with an alarming squeal of his tires, and started forward again, but the dog was caught beneath the front part of the car, or seemed to be caught; there was a sickening thump as Terence pressed down on the gas pedal desperate to escape; he heard the girls screaming now on the roof of 33 Holyoak and he heard the dog's shrieks and he wanted to escape but could not: could not bring himself to leave an injured animal: so, panicked, greatly confused, knowing only that he was very likely in serious trouble, and had brought this trouble upon himself, Terence stopped the car, opened the door, looked out to see—to his immense, incalculable relief—that the burly dog was all right, evidently, having scampered out from beneath the car before the tires went over it. Still barking, with that curious human-sounding quaver, the dog stood in the middle of the street, unharmed, glaring at Terence with amber-bright eyes.

Terence drove swiftly away. In the rearview mirror, the dog's reproachful image grew smaller, and smaller, until it disappeared into the distance.

Never. Never again.
Such reckless, needless behavior—never.

By the time Terence returned home, it was 6:20 P.M.

There were cars in the driveway: guests for cocktails.

He'd forgotten completely that Phyllis had invited the Montgomerys and the Classens over for drinks, before going out to dinner at the Queenston Country Club. There was a $500-a-plate benefit dinner for a local charity—the Save-Our-Schools or the Feed-the-Homeless?

Terence wandered out onto the rear terrace, where his wife and friends were sitting. He was disheveled and perspiring, with the look of a man who has traveled a long distance and no longer knows where he is. Phyllis and the others glanced up in surprise.

Matt Montgomery said, with a chuckle, "*There* he is!—the man of the hour."

"Terry, what on earth—? I've been worried!" Phyllis cried, more sharply than Terence might have wished. "You're late."

A blur of greetings, handshakes, kisses on the cheek—Hedy Montgomery, a stylish, good-looking woman of forty who always seemed to be suppressing nervous laughter; Matt Montgomery, tall and tanned and vigorous and handsome, with his endearing smile and steely handshake (Matt had won his township office in the April election, and was planning, Phyllis said, excited, to run for mayor of Queenston next); Lulu Classen, a sweet beige woman with a breathless manner; and Mickey Classen, who seemed embarrassed for Terence, and whose handshake was limp and fleeting. Phyllis, smiling hard, leaned on tiptoe to brush her lips against Terence's cheek, and asked in an undertone, "Damn it, Terry, where *were* you?" and Terence said, "I was lost, I'm afraid," and his friends laughed, Matt Montgomery the heartiest, and Phyllis said incredulously, "Lost? Lost in *Trenton*?" and Terence said, with a sigh, running both hands through his thin, dry hair, "Yes, I'm afraid so—lost in Trenton."

Because I believe in Justice. Because I believe I can be the enforcer of Justice, if I am so empowered.

Hettie's boy. All grown up.

It was with a sense of guilty excitement that Terence returned to the Mercer County Courthouse the next morning. And a sense of purpose, determination.

Terence and his fellow jurors had been told by the judge that the trial would probably end that day, or the next. Already, oddly, Terence felt a sense of regret; of imminent loss. As if, in this brief space of time, he'd already lived a significant part of his lifetime—commuting each morning to this city in which he knew no one, and no one knew him; driving south, not north, on Route 1, amid a tide of traffic that bore him onward with quickening urgency, as he had not felt in years commuting by train to Manhattan; turning into the parking garage and pointing at the green JURY DUTY pass on the dashboard of the BMW.

"Yes, I'm on official business—I'm a juror."

Entering the courtroom, an hour later, in his place as fifth juror in the lineup, Terence felt a peculiar sense of dread and anticipation: as if, entering the courtroom by this particular door at the rear, taking his place in the jury box, he were trespassing in a sacred space.

But who would stop him, now he was here?

Terence was disappointed that Ava-Rose Renfrew would not be returning—she'd finished her testimony the day before. It remained now for the grave young prosecutor to present his three remaining witnesses to the court.

And what a surprise: The first witness, "Holly Mae Loomis," great-aunt of Ava-Rose Renfrew and a coresident of the house at 33 Holyoak, turned out to be the hefty, ruddy-cheeked old woman from the Mill Hill Tavern, in the quaintly prim pillbox hat!

Except, this morning, Holly Mae Loomis wore a peach satin cloche hat that covered most of her brassy dyed curls. Her cotton dress was a billowing affair printed with bright green parrots; though she wore chunky orthopedic shoes, her stockings were sheer, and green-tinted. Like pretty Ava-Rose, Mrs. Loomis spoke with the open, frank, smiling air of one confident she will be believed.

Mrs. Loomis told the identical story her great-niece had told—of the "bursting into" the house by the defendant; the "mean, crazy" attack on the stairs; the rest. During the cross-examination, when the defense counsel slyly tried to confuse her regarding the precise sequence of events, and questioned whether, in fact, she had even been in the house at the time, Mrs. Loomis lifted her fleshy chin, and glared at him, and exclaimed, in a dramatic manner, "Why! Are you suggesting, young man, that I am prematurely senile?—or, what is more insulting, that *I am a liar?*" The woman's rouged face and air of outrage suggested a stage comedienne of some past era, Ethel Merman, perhaps. Several members of the jury laughed, Terence Greene the most heartily. Even the judge could not resist a smile.

The defense counsel's face, already oily with perspiration, reddened. In an abrupt, despairing gesture, he pushed his horn-rimmed glasses up against the bridge of his nose. His voice was a hoarse croak—"No further questions, Your Honor."

Next, the young prosecutor called "Charlton Heston Renfrew"—another time, to Terence's astonishment. For this young nephew of Ava-Rose Renfrew's, a resident too of 33 Holyoak Street and an eye-witness to the beating, turned out to be the husky blond teenager from the Mill Hill Tavern. He wore, for his appearance in court, the same tight-fitting sports coat he'd worn the other day; his Phillies baseball cap was stuck in one of the pockets.

There was a moment's comic flurry as, before the bailiff could swear in Charlton Heston Renfrew, the judge had to ask him to please remove the gum he was so vigorously chewing. A sheriff's deputy took the wad from him in a tissue, with a look of controlled distaste, and carried it away.

The prosecutor began, "Charlton Heston Renfrew, will you tell the court your age, please, and your relationship to Miss Ava-Rose Renfrew—"

The boy shook his head as if embarrassed. "Naw, the name's *Chick*, nobody ever calls me *that*. I'm fifteen years old, and Ava-Rose, that that guy over there tried to kill, is my *aunt*."

At once the defense counsel was on his feet. "Your Honor, I object!"

Before the judge could reply, the Renfrew boy cried, " 'Object'! What do you know! *You* weren't there! Seeing that bastard punching and kicking Aunt Ava-Rose, dragging her

down the stairs—!'' He waved a fist at the attorney. His handsome, mildly blemished face looked heated and his hair,
dirty-blond, stiffly curly, seemed to rise from his head in
protest.

It was some minutes before courtroom decorum was restored. At a request of the defense counsel, the jury was hurriedly sent out of the courtroom; locked into the jury room;
then, ten minutes later, herded back. Terence very much
hoped that the young witness had not been banished from
the trial, and was relieved to see that he was still on the witness stand, though looking now subdued, boyishly contrite.
For the remainder of his testimony, "Chick" Renfrew spoke
quietly, yet with indignation. He told of T. W. Binder harass-
ing his aunt for weeks—forcing his way into the house—
beating Ava-Rose on the stairs, kicking her as she lay fallen
—shouting "I'll kill you, bitch!" He told of trying to pull
Binder away from his aunt, and being struck in the mouth.
He described in detail Binder's hand tooled leather boots,
with which he kicked his aunt in the head repeatedly. His
story corroborated to the smallest detail the stories given by
Ava-Rose Renfrew and Holly Mae Loomis, and as he gave it
he glanced frequently at the jurors as if confident that they
would believe him. Only fifteen!—Terence smiled at the
boy's combination of innocence and theatricality. You would
almost think that "Chick" Renfrew had given testimony in a
courtroom before.

When the defense counsel began his cross-examination,
rather warily, as if he feared provoking another damning outburst, he did in fact inquire with seeming innocence after
the witness's "juvenile record"—but this line of questioning
was brought to an immediate halt as, simultaneously, the
prosecuting attorney raised an objection and the witness himself turned to the judge and asked, in an aggrieved voice,
"Do I have to answer *that*?"

The judge explained to the jury, at some length, a tech-
nicality of state law that protected any juvenile in the matter

of his or her "juvenile record," which was sealed. But, it seemed, "Chick" Renfrew did have a record of some mysterious kind.

Emboldened by this small gain, the defense counsel, pacing excitedly about, asked the witness if he had not contributed to the incident by fighting with the defendant himself; but the witness denied this vehemently. He'd tried to "pull Binder off," "make him stop kicking Aunt Ava-Rose" —that was all. Seemingly unaware of his tactical error, the defense counsel doggedly asked questions that allowed the boy to dwell upon the beating, to repeat several times "All the while he's yelling, 'I'll kill you!—all of you!' " and to describe the victim's bleeding wounds, so that, after some minutes, one of the woman jurors made a gesture as if she were on the verge of fainting. Terence himself, listening intently, envisioning the brute Binder so savagely beating a woman half his size, felt an unmistakable gastric pang.

If the role of cross-examination in a trial is to introduce doubt into jurors' minds regarding witnesses' testimonies, it was having the opposite effect, Terence thought, in this trial. The more the defense counsel hammered at the credibility of the Renfrews, the more overwhelming seemed the defendant's guilt.

"Yessir, I sure am sure I saw what I saw," the Renfrew boy said vehemently, "—and lucky to be alive to tell it, seeing as how T.W. wanted to kill me, too!"

At last the defense counsel gave up, and dismissed the witness.

"No further questions, Your Honor."

As Charlton Heston Renfrew rose to leave the court, he pulled his baseball cap out of his pocket, gripped it in both hands before him in a clumsy, bashful gesture, and made a bowing gesture with his head, toward the jury: "Have a real nice day, y'all!"

The prosecution's final witness, Ronnie Reuben, was a neighbor of the Renfrews'; a resident of 31 Holyoak Street; a squarely built woman of about thirty-five who described herself as a person who minded her own business, yet could not help but be aware of the ruckus next door on December 27—"You'd have to be deaf, not to be." She'd known that Ava-Rose had been having trouble with her former boyfriend the motorcyclist because the Renfrews had spoken openly about it—"she wouldn't marry him, I guess: He was crazy about her"—and sure enough, two days after Christmas, there came T. W. Binder riding his Harley-Davidson right up onto the sidewalk; and, a few minutes later, a terrible commotion next door, as if somebody was being murdered. Mrs. Reuben told of going over to the Renfrews', though she was scared to death, to see if she could be of help; what she should have done, she realized afterward, was call the police right away. "Was I crazy!—I walked right up to the front door, where it was open, and Binder—yes, that's him, there, sir"—she pointed at the defendant—"came rushing out, knocking me aside like he didn't even see me. I could smell whiskey on his breath—there was blood splattered on his face, and on his hands—I almost fainted, I was so scared!— thinking for sure he'd murdered Ava-Rose! 'Cause, that other time, he'd been arrested, and there was going to be a trial, police saying he'd drowned that poor old what's-his-name— *Applewine?—Wineapple?*"

At once the defense counsel was on his feet, objecting; in such a fury, his glasses nearly flew off his nose. Yet Terence saw too that the prosecutor was also concerned. The judge quickly sustained the objection, and ordered the court stenographer to strike the witnesses' remarks following her statement of having been scared.

Yet this was insufficient for the defense counsel, who requested, and was granted, a consultation with the judge and the prosecutor, on the far side of the judge's desk, out of the jurors' hearing.

Naturally, all the jurors were alerted. So T. W. Binder was not only accused of having beaten a young woman half to death, but had once been arrested for a drowning? Terence recalled the judge having asked prospective jurors if the name "Wineapple" meant anything to them: Those who had answered "yes" had been summarily dismissed from the jury. So this is a murder case too, Terence thought, baffled. And how frustrating, that we jurors must sit here like deaf mutes, unable to ask questions or even to show our impatience!

After some minutes of intense whispered debate, the trial resumed. Ronnie Reuben, a plain, jut-chinned woman with coarse graying hair cropped close as a man's, appeared abashed at the flurry she'd caused; Terence knew enough of courtroom strategy to understand that the witness had inadvertently brought up a subject the prosecutor had not wanted brought up, though, in fact, it adversely affected the defendant's case. From this point onward, the witness spoke in a careful, halting fashion, and when the defense counsel questioned her, he limited his examination to niggling details about the "unfounded rumors" of T. W. Binder's threats against Ava-Rose Renfrew; the precise sequence of events on the afternoon of December 27; and, given that blood is blood, whose blood could Mrs. Reuben swear she'd seen on the defendant's face and hands—"Couldn't it have been, after all, his own?"

Mrs. Reuben pursed her mouth, and thought, and had to concede, "Well!—I s'pose Holly Mae and Chick might've gone after him, too, in self-defense."

" 'Self-defense'?" the defense counsel said, slyly. "How do you know it wasn't an out-and-out attack on T. W. Binder? By your own account, you weren't an eye-witness to the scene inside the Renfrew house, were you?"

Before the witness could reply, the prosecution adroitly raised an objection. Another delay! Terence felt his stomach churn. He could barely bring himself to look at the defense counsel, still less at the defendant, he felt such rage for them. He tried to calm himself by swimming laps in his imagination in the sparkling white-tiled pool at the Queenston Athletic Club. How calming on the nerves, the chaste monotony of the Australian crawl! The solace that, in the pool, naked except for swimming trunks, thus anonymous, one could commit no sin, do no wrong. *I want to be good and I want to do good but I want Justice.* Since the start of the trial, which seemed to be draining all his energy, Terence had not gone to the pool once; he felt the discomfort of unexercised muscles in his neck and shoulders.

And had not Phyllis, the evening before, at the sumptuous dinner at the Queenston Country Club, nudged him in the small of the back and murmured in a pained undertone, "Oh!—can't you stand up *straight.*"

The single witness for the defense was the defendant himself, T. W. Binder, who, called by his attorney, made his way forward in a shambling, swaying gait, like a man uncertain of his surroundings. Everyone in the courtroom watched as the bailiff swore him in: He laid a hand clumsily against the Bible, and mumbled a near-inaudible reply. For a man of thirty-two Binder appeared, to Terence's critical eye, much older. His reddish-brown hair was receding from his bumpy forehead and his muscular body was going to fat; his flushed, formerly handsome face was soft in the jowls. His lips were unnaturally white as if the blood had drained out of them *soft like slugs yet she had kissed him and been kissed by him.*

The defense counsel led Binder through his testimony, which, though clearly rehearsed, was delivered in a faltering, defiant voice. Binder insisted he'd never meant to hurt Ava-Rose Renfrew—"I just wanted to talk to her." No, he had never "harassed" or "threatened" her. He had not seen her in weeks, maybe months. If somebody was bothering her, as she'd claimed, it was "some other guy—not me." In fact, Binder said, staring at the defense counsel with a look of muted rage, as if the man were an enemy and not his only ally in the courtroom, Ava-Rose Renfrew and her family owed him money. He'd gone to 33 Holyoak Street on the afternoon of December 27 to ask about the money they owed him. How much was it?—"A couple of thousand. Maybe more." But as soon as he stepped inside the house, Binder said—"Things happened so fast, I never knew what."

The defense counsel, who appeared both belligerent and nervous, glanced at the jury to see how they were absorbing Binder's testimony. For a fraction of an instant the man's gaze locked with Terence's: He seemed to freeze. Then, "Mr. Binder, continue. Try to approximate what *did* happen."

Binder was slow to speak. He flexed his fingers, shifted his broad, hunched shoulders inside his cheaply cut brown coat. His pale mouth worked oddly, as if these words gave him pain. "Like the first time I ever saw her!—three years ago. And every time I was with her, or went there—to that house. They tried to keep me out after all I did for them, but I had a right! So I pushed my way inside and maybe I was a little drunk, but that wasn't it—what happened. I looked up, and Ava-Rose was on the stairs, and—somehow I was with her. And we were falling. And Chick, and the old woman Holly Mae, and the old man they call the Captain— *he* was there, too—and they were all on me." There was a pause. The defense counsel waited. Binder shook his head vigorously, like a dog. "Naw, I don't remember. It's all a fog. I don't know what happened. I blacked out, and when I came to I was on the bridge over the river, in the wind, my face drying in the wind, sort of freezing, on my 'cycle flying over into Pennsylvania." Binder grinned maliciously. "I went to Philly, where I got some friends. I thought maybe I was finished, here."

A chilling remark! Terence and his fellow jurors listened keenly.

The defense counsel shoved his glasses against his nose and regarded his client guardedly. As if much of this testimony were new to him?—and he dared not risk more? "Mr. Binder, uh—tell us what you were wearing on your feet that afternoon."

Binder stared, and blinked, then nodded, slowly, as if back on course. "Jogging shoes, sir. I was wearing jogging shoes."

"Jogging shoes! And not 'black leather boots'?"

"They were black jogging shoes, sir. I was wearing black jogging shoes. Not boots."

"Not boots! Very good!" The attorney sighed, rubbed his hands together. "Now tell us, to the best of your ability, Mr. Binder, what happened on the afternoon of December 27, at 33 Holyoak Street. Go back to the beginning, to your arrival—"

And so T. W. Binder did, or tried to do, in his halting, stumbling way: until, again, he reached the point of no longer remembering—"I blacked out." *Blacked out!* Terence Greene, so deeply offended by the defendant's obvious subterfuge, as by his crude physical presence, that he could scarcely force himself to listen, sat stiff and detached. Even when, later, the young prosecutor took over the questioning, several times reducing Binder to guilty, sullen silence, Terence could not concentrate. Thinking that, long ago, in a distant part of the country, as in a distant part of his life, he too had been a witness to, if not a participant in, some lost, utterly mysterious event.

Like Binder, Terence had simply blacked out, afterward.

In a place where pain runs wild, like fire. Where words refuse to follow.

The trial concluded late in the morning of the fifth day, with formal closing arguments of the prosecution and the defense; and the examination, by the jurors, of the items of evidence—the detailed medical report on the condition of Ava-Rose Renfrew, admitted to the emergency room at Trenton General Hospital, 4:40 P.M. of December 27 of the previous year; and six black-and-white photographs of the interior of the house at 33 Holyoak, primarily of the steep staircase down which Ava-Rose was said to have fallen. (Of all the jurors, Terence Greene examined these items most thoroughly. He would have liked to make a copy of Miss Renfrew's medical report, just for himself! And the interior of the Renfrew house fascinated him, what he could see of it in the background—an elaborate woven mandala wall hanging, a spiny, grotesquely flowering potted tree of about the size of an orange tree, garish Christmas decorations. At the very top of the stairs, in one of the photographs, lay, deep in slumber, the rough-coated mongrel with the German shepherd's face who had given Terence such a fright the day before.)

Before sending them to the jury room to deliberate, the judge gave the jury detailed instructions regarding the case at hand and the law governing it. They were to vote "guilty" or "not guilty" on a charge of aggravated assault; if "not guilty," they were to vote on a lesser charge of assault. All, including Terence Greene, came away having memorized that part of the New Jersey statute pertaining to "aggravated assault": *that the defendant knowingly, purposefully, and recklessly intended to inflict serious physical injury, or did inflict such injury.*

To Terence's surprise, his fellow jurors unanimously elected him foreman.

"Well! Thank you." He was genuinely moved.

(And humbled: For these men and women, strangers to him, must have been watching him with something like admiration, while, in his characteristic aloofness, he'd paid no attention to them at all.)

Yet, even granted such authority, Terence had, at first, a difficult time guiding the deliberations. He invited discussion from any of the jurors, urging them not to be shy; yet was startled by the vehemence of one of the younger men, who said, flatly, "I'd say I don't know who to believe. *Him,* just now—he sounded spaced-out. But *her,* this 'Ava-Rose'— something about her, she'd eat you up alive, I don't *know.*" He shivered, and laughed; and others laughed with him. The young man's very lack of coherence seemed to make his argument, if it was an argument, the more persuasive. Terence simply stared.

Another man, in his mid-forties, in robust physical appearance resembling Matt Montgomery, though clearly less educated, said, with a snort of derision, "*I* don't think that woman's face looked so bad, like it's anything permanent, or even 'serious,' like they say it's got to be to find him guilty. And if the guy had really kicked her in the head, wearing boots, like her and the kid said, she'd be dead now, or crippled, not walking around!"

A woman said, tentatively, "Well, she *did* have a concussion. It says here on the medical report—"

"Hey, you can get a concussion falling down a stairs, you don't need to be kicked in the head."

"But he pushed her—"

"She says! He said they all attacked *him*."

"You believe *him*? The way he acted?"

"How can you believe any of them? That kind of people—"

Terence sat quietly, listening amazed. He felt his face redden. Was it possible!—his fellow jurors, having heard the same testimonies he had heard, had formed such different opinions?

A faded, pretty woman in her mid-fifties, whom Terence had overheard identify herself as a registered nurse, said, tentatively, "These injuries on the medical report, they *are* minor. And did he mean to do it? 'Knowingly, recklessly'—all that? Was it 'aggravated'?"

"A concussion is *minor*? An eye injury?"

"Yes, compared to—"

"What *I* think happened is—"

"Look, he said he was gonna kill them—"

"*They* said!"

"It's four against one!"

"But three are in the same family."

"He said they owed him money—"

"—and what was that, about some guy—'Wineapple'?"

"Yeah, the neighbor woman said what's-his-name was going to be tried for some other thing, 'drowning'—"

"There's a lot here we don't know, huh!"

Everyone was speaking at once. Terence, though unhappy at the tone of the discussion, recalled his position as foreman, and rapped gently on the tabletop to restore order. At once, the jurors quieted. He said, "I am not a lawyer, but I feel I should speak for the judge. She did instruct us, you know, to exclude that fragment of testimony—that mysterious reference to someone, apparently drowned, named 'Wineapple.' "

"Huh! It's hard to forget something you *heard*!"

"It is," Terence conceded, "—but, in the interests of Justice, we must try."

Inwardly wincing *for certainly T. W. Binder was guilty, and that was Justice!*

An hour passed. Discussion continued. Several of the more clamorous (male) jurors, wanting to go home, suggested that a ballot be taken; but Terence, fearing that a majority of the jurors would vote for acquittal, forestalled the ballot. "We must not act prematurely," he said. "This is a grave responsibility entrusted to us."

As at meetings at the Feinemann Foundation, where it was Terence Greene's responsibility to preside over panels of contentious judges, each an expert in his field, he knew to use his understated, seemingly neutral authority to advantage.

Terence led his fellow jurors through a discussion like that of a university seminar, analyzing the trial testimonies in sequence: that of Ava-Rose Renfrew, that of Holly Mae Loomis, that of Charlton Heston Renfrew, that of Mrs. Reuben, that of T. W. Binder. This required a considerable amount of time—nearly two hours. Like the skillful teacher he had been for much of his life, Terence was careful to draw out the more reserved jurors, one of whom was an elderly black man retired from the post office, another of whom was a very young, diminutive woman with delicate Asian features; and was pleased to discover that both seemed to side with the prosecution. The young woman said hesitantly, "I think, well, she's the victim, here. This Binder, he was threatening her—"

"She says!" The aggressive young man, who had taken such a pronounced dislike to Ava-Rose Renfrew, let his fist fall on the table.

Terence, as foreman, said sharply, "Don't interrupt, please."

The young woman continued, breathless, "It happens all the time, it happened to my sister-in-law: Some guy thinks he owns a woman, beats her up, sometimes kills her. And people blame *her*. *I* think it was aggravated assault. *I* think he meant to kill her."

Terence said, quietly, "Yes. I think so, too."

It was the first clear statement Terence had made indicating his own opinion; he sensed how the others took it in. It pleased him too that the aggressive young man so immediately acquiesced to his authority. *I am the expert, I am the judge. Listen to me.*

After another half-hour, Terence called for a vote. He did not think that a clear majority would vote guilty, judging from the tenor of the debate; yet he could not forestall a vote much longer. He printed GUILTY in block letters on his ballot and sat watching, with some apprehension, as the others voted. It was a curious paradox: The more belligerent, mostly male, claimed to distrust the prosecution's argument, but were really siding with T. W. Binder against the Renfrews; the more tractable and reasonable jurors believed the prosecution's argument, and sided with the Renfrews against Binder. Where was Justice to be found? *Was* there Justice, in such a petty, brutal case?

Terence himself counted the ballots, openly. What! There were seven votes of *not guilty*, and only five of *guilty*.

A flame of pure murderous rage ran over his brain.

Yet he kept his voice under control. In his profession, diplomacy was cultivated to the level of instinct. He even managed a good-natured smile, in the face of his frowning, disgruntled companions. "Well! It looks like we may be together in this room a long time."

A mere statement of fact, and hardly a threat. But his adversaries would know he meant business.

Outside the jury room's single grimy window the warm June day began to slant into afternoon. And then late afternoon. A sheriff's deputy brought them coffee, soda pop. Terence, outwardly calm, gentlemanly as always, felt like a man in a cage. *Your quick temper. Impatience. In the company of people not like yourself.*

Terence led the discussion, which was circular, repetitive, and weary. He tried to keep an air of incredulity out of his voice as he asked questions of those jurors he knew to be his adversaries. How can you justify, do you truly think, why would the prosecution, what of the four witnesses, what of the defendant's claim of "blacking out"? He perceived that Ava-Rose Renfrew was being assaulted yet another time, in the jury room; it was an astonishing example of the stereotyped response to violent crime—"blame the victim." Yet he dared not accuse his adversaries of such primitive thinking, or he would alienate them entirely.

One of the irresolute jurors, who clearly no longer cared what the verdict was, so long as he could go home, suggested, at 5:45 P.M., that they take a straw vote on the reduced charge of simple assault—"I bet we'd be unanimous, on that"—but Terence was reluctant to do so. Obviously, the jurors who believed Binder guilty of the greater charge also believed him guilty of the lesser; the other jurors, distrustful as they were, or claimed to be, of the prosecution's case, nonetheless believed that an assault of some kind *had* occurred. Terence said, "I'm afraid, as the judge instructed us, we are to proceed with the charge of 'aggravated assault' first. And then—"

"But we're deadlocked!"

"—and then, if it seems we are really at an impasse, we can proceed to the other charge."

The man who resembled Matt Montgomery snorted

through his nose, but his voice was pleading. " 'Impasse'—what the hell's that?"

"A deadlock. A 'hung' jury."

"But we *are* deadlocked aren't we?"

Terence smiled. "Not yet."

It was Terence's perception that his adversaries, having no deep moral conviction in the case, but only a sort of spiteful emotional identification with T. W. Binder, would not hold out much longer. (Nor would his allies, probably. But *he* would hold out—forever.) As at the Feinemann Foundation, Terence Greene invited those whom he hoped to eventually defeat to speak at length, so as foreman of the jury he graciously invited his adversaries to speak, for as long as they wished, explaining why they "rejected" the State's case. It was Terence's shrewd conviction that, for many people, especially the more volatile and the less intelligent, the mere act of speaking constituted action; sometimes it was as satisfying. The loud young man, the man who resembled Matt Montgomery, another man of slack-bellied middle age whose bald head shone as if polished: These jurors took turns airing their grievances, in monologues that revealed an intense dislike and distrust of women. All three men claimed to have known women like Ava-Rose Renfrew—"She'd say any damned thing, and just her saying it," the bald man said excitedly, "made you believe it was so. Like if she said, 'It's raining out,' on a day like today, you'd believe, hey, it's raining out! Yeah!" Everyone, even the women jurors, laughed.

Terence said, "But she didn't put anything over on *you.*"

More laughter. The bald man's chunky teeth gleamed. "Hell, I'm still paying alimony, nine years later."

So it went. The sheriff's deputy brought them supper, carried across the street from the Mill Hill Tavern, and the jury's mood was more convivial. Terence at last argued his own position, explaining that he had "an unshakable moral conviction" that the defendant Binder was guilty as charged;

and that it would be a violation of Justice if the jury settled for anything less. Terence chose his words with care; yet he felt buoyant, inspired. *Hettie's boy. Poor child. Yet listen!*

After he finished his appeal, there was a silence. His fellow jurors contemplated him wonderingly. Then the loud young man, who had been restless and sullen for some time, shrugged, and laughed, and reached for a ballot—"Okay, man, you convinced me! Let's just get out of here."

This time, when Terence counted the ballots, he was happy to see that the vote was unanimous: *Guilty.*

And what pride he took, rising in the jury box, in the courtroom, when the judge requested him to stand and deliver the verdict.

"Guilty, Your Honor"—in his even, neutral-sounding voice.

The prosecutor checked a smile; the defense counsel dropped a pencil on his tabletop, in a small gesture of disgust. But the defendant T. W. Binder sat impassive, with downcast eyes, and did not look up.

Terence's only regret was that *she* was not in the courtroom, to hear the verdict.

"Daddy Looked Right Through Me"

*C*indy Greene would remember: It was only a few days after poor Tuffi died that Daddy began to change.

This was in early September. Before Labor Day, when it was still warm and humid as summer. Cindy, who believed secretly that she was her daddy's favorite child, *yes there was some secret understanding between them that excluded Mommy too,* hadn't any word for it, at first; just a sense, a visceral sensation of hurt, unease, resentment—"Daddy, aren't you listening? You never listen to me!"

And Daddy would say, quickly, his gaze shifting from its gray-gauzy look to its sharper, in-focus look, fixed upon Cindy, "Why of course I'm listening, honeybun. You were telling me about—" repeating Cindy's words the way a machine or a parrot might, just the words and not the meaning beneath.

"Oh Daddy! Really! You don't have to humor *me.*"

Cindy might laugh mirthlessly, to show she didn't give a damn, really. Or she might storm out of the room, heavy on her heels, knowing Daddy was staring after her, apologetic and pained.

(Cindy weighed more than ever. She'd abandoned her

diet in self-disgust, during the family's two-week visit, in August, to Grandmother Winston's summer home in Nantucket; it gave her a hateful sort of pleasure, knowing how plain and chunky she was, how she was growing, breasts and hips especially, and would continue to grow, *and there was nothing she or anyone else could do about it.*)

The first strange thing about Daddy, that occurred soon after Tuffi's death, was, in a way, the strangest. When Cindy thought of it, afterward, during the terrible months to come, she would hug herself, the plumpness and solidity of herself, and shudder. *What had it meant!*

It was in fact the first of those numerous Saturdays Daddy had to be away for professional reasons—a conference in New Haven, Connecticut. He'd left before breakfast, and so was cheated of the usual household chores he so loved. Poor Daddy! How quiet the house was, how empty, and ordinary, without his hammering, sawing, whistling, banging about, talking to himself!

Phyllis observed, with a shivery little laugh, "With both of them gone, it's too peaceful, somehow, and too sad."

"*Mom*my!"—Cindy and Kim both giggled, shocked.

(For Mommy was referring to Tuffi, as well as Daddy.)

Daddy had said to expect him home on Sunday afternoon, but, to Cindy's surprise, he came home early, on Saturday night. It happened that Cindy was alone: Aaron had left for Dartmouth, Kim was at a party, Phyllis was having dinner at the Bawdens' on Cherrylane Road. Cindy, who scorned the company of the few girls in her class who might have befriended her, was watching a video and eating lukewarm pizza when she heard a car turn up the driveway— judging, by the sound of the motor, that it was Daddy's car, and not Mommy's.

Daddy?—home early? And only Cindy to greet him?

Cindy hurried into the utility room, hearing her father drive his car into the garage; hearing the motor running—

and running, and running. What was wrong? Why didn't he turn off the ignition? Cindy opened the garage door, poked her head out—saw a sight she would not soon forget: Daddy in his car, behind the wheel, stiff and unmoving and unaware of her, *hiding his face in his hands.*

"Oh Daddy!"—a whisper, not a cry.

After a long moment, Daddy lowered his hands. Was he crying? The overhead light in the garage was on, but its light was indistinct, shadowed. Daddy had no awareness of Cindy, so hypnotized-seeming was he. Could he be sick? drunk? Cindy frowned, watching him. How strange he looked: shadows beneath his eyes deep as grooves, nostrils smudged and black as holes. He did not look handsome as Cindy knew him but disfigured somehow—ugly. Even his necktie was askew, as if someone had flung it mockingly back over his shoulder.

And why did he sit there, still as death?—like some robot or zombie in a movie? Why didn't he turn off the ignition? The garage was filling with poisonous smoke.

Cindy, who was frightened, decided to make a joke of it. She shouted, "Daddy, hey! Carbon mo*nox*ide!"—waving and making a pug face, so Daddy saw her at last, waking from his trance. At once, he switched off the ignition.

Cindy ran to the car, to open the door and to be kissed. "Hey! Hiya! How come you're back home early? You trying to gas yourself, or—" But how peculiar, Daddy had hardly moved from behind the wheel; held back, as if not wanting to be touched, or to show himself in the light. Cindy cried, "Daddy, what's wrong? How come you're—" seeing then the still-moist clots of blood in his nostrils and the bruise beneath his left eye; his swollen upper lip. She screamed, "Oh Daddy, what *happened?*"

Daddy had a wad of tissue in hand, a bloodstained wad, and was hurriedly dabbing at his nose. He said, quickly, in an effort to sound normal, even cheerful, "Honeybun, I had a little accident on the way home, and banged my silly nose."

"Oh Daddy! An *accident!*"

"But it's nothing, really. *Nothing.*" Daddy's voice rose, uncertainly. "Your mother's not home?"—seeing that Phyllis's car was gone.

"M-Mommy's at the Bawdens', and she'll be—back soon."

"Good! Good. I'd hate to upset her, too."

Cindy saw that the front right fender of her father's handsome BMW had buckled in, and part of the grill was dented. The right front headlight was cracked.

"Some damned driver on the Turnpike changed lanes right in front of me, and I couldn't brake in time—" Daddy's voice trailed off in impatience and regret, as if he were about to cry. "Of course, I suppose it was my fault, too, for daydreaming."

Cindy, suddenly a very young child, sucked at her fingers watching her beloved father climb out of his car, stretching his long legs and standing on them tentatively, as if fearing the knees might buckle. Except for his bruised eye and bloodied nostrils, Daddy's face was a sickly-clammy gray, like damp newsprint. His necktie was not only crooked, but speckled with blood; his shirt front was speckled with blood; one of his coat sleeves was torn at the cuff, and both lapels were torn. (This was a modestly stylish beige sports coat, a cotton and linen fabric. The necktie was a plain brown silk.) It would not occur to Cindy to wonder how such injuries to her father's clothes might have been caused by a minor accident on the Turnpike.

Daddy switched on one of the garage lights, and examined the front of the car, where the fender and grill were dented. There was a smear of oil, or something, on the fender, which Daddy hurriedly wiped off with a kerosene-soaked rag; Cindy could hear his audible, agitated breath. Poor Daddy!

Cindy asked, incensed, "Did you get his license plate number? Did anybody *see?*"

Daddy said, shuddering, "No. Nobody saw. The other driver—drove away. And I was left behind." He passed a trembling hand over his eyes. Cindy had never seen her father so—disturbed; so *unlike himself.* He murmured, another time, "I suppose it *was* my fault."

"But, Daddy, what if you'd been killed! Don't say that!" Cindy was wide-eyed, indignant. Reluctant too to surrender the delicious fear, the secret rapport between Daddy and herself, the very *strangeness* of this encounter. Tears sprang into her eyes as she rushed to hug Daddy, who, stooping to hug her, gave a faint groan, as if his knees did hurt. The sinister odor of automobile exhaust hung in the air, for it was a warm, humid September evening, with no wind. Though Cindy was tearful, and agitated, she could not resist a bright schoolgirl's observation—"Carbon monoxide, the poison, actually doesn't *smell.* It's just the exhaust, the smoke, that *smells.* Did you know that, Daddy?"

Daddy gave a hoarse little sob, hiding his face in his daughter's hair.

Phyllis too noted the change in Terence: Though, being more observant than Cindy, and perhaps inclined to be more critical of Terence than Cindy, she would have dated its onset earlier than Tuffi's death: Certainly, it began with that damned trial, back in June.

Terence's distracted, fumbling manner, his dreamy *not-thereness*—these were qualities in her husband some found endearing, but Phyllis found increasingly annoying. During the five days of the trial, there had been some excuse, at least; but, then, after the trial, for weeks; even while they were visiting Phyllis's mother on Nantucket Island, staying as guests in the Winstons' beautiful oceanside house—why, in such a setting, spend so much time brooding, *off in a world of his own?*

One brightly sunny morning on the island, Phyllis said, as she and Terence were dressing, "I wish you wouldn't be so absentminded, around Mother. After all, this is her house. We're guests here, and the children are guests here. And it *is* beautiful."

Terence turned to Phyllis, with his vague querying smile. "Has your mother complained of me? I'm sorry."

"Her arthritis is so painful, she may have to use that awful wheelchair all the time," Phyllis said passionately. "She has a right to expect gratitude from us, and sympathy; and she has a right to expect—well, *gallantry*—from you, her son-in-law. Remember how Father used to pamper her? She's never really recovered from his death."

Terence said, concerned, "Why, Phyllis—I thought I *was* being gallant. Last night, at the yacht club—"

"Yes, but Mother didn't need to be helped with her lobster, not as you were doing it," Phyllis said, "—and that business with her chair, and the edge of the carpet, that just embarrassed her, I think. She's such a sweet, brave woman —we must be more thoughtful with her. I realize, she sometimes chatters, but—"

"Phyllis, I'm very fond of your mother," Terence said, "—as I was of your father. They did so much for us—of course, I'm infinitely grateful."

Phyllis detected a faint air of mockery, or irony, here: Her husband was a literary-minded man, a man who chose his words, when he wished to, with care. "You don't need to be 'infinitely' grateful, Terry, just 'adequately' grateful. The children take their cues from you, especially Aaron. Keep that in mind."

Terence pulled at his nose, as if deep in thought. He stood some yards from Phyllis, in khaki shorts and a white T-shirt that fitted his narrow, rather flat torso loosely; he was barefoot, and his bony white toes kneaded the carpet.

Phyllis, who tanned beautifully, looking, these summer days, years younger than her age (she'd recently had a birthday: her forty-sixth), regarded even Terence's toes, like his pale, if sturdy, legs, with a measure of exasperation. Wasn't it like Terence not to *tan*? How, even in the summer, did he manage *that*?

Terence smiled, that sweet boyish smile that, years ago, had so won Phyllis's heart. He said, "If I've neglected your mother, dear, it wasn't intentionally. From now on, I'll try harder to be nice. This very day. This morning!" He kicked his feet into sandals, and made swiping motions at his wispy hair with both his hands, peering into a mirror on the wall. "And I'm damned sorry for losing that attaché case she gave me."

Phyllis said sharply, "Mother didn't give you that attaché case, Terry. I did."

"Oh—really? I—must be thinking of another case, or a—wallet—or something." Terence's face colored faintly, with embarrassment.

Phyllis asked, "Why do you think of the attaché case, why right now? I'm just curious."

"Why? I really don't know, Phyllis," Terence said, sighing, "—just thinking of your mother, I suppose. Of disappointing her. And you."

"Are you still thinking about that trial? About Trenton? After so long?"

"I'm sure I was *not*."

"Imagine, on Nantucket Island, with this view of the Atlantic—thinking about Trenton, New Jersey." Phyllis laughed, fondly, if with exasperation. She touched Terence's upper arm, feeling the hard, compact muscles: a swimmer's muscles. "Of course you don't 'disappoint,' Terry, either my mother, or me. Don't talk that way."

"I will admit, I've been distracted. I really don't know why." There was a pause. Terence seemed about to continue, but did not.

"Well, I advised you not to sign on for jury duty. I said—"

"Phyllis, why do you make such a fuss over that? The trial was unexceptional, it lasted only five days, it's *done*." Terence spoke with unusual severity. "I was only doing my duty as a citizen."

Phyllis looked at him searchingly, her hand still on his arm.

How open, frank, innocent her husband was!—he could

have no secrets from her, she knew. Her parents' initial disappointment with Terence Greene—with his background, rather more than with him—had been tempered by their perception that here was a good man, an honest man, a man of integrity. At times, Phyllis felt herself the custodian of her husband's very innocence, as if, along with being his wife, she were also his mother: the mother he'd lost as a small child.

Quickly Phyllis stood on her toes, and kissed her husband's warm, mildly indignant cheek. "Sorry, darling! I won't bring it up again."

Because I know something about you, and your early life, which you don't know. Which you've blessedly forgotten.

For the remainder of the Nantucket visit, Terence seemed clearly to be making an effort to be less self-absorbed; above all, to be attentive to Phyllis's mother. He commiserated with her on the subject of her rheumatoid arthritis; he learned to be deft and adroit and gallant, assisting her in the wheelchair when they went out, while sharing with her the fiction that the wheelchair's use was merely temporary, an anomaly in the life of a healthy, vigorous, independent woman; he listened to her reminiscences, and her complaints, and called her "Fanny" instead of "Mrs. Winston," as he'd done for years.

Phyllis's mother was a solid-bodied woman with a strong, bulldog face, eyes direct and level as her daughter's, a mind like a proverbial steel trap when it came to finances; yet, like many widows of her class, she imagined herself made more feminine, thus more fluttery and girlish, since her husband's death. Certainly it was true, in her wheelchair, which she detested, she *was* at a disadvantage. So it seemed quite natural that she hang heavily on her son-in-law's arm, and his hand; that, having drunk too much at dinner, she giggle, and call him "Terry, dear," and address most of her chatter, even intimate reminiscences of Phyllis's childhood, to him.

It was to Terence that Fanny Winston said, sniffing as if

on the verge of tears, "I feel so *safe* around you—and your family. As if I know who I *am*." And, as August neared its end, "This has been a lovely visit, hasn't it? I'm afraid I'm going to miss you, terribly!" And, with a squeeze of Terence's fingers, "Phyllis has invited me to visit you in Queenston this fall—I hope that's agreeable with *you*?"

Terence smiled sweetly, and said, "Why, Fanny, of course, *yes*."

So Phyllis was the more mystified, and the more upset, when, at the time of her mother's visit, Terence was his old absentminded self again; and worse.

The trouble began at once, on the very first day. Phyllis's mother was due to arrive at Newark Airport at 1 P.M. of the first Saturday in October; Terence was to pick her up at the airport; unforgivably, he was fifty minutes late. And when at last he did arrive, looking disheveled, and behaving most distractedly, he could offer the poor woman no better excuse than claiming he'd been "slowed down by Turnpike traffic."

Mrs. Winston complained to Phyllis, that evening: "He hardly *looked* at me. He hadn't even *shaved*. I've never been so rudely treated!"

Phyllis, who was angry with Terence, too, and had had words with him earlier, tried now to defend him. "Mother, Terry is under so much pressure, these days, at the Foundation. One of his associates is giving him trouble, and he has so many extra meetings, conferences—"

"Is that any excuse? Are you offering that as an excuse?"

"Oh no, Mother. Except—"

"Your poor father had as much pressure, or more; there was always at least one parishioner *dying*, and invariably, over the holidays, when we wanted to get away to Coral Gables, three or four. No wonder he had those terrible strokes!"

"Oh, I know, Mother. I realize—"

"And Willard had numerous investments, adding up to quite a bit of money, for which he bore sole responsibility— unlike Terence, I believe?"

Phyllis winced at this remark. She loved her mother,

however a challenge it was at such times to *like* her mother; certainly she felt sympathy for the aging woman in the wheelchair, once attractive, now puffy-faced, with bluish-gray permed hair and drooping eyelids and a perpetually aggrieved air. She said, squeezing her mother's beringed hands, "Now, Mother!—you know that Terry has other qualities, don't you? He *has* apologized for being late at the airport."

"And where is he now?"

"Where—now? In his study, I think. Working."

Mrs. Winston dabbed at her eyes, which were fierce with tears, a bright steely-gray. Seated in her shiny motorized wheelchair she commanded an authority she had not had previously. Unspoken between Phyllis and her mother—as, indeed, between Phyllis and her father: for the Winstons were not comfortable speaking of such things—was the issue of the older woman's estate, which must be worth, by now, no less than several million dollars in cash, property, and investments. There was no one else to whom Mrs. Winston might reasonably leave this fortune than her daughter and her daughter's family—was there? At all times, the subject was unspoken yet underscored such conversations, like an incessant humming noise in the background.

Phyllis said, warmly, her hands still on her mother's, "Terry *is* a perfectionist in his work. I try to get him to relax, but—"

"I thought he wanted me to visit," Mrs. Winston said, hurt. "I just don't feel welcome here."

"Mother, of course Terry wants you to visit. He's been looking forward to this, really he has. It's just that—you know how he is."

"After Willard and I helped you with this house—and it *is* a lovely house, isn't it?"

Phyllis smiled a little harder. "Yes, Mother: a lovely house. And Terry and I were, and are, grateful. As I think we've said."

"I'm not sure I like the new carpeting in the family room, it's too—I don't know: bland. But the new curtains in my room—in the guest room—are *very* charming. I've always loved organdy."

"I picked them out myself, with you in mind. Pink organdy."

"Did you!" Mrs. Winston smiled, though warily. She leaned toward Phyllis, shifting her weight in the wheelchair with some effort. She was not a tall woman, but she'd become quite stout; her poor swollen legs, encased in unfashionable cotton support hose, added to her bulk. It pained Phyllis to see her dignified mother so altered—the more so, in that Fanny Winston so resembled *her*. In an undertone Mrs. Winston asked, "Your husband isn't seeing another woman, is he?"

Phyllis laughed, shocked. "Mother, really!"

It was the most preposterous thing Fanny Winston had ever uttered in her daughter's hearing.

Mrs. Winston visited with the Greenes for twelve days in October, a visit that had its pleasant interludes, but, overall, put a considerable strain upon Phyllis. She had to entertain, daily, her easily bored mother, whose handicapped condition made everything more difficult; she had to keep up, however sporadically, her public relations work. (Not that Queenston Opportunities, with but one or two clients, was anything like a full-time enterprise: But Phyllis hoped to give her friends and acquaintances the impression that it was.) During this time, Cindy behaved, on the whole, surprisingly well; Kim made an obvious effort to *be nice to* her grandmother; but Terence was unpredictable. On those evenings when he actually sat down at the dinner table with his family, he might be courteous, attentive, warm, and engaging—or he might be sombre, ashen-faced, distracted, and without appetite. Or, he might drink too much. Or, he might excuse himself midway in the meal, and disappear into his study to make a telephone call—"Don't wait for me, I don't know how long this will take."

Phyllis did not know whether to be angry, or concerned:

She had never seen Terence quite like this, and his vague explanation, that the Feinemann Foundation was being reorganized, and that, in some quarters, his authority was being challenged, did not seem entirely adequate. Yet, Phyllis chose to believe him, and to defend him to her mother. With wifely solicitude she said, "I just hope Terry's health won't be affected by all this, like Father's was!" Mrs. Winston said, with a grim little smile, "I think it already *has* been."

When it developed that, on the day of Mrs. Winston's departure (she was flying to Hilton Head, South Carolina, for a week's visit at a health spa), Terence would be at a conference in Boston, Mrs. Winston said pointblank to him, "They certainly keep you running, at that Foundation! Willard would be surprised, I think—what he knew of it (he was well acquainted, you know, with several trustees) led him to think it would be—well, more gentlemanly, somehow. A place where you might use your *intelligence*."

"Really!" Terence murmured. It was nominally breakfast: But Terence was having only fruit juice, before hurrying off to catch his train for Manhattan. He managed a lopsided smile, catching Phyllis's eye. "It's very nice to think that, in Reverend Winston's circle, *intelligence* and *gentlemanliness* were not incompatible."

Mrs. Winston, staring at her son-in-law, was not to be deflected. "You had a more comfortable schedule, Terry, as a college teacher, I seem to recall."

"But, Fanny, I made relatively little money as a teacher, didn't I?" Terence asked. He smiled; but Phyllis could see the strain in his face. She was relieved when he left for the depot.

And there was the evening, at one of Queenston's most elegant restaurants, when, having drunk too much wine, Terence fell asleep in his chair—in Mrs. Winston's bemusedly sympathetic words, "like a fevered infant."

And another evening, at the Hendries' (for Alice Hendries' eighty-nine-year-old mother was living with them, and it was hoped the two older women might enjoy meeting each other), Terence fell into a surprisingly heated argument with Burt Hendrie over the issue of gun control and the National Rifle Association: Burt, a self-proclaimed descendant of "pioneer American sportsmen," said that if guns are denied law-abiding citizens, only criminals will have them, and Terence retorted that that kind of stereotyped thinking was in itself criminal—"That damned NRA should be sued for every gun injury and death in this country!"

Phyllis stared at Terence. Remembering afterward, *It was as though a stranger stood in his place—yet with his eyes, his mouth.*

And, next morning, Phyllis's mother murmured, in an ambiguous tone, "Terence *can* be passionate, sometimes—can't he!"

On the final evening of Mrs. Winston's visit, Terence was an hour late for dinner; but apologized profusely, with kisses for everyone, and, unexpectedly, presents as well—"I was walking on Madison Avenue, and there was this exotic little boutique, and I found myself looking in the window, so I thought, 'Why not!'" Smiling happily, as if, perhaps, he'd had a drink or two on the train, Terence handed around gifts to his wife, his mother-in-law, his daughters, and stood rubbing his hands as they opened them. A silk handbag with a shoulder strap, intricately decorated with brightly colored appliquéd flowers, for Kim—"Wow, Daddy! Cool!" A brilliant crimson scarf, for Cindy, whose mouth moved oddly as she lifted it—"Oh Daddy, it's too nice, for me." A necklace of gaudy, chunky glass beads, for Phyllis—"Why, Terry, how thoughtful! Thank you, darling." A pair of earrings for Fanny Winston, made of turquoise and purple feathers, in a sunburst design measuring five inches across—"Why, what *is* this? How—nice!"

"Women can wear such damned pretty things!"—so Terence said, wistfully, smiling upon them all.

The girls left the table, and Phyllis and her mother lingered over coffee, while Terence, still a bit breathless, ate a few mouthfuls of the meal Phyllis had kept warm for him.

He chatted with his mother-in-law, teased her a bit. *Was* he a little drunk?—or just excited? (He'd quickly poured himself a glass of red wine, so, if Phyllis leaned over to kiss him, to smell his breath, she wouldn't really know.) Phyllis watched him closely, considering. Absurd to imagine Terence Greene, of all people, seeing another woman: His behavior was mercurial, and he was becoming ever more eccentric, but, in his fumbling way, he meant well.

So Phyllis forgave him, another time.

Thinking, "I do love him—I suppose."

But what silly gifts he'd given her and her mother—the cheap Indian-style necklace, of a kind Phyllis would have scorned wearing since high school; the utterly inappropriate pair of earrings for her mother, of a kind hippies and flower children might have worn, in the 1960s. Phyllis would pass on her necklace to Kim, who would love it—Kim was so pretty, any sort of jewelry looked good on her. But, poor Fanny!—there she was, preening a bit, holding the outsized earrings up to her ears, the exotic feathers brushing against her flaccid, rouged cheeks. "Why, Terry," she was saying, her eyelashes quivering, "—I certainly don't own anything like *these.*"

And there was Kim Greene's upsetting encounter with her father—which, being Kim Greene, a girl of many secrets, she did not share with her sister Cindy, still less Mommy. No chance!

For one thing, Kim would have had to say she'd been hanging out at tacky Mercer Mall, miles away on Route 1—a place not only forbidden to her, but accessible to her only by way of some guy with a car, forbidden too.

And the guy—could it be Studs Schrieber, whom Kim had promised never to see again, after an unfortunate episode that summer, at Brooke Casey's place, the weekend Brooke's parents were away? (This episode, thank God, had been kept secret from Daddy—it was Mommy's conviction that it would simply upset him too much.)

So, Kim told no one in the family, and tried hard to forget: how, that night, just before Hallowe'en, she'd seen Daddy grinning so, hauling a large brass birdcage to his car, and he'd looked right through her—*his favorite of his three children.*

Mercer Mall, in front of Beno's Pizzeria, was a gathering place for local teenagers—public school kids, kids from outside Trenton, older guys who'd dropped out of school and led mysterious, enviable lives. Very few kids from Queenston Day!—except Studs Schrieber, who drove a new-model chocolate-brown Camaro, and his favored buddies, and his girlfriends. (Kim, who loved Studs passionately, and knew, for all his cruelty to her, that she would never love any man as much in her entire life, had to accept it that Studs had other girls. It was like the stigmata, such knowledge.) While her parents believed that Kim was in Queenston, at one or another friend's house, maybe doing homework, Kim was, most nights, at the mall, from approximately 8 P.M. until 10:30 P.M. (Her curfew was 11 P.M.) There, a rowdy, ever-shifting pack of teenagers gathered, mostly in their cars; eating pizza, drinking beer, passing joints around, in delicious stealth. This corner of the mall was raided occasionally by police, but that was part of the excitement—to outwit the "shithead-Smokeys," as the guys called them.

So far, Kimberly Greene, a junior at Queenston Day School, daughter of Mr. and Mrs. Terence Greene of 7 Juniper Way, Queenston, had not yet been swept up in a police raid, and hauled by van to Mercer County Detention Center in Trenton. Studs Schrieber cheerfully boasted, "I got internal radar, that smells a shithead cop a mile away."

It happened that, one evening, in late October, at about 8:30 P.M., Kim, and Studs, and several of Studs's buddies, were standing by the Camaro trading wisecracks with some beefy redneck skinheads from the far side of Route 1, and Kim glanced up to see, to her horror, her own father driving past!—Terence Greene, in his handsome silver BMW, unmistakable. Thank God, Daddy did not see *her.*

Kim was so astonished, she clutched wordlessly at the sleeve of Studs's leather jacket.

What was Daddy doing here, at tacky Mercer Mall?—at such an hour? Miles out of his way, assuming he was coming from the Queenston depot? (He hadn't been home for dinner that night, he'd called around 6 P.M. to apologize for having to work late at the Foundation—Kim herself had spoken with Daddy on the phone.) Kim watched incredulously as her father parked the BMW close by, and went into, of all places, a pet supplies store called Birds 'N' Beasts; and, perhaps ten minutes later, came out again, briskly, smiling—carrying a rectangular brass birdcage large enough to hold a vulture!

"Fuck!—it really *is* your old man!" Studs said, impressed.

Kim, reckless and sullen by now, defiant—the wind in her hair, two quick cans of beer, several drags from a joint that tasted like burning cat hairs—stood, arms folded, leaning against the front of the Camaro where her father could easily see her, if he chose: But, though it seemed to Kim that Daddy was smiling at her, he did not apparently see her. *Daddy looked right through me.*

And she was carrying, so conspicuously, the beautiful silk purse he'd given her, scarlet, green, purple, gold—roses, lilies, starburst designs in velvet, and sequins, a bag so striking that even Studs had noticed it, approvingly.

After Kim's father drove away, Studs suggested they check in Birds 'N' Beasts to see exactly what he'd bought. The store, like most stores at the mall, was open until 9 P.M.

So they went inside, Studs in the lead, the more curious, inquisitive, asking questions of the salesclerk Kim would never have asked. "That old guy who was just in here—what kind of cage did he buy? How much did it cost?" Studs had a habit of standing at his full height as if at attention; he was only an inch or so taller than Kim, but seemed, in her adoring eyes, much taller. And how handsome he was, despite his mottled skin and narrow, squinty, damp eyes that turned pink as a rabbit's from smoking dope!—his greased dark hair skimmed back, and worn in a tiny tail, "spic-style" he called it, a narrow moustache now on his short upper lip, the gold studs in his ear and the gold ring through his nose glinting shrewdly. Those times he'd done *it* to her sort of against her will and not using a condom —Kim had forgiven him, in the very process of *it*.

But, God!—if Mommy and Daddy *knew!*

So Studs Schrieber learned that Terence Greene, who, like several other Queenston daddies, always looked at him as if wishing him dead, had bought a $300 brass parrot cage, of all weird things. "Since when do you guys own a fucking *parrot?*" he laughed.

Kim, nervous, giggly, but feeling relieved now, and, as they left the store, ready for another joint, said, "Maybe Daddy will be getting us one, for Christmas. Maybe it's a surprise!"

But seeing, afterward, in her mind's eye, her father: that smile of his, that look of a man who's *happy.*

And seeming to know, with adolescent resignation, *It has nothing to do with us.*

Can it be I, who does such things?

It was a consequence of Tuffi's death, one September afternoon shortly after the Greenes returned from Nantucket.

Terence had been on a stepladder clumsily repairing a broken gutter at the rear of the house, trying not to think of the disagreeable meeting he'd had with a panel of fellowship judges at the Foundation the previous day, when, suddenly, there was Phyllis tugging impatiently at his trouser leg, saying she'd been calling him, and calling him—"Terry, for God's sake! Tuffi needs to be taken to the vet. Can you hurry?"

Terence did hurry, to discover, to his horror, the poor dog writhing and squealing on the utility room floor, amid a powerful stench of bowels and vomit. The poor creature had

been visibly ailing for months—the vet had diagnosed pro-
gressive liver failure, for which there was little remedy—and
so this was no surprise, exactly; but it was a shock, and a
piteous sight. Cindy stood in the doorway, hands to her face,
eyes widened—"Oh Daddy! Do something! Tuffi's in *pain!*"
And there was Aaron hovering in the kitchen, with a stricken
expression (for Tuffi had been, since puppyhood, at least
nominally, Aaron's pet), tennis racket in hand—"Jesus, what
a time for this! I have to leave! *Christ!*"

Terence squatted beside the convulsing animal. He saw
that Tuffi's eyes were yellowed, no doubt from jaundice; his
muzzle was frothy with saliva. Gingerly, Terence touched the
dog, hoping he wouldn't bite, or claw—"Tuffi, poor boy!
We'll do what we can."

Phyllis, and Cindy, and Aaron were deeply sympathetic
with the dog's ordeal; but made no offer to ride along with
Terence to take him to the vet. Had Terence not spoken
sharply to his son, Aaron would not even have helped him
carry the dog to his car. "Gee, Dad," Aaron said, in his nasal,
whining voice, "—I'm late already, and I just changed my
clothes."

Terence settled Tuffi in the back seat of the car, atop
some scattered newspapers. The poor dog was so weak, there
seemed no need to put him in his carrying case.

Terence hurriedly climbed into the car, started the ignition. The sight of his son standing in the driveway, tall and
solidly built, handsome in his tennis whites, clearly impatient
for Terence to drive away, and yet simulating a look of grief,
loss, pain, infuriated him. "Why the hell don't you put that
racket down, and come along with me?" Terence asked.
"You might be of some use for once."

"Aw shit, Dad—"

Terence clenched his jaws, hearing the familiar profan-
ity. So familiar! "Don't you care for poor Tuffi, at least? Your
own dog?"

"Sure I do, but—I'm late already for where I'm going."

"This might be the last time you see him alive. Don't you give a damn about *that*?"

"Jesus, Dad—"

Now Phyllis intervened, as, so often, in such circumstances, she did. She had been peering in at Tuffi, making cooing sounds, as if such sounds might comfort the dog in agony; now she turned sharply back to Terence. "Let Aaron alone, Terry! There's hardly any point in *two* people going to the vet, and you know it."

Terence's face was burning. "No, no point. Sorry!"

So Terence, shaken and disgusted, drove the dying dog to the animal hospital by himself. He spoke to Tuffi, hoping to quiet the dog; he was thinking of the poor sweet creature as a puppy, years ago—and of his children, years ago. Aaron as a young boy. Aaron as a baby.

There was, at this time, an unresolved issue between Terence and Aaron, and this too blocked by Phyllis: The previous Christmas, Aaron had asked for, and received, some expensive skiing equipment (Phyllis had made the purchases, but Terence seemed to know the cost had been well above $500); he'd taken it off to Dartmouth, where, supposedly, it had been stolen. But Terence had the suspicion (having heard that one of Aaron's friends had sold similar merchandise, and reported it stolen) that in fact Aaron had simply sold the skiing equipment and pocketed the money. Of course, Terence could hardly prove this. Phyllis had accused him of not loving their son, and Aaron had been furious—"That guy's *sick*, Mom!"

At the animal hospital, it was discovered that Tuffi's liver had so deteriorated, and his kidneys and heart were so weakened, there was no choice but to put him to sleep.

"No choice!" Terence's voice cracked. "Well. I see. Of course."

The vet, a young woman assistant, and Terence held the feebly struggling dog down on the examining table, as the vet injected lethal serum into an artery in the dog's neck.

Dying, Tuffi looked up at Terence with his frightened, dis-colored eyes, as if awaiting a command. He whimpered, but no longer thrashed about. "Tuffi, poor dear Tuffi, we love you, Tuffi," Terence said, in sudden fear himself of the hor-ror of what was happening.

"It will only take a minute," the vet said softly.

Terence stroked Tuffi's coarse fur, and gripped the dog tight in anticipation of a violent death spasm that never came.

Instead, the dog's muscles relaxed; he grew limp, simply as if falling asleep; the terror in his eyes clouded, but his eyes remained open, glassy in death. Terence whispered, "Wait, no—Doctor?—I've changed my mind—"

The vet had been giving Tuffi his shots and treating him for most of his life, and had come to know Terence. He now laid a consoling hand on Terence's arm. "I know, it's hard. But you made the right decision, Dr. Greene."

Dr. Greene!—why did people call him that, when he knew himself so confused, so ineffectual, so at a loss? And, now at this time, so stricken with grief?

Terence tried to make his voice steady. "Did I? Thank you. There's that, at least."

Terence chose to bring Tuffi back home for burial, not to have him cremated at the hospital, as, he gathered, most other pet owners did with their deceased pets. The young woman assistant helped him wrap the body in newspaper, rather tenderly, Terence thought; in his grief-weakened state, her kindness provoked tears. Wiping at his face roughly, Ter-ence said, "He was such a sweet-natured, loving dog. I always felt I didn't love him enough. The children—" But he did not want to be accusatory. He did not want to sound like a disappointed, complaining suburban father. "—loved him, of course. When they were younger."

Terence paused, not knowing what he was saying. Tuffi was now wrapped up in newspaper, his glassy eyes hidden. In death, he would be heavier than he'd been in life. Terence said, his voice cracking, "Damn it, Tuffi was only twelve years old!—that isn't enough of a life."

The young woman in her soiled smock and blue jeans smiled up at Terence unexpectedly. "Gee!—I know I'd feel real lucky at the end, Dr. Greene, if somebody loved *me* like you love *him*."

Terence stared at the young woman for the first time: a heart-shaped, strong-boned face with a good, healthy skin, no makeup, frank brown eyes and wiry brown hair that scintillated as with streaks of mica.

"Gee, yeah!" the young woman said, seeing the sudden look of yearning in Terence's pale face, "—Tuffi's a real lucky old fella!—or *was.*"

And he buried the dog's body by himself, too. At the rear of their two-acre wooded lot, at the foot of a gentle slope fragrant with pine needles.

I will arise and go now. I will arise.

How strangely familiar this neighborhood, the houses run-down, derelict, yet appealing!—and, at 33 Holyoak, the ramshackle residence of the Renfrews, unchanged, except, today, in a golden-sepia flood of autumnal sunshine, the overgrown garden in the front yard was brighter with color than it had been in early summer. Someone—a big-boned stocky woman in overalls and a straw hat—was it Holly Mae Loomis?—was clipping and weeding in the garden. The sunbathing girls on the roof who had so teased Terence were gone—at least, as Terence parked his car at the curb, squinting and smiling vaguely toward the house, he saw no one.

But there was the burly, shaggy brown dog with the German shepherd's face, dozing on the veranda.

Terence's heart was beating hard. As it had done in his childhood, when, urged and bullied by his uncle, he'd pushed off into the cold, deep, metallic-smelling water of the stone quarry where he'd been taught to swim—that initial apprehension, quick-flashing terror, exacerbated by icy currents in the water that attacked his goose-pimpled flesh like knife blades. *I am going to drown, I am helpless.*

But he'd pushed off, anyway. And he'd never drowned.

It was a weekday. A few days after Tuffi had been put to sleep. Terence Greene had done something he'd never done in his entire professional life—he'd called in, pleading illness, simply to take a day off from his work.

Poor old fella!—the words rang, now mockingly, in Terence's head.

Terence had not been to Trenton since the end of the trial, but he'd thought of it—the city, the courthouse, the trial, Chimney Point—a good deal, in the intervening weeks. Often, a ghostly female presence seemed to drift near, invisible yet unmistakable—Terence would turn his head, as if someone had called his name, or touched his sleeve. *Yes? Who is it?* That morning he'd woken with the urgent desire to drive back to Chimney Point; no plan, nor even any expectation of what might occur. He'd had a particularly disagreeable meeting at the Feinemann Foundation the previous day, and could not bear to return, so soon.

As soon as the trial of T. W. Binder had ended, with the verdict Terence knew to be the only just verdict, he'd made an effort to forget it. The interlude had after all been of no significance in his own professional life, and allusions to it seemed to annoy, and upset, Phyllis, for some reason Terence did not understand. (Surely it wasn't because of the stolen Gucci case, merely?) Once Binder had been found guilty, the issue was settled. Though Terence might have been curious, he, a reader exclusively of *The New York Times*, had made no effort to look up Trenton newspapers to read of the trial; nor even to learn what prison sentence the judge had imposed at the sentencing.

He'd meant, too, to look up the mysterious "Ezra Wineapple" in back issues of the *Trenton Times*, but he'd never gotten around to it.

For after all the issue *was* settled.

Yet, in times of reverie, he thought of the experience, so intense and in a way so mysterious, of that short week in

June; yes, he would have to admit, of course he thought of *her.*

And now, today, so impulsively, here. Sitting in his car staring at that rundown house *to which I feel myself so powerfully drawn.*

Chimney Point

va-Rose Renfrew's house. (Was she home, now? Perhaps watching him out of a second-floor window?—one of the windows with panes of glass, not plywood or strips of translucent plastic?) The building had a wry tilted look, as if bucking the waves of an invisible sea; the illusion was marked by a split, of sorts, in the roof, between the older, central part of the house, which was made of crumbling stucco, and the wood-frame wings, covered in weathered gray shingles, which had clearly been added, in stages, over a period of many years. Maybe the place had been an inn at one time; even, long ago, a stagecoach stop. For all its shabbiness and the junk on its veranda (to which had been added, since Terence's visit in June, what appeared to be a long, rolled-up carpet), it had a quaint, "historic" look. Terence recalled that the city of Trenton was an old colonial city, where both British and Revolutionary troops had been quartered.

Phyllis would wince at such a place!—the rotting picket fence, the comical lawn ornaments, the cluttered veranda, the interrupted painting of the shutters (which were, still, a bright robin's-egg blue downstairs, and gray-weathered

upstairs)—the Christmas lights never taken down. That overgrown, weedy garden of seven-foot thistles and diseased hollyhocks, amid the roses. Worse yet, the old slate roof and the
rusting gutters in which, in lurid bright-green patches, moss
grew, like the mange.

Beyond the house was a no-man's-land—a vacant field,
an alley or access road, scrub trees, dilapidated outbuildings.
Then, a railroad track, on raised ground; in the near distance, perhaps a half-mile away, the broad winking Delaware
River. The sky was a hazy blue, given a just-perceptible sepia
cast by air pollutants from Trenton industry, and this sky,
contrasted with the mottled slate roof of the Renfrew house,
seemed curiously near, and flat, with the effect as of a Cé-
zanne painting in which all surfaces appear equivalent—the
expression, not of surfaces, in fact, but of underlying, mysteriously interlocked structures.

"H'lo, mister! Looking for somebody?"

Taken by surprise, Terence saw that the old woman had
pushed her way through vegetation, to stand peering at him
over the picket fence; despite her soiled, mannish clothes,
and the floppy straw hat, he recognized Ava-Rose Renfrew's
aunt Holly Mae Loomis at once. Her smile was wide and
sunny, but there was an edge of suspicion to her voice.

Terence got out of his car, feeling very self-conscious.
He said, quickly, "Why, thank you, no, not exactly. I—"

"You aren't"—squinting at him near-sightedly, and
worriedly,—"that Doctor So-and-So, from the Health Department? Eh?"

"Why, no—"

"Oh, Lord! I know—you're that lawyer from the Transit
Company, eh?"

"No," Terence said, smiling, "—are you expecting
these men?"

"I am *not* expecting any of them," the woman said, with
an indignant, feminine toss of her head. "They are *not* welcome here."

On the veranda, the big dog stirred; roused itself into

prickly consciousness; came trotting in Terence's direction, hackles raised, beginning to growl. With a gesture of the clipping shears she held in her hand, the woman said, "Hush, Buster! Not just yet!"

Terence's face was very warm. Over the dog's excited barking he said, "What a lovely garden you have—"

The woman scolded the dog—"Buster, hush! Buster *Keaton*." Then, to Terence, "He don't mean no harm, he's just cautious of strangers." She raised the brim of her ragged straw hat, exposing crisp brassy-dyed curls at her forehead. Her eyes, near-lashless with age, were a clear amber-green, shiny as glass. Terence wondered if she would recall him from the courtroom—or from the Mill Hill Tavern. "You sure you ain't a lawyer, mister?—you sound like one."

"No, truly," Terence laughed, "—I am not a lawyer."

"So what are you, then?"

Terence smiled, feeling a bit foolish. "A friend."

"Eh? Say what?"

"I believe I have the advantage of knowing you, Mrs. Loomis? Holly Mae Loomis? I mean—knowing your name. And that of your niece, Ava-Rose Renfrew?"

"Ava-Rose?" the woman interrupted. "You want to see *her*?"

"Why, no, I—"

"You wouldn't be the manager of that shoe store by Tamar's Bazaar, would you?—that's always pestering my niece for a date?"

"No—"

"Or who's-it—the 'reverend' from her church?"

"*No.* I was one of the jurors at the trial, in June—when that man, T. W. Binder, was found guilty of assaulting Ava-Rose Renfrew."

Immediately, Holly Mae Loomis's face was transformed. She smiled incredulously. "Oh my, oh my! Mister—uh—*Foreman*?"

How swiftly the mantle of authority, however illusory, put him in good stead with her.

"My name is Terence Greene. I was just in the neighborhood, and thought I'd stop in to say—"

A fawning, crafty look—or was it an old-womanly, intimidated look—passed swiftly across Holly Mae Loomis's ruddy face. She said, with an exclamatory laugh, "Oh! my! what an honor! I *never*—!" Clumsily, as the dog yipped and thumped his stubby tail, she drew off her soiled gardening glove, to shake hands with Terence. Her grip was dry and vigorous, and her hand felt calloused. Almost coquettishly, she said, "I know—it's *Dr.* Greene, eh? If you're not a lawyer—?"

"Well—"

"It's a real privilege, and an honor, to meet you at last, *Dr.* Greene. Those awful days of the trial, when poor Ava-Rose couldn't hardly sleep, and cried her eyes out, being so shamed in public, and so insulted by that nasty-minded lawyer—and you saw how cruel he was to my poor little nephew Chick, who was picked up falsely for that trouble some other boys got him into, when he was only twelve!—all those days, Ava-Rose would tell us, 'There's one man on the jury, I look at *him*, and see a real gentleman. *He* knows.' "

"Really!" Terence murmured. His heart gave a sickening lurch in his chest. "Is that so!"

"It sure is so, Dr. Greene," Holly Mae Loomis said, her eyes damp with tears, and her voice suddenly quavering, "—it's all that kept us going, through that bitter ordeal."

As if Buster sensed the change of mood, he ceased barking and began to sniff about Terence's legs, and lick at his hands. His eyes, strikingly human in appeal, in aspect if not in hue very like poor Tuffi's, snatched at Terence's.

Terence too was deeply moved, suddenly. He patted the dog's bony head. He whispered, "Buster. Good dog."

Holly Mae Loomis, seeing that Terence Greene so admired her garden, invited him to walk through it; and around to the side, and rear, of the house. He flattered her by asking questions—one would not have known, hearing Terence's questions, that he too was a suburban gardener, on a modest scale. Clearly, Holly Mae Loomis took pride in her garden even as she disparaged it for being weedy and out of control. "Well!—all these are trumpet vines, Dr. Greene," she said, pointing at a profusion of vines with sticky, trumpet shaped orange flowers, growing up the side of the house, "and these you recognize, eh?—morning glories—that attract humming-birds, damndest pretty *tiny* things! All that growing there is bamboo—yes, *bamboo*—my great-uncle who lives here with us, Cap'n-Uncle Riff he's called, *he* planted it, just a few stalks, brought back from Borneo or one of them jungle-places, and now, goodness—you see how it's taking over. And these are hollyhocks, that the damn Jap'nese beetles have been eating; and these, you know, are sunflowers, going to seed. These are dahlias, of course. These, day lilies. Oh, this cute thing"—pointing to a lawn ornament, a bluntly rendered fla-mingo standing on one leg, painted a fading pink—"my li'l nieces Dara and Dana did with a fret saw; and that deer, there. Mostly, the girls sell them, they're real popular. Maybe you'd like one, Dr. Greene, for your garden? Eh?" Terence murmured something ambiguous. "All that is wild rose that grows like weed, so watch out for the thorns. It's real pretty when it blossoms, in June; but that's the only time. What I love best are the tea roses—aren't they beautiful?" Terence nodded emphatically, yes the roses were beautiful, and this he could acknowledge without ambiguity; for roses were his favorite flowers, though he had little luck growing them on his shaded property. "—the yellow climber's been hard hit by black spot, but the red's been blossoming like that all summer. These white ones always do well, it's a good, healthy bush. This is a hybrid, 'The Widow' "—pointing to a lavender-blue rose—"and this, my favorite, is 'Double De-light.' "

Terence, a bit dazzled by the beauty of the roses, found himself staring at the hybrid "Double Delight." Had he ever seen this rose before?—he could not remember, yet it seemed to him that if he had, he would not have forgotten. The blossoms were large, multipetaled, exquisitely shaded in white, creamy-pink, and faint crimson; each flower differed from the others in gradations of crimson, so that you looked from one to another, and to another, half-consciously seeking *the* flower. "How gorgeous," Terence said, bringing a forefinger close to, but not touching, one of the flowers, "they're like watercolors, so subtle. What did you say they're called, Mrs. Loomis?"

"Double Delight, Dr. Greene. But, my goodness, you can call me Holly Mae." She laughed, drawing off her straw hat and fanning her ruddy, creased face. "It's been a long time since *I* was anybody's missus!"

Terence laughed, too; but shyly. "Then, Holly Mae, you must call me Terence, or, better yet, Terry, and not Dr. Greene."

"But you are a doctor, aren't you?—that's the difference between us."

"I'm not a medical doctor, I—"

"But you have that degree, eh?—'Doctor of—whatever'?"

Terence laughed, a bit loudly. "Yes—'whatever.' "

Doctor of Philosophy, History, Harvard University. How far he'd come, Hettie's scrawny little boy. Yet, the day before, at a meeting at the Feinemann Foundation, the ex–Poet Laureate Quincy Ryder had referred to him as "Dr. Greene" in a heavily sarcastic voice—and Terence had felt the sting of insult.

"You're real lucky, a man like you—people see it in your eyes that you're special: Nobody better mess with *you*," Holly Mae Loomis said, sighing. Terence saw that, though she must have been a quite attractive woman once, Holly Mae was aging, and, close up, did not appear so healthy; there were myriad broken capillaries in her cheeks and nose, which accounted for her warm, ruddy look; there was even what appeared to be a deep curving scar, amid the wrinkles and creases of her face, running from her left ear nearly to the left corner of her mouth. He was reminded of her niece Ava-Rose's subtly scarred face, and wondered suddenly whether he would ever see that face again. Holly Mae laughed, with an air of appeal—"Gosh! I do wish you *were* a lawyer, Dr. Greene, I sure could use one. I hurt my back bad, slipping on a wet step, last winter, getting off a city bus, and d'you know the bus driver started the bus right up, not minding that an old woman like me was falling!" Holly Mae rubbed the top several vertebrae of her backbone, with a pained expression. "And when we tried to make the Transit Company acknowledge it, or even pay my medical bills—!" She shook her head fiercely.

"Do you mean," Terence asked, incensed, "that the Transit Company has ignored you?—after such a clear case of negligence?"

" 'Negli-gence'—that's what it is, eh?"

"It certainly sounds like it, Holly Mae. Were there witnesses?"

Holly Mae smiled, ironically. "Sure! But—who? I fell on the pavement, this was at 11th Street and Broad, a nasty sleety day, on my way to work at the WDC—Women's Detention Center—in the cafeteria—where I had a steady job, I thought—and the bus driver just drove *on*. Lord, I thought I'd broke my back, just laying there too stunned to cry, till some nice colored woman comes along and helps me. Ava-Rose was real scared, and took me to the doctor, and they make you wait forever, you know—at the welfare clinic—so we gave up there, and tried another doctor, *he* said it was lucky I wasn't crippled for life—he seemed nice, but oh, goodness, what they charge you!" Terence listened with growing indignation to Holly Mae Loomis's account, which went on for some minutes, involving, inevitably, the loss of her job at the cafeteria, prescribed medicine and physical therapy sessions she could not afford, yet-unpaid medical bills, countless telephone calls from Ava-Rose to the Transit Company, a visit to the office, and indifference on the part of the city, or outright rebuffs—"They have this 'legal staff' that lets you know nobody's going to listen to *you*, so why bother?"

Terence, struck by pity, asked, "But is nothing being done *now?*"

Holly Mae Loomis shrugged. "What's to be done, Dr. Greene? Ava-Rose doesn't think we should give up, she's tried to get a lawyer, but—"

"Of course you must have a lawyer, and a good lawyer," Terence said. "I'd be happy to help you out—if you'd allow me."

As if not hearing, Holly Mae Loomis shut her eyes, and continued to rub the top several vertebrae of her back. "Seems life is closing in on me, sometimes! And I ain't that old: I'm seventy-four. Lord, lord. The way a life can turn out, eh?"

Terence said, firmly, "Not at all, Holly Mae. I'm sure something can be done."

"Well, lawyers *are* expensive—"

"Let me worry about that, Holly Mae, will you?—you and your niece?" Terence was embarrassed by his own impulsive magnanimity, and changed the subject, pointing to, and marveling at, a wild, weedy bed of zinnias; he was thinking, excitedly, that he would redress the terrible injustice being done to this powerless woman, he would *help.* They would not accept any cash gift, of course, but, perhaps—a loan?

By this time, Holly Mae Loomis had led Terence around to the rear of the house, where there were fewer cultivated beds; many weeds; and, in the tall grass, discarded debris— lumber, broken household utensils, even the rusted skeletal hulk of a car. The driveway led past the house, rutted, bumpy, and became an access road, to a landfill beyond a stretch of scrubby trees; beyond that, there was a glittering strip, like a piece of tinsel—all that could be seen, from this perspective, of the Delaware River. The September afternoon was warm as summer, and there was a fragrance as of numerous mingled smells—of the earth, of the scented flowers, of the tall grasses in the sun, even of the river. Terence said, almost shyly, "How beautiful it is here!—how private! Why is this part of Trenton called Chimney Point? Is there a point of land, down there, that juts out into the river?"

Holly Mac shook her head, with a vague look. "Maybe so, Dr. Greene. I guess that's it."

"And have you and your family lived here very long?"

" 'Very long'—that depends. Seems like *I* been here forever—but Cap'n-Uncle Riff, who's eighty-two, *he's* only been living here a few years, since he retired from seafaring. Ava-Rose, her and her sister were brought here by their momma, who couldn't keep them, when they were real little, so Ava-Rose has lived here most of her life, anyway off and on she has; her sister, well"—Holly Mae's face darkened—"she wasn't a good girl, I guess, she's long run off. And their momma, too—" Holly Mae shrugged. Terence would have liked to ask more about Ava-Rose, but dared not; he did not want to seem overly inquisitive.

Buster had been trotting about in the tall grasses, sniffing and making the motions of urination; he lunged clumsily at a golden-winged butterfly, then turned, as if Terence had called him, and hurried back to Terence, nudging his damp muzzle beneath Terence's hand. How shivery, the dog's touch! yet how good it felt, since Tuffi was no longer living. *He seems to trust me, and so will the others.*

Impulsively, wanting to keep the topic of conversation closely related to Ava-Rose Renfrew (who was not, surely, at home—not peering out a window at the tall handsome well-dressed "Mr. Foreman" being shown about by her aunt), Terence asked Holly Mae if she'd heard any further news about T. W. Binder. "I assume he was sentenced to prison—for how long?"

Holly Mae, who had been smiling at the way Terence and the dog were getting on, now frowned, severely. "Oh—the judge called T.W. 'dangerous' and a 'threat to society,' like other judges have done with that boy in the past; then, she gives him three-to-seven."

"Years?"

"Yessir! But it don't mean a thing, even so. That brute will be eligible for parole in one year."

"What? One year?"

Terence was astounded. Somehow, he had assumed that the violent young man might be behind bars for as long as twenty years. Hadn't he tried to kill Ava-Rose Renfrew? Hadn't he been convicted of "aggravated assault"?

"Well!" he murmured, crestfallen. "I thought we jurors had done better than that, for you and Miss Renfrew."

Holly Mae shook her head, disgusted. "Some people, 'incorrigibles' they call them, there's no protection against them unless—well, you take the law in your own hands. They steal, and pillage, and murder, and destroy lives, and there's no stopping them. Right now in the state of New Jersey, on death row, there's vicious murderers who have been saved from execution time and time again," she said passionately. "There's no justice anymore, Dr. Greene!"

"Of course," Terence said, awkwardly, "—capital punishment itself is barbaric. We can't really condone—"

"So when T.W. is paroled, and murders my niece, and maybe us all, and burns down the house like he threatened, then what? Some human beings, they *are* barbaric."

"My God, do you think—? Is there a chance that—"

"Poor Ava-Rose! She has had such ill luck, with men! And that girl is so sweet—so innocent! What we're worried sick about, Dr. Greene," Holly Mae said, lowering her voice, and pulling at Terence's sleeve to draw him nearer, "—is that one of T.W.'s friends will do harm to my niece. Now T.W. is in Rahway Prison, *he* can't do it, but there's a friend of his—Eldrick Gill is his name—who has been talking about getting even with Ava-Rose. Cap'n-Uncle Riff and I think he has already threatened her, but Ava-Rose never wants to scare *us*. The other night she came home from evening services at this church she attends—The Church of the Holy Apocalypse it is: *I* don't belong—sort of white-faced, and quiet, and not herself, and Darling leapt at her head—Darling is our parrot, Dr. Greene: a big beautiful African gray—to say 'Greetings!'

like he does, landing on your head if he can, and Ava-Rose panicked, and screamed, covering her head with her arms, like she didn't know where she was." Holly Mae paused, breathing hard. Her flushed face sparkled with perspiration. "Then, later, I went up to her room, where she was sitting in the dark, and I asked, 'Honey, did something happen?' and she said, 'No, Auntie, please don't worry'—so quick, I knew there must be trouble."

"What about the police? Aren't they supposed to—"

"The police! Them!" Holly Mae made a spitting gesture. "You sure can't depend upon them. Everybody knew that T.W. had a terrible temper, he'd done injury to many people, men and women both, before the police could make a charge stick, in court; even so, he won't be in prison long. Up at Rahway, there's all kinds of connections with criminals on the outside—they all know one another, they're *buddies*. This Eldrick Gill, he rides one of them big black motorcycles, just like T.W. They're the same breed. Oh, yes!"

"And you think your niece might be in danger?"

"Dr. Greene, I *know*."

Terence wondered if he should speak with Ava-Rose Renfrew himself. Or if the young woman might misconstrue his motives.

A question occurred to him— "Who was 'Wincapple'? Was he one of Binder's victims?"

Holly Mae Loomis leaned forward, cupping her hand to her ear. "*Who—?*"

" 'Wineapple,' the name was—or was it 'Applewine'? At the trial, the name came up, and the witness was silenced."

Holly Mae Loomis's brow furrowed as she tried to recall the name. She fanned her face vigorously with her straw hat. Then, "*I* never knew this party, nor much of him, Dr. Greene. Nor did Ava-Rose, anything more than a passing acquaintance. He was one of the deacons at that church of hers—I think. Rumor was, T.W. plotted injury against Applewine, or Wineapple, 'cause he believed this party was courting my niece; in fact, there was no truth to that rumor, as far

as I know." Holly Mae smiled, with an air of bemused perplexity. "When you get my age, Dr. Greene, there's lots of
things people shield from you, so you don't truly *know* what
you think you *know*."

"But the man is dead? Drowned, I believe?"

Holly Mae blinked, frightened. "Oh my God. That's
news to me."

Terence saw that he should change the subject; he did
not want to upset the old woman any more than he had.

Terence saw too that it was probably time for him to
leave. *She isn't here, won't be home for hours.*

They had circled the house, crossing a patch of marshy,
dank-smelling wild grass, as Buster trotted affably in their
wake, leaping and snapping playfully at butterflies. Holly Mae
led Terence up the badly rutted driveway, toward the street
where his car was parked; she walked with some difficulty,
favoring her right leg, and seemed short of breath, but continued to speak in her candid, friendly way. "I'd invite you
inside, Dr. Greene, for a cup of coffee, or some herbal tea,
—that's Ava-Rose's specialty: rosehips—or, maybe, some of
Cap'n-Uncle Riff's stout, but, shame to say, the house-
keeping's sort of behind, there's likely no place to *sit*. But
you come back another time, eh?"

Terence said, shyly, "I'd like that, Mrs. Loomis. I
mean—Holly Mae." And, after a pause, "I hope you will allow me to lend you the funds to retain a good lawyer, to bring
suit against the city for that bus driver's behavior? It's really
quite outrageous, what you've told me."

Holly Mae said, humbly, "Long as it's a *loan*, Dr.
Greene, and not, you know—charity."

"Certainly not."

"Cap'n-Uncle Riff would never countenance that, nor
would Ava-Rose. Nor would *I*."

They discussed this matter for some minutes, deciding
that the Renfrews would locate a good, trustworthy Trenton
lawyer (Terence had to admit, he knew no one in Trenton);
and that the lawyer would then contact Terence, and finan-

cial arrangements would be worked out between them. "My family, oh goodness!—we're not very practical-minded when it comes to money!" Holly Mae said. She waved her arm at the rundown house, the overgrown garden, with a wistful laugh. "As I guess anybody with eyes can *see*."

Terence laughed. He felt quite giddy, as if he had in fact sipped some of Cap'n-Uncle Riff's stout. "There are other virtues in life, Holly Mae, beyond being practical-minded about money."

Before leaving, Terence admired the old woman's garden another time. He was thinking that, in Queenston (but he had not thought of Queenston for the past hour), every lawn of every residence was perfectly landscaped. Shrubbery was planted with an eye for symmetry, flowers were color-coordinated. There were no scrawny bushes, no trees in need of pruning, and certainly no weeds. Were any Queenston resident to let his property go as the Renfrews had done, his neighbors would convene to take action against him.

"Yes," Terence said, a bit gravely, "—there are other virtues."

Holly Mae was reluctant to let her visitor go without cutting him some roses from her garden to take home, but Terence declined, saying that he wasn't going directly home; he might not return for hours. His eye alighted upon one of the clumsily executed wooden lawn ornaments, however, and he remembered that these were for sale. Who had made them?—those teasing little girls who'd sunbathed on the roof? He asked Holly Mae if he could buy one or two of these for his own garden, and, flushed with pleasure, Holly Mae said yes, of course—"Dara and Dana made up a bunch of 'em over the summer."

She led Terence up onto the veranda, where a supply of ornaments was stacked, covered by a tarpaulin. (Terence noted wryly that the veranda creaked and sagged beneath their weight. When Holly Mae drew the tarpaulin aside, there was a scuttling as of black-shelled beetles fleeing the light.) "You wouldn't think girls so young would've made these, would you? Aren't they cute!'' Holly Mae exclaimed. Terence picked out a fluorescent-pink flamingo with a cracked beak and a stag with a point of his antlers missing, reasoning that no other customer would want these. How vulgar they were, and yet, how charming! When Terence took out his wallet, and asked Holly Mae how much he owed her, she seemed embarrassed. "Why, Dr. Greene, I don't know—I think the girls were asking five dollars apiece?''

"Five dollars! Surely you're mistaken?'' It saddened Terence to think of the girls working so hard, for so little reward. *His* daughters would never have done so.

Over Holly Mae's protestations, Terence paid her forty dollars for the ornaments. He then carried them to his car, placed them in the back seat, and drove away—waving good-bye with childlike ardor to his new friend, as she stood, bulky in her overalls, her straw hat rakish on her brassy dyed curls, waving good-bye to him.

Buster too was Terence Greene's new friend. The dog yipped, whined, and barked, trotting alongside his car, like an escort, until Terence's speed carried him away. This time, Buster did not slip beneath the car's wheels.

Afterward, Terence could not comprehend what he had done.

Am I mad? Am I sick?

Never in his entire professional career, going back to the early years as a teaching assistant at Harvard, had Terence Greene called in sick, falsely; never would he have wished to do so. And yet, that day, he'd done it—and why?

In pursuit of Justice, still?

Hettie's boy. Pray God he doesn't take after the father.

Terence decided he would not return to 33 Holyoak Street, but he would certainly honor his promise to Holly Mae Loomis about paying for a lawyer: It infuriated him, as a citizen of liberal convictions, that any municipal bureaucracy should so mistreat an old, poorly educated woman and her family.

If needed, he could explain the situation to Phyllis.

"It seemed the least I could do, under the circumstances."

"It *is* a loan. I expect to be repaid."

Before returning to Queenston, Terence stopped at the Mercer Shopping Mall, on Route 1, to get rid of the lawn ornaments in a dumpster behind a pizzeria—*these*, he could never explain to Phyllis.

That evening, at home, in the garage, irritably cleaning his hands with a rag soaked in kerosene. For how to explain, should anyone in the family ask, how he'd gotten fluorescent-pink paint on his fingers, in his office in Manhattan?

Poor old fella!

The following weekend, there was a conference in New Haven—"The Crisis in the Humanities"—in which Terence Greene, as the Executive Director of the Feinemann Foundation, was scheduled to participate; instead, Terence spent most of Saturday in Trenton.

How this came about, he could never quite comprehend. Even before circumstances swerved deliriously beyond his control, he could not have explained.

He'd fully intended to drive to New Haven. He *wanted* to drive to New Haven. Instead, turning onto Route 1, off the Queenston Pike, he found that he was driving south, toward Trenton; and not north, to the Turnpike that would take him to New Haven. *Hereby summoned.*

As, in June, a steady stream of traffic bore him southward. Past the fast-food restaurants, the car dealerships, Mercer Mall, Quaker Bridge Mall, Lawrenceville Shopping Center. Again, it was a balmy, slightly overcast September day. As he neared Trenton, he began to taste grit in the air; his eyes stung, but just mildly. He saw the familiar outer wall—grimy, gray, forbidding as an etching of a prison in a child's picture book—of Trenton State Prison, and realized that it had become, for him, a landmark: He would exit at Mott Street, in a mile, and take Mott over to Holyoak.

This time, Terence wasn't going to drive to the end of Holyoak, but only as far as the Chimney Point Shopping Center.

It was a small, undistinguished gathering of stores, with a working-class character. A Kmart, a video shop, a laundromat, South China Restaurant, Howard's Bargain Shoes, Tamar's Bazaar & Emporium, Discount Drugs, West Trenton Beer & Wine. Two stores stood empty, FOR RENT signs in their windows. Because the day was Saturday, the shopping center was fairly busy; the other day, when, impulsively, Terence had dropped by, fewer than one-quarter of the parking spaces had been taken.

The façade of Tamar's Bazaar & Emporium was glass and simulated bamboo, both in need of a good scrubbing. Glass beads sagged in a giant cobweb behind the plate glass window and there were numerous hand-lettered little signs: EXOTIC GIFTS GALORE, SUMMER SALE, "THE CRAFT OF BEAUTY," YOUR FORTUNE TOLD. The other day, Terence had several times approached the store without going in; he'd glanced in the dark window, seen only his own reflection, and retreated. Today, he did not glance into the window at all, but entered the store *as if he were an ordinary customer for wasn't that what he was?* A bell clanged tinnily overhead and a powerful odor of incense and mildew wafted toward him.

The interior of the store was narrow, like a tunnel; crowded with displays of clothing, jewelry, works of art, and ornamentation; dim-lit, as in a dream where one's vision is unaccountably blurred. Yet Terence saw at once that *she* was there—behind a counter to the left, where a canopy and curtains of some gauzy material provided a sort of stage setting, as for a puppet show. Across the top of the canopy were the letters, in sparkling sequins, THE CRAFT OF BEAUTY.

At once, Terence's stomach clenched; a black mist passed before his eyes.

It isn't too late to flee.

Unfortunately—or perhaps fortunately!—Ava-Rose Renfrew had customers. Several teenaged girls in jeans, trying on earrings, necklaces. One girl, with a dark, dusky skin, held out her arm to Ava-Rose, who appeared to be reading her palm. Terence was surprised that there was so much good-natured chatter and giggling. He would have thought that telling a fortune was a serious business.

Tamar's Bazaar & Emporium was crammed with cheap, colorful, "exotic" merchandise. Terence drifted about, a bit nervously, intent upon appearing like a customer. (He hoped to overhear the girl's fortune being told, but the female voices were not quite audible. Among them, he believed he could hear *hers*.) Wicker furniture, and things made of brass, and bamboo; India-imported fabrics, some of them very striking, threaded with gold; candles—so many; candleholders; heavily decorated satin cushions; beads, shawls, saris, clay figurines (some quite grotesque, multiheaded and -armed: Hindu deities?); mirrors. Terence found himself staring, at first without much comprehension, at his own image in a long skinny mirror framed in cheap stamped brass. The poor lighting made his face look battered, all shadows and dents. A beak of a nose, prissy mouth. And so hopeful, yearning! Kim and Cindy had teased him mercilessly the other day about combing his hair to cover his bald spot, which he'd been doing unconsciously, but it did not appear now that he had any hair at all, only vague wisps of something pale and synthetic as angel hair. *Poor old fella.*

"Hi! I'm Tamar! May I be of assistance?"

A short, busty woman of about thirty-five, in a crimson sari that showed fatty ridges of flesh at her waist, had materialized before Terence, smiling forcibly. She had short, curly black hair like a boy's; but there was nothing childlike about her square jaws and dark, ribald eyes. Even as she smiled, her gaze dropped to consider Terence's shoes, which were expensive, and nicely polished, but utterly conventional American-men's shoes; nor did his sharply creased trousers, and his gray checked gabardine coat from The Queenston

Men's Shop, seem to impress. Terence said politely, "I'm just looking, thanks."

"Looking for what?"

A sly glance in the direction of Ava-Rose Renfrew's part of the shop *as if she knew.*

Terence said, avoiding the woman's eyes, "Well—a present, maybe."

"Yes? For who?"

"A—woman."

"Yes? What kind of a woman?"

Tamar's voice was distinctly New Jersey. *Does she know, but how could she know, don't be absurd.*

"What do you mean, what kind of a woman?" Terence asked, annoyed.

"Young, old—wife, mother, girlfriend—is it a *surprise* kind of thing?" Tamar seemed bemused by her customer's awkwardness.

Terence, his heart beating rapidly, with a quick rising anger that startled him, fingered a floor-length dress, or robe—it was made of a cheap maroon fabric, "on sale" for thirty-five dollars. He tried to imagine Phyllis wearing such a thing, and the vision went blank.

"Or maybe you want your palm read?"—Tamar seemed on the brink of laughter.

Terence blushed. He was examining brocaded jackets, skimpy see-through blouses, wraps that looked as if they were made of hemp. He pretended he had not heard Tamar, or had not understood. *Many men must come in here, is that what she is saying?* As if struck by the artistry of a ceramic deity— frog face, lewd protruding lips, a conical hat—Terence picked the thing up, surprised at its weight.

"Vajradhara—one of His aspects," Tamar said, now solemnly.

"Really!" Terence stared at the slitted, smug, blind eyes. He did not believe he'd ever seen, close up, anything quite so ugly.

"You interested in Tantric yoga, mister?"

"Tantric—? Oh yes: yoga." For a dizzy moment, Terence had thought the annoying woman had said "yogurt." He said, "No, not really," and then, hearing how his flippant reply echoed his son Aaron's habit of speech, he said, "Well, yes—I'm interested in everything."

"Tantric Buddhism is the way of enlightenment through bliss," Tamar said. She stood near to Terence; her scent was musky, like slightly fermented olives. Her fingernails, tapping on the ceramic deity's head, were sharp and red-polished. "This is Vajradhara in blissful union with a Karmamudrā— they are in a sacred state of Dharmamudrā. Y'see?" She tilted the thing, and, to his astonishment, and embarrassment, Terence realized that there were two figures depicted, two ecstatic frog-faces, copulating. The female figure was twisted beneath the male, head upside-down. "We're having a sale right now, it's marked down thirty percent—only $29.98."

Terence said, backing off, "Well! Very nice. But not, I think, for me."

Tamar fussily settled the figurine back in place, with a reproachful glance at Terence.

Terence turned irritably away. He saw, to his disappointment, that those damned girls were still hanging about The Craft of Beauty. Ava-Rose Renfrew was laughing with them, like a girl herself. The dusky-skinned girl, whose hair was braided in intricate cornrows, had taken a thin strand of Ava-Rose's fair, crinkly hair, and was showing how to braid it.

"This woman you're getting a present for, mister—what size is she?" Tamar, at Terence's elbow, was not to be discouraged.

"What size? I—"

"My size, like; or, her size—?"

Tamar meant Ava-Rose Renfrew: tall, willowy, long-limbed.

"I—really don't know," Terence said, suddenly confused. "I have to—put a coin in the meter. I'll be back."

Terence walked out of the store, blindly. Behind him he heard tinkly female laughter, and Tamar's strong voice calling after, "Thank you, mister! Come back, soon!"

Outside, walking swiftly to his car, Terence realized there were no parking meters here, of course. *What a fool, poor old fella.*

He got in, drove off, but only to circle aimlessly about the Chimney Point Shopping Center. Then he turned onto Holyoak, drove a block or two, and stopped at Abbott's Ice Cream where he had a cup of coffee and a single scoop of vanilla ice cream that melted, seemingly with the heat of Terence's breath, in a paper liner set inside a plastic bowl. The cold sweetness, the sudden sugar-rush, hurt his tongue *yet how delicious, you can't deny.*

And then—Terence Greene astonished himself by returning, not to Queenston, but to the Chimney Point Shopping Center.

Was he a fool?—his face felt aglow, as if windburnt, as, another time, he pushed open the door to dim-lit Tamar's Bazaar & Emporium. He winced at the tinny sound of the bell overhead.

God damn! For another customer was having her palm read beneath the gauzy canopy of The Craft of Beauty.

Terence found it difficult not to stare, in frank disappointment. *She* took no notice of him, tracing her forefinger across a woman's upturned palm, speaking in a low, earnest voice. (That voice! Why, he'd virtually forgotten it.) The customer was a woman of about Phyllis's age, sturdy-hipped in polyester slacks, head bowed over her own hand as it was held in the fortune-teller's.

And where was sharp-eyed Tamar?—thank God, at the rear of the store. She was on the telephone, smoking a cigarette, taking no notice of her awkward customer's return.

Terence feigned an interest in a waist-high folding screen, ebony splotched with gilt elephants. It was quite attractive, really—on sale for $69.98. Peering at it, he maneuvered himself into a position only a few feet from Ava-Rose Renfrew; he was closer still to the woman in the polyester slacks. How different their voices, alternating as in a duet— the woman's voice high-pitched and faintly whining; Ava-Rose's a deep contralto, scratchy, like a caress that leaves you startled.

"What I want to know is, will I ever be *happy*?"

"You will—see this wavy line here? You *are*."

"Are what?"

"You *are* happy. *Now*."

"I'm happy—now? *Me*?"

" 'To inhabit bliss is to be blind.' "

"You're reading this, in my hand?"

" 'A small vessel overflows with a small blessing.' See how these lines converge, then break away? And fade out before they get to the edge, here? You see you *are* happy— as much as you can be."

"I am? Shit!"

Ava-Rose Renfrew's throaty voice was chiding, almost prim. " 'The soul exults in its secret glory.' Frankly, I think you should be ashamed of yourself."

The woman snatched her hand out of Ava-Rose's, and laughed, a hoarse hacking laugh. "Well, what else! I mean, hell, what else could I expect!" Then, suddenly, she was crying.

Terence, deeply embarrassed at overhearing this exchange, blundered away. He collided with a precarious display of ivory trinkets and nearly knocked them all flying. *And will I, will I ever be.* As the woman sobbed, and Ava-Rose cooed and comforted her, having come out from behind the counter to hold the woman in her arms, Terence made his way to the rear of the store, where, with a final drag of her cigarette, Tamar was ending her telephone conversation. "Hi, mister! You made up your mind, yet?"

Terence said, "Yes, I think so. That screen over there— with the gilt elephants."

The purchase took some minutes, during which time

Terence steadfastly ignored the scene at the front of the shop. Tamar counted Terence's change out onto the counter—he'd paid with cash—and said, with a wink, "For half price, I could throw in the Vajradhara icon—are you interested?"

Terence said, quickly, "Thank you, but no. I don't think my wife would care for it."

Tamar laughed. For the first time, he realized that the woman wore a tiny red bead in her fleshy left nostril.

As Terence carried the folding screen, with some difficulty, out of the shop, he saw that Ava-Rose Renfrew's customer was preparing to leave. He was breathing hard, and felt a tingling as of anger. At his car, he fumbled with his key; dropped the screen; saw, to his surprise, that in full daylight it was distinctly less exotic than it had looked in the store. Imported from Calcutta? He did not want to consider that he'd been cheated, right now.

Poor old fella.

He shoved the screen into the rear of the car, and hurried back to Tamar's Bazaar & Emporium—seeing, to his horror, that Ava-Rose Renfrew was gone. The Craft of Beauty stood empty, a counter heaped with glittering jewelry and shiny fabrics; the weeping woman too had departed.

Seeing the expression in Terence's face, buxom little Tamar in the crimson sari did not smile in derision, but in sympathy. "If you want your palm read, mister—Ava-Rose will be back later this afternoon."

Terence stared at the woman, not hearing. She said, "Or, like—*I* could do it for you?"

Terence noted that Tamar's Bazaar & Emporium would be open until 6 P.M.

He got in his car, drove away. In a northerly direction, as if returning to Route 1, thus Queenston, but then he turned into a roadside tavern, had a quick lunch and one, or two, or three beers, pondering what to do *as if he had any choice in the matter.* Emerging from the tavern he was vaguely surprised to see that it was still daylight.

Despite the beers, Terence felt sober, judicial. He examined the folding screen and came to the reluctant decision that, like the lawn ornaments, he simply couldn't bring it home to 7 Juniper Way—one or the other of his daughters might like it for her room, but Phyllis would be appalled at Terence's bad taste in buying it, such blatantly shiny gilt elephants stamped on a fake-ebony background, and she might be suspicious.

(It crossed Terence's mind suddenly that his Aunt Megan would have loved such a screen. For that room she'd called the parlor. To divide it from the hallway, so drafty in winter. In fact, hadn't Aunt Megan bought a folding screen in an "Oriental" style, from Montgomery Ward, and Terence's uncle had made her return it?)

Seeing that no one was looking, Terence dragged the screen out of the rear of his car and carried it to a dumpster behind the tavern.

The most expeditious decision, under the circumstances.

Then, he drove back to the Chimney Point Shopping Center.

Terence did not think of his behavior, at this time, as symptomatic of anything beyond itself; as one is inclined, at the onset of a fever signaling a virulent disease, to believe that the fever is only itself, thus finite, contained. He might have rationalized that, yes, he *did* want his fortune told, and so was returning (hadn't Tamar so suggested?) for that purpose. Yet, parking his car a discreet distance from the tawdry little shop, he knew he was not going to enter it another time that day. Quite simply, he could not.

He would wait, and speak with Ava-Rose Renfrew when the shop closed at 6.

The balmy, gritty-tasting September afternoon began to wane. It was 5 P.M., and then 5:30 P.M., and the parking lot

ROSAMOND SMITH / 130

began to empty. Gazing at the glass façade of West Trenton Beer & Wine, which was plastered with exclamatory posters, Terence had a thought of buying himself a six-pack of beer; or a bottle of wine.

But no, he wasn't a man to sit in his car, in a shopping center, and drink out of an object hidden by a paper bag, eyes riveted to the door of one of the stores: waiting.

He did not want to think of the telephone call he'd made so impulsively that morning, to the conference organizer in New Haven, explaining, nervously, but he'd thought convincingly, that a "minor personal crisis" was preventing him from attending the conference and moderating one of the sessions. *And how relieved he'd felt, as soon as he'd hung up the phone: how free!*

He did not want to think that he'd lied to Phyllis, and to his children. That this was the first time *he was certain it was only the first* he'd lied to them, ever.

Nor did he want to think of the problem he was having at the Feinemann Foundation, which he believed must worsen, and which, ironically, he'd brought upon himself: Terence had invited the highly regarded poet Quincy Ryder to be a member of one of this year's committees, not realizing that Ryder, now in his mid-fifties, had become deeply cynical and sarcastic. Though every sort of literary success had come his way (in addition to having been named Poet Laureate of the Library of Congress several years before, he had also won the National Book Award, the Pulitzer, and the Bollingen Prize for Poetry), Ryder was contemptuous of most other poets; he favored certain male Caucasians who were friends of his, or connected with him in some way, but disliked intensely "gays"—"Afro-Americans"—"feminists"— "ethnics"—those who rhymed their verse ineptly, and those who did not rhyme at all. Terence, whose gastric juices turned to acid in Ryder's witty company, had a difficult time controlling committee meetings and luncheons, where Ryder's remarks upset some, and made others laugh. Ryder had a smooth, red, shiny face like Puck, and a deceptively gracious Virginia accent; he wore dapper English-style suits, always with eye-catching vests; his cruelty, masked in wit, seemed to Terence the more inexcusable. The other day, Ryder had sputtered in mock surprise when the poet Myra Tannenbaum's application came up—"The poor silly old cunt—who exhumed *her*?" When Terence protested, "Really, Quincy, I've been reading Myra Tannenbaum's poetry, and I was impressed with—" Ryder retorted, not missing a beat, "Yes, no doubt, Dr. Greene, *you* were impressed." There had been, too, a faint emphasis upon the title "Dr.," which had had the effect upon Terence Greene of a fingernail drawn against a blackboard.

But, of Quincy Ryder, at the moment, *I do not wish to think.*

Chimney Point Shopping Center, like other commercial areas Terence had noticed in Trenton, appeared hard hit by the recession. The parking lot was rapidly emptying, as dusk came on; the only stores with customers were Discount Drugs, West Trenton Wine & Beer, Kmart. Only an occasional customer entered Tamar's Bazaar & Emporium, and Terence had the impression that few emerged with purchases. He felt sympathy for the young women—how long would they remain in business?

Something Holly Mae Loomis had mentioned led Terence to think that she, and possibly other members of the family, was on welfare.

Yet, how beautiful the old woman's garden! Having little money did not mean being deprived of beauty.

As the parking lot emptied of adult customers, it began to be used as a short-cut, or even a raceway of a kind, for teenagers in noisy cars and on motorcycles, who hung out at fast-food restaurants in the neighborhood. There was a 7-Eleven store across the street that seemed to be a gathering place. Shouts, squeals, screams of laughter punctuated the sound of motors. Most of the teenagers were male, but Ter-

ence saw a few girls among them. How could they expect to
be treated, at the hands of such louts! Thank God, Kim did
not behave in such a way. *I could not bear it.*

The Schrieber boy, the one with the ridiculous name,
and the lurid nose-ring, had departed from Kim's life: So Kim
had told Phyllis, and Phyllis believed her. And Terence believed her. *I could not bear it.*

For all his uneasy vigilance, and his keyed-up nerves,
Terence had not consciously noticed the man in the dark
T-shirt straddling a motorcycle a short distance away. Terence
had been peripherally aware of motorcycles and cars without
mufflers crossing and recrossing the parking lot; but he
hadn't realized that the man on the motorcycle was by himself, not part of a group of rowdy youngsters, an adult, with
an adult's purposeful intensity. Only when Ava-Rose left the
shop, and the man quickly approached her, and began speaking with her, did Terence realize what the situation was.

Both Ava-Rose and Tamar left the shop at the same
time, the one tall, slender, with splendid waist-long hair, the
other short, fleshy, with hair close-cropped as a boy's; the one
in a skirt that fell to mid-calf, and layers of filmy garments,
the other in the snug-fitting crimson sari that so startlingly
exposed her midriff. When, at once, the man in the T-shirt
strode up to Ava-Rose, Tamar quickly took her leave of them
and walked away. Terence had the impression that Tamar,
like Ava-Rose, knew the man.

At first, they were talking together, intensely—the man
in the T-shirt pressing forward, and Ava-Rose backing away.
Then, Ava-Rose turned; the man caught her arm, and pulled
her roughly back; Ava-Rose wrenched away, and began walking swiftly; again the man caught her arm, and pulled her
back to face him. Terence was immediately out of his car and
hurrying toward them. "Just a minute, you—are you bothering this young woman?"

The man turned to Terence, surprised, and furious. He
had a round bullet head, disheveled thinning hair, a broad
nose that looked as if it had been broken. He was in his early

thirties and resembled, in manner as well as type, T. W. Binder. "Fuck off, mister!" he said.

Ava-Rose, frightened, began to run, and the man grabbed her by one of her scarves, and they wrestled together, and Ava-Rose screamed, and Terence threw himself blindly upon the man—not knowing what to do, only that he had to do something. Terence felt a blow to his chest and stumbled backward. He saw his assailant's incredulous expression and mean narrowed eyes, lips stretched in a snarl— "I said, *fuck off!*"

"Leave her alone! You can't—"

Perhaps Terence was about to say "you can't do this" —he was not speaking coherently, and would not recall afterward anything he'd said—but his assailant rushed at him, swinging and pummeling, and Terence felt wild, hard blows to his face, chest, belly; he heard a woman's scream of dismay, and a man's infuriated shouts; he too swung his fist, or tried to swing it—striking flesh, but not hard enough to prevent a crude roundhouse right from flying into his left eye. As if struck by a board, Terence staggered, and fell. In the very swiftness and confusion of the moment he heard his uncle's jeering voice of many years ago *If you get knocked down, get up again—fast.* But try as he could, Terence could not get up.

Grunting, cursing, his assailant kicked Terence in the head, chest, belly, groin. Terence, fighting not to lose consciousness, had an impression of Ava-Rose Renfrew, hair in her face, struggling with the man, pleading, "Stop! Eldrick, stop!" Terence tried to grab a booted foot, even as the foot slammed into his side—and then suddenly the blows ceased, and there was a sound of running feet, and a motorcycle's deafening roar; and, above him, swimmingly, like a figure glimpsed in a dream, Ava-Rose Renfrew was stooping, her widened eyes fixed upon his.

"Oh! You! Why, I know you—don't I?"

In the midst of the crisis—the pain, the fright, the rush of adrenaline that nearly burst his heart, the sense of a profound and irrevocable insult visited upon one man by another—Terence Greene heard clearly *Oh! You! Why, I know you—don't I?*

As if his very soul had spoken?

What happened following the attack by Eldrick Gill, Terence was never to recall clearly.

He did recall sitting up, at once, as Ava-Rose Renfrew spoke to him; for even in his distressed state, head and body throbbing with pain, and his sense of himself temporarily shattered, he did not want to appear a weak person in the young woman's eyes. His nose was bleeding, and he was swallowing blood, choking and sputtering, and Ava-Rose Renfrew knelt beside him murmuring words of consolation as, with something gauzy and fragrant, a scarf? a shawl? she wiped blood from his face and dabbed at his aching nose. A scent as of cloves, cinnamon, vanilla lifted from her, loosed by the agitation of her arms, the movement of her thick, springy, fair-brown hair. Terence's left eye was swollen and awash with tears, so that he wondered if he'd lost his sight in that eye yet *how happy he was, how transcendentally how unspeakably happy.*

Terence's numbed lips moved—"Are *you* all right? Did he hurt—"

The young woman's reply was passionate, furious—"Eldrick Gill doesn't have the power to hurt *me*! And he knows it!"

A dozen silver bracelets slid and clattered on her slender arms as she helped Terence to his feet. Terence swayed, his knees buckled, yet he managed to stand; as in a dream in which all things are allowed, because nothing is forbidden, he felt the shock of her arm slipping around his waist, steadying him. "You'll be all right, I'll take care of you, *he's* gone, how brave you were, you saved my life! You *did*!" Ava-Rose was murmuring more to herself than to Terence; she was furious; yet solicitous of him, as a mother of her mistreated child. For a woman so delicately boned, of a height several inches less than Terence, Ava-Rose was surprisingly strong.

In front of the brightly lit West Trenton Beer & Wine, several people stood watching; no doubt, they had watched the entire beating. A man called, "Hey, you want the police?—an ambulance?" and Ava-Rose Renfrew called back, with surprising vehemence, "No we do not! This is a private matter."

To Terence she said, warmly, "Never, never summon the police unless you want *them* messing in your life, too!"

Terence, who certainly did not want the police called, nor any ambulance, said quickly, "I *am* all right—or nearly."

"Maybe some ice on your face, to keep the swelling down," Ava-Rose said, "—some painkiller pills for when it really starts to hurt. *I'll* be your nurse."

Terence saw that, unsteady on his feet as he was, he was walking; this remarkable young woman whom he scarcely knew was supporting him, seemingly leading him, to his car. He'd taken the wadded blood-soaked cloth from her and was pressing it against his face, inhaling its sweet, close fragrance. The fabric was a dark silky cotton, threaded with gold.

"*I'll* drive!" Ava-Rose said. "*You* relax."

Terence reached into his trouser pocket for his car keys—but Ava-Rose already had the keys in her hand.

She helped him into the passenger's seat, and hurried around to the driver's side, briskly efficient, bracelets and necklaces clattering. Terence tried not to groan aloud with pain—in his groin, the pit of his belly, his head where that madman had kicked him. He worried that his body would be covered with ugly bruises, a badge of shame.

If you get knocked down, get up again—fast.

Once some bastard hurts you bad, he'll need to hurt you again. If you don't stop him.

Ava-Rose Renfrew drove Terence Greene to her home at the farthest end of Holyoak Street, as if it were the most natural thing in the world. She sat very straight behind the wheel of the heavy BMW, as a young girl might sit at the controls of a powerful machine that is at the same time a kind of plaything, there to do her bidding. She showed some hesitation approaching intersections, and once or twice had to apply the brake a bit sharply, but otherwise drove with a curious excitable confidence. Her blood too raced with adrenaline: Terence, acutely conscious of her closeness, felt the heat of her warmed skin, and imagined he could see, with his uninjured eye, her beautiful hair crinkle with static electricity.

She was muttering fiercely, as if thinking aloud, "Eldrick won't follow us here, would he dare!—hadn't better, oh no!—that coward!—that beast!—hitting a defenseless man! —threatening to kill!—'the downward path'!—his, and T.W.'s!—two of a kind!—but not *me!—oh,* no!"

Terence asked, "Your assailant—you know him?"

Ava-Rose said, "I know *him,* but he sure doesn't know *me!*"

Ava-Rose had to press down on the brake pedal suddenly, and swung out her arm as if to prevent Terence from being propelled against the dashboard: The gesture was so unpremeditated, and so intimate, Terence smiled despite his throbbing mouth.

Never before had he been a passenger in his own car; rarely, indeed, did he sit passively in any vehicle except taxis and, now and then, in a limousine provided by the Feinemann Foundation. Yet, half-lying in the seat beside this virtually unknown woman as they sped, at dusk, along a shabby street in Trenton, he felt in his passivity, as in his physical weakness, strangely content.

As they approached Ava-Rose's house, however, Terence said, awkwardly, "I—I've been here, you know: I visited with your aunt the other day."

Ava-Rose gave Terence a shrewd sidelong glance. "Oh, I know! I mean, I surmised so. You looked real familiar back there," she said, softly—"and there could only be one of *you.*"

"Terence Greene, one of the jurors—"

"*Dr.* Greene, Auntie said! Oh, you were so kind to *her.*"

Ava-Rose reached out her hand to shake Terence's. Each of her fingers had a ring, sometimes two; her nails were filed short, and looked bitten, but were polished a purplish-silver color. Her handshake was dry, warm, brisk. "I'm Ava-Rose Renfrew as I guess you know?" She laughed, shyly.

Terence too laughed, though his head immediately rang with pain.

"Yes, I guess!"

The sun was disappearing at the western horizon in a massed bank of clouds, shot with red veins; the gorgeous sunset was a consequence of air pollution, yet it *was* gorgeous. At the farthest edge of Chimney Point, at least when the wind blew off the Delaware River, the air was relatively clear. The light had a look of autumnal chill.

And the old wood-and-stucco house with half its shutters painted robin's-egg blue, and patches of moss growing on its roof!—and the jungle of growth in the front yard! Because he could only see with one eye clearly, the house and garden appeared, for all their color, queerly flattened, like a watercolor.

"I—love this house," Terence said. "The first glimpse I had of it—"

"I do, too, love it!—I only hope we won't lose it."

Terence was about to ask about this, but Ava-Rose muttered, "Shucks! Those men!" seeing that a van was parked in the driveway, close to the street. It was an old vehicle, of no color, with letters on its sides that had been scraped off; a fluorescent-orange bumper read HONK IF YOU LOVE JESUS! Apparently wanting to bring Terence closer to the rear door of the house, so that he wouldn't have to walk so far, Ava-Rose drove the BMW around the van, bouncing over ruts and a patch of grassy earth, and back into the driveway. She braked, hard; the engine coughed and died.

"How is that bleeding, Dr. Greene?—how is your poor *eye*?"

It was Terence's groin and lower belly that really hurt,

but he was reluctant to say so. As he slid slowly—very slowly
—out of the car, Ava-Rose ran around to help him, slipping
her arms around his shoulders, and then his waist. Her hair
against his cheek left him breathless; the warmth of her body,
the very shimmering of her gypsylike clothes and excessive
jewelry, left him faint. Quicksilver as a match's flame, Terence felt a moment's panic—he had never desired any
woman so much. *Yet not in his body, for his body was wracked
with pain.*

As Ava-Rose helped Terence up the crumbling brick
walk, the teenaged Chick hurried out to give them a hand.
If he was astonished to see Ava-Rose bringing a bleeding
stranger home, he gave no sign; indeed, he seemed quite
prepared to help. He whistled, and said, sympathetically, "Oh
wow, man!—looks like somebody did *you!*"

Terence began to say, "I think it looks worse than—"
when a stabbing pain in his lower belly weakened him, and
he nearly fell. Husky gum-chewing Chick slung an arm
around Terence's shoulder and all but hoisted him into the
house.

"Lord, Lord! What have they done to you!"—Holly Mae
Loomis stood in the kitchen, staring at Terence in horror,
wringing her hands in her apron.

"Not 'they,' Auntie— '*him.*' You know who." Ava-Rose
seemed on the verge of tears, now she was safely home.

"Eldrick Gill?"

"He went wild and attacked this innocent man."

Chick whistled again, and made a chuckling sound, like
grating pebbles, deep in his throat. "*He's* gonna get his, just
wait."

Both Ava-Rose and Holly Mae Loomis scolded the boy
for so speaking. Ava-Rose said, as if by rote, " 'Tempt not the
darkness for it is soon on its way.' "

There was a high-pitched jabbering as of a jungle bird,
and a dog's frantic barking, and, from elsewhere in the
house, girls' cries and a man's deep baritone voice. Ava-Rose
and Chick helped Terence to a divan in a big, barnlike room;

they lifted his legs, which were leaden, and swung them deftly around so that he lay stretched out, like a hospital patient. At once the throbbing pain in his groin and belly became bearable. Something moistly hot and soft as a chamois cloth soaked in hot water flicked against his face, and Ava-Rose cried, "Buster Keaton, go away!" To Holly Mae she said, "Please bring us some ice, Auntie, wrapped in a towel." With quick, deft fingers she loosened Terence's clothing, unbuckled his belt, tugged at his necktie, and opened his shirt collar, even unlaced his shoes and tugged them off. She drew her fingers tenderly across his forehead as if to determine if he was feverish. "So brave!—so kind! Risking your life for *me*, a stranger! Mr. Terence Greene, you are of 'that bright, blissful legion' the Book of the Millennium promises." There came then the shock, after a moment a deeply comforting shock, of ice lowered against Terence's throbbing left eye.

Terence nearly passed out. Hanging onto consciousness as to the string of a kite lurching ever higher into the sky.

He shut both his eyes and lay unmoving as Ava-Rose gently washed his face, and dabbed at bloodstains on his clothes. He felt a bristling masculine presence, which would be the elderly white-bearded patriarch Cap'n-Uncle Riff, whom he'd seen in the Mill Hill Tavern that day, and heard the man's voice close over his head—"Give him some of this, dear. It will set the man up well." There was a powerful smell of alcoholic spirits, and the touch of a glass against Terence's lips, and a taste of whiskey. Terence sipped some, and swallowed. Liquid flame ran down his throat and up into his nasal cavities. He tried to whisper "Thank you" but choked instead.

Ava-Rose whispered, "Oh, but should we give him painkillers, too? I have some Percodans right here—"

"Perks?" the boy asked. "Where'd you get 'em, Ava-Rose?"

"I *had* them, smartie."

The deep baritone voice of the elder intoned, solemnly, "Perhaps just one, eh?"

A glass of cold water was brought to Terence, and a capsule was nudged against his lips. He did not think of resisting, though he would have to drive back to Queenston soon, and such a drug might make him drowsy.

Holly Mae Loomis whispered, "He's a good patient, isn't he?"

Ava-Rose said, warmly, "He's a good kind courageous man—I'll never forget how he risked his life for me."

Terence protested, "But, surely, anyone in my place—"

They had moved away from him, to let him rest. Terence felt coolness on his face, from an opened window; he did not open his good eye, yet seemed to be gazing into night.

Elsewhere in the house, a bird chattered, whistled, and shrieked as if in complaint of so much attention being paid to Terence—this would be Darling, the West African gray parrot. Closer, yet at a distance, girls' voices were petulant and wondering—"Hey, why can't we come *in*? Who's lying down there?" (These would be the pretty young girls whom Terence had seen sunbathing on the roof: the girls who'd teased him so.) Buster the dog, recognizing Terence, had ceased his barking, and lay now beside the divan, his heavy, warm head on Terence's knees. Terence groped to pet him, and Buster licked his fingers lovingly. "Good dog!" Terence whispered. The interior of his mouth was coated with something like cotton batting that made even whispering difficult.

Not quite out of earshot, the Renfrews were hurriedly conferring. Terence felt like an eavesdropper—but had he any choice?

The elder Renfrews, with Chick joining in, chided Ava-Rose for being too trusting in the matter of Eldrick Gill; and Ava-Rose, her voice husky and quavering, acknowledged that, yes, she'd made a mistake—"But, between faith and doubt in our fellow man, The Church bids us choose faith. And I *had* to attend to my business."

Cap'n-Uncle Riff said, "Speak to me not of 'The

Church.' The Church of the Holy Apocalypse is not *my* church, child."

"Nor mine neither," Holly Mae Loomis said, with a snort. "And this Eldrick Gill, who's done time in Rahway—who in her right mind would have faith in *him*? Why, he ain't half as good-looking, even, as T.W.! Anybody'd think, Ava-Rose, after T.W. almost killed you, you'd have more sense about men."

Ava-Rose began to protest, faintly, but Chick interrupted. He spoke in a bemused adolescent drawl, yet Terence was struck by the boy's intelligence. "Ava-Rose is so far from evil, herself, she can't see it in anybody else. She feels sorry for anybody who's in love with her—or say they are."

Ava-Rose laughed sadly, embarrassed. "Oh I do feel sort of to blame for causing evil—I guess."

The others laughed in derision. Cap'n-Uncle Riff said, in a lowered voice, moving as if to stand with his back to the visitor lying on their divan, "Look here! Ava-Rose is aware now, but what's to be done? Eldrick Gill surely has a gun, and we do not. He has been to this house and may come again. Unless we flee the premises, and—"

Holly Mae interrupted fiercely, "Oh no, oh no, not me. I do not flee. I do not abandon my home to a marauding beast who would put it to the torch—not *me*."

"Nor me neither!" Chick said loudly, in disgust.

Ava-Rose said, "If only the police—"

Again the others laughed in derision. Their voices grew fainter, as if they were moving away; or Terence were growing drowsier, unable to hold onto consciousness. He did not want to sleep, though sleep, an easing away from his aching body, was deliciously inviting. The sweet-natured dog, whose name, at the moment, Terence could not have recalled, but whose coarse, wiry fur was perceptibly different to his fingertips than Tuffi's had been, snuggled closer, with a human-sounding sigh like a groan of sheer comfort.

Nearly out of earshot, there came the teenaged Chick's

defiant voice, "We ain't gonna let him kill us—hell, *he's* gonna get *his,* you wait," and Ava-Rose cried, "Oh Chick, honey, *no.* That's a wrongful thing to utter," and Holly Mae said, "I say it's a *rightful* thing," and Cap'n-Uncle Riff said, his brave words fading even as Terence strained to hear them, "I say we must defend ourselves—somehow. Or—"

A pit opened at the bottom of Terence Greene's skull, and he tumbled through.

"Dr. Greene?—Ter-ence? Excuse me—"

Gentle fingers stroked his cheek, and removed the cold compress from his left eye. Terence woke, with a start. One instant obliterated in darkness, the other fully awake, like a match struck into flame.

His left eye was not so swollen as he'd feared but its vision was blurred, as if he were looking through a veil; the vision in his right eye appeared to be normal, but what he saw—a young woman's beautiful face, amber-green eyes, heated skin, a tiny white scar on her chin like a vertical dimple—was wonderful to him. And how lovely, her scratchy contralto voice, her quaint pronunciation of his name— "Ter-ence"—with both syllables equally stressed.

So I have not dreamt you, then.

Ava-Rose Renfrew leaned above him, smiling hesitantly. "Your eye doesn't look bad at all, only a bit bruised. I think the ice helped."

Terence too was smiling, or trying to. How dazed, how happy he felt! He said, "Thanks to *you.*" As if to impress the admiring young woman, who gazed at him with rapt, shining eyes, Terence got to his feet; declared that, yes, he did feel much better—"Like Lazarus rising from the dead." He'd meant the remark as a joke of some sort, an allusion to the fact (of which, in his male vanity, he was keenly aware) that he looked ghastly. But, as a joke, it fell quite flat; Ava-Rose Renfrew was clearly not in a mood for levity. She clutched both Terence's hands in hers, in a gesture of singular intimacy—a spontaneous response that cut through the surface of a disheveled man's banter, and spoke to something deeper in him, as, Terence was to think later, his very wife Phyllis would not have done—and cried, breathless, "Oh! Dr. Greene! Don't say such a thing! He might have killed you, if you'd been alone somewhere without witnesses."

Terence's smile turned lopsided, then faded. Of course, Ava-Rose was right. Why did he play the fool, at such a time?

As he stood to his full height, a wave of faintness seemed to rise with him. A pulse beat in his left eye and he could breathe only through his mouth; he touched his nose gingerly, and wondered if it had broken. His clothes were blood-splattered—how on earth would he explain himself to his family?

Phyllis, his daughters, the house at 7 Juniper Way—all came flooding back to him. And the conference in New Haven he'd so uncharacteristically missed. *How would he explain?*

As if reading Terence's thoughts, Ava-Rose said, in a childlike conspiratorial tone, "You'll have to say you were in an accident—a minor accident with your car, won't you, Terence! You don't want to involve the police, you know. They're not reliable—they say they will protect you, if you're a witness to a criminal act, or a victim; then they *don't*. The Trenton police told my family, 'We can't give you twenty-four-hour-a-day surveillance forever just 'cause somebody says he wants to kill you.' "

Terence said quickly, "I understand."

"Well, I hope you really don't—fully."

It was a startling, rather touching answer. Terence looked at the beautiful young woman with the fair, glinting, springy hair and the exotic jewelry—long dangling silver-and-turquoise earrings, several necklaces, many bracelets and rings—and the wide-set clear eyes so fixed upon him thinking *How can I leave you, now I've found you* even as Ava-Rose Renfrew, who was, for all her air of romance, a practical-minded woman, slid an arm through his and led him to the rear of the house. "You'd best get back home, your family will be missing you. Your wife." Ava-Rose tapped at the plain gold wedding band Terence wore on his left hand. Terence murmured, as if reproved, "My wife, yes."

The other Renfrews seemed to have retreated, out of tact. From a distant part of the house came a sound of voices, music, a television set—a parrot's shrilly uttered expletives. There were smells of cooking, something warm, yeasty, spicy, mouth-watering. Through a doorway Terence caught a glimpse of an old-fashioned kitchen with cupboards to the ceiling, antiquated stove and sink, aged dotted swiss curtains on the windows; he saw, with a rush of hunger he wouldn't have believed he had, a large crusty and whorled loaf of grainy brown bread, newly baked, on a counter. *Oh! won't you feed me! please!* Saying ruefully, "I've interrupted your dinner, haven't I! Your delicious family dinner."

Ava-Rose laughed, tugging at Terence's arm as if in affectionate reproof. "Dr. Greene, if we are to be friends, you must not utter 'words that seem not what they say, and say not what they seem.' *I* interrupted Auntie's dinner preparation, and a meal is nothing, is it?—when a man has saved another's life."

Ava-Rose had so distinct a way of speaking, such a curious habit of enunciating certain vowels, Terence wondered if she had a very slight speech impediment; or if her native language were not English. He gazed at her, blinking. "I— I'm not sure that I saved your life, Ava-Rose. I—"

"Why, of course you did, Dr. Greene! In any case, you would have." Ava-Rose drew a deep, passionate breath. "As a daughter of the Faith of the Millennium, who sees intentions as deeds, and who takes all things as seriously as if the world is to end at midnight—*I* will never forget your sacrifice."

Terence laughed, embarrassed. His head was mildly spinning. *She is looking at me with eyes of love—isn't she?* "A daughter of—?"

"I'll tell you of my faith, which is a newly found faith, here in Trenton, though with houses of worship throughout the world, next time we meet," Ava-Rose said sweetly. "Now, I'm a bit worried for you—isn't your family awaiting you, Dr. Greene?"

How Terence Greene would have liked to protest *In fact, no: No one is awaiting me tonight.* But he knew the words would sound hollow and unconvincing. He said, so sweetly rebuked, "Why, yes. Of course."

Before leaving the Renfrew house, Terence used a bathroom, more a washroom, off the kitchen. The facilities were more primitive than any he'd seen since his boyhood in rural Shaheen, New York; he felt a moment's repugnance for anyone who could live in such a house. Not only was the plumbing very old—the toilet bowl and sink permanently stained —but the walls were grimy, the linoleum floor worn through, and there was a plastic strip over the single small window, where part of the pane was broken. Couldn't they afford to replace the glass?—or didn't they care?

Or were they a family who transcended material things?

Outside, Ava-Rose led Terence to his car, shivering. An autumnal chill was rising from the earth and there was a gathering wind from the west, off the river. The sun had long since set; it was night; filmy clouds were blown across the face of the moon, so that shadows moved in the Renfrews' overgrown yard. Terence's nerves were strung tight and now he did want to leave *before something further happened.*

Trying not to wince with pain, he climbed gingerly into his car; put the key in the ignition and started the motor. What relief that the BMW started so immediately, its powerful engine leaping into life. Terence had halfway worried that— well, something might have happened to the expensive car in this shabby West Trenton neighborhood.

Ava-Rose too seemed relieved. She smiled, and gave him her hand in farewell. The wind stirred her hair and her long earrings glittered against her cheeks.

She spoke quickly, quietly, glancing nervously back over her shoulder as if fearing someone might be watching. (*Was* someone watching? The wind in the trees, the wind in the tall grasses.) "Dr. Greene, I sense our destinies are linked! —*I* will never forget *you*. And Auntie told me about you offering to help us get a lawyer—what kindness! Auntie Holly has had such a hard life, and has suffered so from that back injury, and not one person among the 'powers of the secular' in Trenton has cared in the slightest. You've given us all such *hope*."

Was it true? Terence had rolled down his car window and was leaning to it, gazing up at Ava-Rose Renfrew with an expression of such yearning, he knew he should be embarrassed. His bruised eye leaked tears, which was more embarrassing still. Yet he could hardly help himself. *Don't send me away, Ava-Rose—I love you.*

He said, "You called me 'Terence' before, Ava-Rose—I hope you will again?"

Shy as a young girl, blushing, Ava-Rose bit her lower lip. For there was no mistaking this stranger's interest now.

" 'Ter-ence.' "

"Yes. Exactly."

They were still holding hands. Impulsively, as if overcome by emotion, yet in the most innocent of ways, Ava-Rose brought Terence's hand to her lips—to kiss.

With which gesture, Terence Greene's life was changed forever.

For here is what happened, as Terence would subsequently determine, in the weeks and months to follow that September evening.

In all the years of his life, to follow.

Eldrick Gill, after punching and kicking Terence in the parking lot, went to get drunk; and, drunk and deeply embittered, for what private reason obsessed with Ava-Rose Renfrew, he'd been unable to keep away from the Renfrews' house where—how many times?—he'd been a visitor. Shrewdly, he hadn't driven his motorcycle along Holyoak

Street, where he would have been seen by neighborhood residents; he took the back route, driving up from the River Road, Route 29, on the unimproved access road that led to the landfill-dump a quarter-mile beyond the cul-de-sac of Holyoak, and behind the Renfrews' property.

There, he'd left his 1988 Harley-Davidson. Partly hidden in underbrush. Where, later that night, Cap'n-Uncle Riff Renfrew and fifteen-year-old Chick Renfrew would discover it after a brief search, preparatory to rolling it down to the Delaware River, and into the river. To sink without a trace.

Like the lifeless bloodied body of Eldrick Gill himself, weighted with debris from the landfill. Later that night.

Eldrick Gill, thirty-four years old, resident of 2822 Sixteenth Street, Trenton; intermittently employed construction worker, truck driver, gas station attendant; with a criminal record of several arrests for burglary, drug dealing, assault and battery, and a single conviction resulting in three years (for assault) at Rahway State Prison. His body never to be found since, in life, he was not to be much missed.

But Eldrick Gill could not have anticipated such a fate for himself, meaning to do injury—to kill?—making his way, on foot, by stealth, to the rear of the Renfrews' house, at approximately 7:30 P.M. He saw that the Renfrews had a visitor—very likely, he recognized the BMW in the driveway as belonging to the well-dressed middle-aged stranger he'd attacked at the Chimney Point Shopping Center—and so he waited, amid the bushes and tall grasses, to see what developed. He'd had six quick ales in a tavern on State Street, yet might have believed himself clear-minded, cunning. He wanted revenge but he hadn't known what he would do to Ava-Rose Renfrew, who had betrayed him, or to any of her family; he hadn't known whether he would do anything at all.

After some minutes of waiting he saw Ava-Rose and the tall stranger leave the house at the rear. He saw the man, with a stooping, wincing walk, get into his fancy silver car;

saw Ava-Rose take the man's hand in hers; saw her suddenly lift the hand, and kiss it—and in that instant, Eldrick Gill lost control.

Rushing at the woman, cursing—"Cunt! Liar! Murderer! *You!*"

How swiftly and terribly it happened, and how clumsily: Eldrick Gill struck Ava-Rose Renfrew a vicious chopping blow, aiming for her neck, to break it, but striking her shoulder instead. She cried out only faintly, falling like a shot to the ground. There was an outcry from the back door of the house, where the white-bearded Cap'n-Uncle Riff and his great-nephew Chick were watching—there was a dog's wild barking—and the man behind the wheel of the BMW, wholly astonished, cried out too.

"Stop! Wait! What are you—"

Eldrick Gill panicked and turned to run—stumbling and swaying back along the lane—as, behind him, there were furious cries from the old man and the boy, directed at Terence. "Get him! Go after him! Don't let him get away!"

So Terence, confused, but eager to obey, pressed down hard on the accelerator and the car leapt forward.

The lane was weedy, bumpy—the car so bucked, bounced, jolted, Terence had to grip the wheel tight with both hands to keep from pitching forward. In the lurching headlights, the fleeing man turned, with a look of fury, incredulity, and terror—his opaque eyes shining like a cat's, the very bristles of his unshaven jaw, dark against his pasty face, illuminated—as, seemingly of its own volition, primed for the kill, the BMW struck him, and ran over him.

There was a short, anguished scream—Eldrick Gill, or Terence Greene, Terence himself did not know.

He jammed on the brakes. The man's body was caught somehow in the bumper, or beneath the wheels; Terence, panicked, not knowing what he did, put the car in reverse, felt the right front wheel pass over the man another time, and again jammed on the brakes—"Oh no oh no oh God no *God help me.*"

All was still, now. No further screams or cries. Even the dog's barking had ceased.

Terence's headlights, at an angle, illuminated a lane of coarse gravel and rutted dirt, bounded by tall grasses. There was no movement of any kind except the wind in the grasses. No human figure was visible, or face.

Terence could not comprehend *oh yes he knew: he knew* what had happened. Except to know that something had happened. Something was caught yet beneath the wheels of his car—something utterly still now, silent.

Terence was sitting paralyzed behind the wheel of his car and though his nose was bleeding freshly where he'd bumped it on the wheel the grogginess of the past two or so hours had lifted and in its place was a terrible, chilling lucidity.

What I have done, I have done. Never to be undone.

The noble-headed white-bearded Cap'n-Uncle Riff limped to the car, to examine what was caught beneath the wheels; Chick in T-shirt and jeans, his Phillies cap reversed on his head, chewing gum furiously, trotted beside him, as did Buster the dog, his eyes glaring yellow and his moist black lips bared from his glistening teeth. Terence was sick with terror hiding his face in his hands yet peered through his fingers at the old man whose bristly snow-white beard seemed all of a piece, hanging stiffly from his face, and whose bushy white eyebrows arched above grave recessed eyes, oddly smooth, pinkened cheeks. The old man too wore a cap—a navy blue nautical cap, rather smart, with a shiny visor; his clean blue much-laundered work shirt was buttoned to his throat, where flaccid flesh hung, in wattles. The boy Chick was as tall as Cap'n-Uncle Riff though he had a tendency to slouch, as if his hefty, muscular shoulders and arms were heavy. Like his great-uncle, Chick stared at what lay on the ground at his feet, and his expression was as blank, as stunned, as the old man's. Then Chick took off his baseball cap to fan his face, and whistled—a long, slow, high-pitched but descending whistle.

Cap'n-Uncle Riff took note of Terence Greene behind the windshield of the car, and came to console him. In his solemn, deep baritone, fixing his eyes on Terence's, he said, "Don't grieve, son. Your secret is safe with us."

The Lover

As a pregnant woman may be said to inhabit her pregnancy, as her pregnancy inhabits her, and to understand that, not merely her body, but her very soul is pregnant with a new, unknown, mysterious life, so too the lover is forever conscious *even if unconscious* of his beloved: whose love he both inhabits, and is inhabited by.

Waking, or sleeping; in the beloved's presence, or in the presence of others; bounding up the walk to her house, or, constrained by circumstance, many miles away—it scarcely matters, for the lover defines himself by his love. His happiness springs from his love, and his unhappiness. His dread, his anxiety, his anguish; his anger and frustration; his hope, his joy, his ecstasy. The very expression on his face—

"Dad-dee, why are you standing there like that, why don't you bring the tree in*side*? Why are you smiling so—silly?"

It was Cindy in the doorway, it was Cindy's anxious teasing voice, and there was Daddy with the six-foot Christmas tree in the lightly falling snow, his skin warmed, his eyes misting over *with a thought of her, an unbidden delicious memory of her, Ava-Rose Renfrew framing his face in her hands kissing him*

*chastely on the lips murmuring how can we thank you? thank you?
thank you? for this wonderful Christmas?*

A twin-tree, as fragrantly evergreen, as full-branched,
and as tall, for the house at 33 Holyoak, Trenton, as for the
house at 7 Juniper Way.

Yet it was a fact, and this fact was *the fact* of Terence
Greene's life in his forty-fifth year, that, when he was at home
in the one house (in Queenston) he was also, in his thoughts,
in the other house (in Trenton); but when, for whatever period of time, an afternoon, overnight, a mere snatched hour
or so, he was in that house (in Trenton) he was rarely, in his
thoughts, in the other house (in Queenston).

To inhabit bliss is to be blind.

She'd taken his hands in hers, gently she'd stroked the
backs, the bony knuckles, the long slender fingers, then turning his hands over to examine the palms, concentrating then
on the palm of his right hand—so tenderly! Her head bowed,
a crystal dove gleaming in her hair, and her fleshy lower lip
caught in her teeth as she drew a slow ticklish forefinger
across the palm, as reverentially as if she were translating the
hieroglyphics of a sacred text—"Oh! Ter-ence! Good news!
'A vessel that overflows yet has no bottom': Your life will be
long, and fruitful, and happy, and will bring happiness to
others."

He would have laid his head in her lap, pressed his warm
yearning face against the folds of her cheaply shiny crinkled-
satin skirt, and the milky, hard-muscled thighs beneath (he
assumed milky, like the inside of her forearm: In fact he had
yet to see Ava-Rose Renfrew's thighs), he would have hugged
her hips in his arms, *Oh love me! never send me away!* but he
did not dare.

Though he had killed a man for her sake, however ac-
cidentally, their relations were quaintly formal.

Tender, but formal.

It *had* been an accident, hadn't it.

Yes, said the Renfrews. Yes you know it was an acci-dent, and no one is to blame. You saw how he'd struck down poor Ava-Rose—"Like the Goddamn Karate Kid," Chick observed—clearly intending to kill her.

Even if it wasn't an accident, exactly, but what the law calls *vehicular manslaughter—vehicular homicide?*—still, that wicked man had deserved it.

A nightmare, recurring like ripples that become waves, waves that diminish to ripples, and then suddenly swell to waves again, pulsing and pounding in the brain.

The mangled broken body caught beneath the shiny grill of the BMW. The dented, blood-smeared bumper. Cracked headlight like a demented eye. He'd felt the car lurch forward out of his control and he'd slammed on the brakes and shifted to reverse and now the car *was* in control backing over the unresisting body. Terence had not seen *yes he'd seen: blood in ribbons streaming from the dead man's nose, mouth, ears* cringing paralyzed behind the wheel whispering "Oh no oh no oh God help me no."

Daddy had an accident on the Turnpike, a minor acci-dent. Nose bloodied and his eye bruised, poor Daddy. Cindy had stared at him *as if knowing that something terrible, irrevocable had happened to them all* but of course she hadn't known, how could she.

For it hadn't been murder, it had been an accident. Terence hadn't known *yes: of course he'd known* what he was doing, pressing his foot down on the accelerator as he had.

And the car leaping away.

And the scream of incredulity and anguish, dragged down beneath the front wheels.

The *thud!* of the body against the front grill and bumper, the sickening *thump!* of the tire passing over living flesh.

He'd known, it had been deliberate. Killing that brute son of a bitch who'd dared lay a hand on Ava-Rose.

Terence had leaned out the opened front door of the car to vomit into the weeds, sobbing and retching. He hadn't meant, he hadn't known. His body was wracked with terror as with electric charges. His teeth chattered, tasting of bile.

Then he was on his feet in the chill night air begging them to call the police, an ambulance, maybe it wasn't too late?—maybe Eldrick Gill was still breathing?—and Cap'n-Uncle Riff gripped Terence Greene's shoulders tight and gave him a shake and said sternly, "Son, no police will set foot on this property, as I live and breathe," and Chick whistled in amazement and resignation, "*His* brains is leaked out his ears—you'd need a shovel for him, not a stretcher."

Holly Mae Loomis had rushed out to give aid to Ava-Rose, lying panting and moaning in the wild rose alongside the driveway. Lifting the poor girl from where she'd fallen, all twisted, Holly Mae had heard the sound of silk tearing and had thought for a terrible moment it was her niece's skin being torn.

At the same time scolding Dara and Dana—"You two! Get back in that house! Don't you dare come out here! Go away and hide! *Do you hear!*"

The little girls stood on the crumbling cement stoop, hugging each other. Crying, "Aunt Ava-Rose?—where are you?"

All these things, Terence Greene had not known, but known.

As Buster the mongrel husky–German shepherd whimpered and nudged his moist nose, yearning mouth, against Terence's hands.

Terence said, "But I will have to notify the police—I *must*," and Ava-Rose said, "No, no! Please! The man is dead, the police can't bring him back," so sweetly lucid despite her own bruised face, her dilated eyes, and Terence said, "It isn't a matter of bringing him back, it's a matter of the law," and Ava-Rose said, "The Book of the Millennium tells us 'When the Rapture is at hand, what of Mankind's Law?' " and Terence said, trying to maintain his eerie composure, which he seemed to know, at the time, was but a form of hysteria, "But the law of the State of New Jersey, the law of the United States of America!—I must report hitting and killing a man with my car," and Ava-Rose said stubbornly, "Oh, Ter-ence, why!—when he wanted to kill *us*," and Terence beginning to weaken, smelling the crisp fragrance of her hair, seeing her gemlike eyes, the pupils blackly dilated, said, "That isn't the point, the point is he's *dead*," and Ava-Rose said, like a tired, careless child, "Cap'n-Uncle Riff and Chick will see to him, and *we* won't need to know," and Terence said, "But, Ava-Rose—" and Ava-Rose said, seizing his hands in hers, leaning close, "Then I will tell you why, Ter-ence: Because if the police come to this house another time, if they learn of Eldrick Gill's death on our property, the city will take custody of Dara and Dana, my sister's girls she abandoned with me eleven years ago—they'll be put in a foster home and I won't be allowed to see them again. Nor Holly Mae, nor Cap'n-Uncle. The family will be destroyed, Dr. Greene, don't you see?"

Terence stared at Ava-Rose, helpless. With grief, and with love.

"Yes. I see."

Before Terence drove home to Queenston that night, Cap'n-Uncle Riff conferred with him in private. "I know what it is, son, and what it will be, in the days and weeks, and months, to come. I too killed a man, by accident—a hunting accident—in Borneo, forty years ago." The elderly man paused, gazing deep into Terence's eyes, as Terence, hypnotized, gazed into his. "You will learn to live with it, son. Like a wound that heals over. Wait and see."

The terrible evening of September 14. *What I have done, I have done. Never to be undone.*

"Oh!—it's *you*!"

A blowy January dusk, and had Terence come home at an unexpectedly early hour?—he could not recall when he'd told Phyllis he would be back, or if he'd told her anything specific at all.

Phyllis looked up startled as Terence blundered into the dim-lit bedroom. She was in her champagne-lace negligee, her bare legs and feet very white, sprawled somewhat gracelessly atop the rumpled bedspread just stubbing a cigarette out in an ashtray (the room was unpleasantly blue with smoke), and was she also replacing the telephone receiver in its white plastic cradle, having heard Terence's footsteps in the hall? As if to make a joke of it, she said, sniffing, "I wish you wouldn't *barge in* like this!—you're never home, and when you are, you—*barge in.*" Terence apologized at once; seeing, to his dismay, that Phyllis's face was puffy and her eyes red from crying.

"Why, Phyllis—what's wrong?"

"Wrong? With *me?*" She wiped roughly at her nose with the back of her hand. "What about you?—what's wrong with *you?*"

Terence stared at his wife, not knowing how to reply.

It is my fault, of course. These weeks, months. She knows.

(Yet, what could Phyllis know? Nothing of Eldrick Gill, surely—no one except the Renfrews, and Terence Greene, knew of him. And the thousands of dollars Terence had spent on the Renfrews, or given them, had been by shrewd indirection taken from certain accounts, converted into checks payable to Terence Greene as Executive Director of the Feinemann Foundation, then converted to U.S. Postal money orders—to Terence's way of thinking, a foolproof procedure.)

Terence had just returned from New York (in fact, from Trenton: He'd left his office early to drive to downtown Trenton, for a two-and-a-half-hour conference with Holly Mae Loomis and the lawyer the Renfrews had engaged to represent Holly Mae in her $12 million negligence suit against the Trenton Transit Company) and was gray-faced with fatigue (though inwardly glowing, burnished—for Ava-Rose would surely call him next morning to thank him for his kindness, and to invite him to visit); stricken now with guilt at seeing Phyllis so upset. He tried not to show distaste for the smoke in the air (Ava-Rose was passionate against smoking: furious, the other day, having caught Chick with a pack of cigarettes in his pocket), nor even husbandly surprise and concern that Phyllis had resumed smoking (*hadn't* she stopped?—he seemed to think she had). He sat on the edge of the bed and touched Phyllis's shoulder, saying, "I—hope it's nothing I've done?—that has made you so upset?"

Phyllis laughed, sitting quickly up, so that Terence's hand fell away. In the lacy negligee her full, heavy breasts were loose, yet constrained, like ripe fruits in netting; her stomach swelled too, and her hips; Terence had a quick dizzy vision of embracing her, that warm womanly body, burying his face against her breasts, or belly. It had been such a long time.

"Would that make it any less of what it is—or isn't?" Phyllis asked, brightly.

"What?" Terence had no idea what she meant.

"What *what?*—have you forgotten what we're talking about, in the space of a minute?"

Terence drew breath to speak, but hesitated. Apparently, he had.

Then he remembered—"I was just asking you, dear, if it had anything to do with me. Your being upset, crying—"

"And I was asking, would that make it—assuming I *am* upset, and crying, which, in fact, I *am not*—would that make it any less significant, whether it had anything to do with *you?*" Phyllis swung her legs around, and sat up, flush-faced, smiling. "Male vanity! Indeed!"

Terence said, humbly, "I meant only that, if I were somehow responsible, I might be able to help."

Phyllis saw that he was contrite; peering at him, she might have seen that he was very tired. Relenting, she squeezed his hand, as she often squeezed Cindy's hand, after scolding her. "I'll be all right, Terry. I'm sure it's just a— phase. A phase we're going through."

"Your father used to say, 'Human history is just phases; but God's history is one single substance.' "

Phyllis appeared startled. "He did?—Father?"

Rarely had Terence been comfortable with his ministerial father-in-law, who'd had a habit of frowning at him over half-moon reading glasses, as if unable to place him. Now that Reverend Willard Winston was dead, Terence felt on easier terms with the man.

He said, "Certainly. I think he was influenced by Hegel."

Phyllis drew her negligee more tightly about herself, crossing her arms over her breasts. She did not trust Terence's remarks about her father, perhaps because she knew that Reverend Winston had not entirely approved of his son-in-law. (But had Terence known, had he sensed?—Phyllis wasn't certain.) In the lamplight, Phyllis's slightly swollen eyes and hurt mouth gave her a childlike, vulnerable look; there was something melancholic about her very posture. Her blond-frosted hair, usually stiff as a helmet, was flattened on one side of her head. Terence gazed at her, but saw instead *his Botticelli Venus: the fine-lashed eyes gleaming amber-green, the slightly snubbed nose, perfect mouth. Even the near-invisible scars, delicate as sparrows' prints in the snow, seemed to the lover exquisite.*

Phyllis blew her nose in a pink tissue. "Well. At least you *are* home."

Terence loosened his tie. He could no longer bear his tight-fitting Italian shoe-boots, and tugged them off. What bliss, suddenly! He seemed to know that, though it was a weekday, and the weather frigid, he and Phyllis were expected somewhere for dinner; but he did not dare ask. The previous weekend, Terence had attended a three-day conference in Atlanta (in fact, Terence had attended only the first day of the conference, had flown back early and spent the remainder of the weekend in Chimney Point—that Sunday, January 12, had been Dara's and Dana's twelfth birthday); next weekend, Terence was to visit the palatial estate of Nelson Feinemann's son's widow, in Rhinebeck, New York (in fact, the visit was planned for Saturday only: on Sunday, Terence was to be in Trenton, with the Renfrews). Guilty, excited, Terence said, "Phyllis, I'm sorry for my part in this 'phase,' as you call it. I think you're right. I—" *Not sorry in the slightest. The soul exults in its secret glory.* "—I'll try to be home more, to see more of you and Kim and Cindy. And keep in closer contact with Aaron. It's a difficult time of year at the Foundation—after the holiday lull, everything begins to accelerate. And—"

Phyllis said, quickly, "Yes, and at Queenston Opportunities, too. Since my wonderful victory with Matt—of course, *he* did it, really: The man is so charismatic—I've had almost more clients than I can handle."

"—and the pressure on me, it's astounding, to swing grants in the direction of friends of friends, connections—"

"—and my assistant Trudy is quitting, so abruptly—"

"—the social life here in Queenston, on top of everything else, is really, sometimes—"

"—the fund-raiser for the Queenston Medical Center, in March—if I can just get through *that*—"

The telephone rang. Phyllis reached for the receiver quickly, raised it, and broke the connection—"Let's not be interrupted *now.*"

Terence agreed. There was no one in the world from whom he expected, or desired, a call: Ava-Rose Renfrew would never call him at home.

Though sometimes Terence, in the privacy of his study, if it was not too late in the evening (the Renfrews, Ava-Rose included, were usually in bed by 10:30 P.M.), quietly telephoned her.

Hello? How are you? I've just called to hear your voice.

Tell me: How is the family? Holly Mae, Cap'n-Uncle Riff—I wish you'd let me do more for you—for all of you.

Phyllis, standing barefoot before Terence, leaned down impulsively to take his hands in hers. With a bright, brisk smile she said, "We have to make an effort, Terry! We've been growing apart. Since last fall, I think. Mother's visit was

difficult, and it seems the children are always making de-
mands, and I—*I* haven't been myself lately. I suppose you
know?''

Terence looked up at Phyllis, uncertainly. Know what?
''Why, Phyllis, I—''
''I want us to try again, Terry. Please?''
''Phyllis, of course. But—''

Tears glinted in Phyllis's eyes, but her smile held fast: It
was a domestic version of The Radiant Smile, which Terence
had not seen in months. Yet there was something fearsome
in Phyllis's intensity.

''*Do* you love me, Terry? As—we used to be?''

Terence said, hesitantly, and then with genuine warmth,
''I love *you.* Of course.''

''As we used to be—? Before—?''

''Before—?''

Phyllis gestured carelessly as if to indicate the room; the
house; all that surrounded them. ''All this!''

Phyllis leaned down, to kiss Terence on the lips; he half-
rose, awkwardly, to embrace her; his heart swelled with an
emotion—love, tenderness, yearning, a need to protect and
preserve as powerful as any sexual need. *All this: all of our lives
together. Yes.*

Terence said, urgently, ''Why don't we stay home tonight, Phyllis?—I could build a fire, and—'' He thought of
the children, as they'd been; the image shimmered before
him, as if seen through the wrong end of a telescope.

But Phyllis pushed at his shoulder in gentle reproof.
Already she was turning away, headed for her bathroom. ''I
wish we could, darling, but Glenda Ryan would be terribly
hurt if we cancelled out at the last minute—and furious. You
know how some of our friends are.'' How swiftly Phyllis's
mood had changed! Terence blinked in her wake, like a man
who has lifted his face to be kissed but has been slapped
instead.

He began to change his clothes, moving about numbly
as, in the adjoining room, Phyllis raised her voice to be heard

over the sound of fiercely running water. With no apparent transition she was speaking of Aaron; alluding, worriedly, to a matter Terence hadn't known about, though Phyllis spoke as if he did. "—seems so unfair, doesn't it!—'social probation'—he and his fraternity brothers—out of *loyalty*—and their friend who'd actually assaulted the girl—or whatever: accounts vary—lied to the disciplinary committee about *them*, and so—"

Terence asked, startled, "What? What are you saying?"

"—a lawyer, if worse comes to worse and the girl's parents sue—I mean, sue Aaron and the other two or three boys—who, she says, lied—and apparently it got into all the papers up there, not Aaron, but—"

"Phyllis—?"

Phyllis had closed the bathroom door. Terence stood for some seconds, immobilized, gnawing at his lower lip.

After a brief spell he came to, and continued dressing. So it was the Ryans' for dinner. And in the morning, *she* would call him, giving an invented name as he'd asked.

I don't feel it's right, "fructifying untruths."

Nor do I. But, for me at least, what is the alternative?

Passing by the bed, where the puckered satin spread showed the imprint of Phyllis's body, Terence caught sight of the receiver, still off its hook. The querulous beeping noise had long since stopped. Terence put the receiver back, with a mild fleeting wonder why Phyllis, who usually answered the phone with girlish enthusiasm, had chosen not to answer it a few minutes ago, in his presence.

Not seeing, as, mornings before dawn, he swam—a vigorous half-mile of laps in the turquoise-glittering chlorine-stinging pool of the Queenston Athletic Club—*the mangled body, the bloodied white face, the greasy tendrils of dark hair* beneath him as he swam, a lean youthfully middle-aged man keeping scrupulously to his own lane, glancing neither to the right nor the left, he swam doing the Australian crawl as he'd been taught, he swam not seeing *what had sunken beneath the choppy moonlit waves, dumped like debris* measuring his strength, knowing he wasn't in the very best condition for a man of his age but determined to swim a half-mile and no less feeling the strength, the thrill of such strength, coursing through his shoulders, arms, kicking legs he swam, he swam seeing nothing beneath him *a shadow at the bottom of the pool but how could it be his, being motionless as death.*

He swam.

Ava-Rose Renfrew at the long, battered "antique" table in the room the Renfrews called the parlor, preparing her appliquéd garments and purses by hand, and with loving patience.

Ava-Rose, gorgeous as a rose, one of those creamy-petaled multifoliate roses shading into crimson, exquisite.

What had Holly Mae Loomis called that rose?—"Double Delight."

Ava-Rose, a faint smile on her lips, the tiny white scars invisible in lamplight, fair crackly hair subdued in braids wrapped around her head like a coronet.

Ava-Rose in a long peach-colored woolen skirt trailing on the floorboards, a purple taffeta blouse with ruffles, a black satin jacket with boldly iridescent appliqué designs on the back—a rainbow of tiny butterflies, dragonflies, bumble-bees, hummingbirds.

Ava-Rose biting her lower lip as she stitched, rapidly, fingers flying, rings glittering, bracelets chiming, bright colored scraps of velvet, silk, satin, taffeta, terrycloth onto jackets, smocks, sarilike dresses, robes, shawls, wraparounds lavish as drapes—garments purchased at secondhand clothing shops and refurbished.

Ava-Rose, humming under her breath. A just perceptible pinkness rimming her nostrils—she'd been blowing her nose, but denied she had a cold.

"What is called 'disease' is but 'dis-ease'—a confusion in the mind of man."

Ava-Rose laughing, as, as Terence entered the room,

Darling the magnificently feathered West African gray parrot, mad-yellow-eyed, scimitar-beaked, blood-bright tailfeathers flashing, flapped his wings and clambered out of his handsome new brass cage to perch atop the cage (except when Cap'n-Uncle Riff was home, Darling's cage door was kept open—the fastidious old man disapproved of the bird's liquidy droppings throughout the house, but the other Renfrews seemed scarcely to notice), and to shriek a greeting at Terence—"B'njur M'zzrrr! G'tt'ntag! M'zzrrr! Beeeyt PEEZE!"

Ava-Rose lifting her lovely face to be kissed—but lightly, chastely on the lips.

Knowing that her devoted friend and benefactor Dr. Greene of Queenston was a married man, and the father of three children.

Ava-Rose, so beautiful. Ava-Rose, won't you love me. Ava-Rose, for whose sake a man died.

With a gesture of her arm (loose flaring sleeve trailing into a saucer of blue sequins, bracelets clattering) Ava-Rose indicated where, amid typical Renfrew-clutter, her visitor might sit. At the end of the long table, beyond the tarnished silver candlesticks and dust-coated wax fruit, in a brokenbacked, but comfortable, old wicker easy chair.

"Thank you! But don't let me disturb you."

Ava-Rose's lips mysteriously twisted—"Ter-ence! No one *does* disturb me."

And Darling, stretching his long snaky neck, continuing to shriek—"B'njur M'zzrrr! *Beeeyt PEEZE!*"

(Which Terence interpreted as "Be at Peace"—the formal greeting of the members of the First Church of the Holy Apocalypse of Trenton.)

And who was snoring beneath the chair, waking with a growl deep in his throat and fangs bared, until, identifying the intruder, sniffing at hands, crotch, boots, the burly dog began to yip happily and lick at Terence's face—"Why, Buster Keaton, my old ally!"

Ava-Rose scolded Buster for jiggling the table, even as

the saucer of sequins overturned, and some pearl buttons rolled rapidly across the table, setting Darling into a flurry—did the big bird think the buttons were insects, and edible? Terence laughed in delight, having no sooner settled down in the easy chair than he jumped to his feet, scooped up the buttons to return to Ava-Rose; and kissed her again, breathlessly, yes but chastely, on her mysteriously smiling mouth.

Ava-Rose, my beloved.

"Dr. Greene, Ter-ence!—*kiss us, too!*"

It was Dara and Dana bursting into the parlor, just home from school, their pretty pale-freckled faces aglow from the winter cold and their braces glittering. For such petite girls, they made a considerable racket—"Dara and Dana, mind your manners!" their aunt scolded, but as usual they paid no heed.

Terence could not help but be flattered that the twelve-year-olds, who were inclined to be snippy with their elders, seemed so admiring, and so respectful, of him. Everything about Dr. Greene impressed them—the new-model white Oldsmobile he drove (he'd traded in the BMW in December); the way he talked, and dressed; the fact that he lived in prestigious Queenston, New Jersey. (Terence was surprised that mere children knew of such matters, but, as Holly Mae said, sighing, "There almost *aren't* children, nowadays!") There was something innocently flirtatious about the way they hovered about him, vying for his attention, boldly tilting their cheeks up for his kiss. Terence kissed one girl—was she Dara?—and the other giggled jealously. "Now me, Dr. Greene!—*me!*" and when he kissed the second girl—was she Dana?—the other giggled jealously. "Now me, Dr. Greene—you didn't kiss *me.*" And so, laughing, he kissed the first girl again; and naturally had to kiss the second girl again. Identical twins! Their wire braces tickled his lips.

Do Dara and Dana know about Eldrick Gill?—the accident?

No, impossible—they wouldn't want me to kiss them, if they did.

The girls leapt about so excitedly, they overturned a saucer of brightly colored glass beads Ava-Rose had been sewing on a black felt vest; Ava Rose sprang to her feet, exasperated, but laughing, as she slapped lightly at the girls—"Dara, Dana! Aren't you ashamed! Pick up every last bead you've spilled, and put them back in this saucer, and go upstairs and do your homework, d'you hear?"

The girls cringed, though Ava-Rose's aggression was merely playful. "Yes, Aunt Ava-Rose," mumbled the one; and the other, "Yes, Aunt Ava-Rose, we're *sorry.*"

Terence helped the girls pick up the glass beads, making a game of it—who could find the most beads, most quickly. He was reminded of similar delightful games he'd played years ago with his own children; a long-forgotten game played with Aaron when the boy was no more than two or three, collecting toys scattered across the nursery floor.

Dara and Dana fascinated Terence, for there was, to him, a mystery in twins; identical twins; two human beings sharing the same genes, precisely. How very different from Terence Greene, as a child, and, yes, as an adult, knowing himself so profoundly alone in the world—isolated in his "uniqueness."

Dara and Dana were sweet girls, if sometimes overexuberant. Terence tried, but could never tell them apart. Looking from one to the other, and back, he felt the more mystified. They were not quite so pretty as Kim, but they had certain of her mannerisms—intonations of voice, facial gestures. The shared subculture of American youth, from which, too, Terence felt permanently estranged.

And, too, the girls' uncanny resemblance to Ava-Rose— except for the pale freckles scattered across their faces, and darkish strawberry blond hair less curly than Ava-Rose's, and the charmingly crooked front teeth, they were child-versions of their aunt, thus rather seductive. Even their voices were unusually low and throaty for girls so young.

The glass beads were recovered, presented to Ava-Rose in the old cracked saucer. The girls ran off, giggling—one cried, "Bye-bye, Dr. Wineapple!" and the other, giving a hard shove to the first, corrected her, "—Dr. Greene! *'Bye!"*

In their wake, there was a moment's awkward silence.

Determined not to inquire after "Wineapple," for fear of seeming a jealous lover (which, assuredly, he was not), Terence observed, "How much the twins resemble you, Ava-Rose! I suppose you and your sister look very much alike?"

Ava-Rose had taken up her needle and thread again, and said, stiffening slightly, "No. Not really. We have a common mother, of course—that's the genetic inheritance. Grace is three years older than I am, a Cancer, with a Moon in Capricorn and a Fixed, Aquarius Ascendant. Very cold, calculating. Detached. She long ago divorced the man who was—is—the twins' father; he seems to have disappeared." Ava-Rose paused, stitching. She regarded Terence with eyes brimming with sudden moisture. "Grace had a hardness in her even when we were children. She used to say, '*Our* mother abandoned us like stray kittens—that's what *we* owe the world.' I love her, Ter-ence, but I have cast her out of my thoughts, because I know that's what Grace wants. I have not seen my sister in eleven years."

"I'm so sorry!" Terence murmured.

Abandoned. Like me.

That was the snow-swirling January afternoon, shading into evening, when Terence Greene told Ava-Rose Renfrew certain secrets of his life, which he had never confessed to anyone previously. Not even Phyllis.

Especially not Phyllis!—who would have been revulsed.

How, as a child of two, he'd been abandoned by both his parents. He could scarcely remember either of them. A woman who'd been his mother, a young woman, with no distinct features—a man who'd been his father, big, bearded, or perhaps just unshaven, with bulging blood-threaded eyes, an angry hacking cough. (Had Terence's father coughed blood?—Terence seemed, vaguely, to recall this.) "Something terrible had happened, because I remember being in a speeding car—my mother screaming—a siren?—an ambulance, or a police car?—and a crash—I'm sure it must have been a crash—though my memory is blurred, like something glimpsed through water." He paused, seeing that Ava-Rose was listening closely, sympathetically. But should he pour out his heart, and risk this lovely young woman's pity? He drew a deep breath. "Even now, sometimes, I hear a woman's voice—I look around, and no one's there. I see, sometimes," he held out his hands, which trembled slightly, "ghost-splotches of blood, on my hands. Of course, there's nothing there."

"Poor Ter-ence!" Ava-Rose shivered.

"And, afterward, there was a courthouse—a courtroom—though I can't remember whether I actually was there; or just knew about it. I'm inclined to think that I just knew. No one told me, no one would tell me anything as I grew up, living with one relative of my mother's after another. 'Hettie's boy,' they spoke of me, 'Hettie's poor boy,' as if I couldn't hear. My mother's name was Hettie Greene. I don't even know if she and my father were married, but— my name is hers. It always has been."

Terence spoke with an odd passion, and was immediately embarrassed.

It always has been.

What I have done, I have done.

Ava-Rose said, feelingly, "You've suffered!"

So Terence unburdened his soul. He glided quickly over his marriage, his children; he would not exploit them, for the sake of winning sympathy from Ava-Rose. He spoke of his "unresolved" life—his earlier academic career, which had gone unexpectedly well, and which, indeed, he'd liked, very much; his subsequent position as Executive Director of the Feinemann Foundation, which seemed to be grinding him down, to a fine gritty powder. "The Foundation is wealthy, and so we're besieged by applicants. My Aunt Megan used to say, 'Beware of being honey set in the sun—it attracts flies.' We give grants to museums, theaters, dance companies, individual artists, and most of it, certainly, is deserved; but there is no provision for—well, art of the kind *you* create, Ava-Rose." Terence had not known he would say this, nor that he would speak with such warmth. "Those lovely appliqué designs!—the things you do with feathers, sequins, beads! It's really quite remarkable. 'The *Art* of Beauty.' My daughter Kim loves that purse of yours I gave her—she carries it with her everywhere. And my mother-in-law, who's famously hard to please—" But now that Terence thought of it, he hadn't once seen Mrs. Winston wearing the exotic feather earrings, though, that evening, she'd professed to find them beautiful. "Well—you *are* a genuinely gifted artist, Ava-Rose. Unfortunately the snobbish cultural establishment has its own rigid definitions of 'art,' and much that moves us greatly is excluded."

Ava-Rose said, negligently, "It is said, 'Covet not thy neighbor's riches, else you covet his sorrow as well.' "

Terence rubbed his chin. "That's so. But—who said that?"

"It is written in the Book of the Millennium, which has come down to us through the generations."

Terence had several times asked Ava-Rose about the history of the Church of the Holy Apocalypse, but her answers were vague and elusive; he had the idea that she didn't know much about it, and did not want to embarrass her. Having no religion himself, Terence envied others the apparent solace of their beliefs. Like many a humanist-agnostic, he was inclined to take religious men and women at their word.

"I see," Terence said. "Still, there is the principle of human justice."

" 'Justice'—!" Ava-Rose laughed, with melancholic irony. "That too excludes *us*."

By this time, it had grown cozily dark.

Cozily dark, and would Terence stay for dinner?

He murmured, "Thank you, but I—" and Holly Mae

Loomis protested, "Yes, yes, Dr. Greene, please! After all you done for *us*—" and Ava-Rose laughing and tugging at his arm, like a little girl, "Oh now Ter-ence, please do stay! Auntie has made cornmeal biscuits, and I—*I* have made chocolate fudge cake, just for you."

How then could Terence Greene refuse?

(In hope of being invited to stay for dinner, Terence had shrewdly told Phyllis he'd be having dinner in New York that night. Wouldn't be home until late.)

So a place was set at the big battered dining room table for Terence, between Ava-Rose and Holly Mae. Cap'n-Uncle Riff in navy blue brass-buttoned coat, smart nautical cap on his stiff white hair, beard freshly trimmed and brushed, sat at the head of the table, and did the carving. With a flashing silver knife the size of a dagger. (Dara and Dana, seeing Cap'n-Uncle wield the knife against the roast, giggled in a shivery-silly little-girl way, "Cap'n-Uncle, where'd you get *that*?" and Cap'n-Uncle and Chick answered in the same voice, "It came into the store today." Cap'n-Uncle Riff had a second-hand goods store, or perhaps he managed such a store, on lower State Street, which Terence had not yet seen.) Hefty good-natured Chick, who seemed to have grown an inch or two, all around, in recent weeks, sat across from Terence, and between Dara and Dana—there being an old family tradition of keeping the twins separated at meals. For a boy of sixteen (Chick's birthday had been on December 24), Chick was remarkably adult in his manner and attitude; and in his cheery deference to other adults, like Terence Greene, whom he called "Dr. Greene."

Months ago Terence had said, gently, to correct the boy, "I'm more comfortable as 'Terence,' not 'Dr. Greene.' I'm not a medical doctor, after all."

Chick beetled his forehead, shifted his Phillies cap about on his head, then said, with a sly sideways grin, "D'ja ever *try*?"

"Try—?"

"Like, making out 'script?'"—seeing Terence's baffled expression—"*pre*-scriptions, like? Valium, oxycodone, Percodan? Like, for a drugstore?"

Terence laughed, uneasily. He guessed that the boy was making some sort of joke; as with Aaron, such humor struck an awkward note, pointing up the gap between the generations.

Yet, most of the time, Terence was impressed with Chick's maturity. At dinner, Chick maintained his part of the conversation, while eating with the gusto of a teenaged boy: He asked astute questions of Terence, Holly Mae, and Ava-Rose on the subject of Holly Mae's lawsuit (which had become quite complicated, involving now a second high-priced lawyer); he spoke most respectfully to, yet joked with, Cap'n-Uncle Riff (for whom, or with whom, he worked: Apparently he was no longer in school?); and resisted, with big-brother stoicism, Dara's and Dana's giggly asides and nudges. Holly Mae Loomis was one of those breathless excitable women who are always leaping up from the table to run into the kitchen, or to pass a serving bowl about, scarcely enjoying their own cooking, and so Chick teased Holly Mae even as he reprimanded her—"Auntie Holly, no wonder your blood pressure's high! Sit still, or we're gonna tie you in your chair!"—jumping up himself with surprising alacrity.

And there was Buster the dog who'd taken such a liking for Terence, dozing with his warm heavy head on Terence's feet beneath the table—a pleasant sensation. And there was Darling the parrot wheeled into the room in his showy brass cage, chortling, preening, clowning, "cake-walking" about the bars, shrieking for attention—"H'lo! H'lo! H'lo! B'jurr! Beeyt PEEZE! PEEZE!" (Poor Darling: In Cap'n-Uncle's presence, the parrot had to be shut into his cage. But everyone, including the bearded patriarch, talked cheerfully to him; and those within reach of his cage pushed tidbits—including meat, gristle, skin, tender bones—through the bars. Terence was impressed with the bird's voracious appetite!) And, too, there was Marcellus the Mystery—a declawed Siamese cat, a neutered male, sleekly beautiful, with bluish-creamy fur, light blue eyes, a blue collar stamped MARCELLUS, and a throaty, crackly mew—who, found wandering by Chick down along the busy River Road, now prowled about the Renfrew household as if he owned it, demanding to be fed from the table. Clearly, the expensive pedigree animal had a strong sense of his own worth.

Chick said, of the rescue of Marcellus, "I got a soft-touch face, is all. Any lost cat or dog, they sort of got *radar* for me."

Dara, or was it Dana, told Terence, "Last time, Chickie found a poodle along by the river—those real nice houses, y'know? Her name was Tiffny—"

"Tiffany"—the other twin interrupted.

"—Tiffny I *said*. Biggern you'd think a poodle would be, all white fur so curly and fluffy-pretty it's like angel hair or something? on a Christmas tree, y'know? And—"

The other twin interrupted breathlessly, widening her eyes at Terence. "Tif*fany* it was!—Tif*fany* was worth $500, Dr. Greene! They had this ad in the paper, like 'Reward—' "

"—'and no questions asked.' "

Holly Mae said in a cheerful, resigned voice, to Chick, yet in such a way as to divert Terence's attention from the twins, "Lord, *I* worry about my asthma, all these fancy cats and dogs. Seems like their fur is the most troublesome! You had any luck with the wants ads, yet?"

Chick said, "Auntie, it ain't *want ads*, it's *lost-'n-'found*—think you'd know that by now."

"Don't you sass me, boy. You know what I'm saying."

Chick's broad, handsome face, mildly blemished by pimples on his forehead, pinkened with blood. "I'm looking, sure; but I ain't seen any ad, yet."

"Marcellus is such a kingly creature, his owners are sure to miss him," Ava-Rose said. She'd been feeding the cat slivers of fatty meat, and now he leapt into her lap, causing a bit of flurry at the table, before, with Terence's help, he was encouraged to jump down again to the floor. "*I'd* offer a rich reward, for such a beauty."

Terence was going to ask Chick if he'd made inquiries at houses along the River Road, but remained silent. By this time he'd had several foamy glasses of Cap'n-Uncle Riff's home-brewed Chimney Point Stout, as the old man called it —a tart, briny, wood-grainy, delicious-dark, simmering sort of ale, like no other spirits Terence had tasted.

Since coming to know the Renfrews—this wonderfully eccentric, unpredictable family—Terence often remained silent, and listened. Just when he thought he might have figured out a relationship or two, he was made to see otherwise. In their household, he laughed a good deal, not always knowing why. He had trouble thinking—was it *sequentially?*—even when, unlike this evening, he hadn't drunk a little too much Chimney Point Stout.

The twin on Chick's left side—Dara?—leaned forward and said, excitedly, "One time, Chick found a lost *pony*—"

"—acrost the river, in Yardley?—by the canal?—" the other twin interrupted.

"—they brought him back in the van. And—"

In his deep bemused baritone, with a touch of impatience, Cap'n-Uncle Riff cut the girls off. "And there's pony manure in the cellar, to this day."

"Cellar?" Terence said, frowning. "But why the cellar?" Seeing how the Renfrews were watching him, he felt a ticklish sensation all over his body. "Why not outside?"

"Because, Dr. Greene, that's where the damned pony abided, during his stay with us." Cap'n-Uncle smiled in his lofty yet charmingly self-mocking way; and asked Terence if he would like more stout.

Terence began to say, "No, thank you, sir," but heard, instead, "Yes, thank you, sir." He laughed, startled. What was happening to him? Ava-Rose poured the dark, foamy brew into Terence's glass, and sipped a little from the glass; on principle, Ava-Rose did not imbibe alcoholic beverages, but sometimes took tiny sips from a glass of Terence's, which pleased him enormously. Terence took a hearty swallow, so happy suddenly that the tip of his nose went icy-cold. "Cap'n-Uncle, why is Chimney Point so named?—no one seems to know."

As he often did when he meant to be funny, Cap'n-Uncle tugged at his beard. "Maybe, Dr. Greene, this part of Trenton is named for my stout?" The elderly man's deadpan delivery made them all laugh, even Terence. Chick, who'd lapsed into a fugue of sullenness, woke from it and laughed loudly.

Cap'n-Uncle reminisced for some fascinating minutes of his years at sea, in Malaysia, the Indian Ocean, and the South China Sea in particular; his voice took on a wistful note as he told Terence of "the old, lost days" of mercantile trading. He'd run off to sea at the age of seventeen, retired at the age of seventy-six, and then only because the ship he commanded was dry-docked in Taiwan. In 1939, he'd married a beautiful Sulawesi princess in a sacred rite in which he'd had to drink human blood; he'd been madly in love with the princess, and had sired a son with her, whom he'd only seen once—"Tragic European history intervened!" It was in northern Borneo that he'd first drunk the highly potent ale he now brewed himself, given him by an exiled Englishman, a refugee from the British Navy who'd taken a liking to Riff Renfrew (at the time in his early thirties), and willed him his small cache of jewels, gold, stolen icons, and devalued British currency, at his death. With this modest fortune, constituting about twenty-five thousand American dollars, Riff Renfrew had been able to invest in a Greek mercantile ship; and so began his career as an officer, and not merely a slavey under others' commands. "I never drink this ale without thinking of my old, lost friend," Cap'n-Uncle said soberly, raising his glass, "—whose name I have forgotten, to my sorrow."

Terence was deeply moved. He asked, "Do you miss the sea badly, Cap'n-Uncle?"

"No, because I carry the 'sea' within me," the old man

said, with unexpected candor, fixing his deep-set, steely eyes on Terence's. "As, in age, we carry 'youth' within us; or, as the lover, if he is true to his love, carries her within him at all times."

A moment's awkward pause. One of the twins giggled, jamming her knuckles against her mouth; the other joined in, snorting.

"Oh," cried Ava-Rose, "—aren't you two *silly!*"

Then Marcellus the Mystery leapt boldly up onto the table, seized in his jaws the greasy remnants of some meat on Terence's plate, and leapt down to the floor again, already in flight—so sinuous in motion, the entire maneuver seemed but a single fluid gesture, as of a magician's sweeping wand.

Ava-Rose sprang up from the table, smiling. "Auntie Holly, stay right where you are. I'll get dessert."

And Terence, emboldened by stout, sprang up, too, to follow Ava-Rose out into the kitchen. "I'll help, dear. Tell me what to do."

At first, Ava-Rose seemed genuinely opposed to Terence being in the kitchen with her. She said, almost crossly, "You've done so much for us, Ter-ence—I'm plain ol' *embarrassed.*"

Terence said happily, "But I've only begun."

It was true, though Terence had kept no records, he'd loaned, or given, the Renfrews a considerable amount of money in the past several months; and had impulsively bought them numerous gifts, like the $300 brass parrot cage. (Darling's former cage had been a cramped, shabby affair, unbefitting a bird of such dignity and character. To see him in such quarters had wrung Terence's heart.) Without Cap'n-Uncle's knowledge (for the elderly man was proud, and would not have accepted charity), Terence had helped pay the mortgage on the house, and the insurance; when, on the first really cold day of the year, in December, the Renfrews' antiquated oil-burning furnace had broken down, Terence had helped Ava-Rose buy a new one. (Conferring with her, in husbandly fashion, had seemed to Terence well worth the price!) There were medical bills of Holly Mae's; and sizable retainers for her lawyers. There were household repairs, minor, but urgent—windowpanes to replace long-broken panes, new plumbing fixtures for the bathrooms. It had long been a dream of Ava-Rose's that her nieces should wear braces to straighten their teeth—"For facial beauty, however superficial, *is* the way in which women in our culture are judged"—but, until Terence came along, taking the girls to an expensive orthodontist was out of the question.

A twenty-two-pound turkey for Thanksgiving, a six-foot evergreen, poinsettias, a lavish basket of fruit, nuts, and candies for Christmas. Noting the shabby condition of young Chick's windbreaker, Terence had slipped $200 to Ava-Rose for the purpose of buying him a new one—without telling that Terence was paying. (Terence sensed that Chick too had his pride, and did not want to offend him.) For Dara's and Dana's birthday, Terence had arranged for Ava-Rose to buy the girls new winter overcoats, which they'd badly needed; and then, in a reckless gesture, he'd taken the entire Renfrew family, including Cap'n-Uncle, out to a lavish Sunday brunch at the Washington Crossing Inn across the river in Pennsylvania. He'd seemed to know that none of his Queenston acquaintances would chance to see him there, at the head of a motley sort of family and beside a young woman of startling gypsy-beauty.

After Eldrick Gill, perhaps nothing and no one could touch him.

Half deliberately, Terence hadn't been keeping records of these abrupt and often impulsive expenditures. Usually, he gave Ava-Rose cash; which the sensitive young woman would accept only if convinced by Terence that her family needed it, and then only if it were presented as a loan. (Ava-Rose's peculiar Church, which Terence hardly wanted to challenge, at least in this stage of their relationship, seemed to forbid any kind of "material transaction" at all.) Terence had little financial acumen, but thought it an easy matter to transfer funds from one account to another, and to another; from a personal account in Queenston to his expense account at the Feinemann Foundation, and sometimes back again, in a convoluted yet surely quite innocent paper trail which could be explained (but why should it be explained?) should anyone, from Phyllis to accountants and auditors at the Foundation, make inquiries. *I exceeded my expense allotment for that month at the Foundation, and made it up with personal funds; the time I was short, I sold x, y, z stocks, and transferred the cash to another Foundation account. And then—*

But Terence broke off such calibrations, impatiently. Who would question *him?*—with his reputation for honesty, probity? It was a lucky thing too that Phyllis had money of her own; and that her mother, who could not live forever, would leave her—and surely Terence, too—millions of dollars.

Terence, lost in thought, realized that he wasn't helping poor Ava-Rose, much—he saw her reach for plates on a high cupboard shelf, saw her odd, bunchy little black satin jacket hiking up, exposing her waistband, and the purple taffeta blouse hiking too, to reveal a creamy crescent of skin—and a wave of vertigo overtook him.

My love, my only love.
How can I be worthy of you!

Quickly, Terence got the plates for Ava-Rose, and together, in cheerily clumsy fashion, they dished out prodigious amounts of peaches and ice cream atop thick squares of chocolate cake. Though Terence had eaten a good deal already of Holly Mae's delicious food, and his stomach was bloated with Cap'n-Uncle's ale, his mouth watered, like a child's, for Ava-Rose's dessert.

And, at the Renfrews' crowded table, in his place between beautiful Ava-Rose and Auntie Holly Mae, Terence ate as hungrily, even, as Chick.

Terence asked Ava-Rose if her chocolate cake had any name, and Ava-Rose and Auntie Holly Mae answered, laughing, in unison—"Double-chocolate-fudge-devil's-food-delight. An old family recipe."

"Is it!" Terence said, picking up the last crumb from his plate with his fingers. "It's the most delicious dessert I've ever tasted."

It would have been wise for Terence then to leave, but, hoping for what, exactly, he did not know *knowing exactly: to consummate his love for Ava-Rose, this very night and in this very house,* he lingered, over coffee; so enjoying himself in this warm-lit, cozily shabby place he could not bear to think of leaving. The wind! the swirling snowflakes! And, in the house at 7 Juniper Way, Queenston, a woman's stiff face, hurt and sarcastic voice—*I thought we'd made a joint New Year's resolution, but, evidently, I made it alone.*

Then, abruptly, the tone of the evening changed.

Dara and Dana excused themselves from the table, with a bustling commotion of kissing everyone good night (including "Dr. Greene," who was most moved); to his surprise, the twelve-year-olds were going out to a classmate's house to spend the night—a "slumber party," as they called it.

Terence, recalling certain unhappy events in the Greene family history, when, it seemed, Kim had not told the exact truth about who would be at one of these parties, or even at whose house the party was to be, felt a tinge of apprehension. Yet, could he speak?—dare he speak? He was not Dara's and Dana's father, after all.

Terence said, uncertainly, "On a school night?—it doesn't seem—"

No one heard. Chick sniggered deep in his throat.

Ava-Rose went away upstairs with the girls, and, when the doorbell rang, came herding them down. There was much good-natured chattering and scolding. Terence drifted out to see the girls off, watching Ava-Rose help them into their attractive new winter coats (a deep burgundy for Dara, a bright green for Dana), feeling a distinct sense of unease.

And there was Ava-Rose's somewhat nervous, fussy manner as the girls prepared to leave for the night. *She should have children of her own. This peculiar self-sacrificing "family life" of hers is unnatural.*

The father of the twins' classmate was a stranger, of course, and unexpectedly dapper in his dress. He wore a camel's hair coat, and a matching fedora tilted on his head. He was about Terence's age; with a sallow skin and a small, rosebud mouth. Seeing Terence, he frowned, muttered something inaudible to Ava-Rose, and turned quickly away, as if to avoid Terence's scrutiny. Without a backward glance, Dara and Dana ran out to his car idling at the curb.

Ava-Rose quickly shut the door, shivering. When Terence touched her arm, she turned to him, as if in appeal, and said, "It's only for overnight, but I *worry.*"

Terence said, hesitantly, "It does seem that, on a school night, a slumber party isn't a good idea. My daughter Kim—"

Ava-Rose murmured, "Yes!" and led Terence back into the dining room, where, to his surprise, the atmosphere seemed suddenly to be tense. Holly Mae was loudly blowing her nose, and Chick, seeing Terence, went sulkily silent; Cap'n-Uncle, face reddened from many glasses of stout, let fall his fist against the tabletop, as if concluding an argument. He said loudly, "As Abraham Lincoln said, 'A sucker is born every minute.' "

Terence felt a pedantic tinge. "Abraham Lincoln?— why, no, I think it was—"

Curtly, Cap'n-Uncle cut him off. "The principle is the same, Doctor. 'A sucker is born every minute, and what are *you* going to do about it?' "

Holly Mae laughed, as if scandalized. Despite her various ailments (apart from her back injury, and asthma, she complained of inflammations of her joints, and an occasional "spinning head") Holly Mae was looking robust, with plump reddened cheeks and brassy curls ringing her head like a gilt crown. "Cap'n-Uncle, for *shame.*" She shook her forefinger in his direction as if he were a naughty old boy.

Chick, toothpick in his mouth, suddenly shoved back his chair and stomped out of the room. Evidently the big blond boy's feelings had been hurt—Terence, comparing him with Aaron, marveled at his sensitivity. In an exasperated voice, Ava-Rose said, "Oh, what *is* this all about? The twins going off, overnight? I thought we'd all agreed—they're twelve years old, my goodness. When I was that age—"

"When *I* was—!" Holly Mae was laughing so, she had to wipe her eyes on the edge of her apron.

Terence looked from one Renfrew to another, baffled. Seeing how out of embarrassment, or anger, Ava-Rose avoided his eye, he thought for the first time that it might be her own family, loving, and yet suffocating, from whom Ava-Rose Renfrew might be rescued.

By whom?—by a lover who would sacrifice everything, for her.

But Terence had no time to pursue this insight, for, stomping as heavily back into the dining room as he'd stomped out, Chick, a vengeful shine to his eyes, returned, tossing down, in triumph, on the table in front of Terence, an item that was distressingly familiar—Terence's lost Gucci attaché case.

A painful silence.

Recalling that moment afterward—the missing attaché case flung down amid the dirtied dinner plates, the initials *TCG* gleaming as if in mockery—Terence could scarcely remember his response. Perhaps, as in a crisis of metaphysical paralysis, he'd had none?

He stood baffled, speechless. Sensing how the glowering boy with the toothpick in his mouth had brought the attaché case out less for Terence's benefit than as a taunt to the elder Renfrews.

Chick said, boldly, "Look familiar, Doctor? We been keeping it for you."

"*Safe*keeping," Cap'n-Uncle said quickly.

And Holly Mae, who'd seemed to have had the breath knocked out of her, recovered sufficiently to mumble, "Why yes—*safe*keeping.'' She then turned to Ava-Rose, who seemed utterly perplexed, saying in a loud, exclamatory voice, "Ava-Rose, hon, *you* don't know a thing about this: how, some time before we made Dr. Greene's actual acquaintance, not even knowing his name, we'd discovered this briefcase that he'd lost, in a restaurant by the courthouse. Oh, the days of that trial! No wonder we weren't thinking straight! We found it, and—'' Holly Mae paused, frowning. She pressed a hand against her heaving bosom. "—and brought it back home, and just plumb forgot it. Till tonight.''

Chick protested, "Till *I* remembered, Auntie! Noner you.''

Terence picked up the attaché case, for he saw it was expected of him. How chill, the smooth gleaming leather—as if the case had been stored in some unheated closet or cubbyhole, of which the big old ramshackle house had many. It was shockingly empty—the applications, documents, letters gone. *What does it matter, they were worthless.* "Why, thank you,'' Terence managed to say. "I—it's—yes, this *is* it. A birthday gift from—a family member.''

Ava-Rose was so stymied by all this, and so exasperated by being so stymied, she tried to make a joke of her situation; pouting, "Well! *I* see *I'm* the one in the dark, here.'' She cast her cousin Chick a furious glance. She turned on her heel to confront Cap'n-Uncle at his end of the table. "*I'm* going to want some decent explanation, you know—as I'm sure our dear friend Ter-ence does.''

In the midst of such strain and awkwardness, Cap'n-Uncle Riff retained his patriarchal dignity; managing, even, to drain his glass of stout. He then rose—tall, bulky, yet, for a man in his eighties, surprisingly majestic—and came to Terence, to lay a warm, fatherly hand on Terence's shoulder. His expression was the alert, enlivened one of a man who is thinking rapidly and purposefully. "Ava-Rose, one day when you were with the district attorney's people, preparing for the trial, remember?—the three of us had lunch at the Mill Hill Tavern, across from the courthouse, and there, why, we found this briefcase of Dr. Greene's, where he'd walked off and left it. We didn't rightly know what to do—couldn't trust the folks there to give it to him, if he came back looking for it; a leather item like this, 'Guc-ci,' what might it cost? One hundred dollars? Two hundred dollars? So, we ran an ad in the *Trenton Times* classified, saying what we'd found, maybe a week, ten days, was it, Auntie?—and when we didn't get any response, we just put it away here. For safekeeping. And then forgot."

Holly Mae was nodding vigorously. "Just plain forgot."

Ava-Rose, hands on her hips, looked from one of her relatives to another. It was clear that she was displeased; yet, there seemed no pressing reason for her to be displeased. Chick, shifting his broad shoulders inside his shirt, seemed particularly uneasy. "Aw, Ava-Rose," he said, with a sheepish grin, "—*you* were with the D.A., it was that long ago."

Holly Mae said, to Terence, "They have to help you with your testimony, you know, for a trial! Telling the truth isn't enough for a murderer can walk free if the jury doesn't believe. A jury—"

"—is mostly a pack of fools," Cap'n-Uncle said dismissively.

Terence was turning the attaché case in his hand, as if it were a part of his body restored to him. "Well, thank you! I'm very"—he felt that curious sensation over his body, like myriad tiny tongues of flame—"grateful." He laughed, and the others laughed with him, even Ava-Rose.

Even Darling, hanging upside-down in his handsome brass cage, cackled.

Don't grieve, son. Your secret is safe with us.

She would not make him leave, surely!

Knowing how he adored her, and so seemingly grateful for all he'd done for her!

Would she? *Could* she?

It was nearing 10:30 P.M., time for Terence Greene to

leave Chimney Point, Trenton, and return to 7 Juniper Way, Queenston. The other Renfrews had drifted off and he and Ava-Rose were alone, as before, in the parlor. The wind continued to worry the shingles, shutters, high chimney, and windowpanes of the aged house, and Terence had a sense of a vast snow-swirling space between him and that other home of his of which, in this house, he could scarcely bear to think.

Perhaps indeed it did not exist. He had dreamt it, invented it.

Hettie's boy. Pray he doesn't take after the father.

He had not wished to discuss the attaché case, nor even to think of it, and Ava-Rose too showed no inclination to allude to the awkward subject; as, he'd noticed, both charmed and annoyed by such a trait in an adult woman, Ava-Rose so often ceased to think of, or in any case to allude to, crucial matters safely *past.*

He was holding, indeed he was stroking, one of her fine-boned warmly dry hands. She had been telling him—he'd asked her—of certain of the beliefs of the Church of the Holy Apocalypse, though really, at this time, he did not care to know *I love you, I adore you, I want to make love to you: you must not send me away, again* of such quaint, curious, primitive, New Age–fatalist notions, even in Ava-Rose's husky, seductive voice. ("It is written in the Book of the Millennium, 'All things are possible, for all things are ordained.' ")

Terence shivered, but had to laugh. How calmly this beautiful young woman uttered paradoxes of logic, refutations of ethics, sweeping erasures of sanity itself, like so many "religious" people of our time, as if she not only accepted such paradoxes, but embraced them joyously. And seeing Terence laugh, she mistook his laughter as an expression of that joy.

The Church of the Holy Apocalypse. Was America of the 1990s itself the Church of the Holy Apocalypse, exulting in the possibilities of its own collapse?

Ava-Rose clasped Terence's hand in both her own, smiling happily at him. "You *are* beginning to understand, Terence, aren't you? You are not really an 'agnostic,' as you've said."

"Maybe." Terence would no more have argued with Ava-Rose than he would argue, any longer, with the way Aaron wore his hair, the way Kim shifted her gaze about as she lied, the way poor Cindy made a fetish of weighing herself three times a day. The way Phyllis berated him for not loving her even as, half-consciously, she pushed him from her.

Terence asked, unexpectedly, "Ava-Rose, is there another man, or men, in your life?" He knew that there could not be, for he kept careful tabs on her time; but he wanted to be reassured.

And indeed Ava-Rose protested, "Of course not, Terence! How can you ask?"

"You've never been married, you said?"

Pettishly, yet provocatively, Ava-Rose drew her hands away from Terence's hand. "If ever I'd been married, even in a secular ceremony, I would cling to my husband all the days of my life. Even if *he* abandoned *me*."

It was a cruel remark. Yet the sting of it heightened Terence's desire.

"About T. W. Binder—" Terence began.

"Oh, him!—he's dead."

Terence stared at Ava-Rose, who had spoken quickly, as if carelessly. "He's—what?"

Ava-Rose detached an oversized silver barrette from her hair, and one of the thick braids fell loose. She seemed composed; yet her eyelids trembled. Terence had half-consciously noted, over the past several months how, as Cap'n-Uncle tugged at his beard when he intended to be funny, or spoke hyperbolically, so too did Ava-Rose fuss with her hair when she believed she might have misspoken. At such times, she seemed to Terence exquisitely beautiful, vulnerable.

He had to will himself not to become distracted. He asked, "T. W. Binder is *dead*?"

"I don't know. I think I've heard, so."

"But I thought the man was in prison?—up at Rahway?"

Ava-Rose bit at the end of her braid, like a girl; raising her eyes to Terence as if in mild incredulity, that he should be so dull-witted. "Men do die in prison, Ter-ence, don't you think?"

"But—how?"

"Why, *I* don't know. I'm not even sure that—it's so." Ava-Rose frowned, thoughtfully. "Many things are just rumors, in Chimney Point."

"If T. W. Binder is dead, he didn't die from natural causes, did he?"

" 'All that happens is Nature, for there is nothing not-Nature.' "

"Ava-Rose, who said *that*?"

"It is written in—"

"No, no. Someone wrote it, someone human. No book writes itself."

Ava-Rose undid her other braids, bracelets chiming. Her face, warmed from the long festive dinner, and from this discussion, had taken on a rosy, slumberous look; Terence moved nearer to her, so that, as if half consciously, she took a step backward.

And then another.

Snow swirled dreamily against the windowpanes. On Ava-Rose's worktable, folded garments and pieces of fabric lay like sleeping figures. The saucer of blue sequins winked lewdly in the lamplight.

"Ava-Rose, darling, when did T. W. Binder die?"

"As I said, Ter-ence, I'm really not sure that—"

"But if the man did die, when was it likely to have been?"

Ava-Rose laughed, as if exasperated. "Dr. Greene, really! Is this an interrogation?" She paused. Edging gracefully backward, she had pressed against the edge of a massive old sideboard. Terence had a vague impression, without looking closely, that the shelves, behind the glass breakfront, were crammed with purses, handbags, old briefcases and attaché cases—a miscellany of leather goods. Indeed, the house was cluttered with such stray, anonymous, seemingly cast-off items.

"Ava-Rose, don't you think I have a right to know?—I'd been worried, that the man would hurt you, somehow. When he got out on parole, or if he asked a friend of his, like Eldrick Gill, to—"

Ava-Rose interrupted, "Auntie Holly said she'd heard that T.W. died around New Year's. One of the inmates up there must have done it. I don't know! Don't blame *me*!" Tears glinted angrily in her eyes. "I did not love T.W., and T.W. was not, as you seem to think, my lover. Aren't you ashamed of yourself, forcing yourself in my life, poking about in other people's business!"

To Terence's astonishment, Ava-Rose's slender hand flashed—she slapped him across the face.

"What—!" One of her spiky rings must have caught him in the cheek, he felt blood begin to trickle down his chin.

Then he'd grabbed her and was embracing her, struggling with her. They foundered against the sideboard, and against the wall. There was a sound of breaking glass. Terence buried his feverish face in Ava-Rose's neck, feeling one of her thick, scratchy, fragrant braids against his mouth. Ava-Rose tried to free her arms, to push at him, claw at him, but Terence held her fast. Never in his life had he felt such desire! such fierce exultation, in desire! He was kissing the squirming woman, pressing himself against her, unheeding how she whimpered in astonishment and pain, and panted, "No! no! Ter-ence, no!"

He knelt before her, pulling her down, hugging her about the hips. He tugged at her clothes, pushed up the black satin jacket, and tore at the taffeta blouse—what pleasure, hearing it rip, feeling Ava-Rose stiffen in genuine fear. He heard, as from a distance, the woman's hoarse, panting, pleading voice, "Ter-ence! No! You're a married man, and not free to love me! *Ter-ence*—"

And then all was exquisitely, explosively blank: Terence Greene had stopped listening.

"All Things
Are Possible..."

"*T*erry?—what *is* this?"

Woken from his reverie *his shameless dreamy thoughts of her whom he adored, and of making love to her, which, even in reverie, left him dazed, giddy as a man unaccustomed to drink who has downed several quick glasses of champagne* Terence turned startled yet guarded toward Phyllis, who had pushed open his study door without knocking, and had entered the room without being invited.

The tone of Phyllis's voice—its sharp soprano raised, quizzical, yet not, at least immediately, accusatory—straightened Terence's backbone, and forced a genial smile to his lips. It was a weekday in mid-March; nearing eleven o'clock in the evening; Terence had returned home from New York (not from Trenton: He'd visited Trenton the day before) well in time for dinner at seven-thirty with Phyllis, Kim, Cindy, and Mrs. Winston, who was visiting for the week. The meal had passed pleasantly if, on Terence's side, a bit blankly, and Terence had been under the impression that he and Phyllis were on amicable terms again. After dinner Terence had retreated to his study, and to his desk, where he'd been trying gamely to decipher Quincy Ryder's negligently hand-scribbled evaluation of a candidate for a Feinemann award, or, at any rate, would be perceived by Phyllis as doing so; fierce in entry, she could not know that Terence had been staring at the same paragraph for *how long, how many languorous drugged minutes recalling not only his own explosive sexual pleasure but Ava-Rose's as well, so sweet, a mere breath, a mere sigh* scarcely aware of his surroundings.

Quickly Terence said, "Yes, Phyllis?" as if it were altogether natural for her to interrupt him at his work, without even the courtesy of knocking. "What is it?"

Phyllis said, advancing upon him, waving a thin piece of paper in her fingers, "I was going through the accounts, the receipts, looking for something of my own, and"—as Terence continued to smile, steeling himself, thinking he could not be found out, surely, there were no records, no checks made out directly to Ava-Rose Renfrew or to any of the Renfrews, hadn't he seen to that?—as Phyllis hovered over him —"a Visa slip of my own, and I came across this—this enormous bill—dinner at the Washington Crossing Inn?— back in January? What on earth were you doing there?"

Terence took the receipt from Phyllis's fingers, frowning at its carbon copy blurriness, its smudged numerals and guilty backhanded signature: *Terence C. Greene.* Unmistakable. The bill was for $155.56 including tip. The date was January 12.

"It *is* your signature, Terry, isn't it?" Phyllis asked.

"It does look like it, yes," Terence said thoughtfully.

Recalling the occasion perfectly: that bright sunny Sunday of the Renfrew twins' twelfth birthday. Terence treating the Renfrews to a lavish brunch at the historic old inn, Terence beaming with a shy sort of happiness at being the cause of the Renfrews' happiness. Through the long boisterous meal, Dara and Dana had sat on either side of dashing Dr. Greene, vying for his attention; Ava-Rose had sat across from him, smiling at him, gazing at him with her lovely eyes—what ecstasy! Afterward, in the cloakroom, Ava-Rose had given Terence a quick, furtive kiss on the cheek—"Thank you, thank you, thank you, Ter-ence! This was the nicest surprise-birthday ever!''

How could he have been so careless as to have used a credit card?—it must have been the day he hadn't enough cash in his wallet.

With a harsh, hurt little laugh, Phyllis said, "The name of the restaurant flew up at me, while I was leafing through the accounts. 'Washington Crossing Inn.' How many years has it been since *we* were there?" The question hovered in the air, as Terence continued to study the receipt. "Who were you there with, of all places?"

These past several months, Terence's increasingly intimate relations with the Renfrews, and with Cap'n-Uncle Riff above all, had given him a certain style in which to deflect others' suspicions or accusations. He'd more than once happened to be in the old man's presence when something Cap'n-Uncle said was challenged—by Holly Mae, for instance; and there was the episode of the mysteriously missing, or stolen, attaché case, which Cap'n-Uncle had explained so tactfully, Terence had felt flattered. He respects my intelligence, Terence had thought.

Confronted now with the receipt, Terence tugged at his chin, as at an imaginary beard, and said, with an air of surprise, yet not the slightest touch of annoyance, "Phyllis, I'm sure I told you about this. It wasn't a dinner but a luncheon. A business luncheon. Feinemann business."

"In Pennsylvania?" Phyllis's voice sharpened in doubt.

Terence glanced up at her mildly. "You must remember, dear, *I* wasn't very happy at the inconvenience, but Gordon Laird—the curator at the Philadelphia Museum of Contemporary Art—thought we could compromise between Philadelphia and New York, and meet there. They'd applied for a $600,000 grant at the museum, and—"

Terence could usually count on his wife's eyes glazing over when he began to speak of Feinemann matters; though Phyllis had once been genuinely interested in Terence's work, and above all in the intrigues and feuds that occasionally enveloped it, that time was long since past. Now, however, she continued to stare at him. "But you were in Atlanta on January 12, Terry. And it was a Sunday."

Terence said quickly, but now he did stammer, "Then the date is wrong, I'm sure I—I know I—It was a Monday, I'm sure. It must have been January 13, and whoever made this out—" He paused, and collected his wits, and said, more calmly, though with a flicker of wonderment at Phyllis, that she should make so much of an utterly inconsequential matter, "—Just an innocent mistake, I suppose, on the part of the waiter. Why is it so important?"

Phyllis peered at the receipt as if it were somehow to blame. She'd been drinking white wine at dinner, which she rarely did except when they dined out; the color was up in her cheeks, giving her a ruddy, girlish appearance. It was true, she and Terence were on easier terms lately: Terence was absent from home no less than before, but his love for Ava-Rose, and the young woman's obvious love for him, had restored peace of a kind to his soul; for her part, Phyllis had one or two new, important clients at Queenston Opportunities, occupying a good deal of her time, too, and pleasing her enormously.

After a moment Phyllis said, with a shrug, and a smile very like Cindy's, as hurt dissolved to indifference, or even to whimsy, "I don't suppose it *is* important, Terry." She took the receipt back from Terence, and went to the door. "I'd only thought it was, and I was wrong. Sorry to disturb you!"

Terence looked after Phyllis, feeling that familiar half-pleasurable guilt in the pit of his belly. "I'm sorry to have disturbed *you*," he said, but too late—Phyllis had shut the door quietly behind her.

Taking up, more emphatically, the evaluation sheet before him, an assessment of a Native American poet who was a candidate for one of the coveted "American Master"

Feinemann fellowships, determined to read the snarled, crotchety, downward-slanting handwriting even as his thoughts slid like sand in a vertiginous sensual spill *Oh love, my love, my Botticelli Venus, how can I be worthy of you* his vision misting over with desire.

And he would have forgotten the incident regarding the receipt, would simply have pushed it out of his mind, as, lately, he was pushing so much out of his mind, with an odd fatalistic cheerfulness, for, increasingly, his life in the house at 7 Juniper Way, Queenston, was somehow not fully real, any more than the handsome house itself (for which he had little time: hadn't taken up his once-beloved handyman's tools since last September!), except, a day or two later, he happened to overhear his wife and his mother-in-law conferring in low, querulous voices.

One murmured as if plaintively, "—don't understand, I swear I—" and the other, "No one expects you to!" and the first (this was Mrs. Winston), aggrieved, "—what things are coming to!" and Phyllis, as if to humor, "Yes, Mother, and so—*why?*" and Mrs. Winston, "Your father and I—" and Phyllis, "Yes, Mother—but that was fifty years ago—" and Mrs. Winston, now a bit snappish, "It was *not!*—and anyway the principle of marriage—" and Phyllis, as if pleading, "Now, Mother—" and Mrs. Winston, "But you and *your* husband, you—" and Phyllis, quickly, "Mother please, not so loud—" and Mrs. Winston, pettishly, "*I* would not allow—" and Phyllis, "Oh for God's sake, Mother—" and Mrs. Winston's response was muffled, and Phyllis's rejoinder as well, as if, abruptly, the women were moving away, their backs to Terence, edging out of earshot.

Terence was on the stairs coming down from the second floor, and the women were in the hall, walking in the direction of the kitchen. At once he froze. *Don't: don't eavesdrop: turn around and go back upstairs: such behavior is not worthy of you.* He felt mildly sick, having overheard a conversation not for his ears, in his very house.

What was Mrs. Winston speaking of?—and why in such a tone of moral disapproval?

Surely she could not know, or suspect—?

"Of course not. Neither of them has any idea."

Lately, Fanny Winston's visits to Queenston were becoming more frequent, and more prolonged. She claimed—and this was of course good news—that her arthritis was less painful, for some reason, in her daughter's house; she rarely used her wheelchair in Queenston, and often got about quite handily, using a walker or a cane. Since she'd come to stay with them this time, arriving the week before, she'd been using just her cane. The sound and weight of her footsteps, augmented by the hard, hammerlike rap of the cane, had become a familiar feature of the household.

Terence was fond of his mother-in-law—he believed he was fond of his mother-in-law—who was after all a generous, well-intentioned, lonely woman, a widow, *yes and a millionairess: who intends to leave most of her estate to her daughter and her daughter's family*—but he felt a certain strain in the atmosphere when she came to visit; he had the impression, even without eavesdropping, that Mrs. Winston frequently criticized him to Phyllis behind his back, even as, to his face, she was warmly friendly, and even at times a bit flirtatious.

Ava-Rose understood Terence's ambivalent feelings about Fanny Winston, as about so much else in his life. How attentive the young woman was, how sympathetic! Saying, when Terence ruefully remarked that he hardly felt at home in his own house, when Phyllis's mother was there, "Now, Dr. Greene, you can afford to be kind. *The old woman won't live forever.*"

Now that they were lovers, or, at any rate, lovers most of the time—for Ava-Rose, mysteriously, was not always receptive to Terence—Ava-Rose sometimes called him, with quaint, playful formality, "Dr. Greene."

"Dr. Greene"—with a slight emphasis upon the "Dr."

Unlike "Ter-ence"—the two syllables equally stressed,

so that the name, which Terence himself had never liked, had acquired an exotic, foreign-sounding ring.

Dr. Greene, Ter-ence, you are the kindest man I know, the most generous and courageous man, if only you were truly free to love me—

Terence stood on the stairs, nerves jangling, considering what to do. He decided to go back upstairs and come down again loudly, whistling, to give the women sufficient warning; out of the range of temptation, for he loathed any sort of duplicity, particularly deceit in his own household. Yet, oddly—his heart pounding as in a dangerous child's game— he found himself in the hall, approaching the kitchen so stealthily that his footsteps were not only soundless but his body seemingly weightless. Just outside the kitchen doorway he heard Mrs. Winston's now tearful-angry remark, "Oh! I'm just a contemptible old woman, what do *I* know!" and Phyllis's rejoinder, "Now, Mother, please, you'll just upset yourself—" and Mrs. Winston, "—yes, I mean it: you'd better lay down the law to her: children, it seems, almost aren't children, nowadays!" And she rapped on the floor sharply with her cane, for dramatic emphasis.

So Terence relaxed, retreated. The women were discussing Kim now.

This, Terence did not want to hear.

(He would have said yes he was thinking of his children, he who had become so passionate and infatuated a lover, yes certainly he thought of them, suffered pangs of guilt about them, yes. He worried about Aaron, and he worried about Kim, and he worried about Cindy yes certainly except he hadn't time, he meant to think seriously about them, Aaron's mediocre grades and vague plans for the future, poor sweet Cindy whose latest notion was to become a performance artist, you don't have to be beautiful you can be yourself, that's the whole point of performance art *you can be yourself,* but most of all he meant to think seriously about Kim, so sweetly plump as a small child cuddling in Daddy's arms now tall as Phyllis and defiantly skinny her heartbreak face her sly smile and gaze shifting rapidly about as she lied to Daddy and Mommy about where exactly she was going, and who would be there, and when she would be back, and even, if they challenged her, about why she lied—these were the things Terence meant to think seriously about, except he hadn't time.)

Your secret is safe with us and this Terence believed unquestioningly but elsewhere wasn't he vulnerable?—forever at risk?

For instance, the very evening of the day he'd overheard Phyllis and her mother talking surreptitiously together, Terence walked into his study and saw, to his surprise, Mrs. Winston positioned with her cane in front of his cluttered desk, brazen, unapologetic, sturdy as a three-legged stool. As Terence entered, the elderly woman merely glanced around at him, and smiled complacently. "This desk brings back happy memories," she said, and seeing Terence's blank, startled expression, she added, a bit pettishly, "—it *was* Willard's, you know. Surely you haven't forgotten?"

The massive, heavy mahogany desk, wonderfully broad, with three drawers on either side and a capacious center drawer, was one of the household antiques, yet so long a possession of Terence's, as a castoff of Phyllis's parents, that he had more or less forgotten its origin.

"Of course not, Fanny. I—"

"I *hope* not." Mrs. Winston reared back, as if to demonstrate that she scarcely needed her cane at all. She fixed inquisitive eyes upon Terence, yet she meant to be fondly chiding, coquettish. "I wonder what poor Willard would say, if he saw how disorganized his desk has become?—so much *miscellany.*"

Terence was speechless. He'd seen, to his horror, amid the letters, documents, manila folders scattered across his desktop, the sheet of yellow notepaper upon which, working late the night before, he'd dreamily written AVA-ROSE, AVA-ROSE, AVA-ROSE, and HOLYOAK, and CHIMNEY POINT, and RENFREW; even, appallingly, ELDRICK GILL. Had his mother-in-law seen?

"Terence, is something wrong?" Mrs. Winston's voice, rising sharply, had an edge to it very like Phyllis's.

Terence stammered, "Wrong?—what?"

"You're looking at me so—strangely."

Terence felt his lips draw back from his teeth in a ghastly semblance of a smile. For a long moment he and Fanny Winston stared at each other. Then, with a faint shudder, the elderly woman drew back. "Well! I can see I'm not exactly welcome here, am I!" she said, hurt.

Using her cane emphatically, favoring her right leg, with its pitifully swollen ankle, Mrs. Winston brushed past Terence and left the room. Terence, rooted to the spot, did not so much as look after her. He was clenching his fists so tightly, his nails sank into his flesh.

The old woman won't live forever.

"How happy I am! How rich and splendid life is! *If only I can hang onto it.*"

In places hostile to romance Terence Greene thought of her whom he loved. It might be said that, in those fevered months, there was rarely an hour, a minute, a passing moment, when he was not thinking of her.

Especially he thought of Ava-Rose Renfrew (had it something to do with the flurried sensation in the pit of his belly, in his groin?) ascending in one of the elegant glass-backed elevators in his Park Avenue office building, rising swiftly and soundlessly to the ninth floor. The interior of the stately old building had been lavishly renovated to accommodate an atrium that opened to the very roof, which was made of tinted glass and aluminum; the foyer was mauve marble, with a circular fountain, classical in design, spouting streams of bubbly water, at its center. Visitors to the Feinemann Foundation invariably remarked upon the beauty of the atrium, but only recently had Terence begun to notice it again.

In the beginning, during his first year or so as Executive Director of the Foundation, Terence too had appreciated the airy spaciousness of the building. Then, by degrees, he'd ceased to see it.

Now, Terence not only saw the dazzling play of lights, glass, polished marble, reflecting metallic surfaces and leaping streams of water, he seemed sometimes to feel it thrumming along his veins; radiating out from the pit of his belly, his groin. Like a man in a waking delirium he thought of the woman he loved, missing her with his body. *Oh my love, what can I do to keep you. How can I hold onto you.*

Often now when Terence left the elevator at the ninth floor, if he were reasonably alone, and unobserved, he paused to linger at the railing, to look back down. He pressed his forearms hard against the railing, balancing his weight, and peered over, nine floors below to the alabaster-white fountain with its leaping, darting, scintillating rays of water. The railing was latticelike, and sturdy, open to the height of an average man's waist; assuredly, there was little danger of falling unless one leaned far over. Yet Terence felt a half-pleasurable sensation of vertigo, dread.

"And if I fall?—if I fell? What then?"

It was the morning after he'd surprised Phyllis's mother in his study; that week when it began to seem that his secret life might be close to exposure, or at any rate more vulnerable to exposure than he'd believed. He'd set his attaché case down, and leaned over the railing, staring down at the foyer until he grew dizzy, and a roaring started in his ears; he felt his body's helplessness, as at the onset of that plunging sensation that precedes orgasm. *My love. My love. Oh my love!*

Then, abruptly, Terence drew back. He was thinking that he dared not fall—"They would audit my accounts, and discover why."

———

Even at meetings of committees, where discussion was likely to be lengthy and acrimonious, and where Terence Greene, affable and courteous and soft-spoken, had to moderate, *slyly he thought of her whom he loved.*

Meetings were held around the long executive table in Terence's office, which could comfortably seat fifteen people. The office itself was large and handsomely furnished; a corner room with a striking view, on clear days at least, of midtown Manhattan looking toward the East River. Clever Terence so positioned himself that, during his expert judges' remarks, which were frequently monologues, he could gaze over their heads and out the window *dreaming of her whom he loved* while frowning and nodding in such a way that flattered the speakers.

"How well you get along with everyone, Dr. Greene!" his secretary Mrs. Riddle exclaimed, when Terence was new at the Foundation, "—not like poor Dr. Swain, who was always coming down with migraine after these meetings." Terence did not want to confess that he got along well with egoists because he cared little for his own ego. Those traits of modesty and self-effacement that so exasperated Phyllis, as being insufficiently manly, endeared him to others. Even Quincy Ryder seemed intermittently approving of Terence— in the men's lavatory at the Foundation, Terence, while in one of the toilet stalls, once overheard Ryder say to an unidentified party, in his droll Virginian accent, "At least, Greene shuts up and lets one talk. He may be a fool, but he knows to do *that.*"

But what did Terence care, really—he would preside over the day's meeting with his "expert judges," which would include luncheon, with cocktails and wine, and would continue well into the afternoon, and then adjourn. At the midpoint, as lunch was breaking up, he would slip away to call Ava-Rose at Tamar's Bazaar & Emporium, the telephone number of which he'd long since memorized.

"Hello darling!" he would murmur, as if, in utter privacy as he was, he might yet be overheard, and at the other end of the line Ava-Rose would give a little cry, in her husky, surprised-sounding voice, "Why—is it Ter-ence? Hel*lo!*" and Terence would ask a flurry of little questions, how was she, what had she been doing, and Ava-Rose would delight in telling him, describing even the customers she'd waited on that morning, or a funny conversation with a man who sold her gas for the car (a new-model canary-yellow Corvette) Terence had bought her for Valentine's Day, or what had happened at the Renfrews' the evening before, and Terence would listen with half-shut eyes picturing her whom he loved, how anxious he was to keep the conversation flowing, eager, a bit breathless, sparkling like the gushing streams of water in the fountain down in the foyer, and at last he would ask if he could see her that evening? next evening? when? and his heart would seem to pause between beats, awaiting her reply: For even now that they were lovers, and had in fact slept together several entire nights, Ava-Rose declared herself a woman of independent spirit—"I could never be *possessed,* even by love."

Sometimes, however, when Terence excitedly dialed the number of the store, Tamar answered, "Oh, it's you," in her flat New Jersey voice, "—sorry, Ava-Rose isn't in, and I don't know when to expect her."

And when, disappointed, he dialed the number of the house at 33 Holyoak, it was invariably Holly Mae who answered, in her loud, cheery voice, "Hey, h'*lo,* Doctor! Naw, Ava-Rose ain't here—this time of day, she'd be over at Tamar's."

He was not jealous of her, and vowed he would never be.

Seeming to understand that that was the fate of the others: T. W. Binder, Eldrick Gill. *Yes and both of them now dead.*

He was not even certain at times that he loved Ava-Rose, maybe he only adored her? Or did he (and this was a subtle point) love the person he himself was, in her presence?

Recalling her murmured words, after Terence had

forced himself upon her that night he'd drunk too much, the night of the attaché case—"Why, Dr. Greene! I never expected such behavior of *you!*"

Terence had not expected it of himself.

He'd begun to apologize, suffused with shame, but Ava-Rose had silenced him with a forefinger to his lips: "It is written, 'Love that is violence is yet love.' "

To Terence's astonishment Ava-Rose continued, in a soft, sleepy, ruminative, rueful voice, "Oh! I do allow I did provoke you just now, Ter-ence! I have that way—I've been told." Kissing the small but bloody wound on Terence's cheek where her pronged ring had caught his flesh. "And when a woman so provokes, she must be accepting of the consequences—'All things are ordained.' "

Terence had felt his heart swell nearly to the point of bursting.

To be forgiven for having behaved like a drunken brute!—to be so understood, so loved!

For how could any man doubt, *this is love?*

And how vigorous and inspired a lover Terence had become, these past months. Like a young man again. Like the young man whom in fact he'd never been.

Ava-Rose Renfrew seemed by her nature to want him to . . . force her, somewhat. Even, sometimes, to hurt her. Just a bit.

Sometimes, after lovemaking, Terence discovered Ava-Rose's face streaked with tears; her lovely eyes blurred, reddened. She buried her face against his neck as he embraced her, murmuring, "My darling, have I hurt you? I didn't mean to."

Perhaps it is in the nature of lovemaking, that a man does force a woman . . . somewhat.

That the woman does resist, just a bit.

And afterward sighing in her lover's ear, as Ava-Rose Renfrew sighed in Terence Greene's ear, "Oh Ter-ence, *oh!* —you're so strong."

How flattering, to a man's virility. How irresistible, and wise.

"So this is the man I really *am*. And the other—"

With Phyllis, Terence had long felt merely tolerated; "loved," of course, yet "loved" as a sort of useful appendage of the household, an amiable if exasperating presence, an escort to social events. In matters of lovemaking, he'd long felt somehow automated, and hollow: Phyllis pushed buttons, and Terence responded.

Or failed to respond.

"—the other is someone *else*."

How hurt he'd been, how he'd managed to forget, that time, that humiliating time, when Phyllis, frustrated, tearful, had lashed out at him *It's selfish to begin something you can't finish.*

Yet Terence loved Phyllis. He loved Kim, Cindy, Aaron.

Even in the delirium of passion he could not bring himself to suggest to Ava-Rose that they marry; nor even that he leave his family, to live with her. "I know I should begin to think of the next phase of my life," he told Ava-Rose worriedly, "—but, somehow, I can't. Not yet."

Ava-Rose laughed, and kissed Terence on the forehead. " 'In time, all is resolved.' "

Terence knew that he should begin too to think of the "expenses" (the sum of the numerous financial calculations, withdrawals and deposits and rewithdrawals) he was incurring, in his eagerness to befriend the Renfrews, but somehow he could not—"Not yet."

Occasionally in the news it is revealed that some semipublic figure has embezzled funds, or stolen money from clients, or, hardly less inexplicably, failed to pay his income taxes, and one's response is *How could he think he could get away with it?—at least, for very long?*

The answer is, as Terence Greene might have acknowledged, *You don't think. Quite simply, you don't.*

"Expenses"—so the problem was designated, succinctly and seemingly neutrally, in Terence's mind.

"The hell with 'expenses'! I am a lover, not an accountant."

The Renfrews by their very nature reinforced such a sentiment. They were unjudging—"the salt of the earth." If they disapproved morally of Terence, a married man, conducting a love affair with Ava-Rose, they did not so indicate; in fact, it seemed to Terence that, like Ava-Rose, they were becoming ever more fond of him. The proof of it was (so Terence surmised) that they accepted gifts from him, and occasionally even cash. Ava-Rose was delighted that her family had grown so fond of Terence, for, he gathered, there was a history of "things not working out quite right" with Ava-Rose's man friends and the Renfrews. The family was not always predictable, Ava-Rose said, except in one matter: pride.

"It's a true failing, and a sin in the face of the Divine," Ava-Rose said, frowning, "—this blindness called 'pride.' But I do love them! I swear, I would die for them! Family's about all a person has, in the human world."

Terence would have liked to retort that, to him, the Renfrews were the true, the authentic, the American—so unlike the materialistic, loveless hypocritical families of such affluent suburban enclaves as Queenston, New Jersey. But he was so enchanted by the beautiful young woman when she spoke in that apologetic way, begging a forgiveness any lover would be eager to give, he could hardly bring himself to contradict her. He said instead, warmly, "I see nothing wrong with pride, Ava-Rose, if it doesn't interfere with—matters of the heart."

All had to cooperate to shield Cap'n-Uncle Riff from knowledge of Terence's financial support, and this led to some comical conspiracies. When Ava-Rose and Terence drove home in the splendid new Corvette, Ava-Rose at the wheel giddy as a young girl, for instance, the explanation was that she had won the car in a raffle!

"Which raffle was this, exactly, my dear?" Cap'n-Uncle asked, as the family stood about in the driveway admiring the car, "—a raffle at the Church of the Holy Apocalypse?" The old man stroked his beard thoughtfully, waiting for his niece to reply.

"Cap'n-Uncle, no!" Ava-Rose exclaimed, a bit piqued. "You know the Church of the Holy Apocalypse doesn't countenance such things as *raffles*. This was the Catholic church over on Pennington Avenue, I've forgotten the name."

"I see," said Cap'n-Uncle. He ran his hand along the polished flank of the Corvette, and let it drop away, with an elderly sort of sigh. "Well. Catholic or Protestant, it *is* damned beautiful."

And so, Terence thought proudly, it was.

It was on the first warm, springlike day in April that Terence Greene's happiness was nearly destroyed.

The morning began awkwardly enough: When Terence stepped into his office at the Feinemann Foundation, he saw, to his surprise, portly Mrs. Riddle standing at his desk, hurriedly sorting through a stack of applications. She glanced up at him, smiling, though with the slightest suggestion (unless Terence imagined it?) of a squint. "Ah, Dr. Greene! Thank goodness! Marcia"—Marcia was Mrs. Riddle's assistant, primarily a typist—"is desperate thinking she's lost that long application from the Corcoran Gallery, and I'm wondering if it's here on your desk?"

Terence said, quickly, "Why, I'm sure it is. Let me look for it."

He saw that Mrs. Riddle was embarrassed, and hoped to put the woman at her ease. Hoping too she had not seen that flash of blind panic in his face.

Not that there was any reason for panic, surely not, not in this office. Or, at any rate, so carelessly exposed atop Dr. Greene's desk.

Like my mother-in-law, with that pose of innocence. Going through my private things.

The application from the Corcoran Gallery was found, and handed over to Marcia, and the incident was forgotten.

Or would have been, if Terence had not noticed (*had* he noticed? or was it his imagination?) the women in the outer office, Mrs. Riddle, Marcia, and another secretary, laughing together and then growing suddenly silent when Terence appeared.

The main business of the day was the final meeting of the committee on selection, the completion of a series of meetings begun months ago. Because of the prestige and monetary value of the Feinemann fellowships, and the intense degree of rivalry among applicants, and even among those recommending applicants, the Board of Trustees had wisely set up a division of powers under the guidance of the Executive Director: There was a committee of nomination, consisting of fifteen men and women of established reputations in the arts, which accepted applications and nominations for various Feinemann awards, and had the power too to nominate; there was a committee of evaluation, similarly constituted, which winnowed through thousands of applications and nominations, cutting the number by nine-tenths; finally, there was the committee of selection, which had the power of making the final selections, but could make these selections only on the basis of the list provided by the committee of evaluation. With so many checks and balances, and no committee member with the power of simply handing over an award to a protegé, which is usually the case with such awards, it was believed that the Feinemann awards were made as justly as possible.

Since Terence Greene had become Executive Director, he had inaugurated a policy too of strict honesty regarding committee members' connections with candidates for awards and with one another—"Ideally, we want to avoid not only impropriety, but the appearance of impropriety. I'm sure you can all see why."

Everyone did; but, now and then, one or another committee member objected. As an elder dramatist, serving this year on the committee of nomination, said, jokingly, "There doesn't seem to be much point in getting to be my age, and not being allowed some 'impropriety.' "

Because their work was preliminary, the first two committees, though disputatious, were generally less disputatious than the third: The third, the committee of selection, had the power of giving away $4 million, yet, ironically, could not give this money to any but candidates passed on to them. This year, of the fifteen distinguished members of the selection committee, it was Quincy Ryder who most vociferously objected to the list his committee had inherited. Months before, Terence had been shocked by the man's flippant rejection of the poet Myra Tannenbaum; yet Ryder rejected others with equal contempt—"I really must insist that we make our *own* nominations, in the interests of maintaining cultural standards in the United States!"

In Ryder's droll Virginia accent, his shiny puckish-red face screwed up as if there were a bad odor in the room, the statement had a floridly comic tone. But few of Ryder's fellow judges laughed.

Terence, whose thoughts yearned toward Ava-Rose Renfrew, but whose responsibility was to maintain order in the meeting room, responded courteously to Quincy Ryder, as always—what else could one do?—and proceeded with the day's business. Certainly, Quincy Ryder knew that the selection committee was forbidden to name Feinemann winners directly.

One by one, judges spoke. These were serious, intelligent men and women, nine men, six women; yet rather soft-spoken and deferential, compared to the assertive Ryder. The most strong-minded was a black woman novelist of about fifty, who could be counted upon to stare stonily at Ryder when he launched into one of his cruel comic monologues, and who frequently challenged him when he overstepped the apparent boundaries of his knowledge. Today, Adele Brown blew her nose repeatedly in tissues which she left crumpled and scattered about the table in front of her. Her plum-dark skin seemed darker, her heavy-lidded eyes sullen. Terence hoped that the animosity between her and the conservative white man would not flare into a public quarrel.

The list of candidates stood at two hundred seventy-two, and would have to be cut severely to one hundred forty; within the one hundred forty, there were twenty-five "Americans of Promise" awards which were slated for younger artists whose major work lay before them. These awards were especially coveted because they brought with them not simply a single year's grant but a five-year grant of $40,000 yearly, tax free; Quincy Ryder seemed to feel most strongly about them on the grounds that the "most brilliant young artists of my personal acquaintance" had been rejected by a previous committee, or had not been nominated at all.

Ryder was particularly incensed about the absence from the list of a young poet named T. C. Tucker, of whom Terence had never heard—"I say we restore this excellent poet's name to the list, from which it was so ignorantly cut! Otherwise, I don't see how we can take these deliberations seriously."

"Now Quincy," Terence said, in the reasonable voice with which he met all unreasonable suggestions, "you know the by-laws of the Foundation. Even if this committee voted to—"

"Fuck the committee, I'm talking about justice!"

"We have two hundred seventy-two highly recommended candidates, and of these—"

"T. C. Tucker is in the great tradition of Yeats, Eliot, Auden—he has already won numerous prizes for his books! It was an act of personal vengeance that that old fool—" and here Quincy reiterated a charge he'd made at previous meetings, that an enemy of his had purposefully cut young Tucker from the list when the committee of evaluation made its decisions. Ryder's voice quavered dramatically. *"I am talking about justice."*

Adele Brown said, politely, "This 'Tucker'—he's a friend of yours, yes? Or maybe a relative?"

Ryder said furiously, "Why should he *not* be a friend of mine? *I* choose my friends *discriminatingly.*"

Several others joined in. T. C. Tucker was, or was not, a leading young poet. T. C. Tucker was, or was not, especially young—thirty-nine years old. (The suggested cut-off age for "Americans of Promise" was thirty-five.) Terence listened with rising dismay, recalling his experience as jury foreman in Trenton. How easily led people were by those with ulterior motives, even intelligent men and women like those on this committee. In groups, something came over them, clouding judgment; something ignoble, demeaning; a kind of consensus-consciousness. Ava-Rose had told him of the "rapture-awakening" that sometimes transformed services at her church, everyone in the congregation weeping for joy, speaking "unknown" tongues, and while Ava-Rose's lovely face shone with the conviction that such ecstasy was not only desirable but divinely inspired, Terence was secretly appalled. (Ava-Rose, sensing his agnosticism, had never invited him to accompany her to church, and changed the subject when Terence brought it up. Maybe he was simply jealous?) From the initial meeting of this committee, most of the other judges had taken a dislike to Quincy Ryder's haughty tone and transparent maneuvering; yet, now, with so little time to spare, they allowed themselves to be led by him into a pointless debate. Terence saw how they *wanted* to placate him, somehow—"Pitiful, the concessions good will make to evil!"

Terence had not spoken aloud, but only sort of murmured, shuddering, under his breath. Marcia, seated beside him to take notes at the meeting, glanced at him curiously.

It was a season now in Terence Greene's life when people, whether strangers or trusted associates, had begun to glance at him curiously. Not without sympathy, but—curiously.

Did Dr. Greene see?—or did he, prudently, not see?
To inhabit bliss is blind.
Several times since Wednesday (it was Friday today) Ter-

ence had tried without success to telephone Ava-Rose Renfrew. Was she angry at him? Disappointed? (He had not been able to help much with household expenses lately, for his inexhaustible source of funds was beginning to seem distinctly less inexhaustible—but surely that would not matter to dear Ava-Rose and her family?) He would try again, after lunch. He would call Tamar's Bazaar & Emporium. On such a fine spring day, when shoppers were likely to patronize the Chimney Point Shopping Center, Ava-Rose would surely be behind the counter of The Craft of Beauty.

Terence interrupted the discussion, which had grown a bit heated. Quincy Ryder was "questioning the merits of" a black dramatist whom Adele Brown had championed from the first, and Terence wanted to avoid an explosion. He said, hating himself for that air of *reasonable placating* he now heard in his own voice, "Now, Quincy, the issue isn't your candidate measured against another, and you must know it. Your candidate is not on the list. And so—"

"Fuck the list, 'Dr. Greene'! I'm warning you, I'll go to the media. I have friends at the *T.B.R.*"—*The New York Times Book Review*—"who would see it as their professional duty to expose the corruption of this committee!—this 'Feinemann Foundation.' Everyone knows that Nelson P. Feinemann was a vulgarian and a crook."

Terence said quietly, "The founder's business virtues, or lack of them, have no bearing on our business today, Quincy, and you must know it. Before we break for lunch, at least let's—"

Ryder glared at Terence with eyes small and glinting like slivers of mica. "Stop saying I 'must know it,' Greene. I must *not* know it, if it is false. I beg you all—justice is the principle here. I *will* go to the media."

Terence hesitated. He knew that Quincy Ryder had no case to bring to the media, yet—might not a scandal of some kind follow, however unjustly? Even responsible publications like *The New York Times* printed such internal disagreements as news.

Terence said, "This committee will not be blackmailed, Quincy. *That* you must know."

Ryder drew breath to reply, but seemed not to know what to say. He glanced about him, and saw no allies; Adele Brown was derisively blowing her nose. The little man visibly reddened. Even the glassy whites of his eyes were bloodshot. In his black-and-white-checked double-breasted suit, lavender Liberty-print bowtie and matching handkerchief, he appeared dapper as a store mannequin; yet his hands trembled. He sniffed, and shrugged, and said negligently, "Oh, fuck. When's lunch? I want a vodka martini."

"Is Ava-Rose there?—may I speak with her?"

"Oh, it's you." A pause. "Naw, she's out for the day, I guess—wanna leave a message?"

And, next: "Holly Mae? This is—"

"Why h'lo, Dr. Greene! Naw, gee, Ava-Rose ain't here, whyn't you try Tamar's, okay?"

"No, wait, Holly Mae, don't hang up—can you tell her I called, and I'll call again this evening? Or maybe I should drop by?—I might have some good news for Ava-Rose, I— might. Maybe."

"Yeah? What kinda good news?"

"I—I'd better wait, to make sure. Tell her I'll call to-night at seven?"

"What kinda good news? Something personal?"

Terence was baffled how to reply. His heart was pounding rapidly, and his stomach so churned, he regretted the meager lunch he'd gobbled down. "Well, I guess—maybe."

At the other end of the line, Holly Mae laughed, Ethel-Merman style. The sound was disagreeably similar to Adele Brown blowing her nose. "Sounds pretty am-big-rous, 'Dr. Greene'!"

Following the lengthy lunch, during which Quincy Ryder downed four vodka martinis, the committee moved forward with surprising dispatch. Either Ryder had lost spirit for promoting his poet, or his adversarial edge had been blunted by alcohol. (Ryder was not the only judge to sit for long minutes with his eyelids shut.) Balloting began for the "Americans of Promise" grants, and Adele Brown argued so forcibly for the black dramatist that he won nearly unanimously—fourteen votes for, one abstention. (Ryder, of course.) Terence thought, *Yes probably Adele is a friend of the man's* but the thought glimmered past, and dissolved. Terence wanted only that the selection process be completed, and the committee disbanded, and that he hold beautiful Ava-Rose Renfrew in his arms again. What else mattered!

For what does *bliss* most desire, but *blindness.*

As the list of candidates was cut, and a new, final list of winners established, Quincy Ryder sighed, and muttered to himself; seemed several times about to raise objections, and thought better of it; participated in the balloting, but with an ironic detachment. When others spoke, he looked rudely at his watch. (A watch so closely resembling Terence's, with a black suede band, Terence checked to see that his own watch was on his wrist.) At four-thirty, in the final hour of business, when one might have thought that Ryder was no longer a threat, something set him off, and he said, "Are you satisfied!—the lot of you!—*this list!* It is shameful, and it is despicable! I know virtually no one of these 'artists' and those I do know I abhor!" Before Terence could interrupt, Ryder launched excitedly into one of those cruel, presumably witty monologues for which, in certain circles, he was famous. His small, merry eyes gleamed with malice as he ticked off names on the list: "—*this* has-been fag with his anti-American diatribes!—and this 'feminist' creature in combat boots and serape!—and *this* seedy arriviste with his Warhol-plagiarized 'action paintings'!—and *this* bellyaching 'ethnic'-Jew, wouldn't you think the generation had died out by now?—phony Holocaust-exploiters writing treacly verse to make the goyim feel guilty but I refuse to feel guilty, and where poetry is trash *I say it is trash.* And this 'environmental artist'—what passes for lesbian chic—balloon-phalluses on posts! And here we have one of our dear 'persons of color'—and here, a 'physically handicapped'—'ethnic-American'—two for one!''

Terence said angrily, "Quincy, that is enough."

"It *is* enough, 'Ter-ence'!" Ryder said, tossing the sheet of paper down on the table, and pushing back his chair. "Conclude your contemptible business without me!" And he stalked out of the room, and slammed the door behind him.

Terence sat stunned for a long moment: not because of Quincy Ryder's departure, which was a tremendous relief to all, but because he seemed to have heard the man mock Ava-Rose's pronunciation of his name—a lilting, derisive *Terence*.

But how could Quincy Ryder know?

Quincy Ryder could not know, of course, and Terence quickly came to that conclusion, and dismissed the notion, in a flood of good feeling at the end of this long, exhausting day. The committee finally disbanded at 5:20; by which time only Marcia, of the Foundation staff, remained in the office. Terence sent her home, and worked at his desk another forty minutes, putting off his telephone call to Ava-Rose as if in teasing anticipation *no: in fear of being denied her* despite the good news he believed he might tell her now.

He was just about to pick up the telephone when there came a buzz at the door of the outer office. Odd, a visitor to the Feinemann Foundation at this time of day—six o'clock. It had to be someone whom the security guard downstairs had cleared, so Terence felt no hesitation about hurrying out to open the door; even as he opened it, the buzzing continued, rudely. " 'Dr. Greene'! Ever the workaholic! May I come in?" It was Quincy Ryder, voice slurred and menacing.

Terence would have liked to tell Ryder simply to go to hell, but rudeness was not one of his strengths. Unfortunately.

Ryder, who had clearly been drinking, blustered past Terence, and, before Terence could prevent him, back into Terence's private office; Terence had no choice but to follow him. "I want to see that final list, I want to check one or two names, where is that list, I want to see that list, Ter-ence!" Ryder muttered. "I want to see what you cunning people did behind my back, I want to see whether you omitted—" here naming the names of several candidates for whom he'd voted. Terence was appalled by the rude little man's intrusion—how like a nightmare this was!

Quickly Terence said, "Quincy, really!—you can't seriously believe—"

"Don't think you're going to defraud me of my fee"— there was a five-thousand-dollar honorarium for judges— "because I walked out at the very end, either! Oh, no! *Where* is that list, my friend?—I demand to see that list—"

The typed-out list of award winners lay in full view atop Terence's desk and there was no stopping Quincy Ryder from snatching it up, short of physical restraint.

Fussing and muttering, peering nearsightedly at the names, with that look on his flushed face as if he were in the presence of a bad odor, Ryder scanned the columns; to Terence's horror, he paused at the last name, and said, suspiciously, "What's this—someone has typed in a name I've never heard of: 'Ava-Rose Renfrew, artist, 33 Holyoak—' "

Terence pulled the sheet of paper from Ryder's fingers. His voice was loud and quavering. "Never mind, Quincy! That's none of your business."

Ryder said, "What? What isn't my business? What's going on here?"

Terence could feel the blood rushing into his face. He stammered, "Why, any of this, any—anything." He folded the list of names hastily, and shoved it into a drawer. "Now get out of here, will you?"

" 'Ava-Rose Renfrew, artist'—I saw it, my friend. An address in Trenton, New Jersey. Trenton! What *is* going on here?"

"Just get out, Ryder. Please."

Quincy Ryder stared up at Terence, hands on his hips. He was a short man who had long learned to stand with such aplomb as to make himself appear taller. Since departing Terence's office, he had soiled the front of his dapper checked coat; a stain of what looked like ketchup or barbecue sauce was prominent on the left lapel. Ryder's honeyed mid-Southern accent was particularly mocking—"Well, well! The upstanding Terence Greene, of all people! 'Ava-Rose Renfrew, artist'—well, *well*!"

"Please get out."

"I certainly *shall.*" Ryder turned on his heel, not so smartly as he might have wished—he was quite drunk—and stalked out of Terence's office, and out of the outer office. A profound and terrible silence pulsed in his wake.

Yes how like a nightmare, and how! how would it end!

"We will have to run away together—Ava-Rose and I."

Terence sat back weakly on the edge of his desk. Never in his life had he felt so utterly exposed, humiliated, crushed. For some minutes he simply sat there, breathing quickly, perspiration broken out on his body. He tried to think, but could not. He fumbled for the telephone receiver, thinking to call Ava-Rose, but it slipped from his fingers.

So desperate was Terence, he took the list of Feinemann winners out of the drawer, and checked the final name, in the hope that, somehow, it was not "Ava-Rose Renfrew" after all.

But of course it was. For had not Terence Greene himself typed in *Ava-Rose Renfrew, artist, 33 Holyoak Street, Trenton, New Jersey* shrewdly positioning it in such a way as to blend in with the rest of the column? Ava-Rose Renfrew was designated as an "American of Promise."

Terence could have wept with frustration, anxiety. "God damn it, she deserves it. She *is* an artist, as much as any of the others."

It came to him again, more forcibly, that he and Ava-Rose must run away together. But where would he get enough money? Phyllis's mother had entrusted Terence with investing several hundred thousand dollars out of her pension plan, and, indeed, some of this money Terence had siphoned off for Renfrew expenses; but to take a sizable chunk of it—"That would be theft. Grand larceny."

No, he could never steal outright from his own mother-in-law.

Even though it was no secret that, in her will, Fanny Winston was leaving most of her money to the Greenes.

Terence was on his feet pacing about his office, necktie askew, when, to his surprise, *the buzzer to the office rang again.*

His heart leapt—"Maybe it hasn't happened yet?"

Maybe Quincy Ryder had not seen Ava-Rose's name, and the last ten minutes or so had been a hideous waking dream?

Again, Terence hurried to the outer office; again, he opened the door. *Again, Quincy Ryder stood in the doorway, smiling.*

Terence saw at once, however, that of course Ryder knew: It had already happened, and there could be no reprieve.

This time, however, Terence did not invite Ryder into the office. Whatever Ryder had to say could be said in the corridor, since the building was deserted. (It was now 6:25 P.M.) Even if the drunken Ryder raised his voice, his words could not carry nine floors down to the foyer, where the single security guard on duty might hear; in the improbable case that the guard, a soft-spoken Haitian-American, did hear, he could have no idea what the white men's quarrel was about.

Ryder said, squinting his left eye in a semblance of a wink, "We *could* make a deal, Terence, my friend. I was about to climb into a cab when it occurred to me: T. C. Tucker too might be added to the list, and some trifling name crossed out that no one would ever miss—which is what you did, eh? What d'you say, 'Dr. Greene'? Tit for tat?"

Terence's eyes swam with tears of rage and indignation. As calmly as he could manage he said, "Quincy, I don't know what you're talking about. I suggest you go home."

Ryder laughed delightedly. "What an act! Who do you think you're fooling? *I* saw the name, *I* didn't imagine it—

'Ava-Rose Renfrew, *artiste.*' What is she, your girlfriend? From Trenton, New Jersey?"

"Miss Renfrew is not my—my friend. She is a serious, highly regarded visual artist—"

"Oh, fuck! Nobody's ever heard of her, and you know it," Ryder said. In a playful though rather rough gesture, he poked Terence in the chest, as one boy might do to another. "At least my poet-friend Teddy-C. *is* known, and *does* have a national reputation. Yes?"

Terence flinched at the man's forefinger in his chest. A mist passed over his eyes tinged with blood.

"I've told you—go home, get away from here. I can't bear the sight of your face."

"What? Whose face? Who the fuck do you think *you* are, Greene? Your high moral tone doesn't square with—what's the girl's name—'Ava-Rose'—" Ryder spoke in a crude bullying singsong; he poked Terence in the chest again. He belched, and smelled of alcohol.

White-faced, Terence said, "Don't touch me, God damn you!" He shoved Ryder away, and Ryder shoved back, with surprising strength, sending the taller man back against the wall, hard. Now this was truly a nightmare, for in an instant Quincy Ryder seemed to have gone berserk, red-faced, bulging-eyed, shouting incoherently, striking Terence blows in the face and chest. In the confusion and horror of the moment Terence could make little sense of what Ryder said, hearing in his own ears a sharp, percussive voice *If your opponent hits you, counterpunch. Roll with the blow, and counterpunch: a left hook to the head or the body. Once some bastard hurts you bad, he'll need to hurt you again. If you don't stop him* and suddenly furious at being pummelled by Quincy Ryder Terence shoved him, hard—and the little man staggered backward, a look of rapt attention on his flushed face, and his mouth opened in a gaping O like a fish's even as momentum carried him against the railing over the abyss of nine; against the railing with such force that, like an acrobat performing a quicksilver trick, he fell—arms flailing, legs in the black-

and-white checked trousers kicking, black polished shoes showing their scuffed, sand-colored soles!

Terence rushed to the railing, to grab at the falling man, but it was too late—he saw, appalled, Quincy Ryder's body plummeting down like a dead shot, heard the strangulated scream, and then the echo of the scream, as his enemy fell nine floors to death in a gushing white fountain of classical pretensions.

"... Because All Things Are Ordained"

Aprematurely hot May first. Bits of invisible grit flung about in the gusty Trenton air. There was a taste of something oily and sepia-sulphurous that coated the interior of his mouth. His smile which had been a lover's smile of happy expectation was fading.

Ava-Rose? Where—?

Hadn't he seen, yes certainly he'd seen, the canary-yellow Corvette descend Broad Street, to make a left turn into the parking garage adjacent to the Metropolitan Life Plaza where, inside the tall plate glass doors of the building, he was waiting *patiently and hopefully as any lover. Smiling and then his smile faded* for he was certain the Corvette must be Ava-Rose's—*his*—that is, his gift to her on Valentine's Day (the car was registered in Ava-Rose Renfrew's name, of course) — *but where was she?* It would not require ten minutes for her to park the car.

Already it was three-twenty-five. Ava-Rose had promised to meet Terence at three o'clock, promptly.

He had not seen her in twelve days. Had not held her in his arms, kissed her. In twelve days.

Had not made love to her for *but why think in such terms,*

why enumerate, no point in keeping a record of such intimacy, the main thing was their love.

Terence had taken a half-day off from work to drive to Trenton to meet Ava-Rose on this balmy, summery-warm first day of May. Since the tragic accidental death of Quincy Ryder in the Feinemann Foundation building, Terence Greene, as Executive Director of the Foundation, and as one of the last people to have seen Ryder alive, had had numerous inter-ruptions of his work; police had questioned him of course, and even an insurance investigator; two-thirds of his tele-phone calls, it seemed, for days at a stretch, had had to do with Ryder. Terence's nerves were so tightly strung he winced at the slightest unexpected noise, and so his devoted secre-tary Mrs. Riddle insisted he make an appointment to see a doctor, and Terence agreed—in principle.

It had come to seem a brilliant idea, but one he felt guilty about exploiting—taking time off from work at the Foundation in order to see a doctor. Or to offer that as an excuse for driving to Trenton.

But so Terence had done today.

In hot May.

He'd gone to Manhattan in the early morning, and, shortly after noon, he'd taken the commuter train back again, to Queenston. Running the risk of being seen by some-one who knew him, even, if luck ran against him, by Phyllis —"But it can't be avoided." He owed it to Ava-Rose to do this for her. He knew she would be grateful.

So he returned to Queenston, and to the commuter parking lot, and drove south on Route 1 to Trenton, into the interior of the city. The plan was to meet Ava-Rose at three o'clock sharp at the Metropolitan Life Plaza. He'd made an appointment to meet with a Mr. Post at three-fifteen and al-ready they were late *and where was Ava-Rose?*

Terence hurried out onto the windswept plaza, shading his eyes. He'd seen the Corvette turn into the parking garage and had lost sight of it but there was a slash of yellow on an

upper level of the concrete structure, maybe that was it?—
but where was Ava-Rose?

It was true, and yet not true, that Terence Greene was
unwell. Certainly, the strain of the past several weeks in particular showed in his face, which was looking gauntly handsome, like a face in an old etching; his hair, until recently a
silvery-sand color, was now almost entirely silver. It was observed that he ate cautiously, and sometimes wincingly, with
that look of rapt attention and apprehension that sufferers
of stomach trouble show. (And hadn't he lost weight? It
wasn't just his face that looked gaunt.) Nights were unpredictable and turbulent—he squirmed, and kicked about, and
ground his teeth, and perspired so that his pajamas were
soaked through. (Phyllis had had to ask him please to sleep
in the guest room.) In public, as at home, his manner was
persistently affable *off in a world of his own.* His smile was so
fixed that deep creases had begun to bracket his mouth.
Never had he been so happy.

To Terence's way of thinking, he was in excellent
health. He ate quite normally. He drank perhaps slightly
more than he had in the past—his life before Chimney Point.
No matter what Phyllis said, he slept deeply every night, and
sometimes had difficulty waking, his sleep was so profound.
Several times a week he swam laps at the Athletic Club and
his time for one mile was more or less what it had always
been.

Even his beard seemed to be invigorated!—by the latter
part of the day, sharp little silver-glinting hairs pushed
through his skin, so he had to shave another time. *This unexpected virility, a second coming-into-manhood.*

"Ava-Rose—?"

Terence half-ran down the steps to the parking garage.
He did not want to shout loudly, and call attention to himself.
(In his lightweight gray suit, carrying his leather attaché case,
he looked very like other professional men of his age and
background who worked in and near the multimillion-dollar

Metropolitan Life Plaza, one of Trenton's most publicized new urban complexes. Such men never shout—at least in public.) Terence debated whether to take the stairs or the elevator up to the fourth level, where the yellow Corvette was parked; he did not want to miss Ava-Rose, and cause them to be even later for their important appointment with Mr. Post.

He decided to take the stairs, and, as he turned a corner, now beneath the low, girdered roof of the garage, he saw her—not twenty feet away, in conversation with a light-skinned black man in a uniform. Ava-Rose was in profile, laughing happily, as the uniformed man was laughing too; Ava-Rose brushed her wind-blown hair out of her face with quick, nervous movements of her beringed hands, and the uniformed man stood with the heel of one hand resting lightly against the holster at his waist. Terence, drawing quickly back, recognized the man—he'd been one of the Mercer County sheriff's deputies assigned to the courtroom at the time of the trial of T. W. Binder.

Ava-Rose was wearing one of her filmy-layered gypsy costumes, the predominate color that bright arterial crimson of Darling's tail feathers. There was something drooping in her hair—a creamy satin rose?—and her feet in flat black ballerina slippers had an adolescent narrowness and length to them. Bracelets flashed and chimed on her arms, strands of glass beads shone on her high, small breasts, loose inside her muslin, somewhat transparent shirt. How beautiful she was! The sight of her seemed to hurt Terence's eyes.

The sheriff's deputy wore his smart, olive-gray uniform with a slight swagger. When he smiled at Ava-Rose, he looked boyishly handsome as one of the teenaged rock stars in the posters on the walls of Kim's room; he might have been thirty years old. As Terence stared, the young man scribbled something on a card, and handed it to Ava-Rose, who put it in her gaudy woven over-the-shoulder bag.

Terence retreated, not wanting to be seen. His heart was beating in a way disagreeable to him.

" 'Jealousy is the heart's first death' "—so Ava-Rose had

chided Terence when he'd complained that it was difficult to get hold of her by telephone.

Terence quickly retraced his steps to the Plaza, and was waiting there, leaning over a railing, when, a minute later, Ava-Rose appeared, running. In her long, filmy skirt, gypsy-jewelry flashing, waist-long crinkly cloudlike hair whipping in the wind, she had an appealingly girlish-gawky look; two middle-aged men with attaché cases, descending the Plaza steps as Ava-Rose flew up, stared at her openly. Terence was reminded of the first time he'd seen this mysterious young woman, on that June morning, gusty and sun-lit like this, nearly a year ago—she'd been running, like that, heedless of traffic as she crossed Market Street against the light. Legs in daffodil-yellow tights, an emerald-green silk jacket with a rainbow stitched to its back. Beautiful girl. A stranger to Terence Greene.

And where, so unexpectedly, had she run—*up the steps and through the revolving doors of Trenton Police headquarters.*

Terence had many times wanted to ask Ava-Rose about her involvement with the Trenton police and the Mercer County district attorney's office: Had they helped her prepare her testimony for Binder's trial? Was T. W. Binder a local problem authorities wanted behind bars, whatever the charges? But he dared not ask, for such questions displeased Ava-Rose. "It is written, 'Seek not confusion, lest ye find it.' " If she was unhappy, Terence was quickly made to become unhappy.

Nor had he pressed her on the death (murder?) of T. W. Binder in prison; or on the details of her relationship with either Binder or Eldrick Gill. And there was the mysterious matter of, what was the man's name, Applewine, Wineapple—"Ezra Wineapple."

Once, casually, Terence had asked Chick who "Mr. Wineapple" was, and Chick had said, with such affable readiness it was impossible to suspect he might be lying, that the "old guy" had been "one of Auntie Holly's boyfriends" from the Chimney Point Senior Citizens' Center where "the whole gang of 'em used to play bingo, Thursday nights, and Auntie finally got kicked out she won so many jackpots they thought she must be cheating somehow, but, shit—how d'ya cheat at *bingo?*" Chick had squinched his mouth so, pronouncing "bingo," as if there were no other word in the English language so preposterous, Terence had had to laugh.

No, Terence had to admit, he hadn't the slightest idea how one might cheat at bingo.

"Ter-ence! There you are!" Ava-Rose cried, with the slightest suggestion of a pout, "—I didn't know which side to come, this darn ol' place is so *big.*"

Long-legged and energetic, Ava-Rose came rushing to Terence, who greeted her fondly, and kissed her on her lips, rather hard, as she didn't quite enjoy, in a place so public.

Just in case you're watching, Officer.

In the elevator going up to Metropolitan Life Insurance offices on the eleventh floor, Ava-Rose squeezed Terence's hand, shivering.

"It's an adventure, just being here with you—this place I've never been." Ava-Rose was wide-eyed; and spoke sincerely. One of the traits in her Terence so loved was the young woman's childlike wonder and appreciation of life.

"I was a little worried, waiting for you," Terence said. "I'd hoped nothing had happened to you, dear."

Ava-Rose bit her lower lip, and looked at Terence quizzically. She squeezed his hand again in her thin, strong fingers, as if to gently reprove him. "Ter-ence, nothing can happen to *me!* Not in this quarter. Didn't I tell you, my progressed Venus has quincunxed my natal Moon and semisextiled natal Pluto, so there's a sesquiquadrate to natal Moon and a *semisquare* to natal Pluto." She laughed, seeing his expression. "*I'm* fine."

Terence laughed, for the issue of astrology was one of the lovers' conflicts; not a serious conflict, but one that allowed Ava-Rose to lecture him, and chide him a bit, and allowed Terence to tease her, fondly as he'd used to tease his children about one or another of their silly, harmless pastimes. Laughing, though the rapid ascent in the elevator was making him short of breath for it reminded him of the elevator in his building in Manhattan *reminding him of his enemy's flushed hateful face and its transformation into a face of unspeakable horror as he staggered backward and fell against the railing and—*

Ava-Rose had slipped her arm through Terence's, turning her snub-nosed face up into his, prettily chiding. "I wish I could cast your horoscope, Dr. Greene!—you'd see, then, how 'All things are possible, because all things are ordained.' Can't you find out the exact time of your birth, somehow? Your mother—"

Terence said flatly, "My mother has been dead, Ava-Rose, for—most of my life."

The statement seemed simply to utter itself. Terence had not known this fact, if it was a fact, until this moment.

"Dead—?" Ava-Rose's smooth forehead crinkled in immediate sympathy. "You said she and your father had abandoned you, but—"

"Never mind, dear. We won't talk about it now."

"But—are you sure? I mean, if you hadn't seemed to know, and—"

The elevator stopped at the eleventh floor, and now Terence's shortness of breath was pronounced. But he would overcome it. As soon as he stepped into the corridor, seeing there was no open space before him, no atrium, he would be all right. *And so it was.*

Terence said quietly to Ava-Rose, who could always be depended upon, out of instinctive sympathetic tact, not to ask questions of him he did not want asked, "We'll talk about it another time, Ava-Rose."

"Or never," said Ava-Rose gently, "—if you prefer."

Arm in arm Terence and Ava-Rose entered the glass-fronted reception room of the Metropolitan Life Insurance office, and more than one person, male, female, visitor or office worker, glanced curiously at them. A distinguished-looking middle-aged man in a business suit, a flamboyantly pretty hippie-style girl spangled with inexpensive jewelry—a striking couple, yes? Terence's vanity was excited by such attention from other men; yet he knew it was a brazen, reckless thing to do, appearing in this corporate setting with a woman hardly his wife, nor any woman who might be plausibly explained to his wife should a report somehow make its way back to Phyllis.

(Did Phyllis suspect?—or, somehow, *know?* Terence was feeling less guilty about his family than he had at the start of his infatuation with Ava-Rose, for it seemed to him lately that they hardly had time for *him*. Phyllis was caught up in Queenston Opportunities, and in suburban social life, which seemed endlessly to excite her; Kim had her equally demanding teenaged life, to which high school work seemed but an appendage; even Cindy was demonstrably less interested in Daddy, now that she'd joined the drama club at Queenston Day. More than ever, Terence needed the Renfrews—"How lonely my life would be, without them!" He felt so estranged from Aaron, he sometimes forgot he had a son at all.)

Seated in the reception area, waiting to see Mr. Post, Terence at last weakened, and asked Ava-Rose, who was flicking through back issues of *Fortune* and *Business Life*, the question he'd vowed, down on the plaza, he would not ask. "That man you were talking with in the parking garage—who was he?"

"Man? What man?"

"It looked as if he was a policeman. A sheriff's deputy."

Ava-Rose shook her head, slowly. Her lovely amber-green eyes were perfectly clear. "I didn't notice any man," she said. "*Where* was he? In the parking garage—?"

"I might have been mistaken. I thought I saw you and a sheriff's deputy talking together. But never mind."

Ava-Rose's lower lip protruded in that way Terence had come to adore—the mock-pouty, mock-sullen, "misunderstood" Renfrew mannerism. She gave a little cry, "Ter-ence, you know I don't like policemen—they give me the shudders! Walking around ready to shoot one of us down dead with their darn ol' *pistols!*"

That was May first: the day Terence Greene took out a $500,000 insurance policy on his life, the sole beneficiary Ava-Rose Renfrew, 33 Holyoak Street, Trenton, New Jersey. It was an extravagant gesture but, Terence thought, the least he could do—seeing that, in panicked cowardice, he'd crossed out Ava-Rose's name on the list of Feinemann award winners, before the police arrived.

"Death by misadventure"—so the New York City coroner had ruled in the shocking case of the ex–Poet Laureate Quincy Ryder. Still, weeks later, rumors circulated in literary circles that the poet had committed suicide. Ryder was known to have been an alcoholic, and deeply unhappy; he'd studied with, and been influenced by, the poet John Berryman, also an alcoholic, who had committed suicide years ago by jumping off a Minneapolis bridge. There was even the rumor, denied by Ryder's survivors, that he'd had AIDS.

Ryder had died immediately upon impact, after having plunged nine floors through the atrium of the near-deserted building; the coroner's autopsy showed alcoholic intoxication, and the security guard who'd let Ryder into the building (twice, within a few minutes) testified that Ryder was "so drunk, going up, both times I had to press the elevator button for him. And all the man done was say, 'Thank you, boy,' and not even look at me."

The security guard was believed to be the last person to have seen Ryder alive.

Terence Greene, Executive Director of the Feinemann Foundation, with which Ryder had been associated for the past nine months, had been interviewed at length by investigating detectives; though clearly shaken by the poet's death, Terence had been fully cooperative. He had not known

Quincy Ryder well, and had never had a conversation with him not related to official matters, but he'd respected the poet enormously for his contribution to American letters and for the outspoken honesty of his opinions. On the day of the accident, Ryder had had a disagreement with the other fourteen members of the committee he was serving on, and walked out; the implication was that he would not be back. Yes, he'd been drinking, a bit.

The investigating detectives asked Terence if, in his opinion, Quincy Ryder had had a "drinking problem"; if he appeared to be "despondent" about anything. Terence said, after a pause, "Yes, Mr. Ryder certainly had a drinking problem, but I didn't have the impression he was despondent, exactly. Rather more, he seemed to me angry."

Angry—about what?

"That was the mysterious thing, and all who knew him commented on it," Terence said softly. "He appeared to be angry at all of mankind. At *life.*"

As for the circumstances of Quincy Ryder's actual death, Terence could provide little information. He gave his account several times of what he knew—"After the committee disbanded, I stayed in my office working, as I usually do. It was a little after six, when I heard a noise out in the corridor, like a raised voice or voices, and by the time I went out to investigate, Quincy Ryder had already fallen. His body was down below—on the fountain ledge. I looked over the railing and there was Mr. Jamahl"—it was Terence's custom to address the security guard in this formal, courteous way—"by the body, shouting for help. By that time, of course—" Terence's voice quavered and trailed off into silence. His eyes flooded with tears and his rather gaunt, distinguished face seemed suddenly the face of a mourner.

One of the detectives asked Terence if he thought that Quincy Ryder might have thrown himself deliberately over the railing, and Terence said, again after a pause, quietly, "I think it must have been—an accident. A tragic accident."

And not suicide?

"Well—wouldn't suicide be, in such a case, a tragic accident?"

And was Terence Greene sick with guilt over the death of Quincy Ryder?—this terrible secret he could share with no one on earth, not even Ava-Rose Renfrew for whom the man had died?—yes certainly he was *certainly not: once some bastard hurts you he'll need to hurt you again if you don't stop him* carrying the knowledge of it, the horror, everywhere with him for he was after all a man of integrity, a decent law-abiding and -respecting man, husband, father, member of a highly paid American professional class, yes and with a Ph.D. as well *an adulterer who exulted in sin and had never been so happy in his life until now in terror of exposure, and all coming to an end: his very life.*

One thing Terence knew, and vowed—"I must *never* kill again."

The old woman won't live forever. You know that.

And now to Terence's secret "expenses" was added the costly quarterly premium of the $500,000 life insurance policy. (Of course, the policy was worth it: In case of Terence's sudden death, how would Ava-Rose and her family be provided for, otherwise? Terence could not be so selfish and short-sighted as to fail to think of their welfare.) And there were the monthly payments on the Renfrews' mortgage; and a sizable bill, for May, from a Trenton plumber for "emergency" repairs (a pipe had broken, the basement was flooded); a painter had been engaged, and then, for some reason (a disagreement with Cap'n-Uncle Riff?) disengaged, to do some painting on the outside of the house, and there was a bill for his services—a surprisingly high one, considering how little he'd finally done. And there was the twins' orthodontist's bill. And more money to be paid to Holly Mae's team of lawyers (who were hinting of nearing a "substantial settlement" with the Trenton Transit Company). And the monthly payments on Ava-Rose's Corvette.

All these, "expenses."

For a secret life is expensive.

Yet more: In a sentimental gesture, lying one night in Ava-Rose's arms, upstairs in her prettily decorated little bedroom, in her funnily creaky old brass bed, Terence had impulsively agreed to buy Chick a new bicycle; since, as Ava-Rose pointed out, Terence was so generous with Dara and Dana, she was afraid Chick's feelings were beginning to be hurt. But, to Terence's astonishment, the bicycle, which Chick himself selected, turned out to be a sleek Italian model with twenty-one speeds, priced at $640!

Yet more upsetting, this very bicycle was stoken from Chick within fourteen days of its purchase—"Some black kids, with knives, I sure wasn't gonna mess with *them.*"

To add to all this, another greater expense loomed: Ava-Rose had long yearned to move out of Tamar's Bazaar & Emporium and set up The Craft of Beauty in a stylish little boutique of her own; not at the rundown Chimney Point Shopping Center, but at upscale Quaker Bridge Mall on Route 1. This Terence wanted too, for Ava-Rose's sake, and of course he intended to finance the move; but he knew from Phyllis's experience leasing a tiny office on Queenston Square that such properties were expensive. What a pity, though, that Ava-Rose's lovely things had been hidden away, for years, in that dreary store in Trenton! Her distinctive clothes, purses, jewelry—Terence would have liked to set the gifted young woman up in a boutique on upper Madison Avenue, but the expense was prohibitive; also, shrewdly, he would not have wished, perhaps, for her to be exposed to New Yorkers. To male rivals, suitors.

Poor Ava-Rose: Terence had never dared tell her that she'd been slated for a $40,000 annual stipend for five years, courtesy of the Feinemann Foundation; except, in panic at being found out, and linked with Quincy Ryder's death, Terence had eliminated her name after all.

"She would be so hurt!—and never forgive me."

———

Terence was thinking of these things, and other related matters *so many expenses! hidden costs!* driving to pick up his mother-in-law at a hairdresser's in the village, one Saturday afternoon in late May. His brain fairly buzzed. He would have felt guilt *but why? hadn't both men deserved to die?* but, increasingly, he had no time; he was forced to think of financial matters. He, Terence Greene, who yearned only to think of romance, and love; and doing the right thing by the Renfrews.

What had that sympathetic young woman assistant at the vet's said—*poor old fella?* Or had it been *lucky old fella?*

So far, Terence had been lucky. Damned lucky. Not in having gotten away with murder *no: those were accidents, not murders* but in shifting "expenses" about, from one account to another; instead of continuing to have his Foundation salary automatically credited, in full, to his Merrill Lynch account in Queenston, he now had the check, which was precisely $12,500 a month, converted into cash, so that he could use as much as he needed, or dared, before putting it into the account. The Feinemann Foundation, lavishly endowed, was generous with its executives' claims for miscellaneous expenses, and so Terence did not hesitate to claim, for instance, $1,000 while away at a conference in another city—even if, some of the time, he was in fact in Trenton. (He had learned too the conventioneer's trick of acquiring a dinner tab for a table of associates, each of whom paid for his own meal. What a windfall, a few weeks ago, at the Ritz Carlton in Boston; Terence had "hosted" a dinner for twelve men and women, like himself attending a conference in the humanities at Boston University: The bill had come to a staggering $1,460.) At about the time Terence signed on for the $500,000 life insurance policy, he'd begun a new, damnedly belated, procedure: When he dealt with Phyllis's mother's actuary, who was entrusted with investing money from her pension fund, he insisted that the actuary split all commissions with him—otherwise, he would not consent to a deal. (Mrs. Winston, though shrewdly money-minded, was finicky about small matters rather than large; it would never have occurred to her, as rarely it occurs to elderly widows of her type, to question her very advisors.)

Mrs. Winston's actuary had so readily consented to Terence's request, Terence had the idea that such arrangements must be made all the time.

"And it isn't illegal—I'm sure."

Still, Terence could not continue at such a frantic pace, indefinitely. And new expenses looming, new hidden costs. *I must never kill again. Must never.* His brain buzzed as if with a malevolent interior vibration that, sourceless, could not be switched off.

Fanny Winston, hair newly colored and permed, had that festive, somewhat florid-cheeked look of a woman who has been through an ordeal for beauty's sake, and is determined to believe that the ordeal has not been in vain. As Terence helped her walk from the hairdresser's salon to his car parked at the curb, she leaned heavily on his arm, though she was using, too, her aluminum walker, and peered up at him with a coquettish sort of petulance, saying, "Well!— *you're* diplomatic, aren't you!—silent as the *tomb*." Terence realized that he'd been expected to comment on his mother-in-law's hair, which was an eerie bluish-silver, synthetic as spun glass, permed in such a way as to lift in swirls from her scalp, to disguise the hair's thinness; this was in fact the style in which Mrs. Winston had been wearing her hair for years, and Terence thought it quite becoming. It was the elderly woman's puffy, sagging, rouged face that was the problem.

"Your hair is very becoming, Fanny," Terence said, smiling. The harsh chemical odor of the permanent wave, thinly disguised by something sweet and perfumy, made his eyes water. "I like it that way, very much."

"It's the same way I've been wearing it for years."

Before Terence could speak further, Mrs. Winston grunted, swinging herself around into the passenger's seat of the Oldsmobile, as Terence held the door open. Once, helping Mrs. Winston into the car, at a time when she was still using her wheelchair, Terence had inadvertently let slip the heavy door, and it had struck her swollen knees.

As they drove out of the village and into the semirural suburban neighborhood where the Greenes lived, Mrs. Winston chattered and Terence listened, or tried to listen. Trying to keep his thoughts from flying to Trenton, to Ava-Rose: *Would she love him less, if he could not help her relocate The Craft of Beauty, soon?* Mrs. Winston was visiting the Greenes for a week, or was it two weeks, or was it forever, and in her chatter she oscillated from being grateful she was in Queenston— "You can't imagine, at your age, how lonely my life is now" —to complaining, as if conspiratorially with her son-in-law, of her daughter—"I may be old-fashioned, but I simply don't approve of a mother with two young girls spending so much time out of the house. What an active circle of friends you two have!"

Terence, who had seen virtually nothing of his Queenston friends for months, murmured, affably, "Yes."

Mrs. Winston complained too of Kim, who seemed to have no time at all for her grandmother any longer—"It's rush rush rush, no wonder she's so skinny, and if it isn't her friends it's gymnastics now, did you see the bruises on the poor girl's arms?—from falling off the bars, she says. There's something unhealthy about all this *activity*."

Terence, driving his car, murmured, "Yes." Though he had not known that Kim was interested in gymnastics. Hadn't that been Cindy?

Mrs. Winston continued, vigorously, "Isn't it a surprise, Cindy in a senior high school production?—at her age? It's done wonders for her morale, and she's lost weight, but I do worry—you know what actors are like. I wouldn't doubt they all smoke *marijuana*."

The last time Terence had seen one of Ava-Rose's young nieces, the lanky, curly-haired girl had been lounging on the top step of the sagging veranda at 33 Holyoak, smoking a cigarette. A cigarette! At her age! It was a warm, muggy day, and the girl wore alarmingly short denim shorts, and a yellow elastic halter top in which her small pale breasts swung disconcertingly loose. Terence had been upset to see the girl so provocatively dressed, for anyone to notice who drove by, and he thought it shocking that she was smoking—"Is this something new, Dana? Or—Dara?" The girl stared at him, and laughed, as if he'd said something inadvertently funny. "If you don't even know my name, Dr. Greene, maybe it ain't up to you to tell me can I smoke or not, huh?" She spoke in a throaty voice, and she'd stuck out her lower lip in the pouty, seductive Renfrew manner; not so hostile as her words might indicate, but rather more flirtatious. Terence, blushing, could only think to mumble, "Well, I hope your sister doesn't smoke, too," and the girl continued to stare at him, cool, bemused, "What sister? I don't have a sister, Dr. Greene. Who told you that?"

The chemical fumes from Mrs. Winston's hair assailed Terence's nostrils and eyes, and he was beginning to feel slightly nauseated. Mrs. Winston did not want the windows of the Oldsmobile lowered more than a crack, so that her hairdo wouldn't be disturbed. "—on TV, all the time. So upsetting! But if it isn't marijuana it's *crack*. Oh my yes, we all know about *crack*."

Terence had lost the thread of their conversation. He said, tentatively, "None of the kids smokes, thank God."

"Oh but Phyllis has begun again, hasn't she? She's looking very good these days, all that tennis, but I do worry—"

Close ahead was the Queenston River, a narrow but deep stream which Terence must cross by way of a quaintly rattly single-lane bridge; a sturdy enough bridge, having been refurbished years ago, even as, to much local outrage, its weathered wooden sides and roof were removed, for visibility's sake. The unpaved road approaching the bridge was tortuous, and posted at fifteen miles an hour, and the bridge itself at five, but no one would wish to speed in such circumstances for what if the car veered suddenly off the road on the ramp leading to the bridge, what if the car crashed through the bridge's narrow railings, *what if we plunged into the water?*

What if the old woman was trapped in the car, and drowned? "Terence?—why are we going so fast? That bridge—"

Before Terence had stopped by the hairdresser's salon to pick up Phyllis's mother, at Phyllis's request—for Phyllis herself was busily caught up in a fund-raising luncheon for a local state senator—he'd had a drink at the Queenston Inn; a vodka martini. He was not an afternoon drinker and vodka martinis did not appeal to him but, somehow, he'd had the drink, or was it two drinks, which had helped to quell the curious buzzing in his head, unless it had contributed to the buzzing, and, now, as Terence pressed down on the accelerator, staring transfixed at the narrow bridge ahead, a delicious sort of vertigo flooded him, like a reprise of the vodka going down, coursing sharply, yet warmly, through his blood. *How happy I am! How happy, knowing what I must do!*

As in a film, Terence saw the white Oldsmobile crashing through the bridge railing, sinking beneath the surface of the rushing water, saw Fanny Winston trapped inside, in the passenger's seat, saw himself rising gasping and white-faced to the surface, then diving back, with the intention of extricating the terrified woman from the car—for Terence Greene was a moderately good swimmer for a man of his age and physical condition *and this would be expected of him.* He saw himself trying, and failing, to save his mother-in-law, maybe she was wedged into the seat?—maybe her heart had given out, with the shock? Still, he would try! he would try! heroically, he would try! And by this time another car would have come along, there would be at least one witness to Terence's effort, and to the desperation with which, *as if it were his own mother trapped there in the car,* he insisted upon diving back into the water another time—

"My God, no—!"

Panicked, Terence pumped at the brake pedal; turned the steering wheel straight so that, bouncing and clattering over the plank floor, the heavy car rushed over the bridge, and not through the railing: He'd been aiming it, at a subtle slant, to the right. Cold sweat broke out over his body, his heart pounded with adrenaline—how close he'd come to a terrible accident! Close beside him, Fanny Winston was exclaiming in a high, breathless voice, "Oh!—oh!—*oh!*"

The Oldsmobile plunged on, holding the road; Terence brought it so quickly back into control, perhaps it had never been out of control. Cold sweat broke out over his body and his teeth were chattering with the enormity of what had almost happened, but he managed to apologize to Mrs. Winston, and to explain: "This damned car, the brakes need relining. I'm so sorry, Mother—"

It was the first time Terence had ever called Fanny Winston "Mother," though, from time to time, rather wistfully, she'd suggested to Phyllis that he do so.

Now, it did not seem that the badly shaken woman heard; or, if hearing, that she comprehended. She was gasping for breath, one hand pressed against her bosom. "Oh, oh!—my God!" Terence saw that her face, beneath her makeup, had gone a ghastly ashen hue; her quivering mouth hung slack.

What if she should die after all, of a heart attack?—as a result of his careless, absentminded driving?

Fortunately, Mrs. Winston recovered from her fright by the time Terence turned up the drive at 7 Juniper Way. He worried that she would be furious with him, as well she might have been, but, when he stooped over her, to help her out of the passenger's seat, she smiled weakly at him and gave him both her hands so that he could pull her out; her manner was subdued, chastened. Breathily she murmured, her eyelashes fluttering, "Oh my that was a close call, wasn't it, Terence! God was watching over us, that's all!" looking up at Terence in anxious appeal.

Terence said, gravely, "Yes. He was."

———

Ava-Rose, I am in terror of what I am becoming.

Ava-Rose, I must stop seeing you.

Late one evening Terence hid in his study and telephoned Ava-Rose. The phone at the other end rang and rang, as if in mockery.

My darling Ava-Rose, I can't live without you: We must marry.

At last, on the eleventh ring, the phone was answered, and then somewhat rudely—"Yah? Who's this?"

Terence was disconcerted, for the voice was no one's he recognized. He could not even have said whether it was male or female. Had he not heard, amid the background noises (voices, laughter), Darling's unmistakable shrieking, he would have supposed he'd called the wrong number. "Who is *this*?" he demanded.

"Look, mister, y'wanta talk to somebody, or what?"

"Yes, I do. I want to speak with Ava-Rose, please. This is—"

"Yah? What? Can't hear ya."

"—'Dr. Greene,' tell her. 'Dr. Greene.' She'll know who I am."

The noise at the other end swelled, as if the receiver had been flung down facing it. What a mystery, and how disagreeable—the Renfrews always went to bed by ten-thirty, and it was now ten-twenty. Clearly something was going on. A party? House guests? (Terence seemed to recall that Ava-Rose had mentioned Renfrew relatives coming to visit them, from West Virginia.) He could hear laughter very like Holly Mae's, rising, raucous.

Seconds passed, and no one picked up the receiver. Terence muttered, anxiously, "Hello? Hel*lo*?"

Indeed, the receiver must have been flung down, and forgotten. Darling the parrot shrieked happily, "Beeeyt PEEZE! Beeeeyt PEEEZE! *BEEEEYT PEEEEZE!*"

This went on for some time.

Anticipating hours of sleeplessness, alone in the bed in the upstairs guest room to which Phyllis had exiled him, Terence decided he would stay up for a while and work. Since Quincy Ryder's death, Terence had fallen behind in his work at the Foundation. Documents to peruse, reports to prepare, dozens of letters to answer. Phyllis remarked upon his looking "haggard" and Mrs. Riddle continued to worry that he was "under such a strain," but the truth was, work had always been a solace for Terence, even as a boy. There was pleasure in getting something done, and in occupying the mind. Aunt Megan would call out cheerfully, seeing the boy's melancholy face, "Here, kid, might's well make yourself useful!" And so he did, and was.

How lonely I am. Ava-Rose, have mercy.

Terence would have preferred working with his hands to work at his desk, but there was no question of that, in the early hours of a Sunday morning. (His handyman chores about the house—why hadn't he time for them, any longer? Or was it that, deeply in love with another household, he had little passion left for 7 Juniper Way? Yet the Renfrews did not want Terence Greene hammering and fussing *there*. Ava-Rose explained, "Cap'n-Uncle and Auntie would feel, oh I don't know!—like somebody was spying on them, somehow.")

So Terence worked at his desk. Past 1 A.M., past 2 A.M. Until print swam in front of his eyes, his eyelids grew irresistibly heavy, he laid his head down on his arms—and fell asleep, as into a dead faint, within seconds.

Sensing that he was asleep and dreaming, sensing too, by his body's clammy heat, how he was slipping helplessly into a nightmare of spellbinding terror, Terence was aware both of his head on his arms, and of a ghostly movement outside his window. Someone had jumped down from the garage roof, which, due to the slope of the land, was not so high at the rear as at the front; he was moving, in a walk, not a run, in the direction of the woods. Beyond the woods, on the other side of the Greenes' property line, was an unpaved road and on that road Terence seemed to know *there was a car, a sporty-ugly Camaro parked.*

How Terence Greene knew this, he could not have said. But he knew.

As he knew too that the ghostly figure had crept across the garage roof from one of Kim's bedroom windows on the second floor of the house.

With an alacrity rarely his by day, Terence got at once to his feet, ran from his study and through the darkened downstairs to the rear door off the utility room. Where by day he might have had to search for long minutes, and then futilely, for a flashlight, the urgency of the dream provided him with his flashlight at once—for there it was, suddenly, in his hand.

Outside, the May night smelled of cool earth, damp leaves. The trees that were newly budded by day were skeletal by night. In the very exigency of the moment Terence had time for a stab of regret that, since Chimney Point, he had neglected his property—a lawn crew came weekly, as to the homes of Terence's neighbors, to service grounds at which property owners scarcely glanced.

Terence sighted the moving figure, about to disappear into a stand of evergreens about thirty feet away. "Hey, you! Wait!" he called out. The flashlight was already on, illuminating a thin, wiry boy clad in black. He turned defiantly to face Terence, grinning into the beam of light as into stage lights. Gold chains and a heavy gold medallion around his neck glittered; there were bright studs in both his ears, and a thin gold ring through his nostrils. His skin was pale as parchment and his eyes glassy and manic. Studs Schrieber.

"Yah? You talking to me, 'Mr. Greene'?" His question was a drawl, mocking.

Terence stammered, "You—what the hell are you doing here!"

Now the nightmare began to build, pulsing with rage, and horror, and a profound visceral revulsion, as if one species of life were confronted with another, in a bitter death struggle. *An animal, upright.* Though Terence was seemingly paralyzed with terror he was at the same time so charged with adrenaline he sprang forward to meet his enemy with something like passion. *How happy! Knowing what we must do!*

Yet Studs Schrieber stood his ground, brazenly. Hands on his hips. Knees slightly bent. It was clear from his bright, manic eyes and slip-sliding grin that he was high on some drug—"stoned." His black T-shirt hugged his skinny ribs, damp with sweat; his lurid gold jewelry winked.

Terence swung the flashlight menacingly. "You're forbidden to come onto this property, you little bastard! You know that!"

"So what, man? I do what I wanta do." Bemused, Studs Schrieber ran his hands through his punk-style hair. He did not seem to mind in the slightest the flashlight beam in his face. The pupils of his eyes were tiny as caraway seeds. "Just like you, man." He giggled.

"What—are you talking about?"

"Man, *you* know."

Terence stared at the boy. It was at this point, he would recall afterward, that the dream-logic queerly shifted, so that, though he stood facing the jeering boy, he was also, simultaneously, back in the house, asleep at his desk; his head, so heavy! heavy as death! on his folded arms. He was both pleading with Studs Schrieber, and threatening him. He was both advancing upon him, swinging the flashlight like a club, and retreating from him, that look of recognition, hideous filial recognition, in the boy's eyes. Yet: *how happy! Knowing what we must do!*

"—Kim's told me plenty of shit about you, man," Studs Schrieber said, baring his damp teeth in a mock-smile, "you and your old lady both, how you screw around. Wild! Weird!—like, you think *you* can tell Studs Schrieber what to do, huh? No way, man!"·He was making a windmill-like motion with his fists, as if mimicking an elderly man's pose of aggression. "Hey look, 'Mr. Greene,' I saw you once, myself —buying some goofy three-hundred-buck birdcage, out on

Route 1. Kim says you got some girlfriend or something, but what the hell, man—live and let live, huh?'' He was giggling even as the flashlight smashed down on his head, shattering the glass.

Seemingly in the same instant, Terence woke at his desk.

How heavy his head on his arms, how dazed his brain, as if stuck to the inside of his skull! His mouth was parched, coated with something oily and acrid. He was both excited and deathly tired. The time on his wristwatch was 5:05 A.M.

"The night—where has it gone?"

Outside his study window it was still dark; yet a porous, misty dark, yielding to dawn. Terence made a motion to rise, thinking to use his bathroom, and to try to sleep for another hour, in bed, but his left leg was numb. Then in a sickening rush his dream came back to him and he saw himself, disheveled, panting, jaws clenched, hauling the rolled-up length of carpet out from behind the basement steps where it had been hidden for nearly a year, and up the steps; hauling it into the back yard; and, by moonlight, on the pine needle–scattered hill at the foot of which Tuffi lay buried beneath a flagstone marker, undoing the twine that held the carpet, opening the carpet, *and rolling the lifeless body of Studs Schrieber onto it.*

"My God!—what a nightmare."

Next, Terence saw himself dragging the carpet, with the body inside, the twine neatly binding it up again in a roll, up to the driveway; he backed out the Oldsmobile, opened the trunk, and, clumsily yet resolutely, managed to get the rolled-up carpet into the trunk, one end protruding. He located more twine in the garage—he who, by day, would have searched futilely!—and secured the trunk top, with such eerie dispatch that it would surely have seemed, to an observer, *that Terence had long planned all this, beforehand.*

Abruptly then the dream shifted, and Terence was both driving his car, and paralyzed in sweaty, heart-pounding sleep, back at the house, at his desk. He was thinking, in dream-logic, that he would have the alibi, this time—"I *am* asleep." He shivered, and laughed. And kept on driving.

Quickly he was out of Timberlane Estates. North on Route 33, skirting Queenston, driving his car with its terrible burden like one possessed, *or a man who has carefully premeditated his actions.* (Why else had he kept that carpet remnant for so long, hidden behind the basement steps?) Swiftly and unerringly Terence drove into rural Hunterdon County where, years ago, he'd sometimes taken his young family on Sunday excursions. Again, by dream logic, he located a ravine close by, but not within sight of, Route 22, bouncing along a lane into an area strewn with debris—a no-man's-land of a dump. Terence backed the Oldsmobile as close as he dared to the edge of the ravine, which was quite steep; he dragged the carpet out of his trunk, and let it fall—rolling, sliding, tumbling—to join shadowy refuse at the bottom.

I do what I want to do, man. Just like you.

"My God! How horrible."

Terence was leaning over his desk, fighting a sensation of nausea. His left leg tingled with pins and needles now. He did need to use the bathroom; and he did need to sleep. Yet he was so exhausted, and so sickened by his dream, he could not move.

Not Kim. Not that. No—I can't believe any of it.

And it was improbable (even for a nightmare) that Studs Schrieber would die from a mere blow of a flashlight to his head. Improbable that, despite a gash on his forehead, he'd bled fairly sparingly.

Except—wasn't there blood, or something resembling smudged rust, on Terence's fingers? beneath his broken nails?

And on the front of his rumpled khaki trousers.

"What?—this can't be."

He shivered, and laughed. He was feeling very strange now.

In a haze of dread, Terence went downstairs into the

basement, to check behind the steps: To his horror, he saw that the old carpet was gone. The space where, on the concrete floor, obscured by cartons and a cast-off bicycle of Aaron's, it had lain, was now empty—vacant.

But what about the Camaro, parked across his property line?

Repentance

*T*hen it was summer. Humid, seemingly airless. As at the bottom of an ocean. Terence Greene carried himself with the air of a sleepwalker who fears of all things being wakened, yet knows it is inevitable.

A voice sounded vehemently close by his ear. "The damned thing is, contrary to what most people are led to believe, only a small fraction of crimes in this country is ever 'solved.' Even when the police manage to arrest someone, it's rare there's a trial—more likely a plea bargaining, with charges reduced. And if there's a trial, because of our exclusionary laws, a verdict of 'guilty' is hard to come by."

"Matt, really—you sound so cynical. You, of all people!" A woman's voice trilled with concern.

"I'm not cynical, God knows—I'm a realist. A hardheaded realist. In my position, in the township, I have to be. Crime here is definitely on the rise, and people look to their elected officials for help, and what the hell can we do in such an atmosphere? Say a criminal *is* caught, *is* found guilty, he has an excellent chance never to see the inside of a prison. This kidnapping case, or 'hit,' whatever it is—"

Since ascending to public office, however minor an of-

fice, Matt Montgomery was given to such earnest pronounce-
ments, even at social gatherings; his voice pulsed with
excitement and indignation, as if he were declaiming from a
dais.

Terence asked, with a melancholy smile, "What, then,
of justice?"

Matt Montgomery laughed, and let a heavy hand fall on
Terence's shoulder. Evidently he did not consider Terence's
question serious enough to answer.

They were at the Classens'. Unless it was the Hendries'.
Or, indeed, the Montgomerys'. Among their friends, in any
case. Terence knew that they were not in their own house
because they'd driven here, in his car.

He sipped at his vodka martini. How strange, his hand
did *not* shake.

Earlier, as Matt had ambled off whistling to bring them
their drinks, Phyllis had whispered, "What is this—vodka
martinis, suddenly? Why don't you have wine, like you used
to?"

Terence said, annoyed, "Vodka martinis have always
been my drink."

Phyllis stared at him; then cuffed him lightly on the
sleeve, as if he'd blundered at making a joke. "Oh, Terry—
really!"

It was the evening of June 17, a full year since Terence
had first glimpsed Ava-Rose Renfrew; a full year since the
pink summons had brought him to the Mercer County Courthouse in Trenton. He took a large mouthful of his drink,
hoping to forget *yearning to be with her tonight, and not where
he was, amid strangers.*

One of the women called out playfully, "Phyl, Terry is
so *sweet*. Such an *intellectual*."

Phyllis, who was looking very striking tonight, in a white
cotton dress that showed her shapely figure to advantage,
smiled as if mysteriously. "No need to tell *me*!" she laughed.

When they were alone together, Phyllis rarely laughed.

Terence felt her brooding, assessing eyes upon him, and thought, She knows.

And yet—what could she know?

Matt Montgomery and the others had been talking of the disappearance, in May, of the Schriebers' son Eddy, Jr. Since the boy had vanished several weeks ago, the *Queenston Chronicle*, a weekly, had devoted columns of print to the story, though there had been no witnesses to any sort of struggle, nor had local police any leads—they were "continuing their investigation." The consensus seemed to be that Eddy Jr., though of a prominent local family, had been involved in drug dealing for the past two years; he was said to have been part of a ring operating out of Philadelphia. Anonymous sources were quoted in the *Chronicle*—"Studs was mixed up with some real tough guys, not like around here," a senior at Queenston Day School had said. A former girl of his claimed, "Studs used to tell us, *he* wasn't afraid to die." Photographs of the missing boy printed in the *Chronicle* were not recent, Terence had noted, no doubt because the parents could not bear to see their son, in the community newspaper, in his punk-style phase, with spiky hair, ear studs, and nose ring. Instead, "Edward Schrieber, Jr." looked to have been a narrow-headed boy with eyes set so close together as to appear mildly crossed, a receding chin, and a boyish, smirking smile. His age might have been anywhere from fifteen to nineteen.

In fact, Studs Schrieber was nineteen years old—or had been, while living.

"Edward Schrieber, Jr." had been reported missing to Queenston police by his parents, when he'd failed to come home after an eighteen-hour absence. His car, a new-model Camaro, was found parked, and locked, at the end of a cul-de-sac in Fox Haven Estates, a residential community two miles north of Queenston; no one in the neighborhood knew him, or would admit to knowing him (though there were several upper-form Queenston Day students in Fox Haven

Estates); residents of the road on which the car had been found insisted they'd seen and heard nothing out of the ordinary that night. According to the *Chronicle*, police believed that the car had been abandoned there after the boy had been taken away.

Several ounces of cocaine had been found in the Camaro's glove compartment, wrapped in plastic, inside a greasy take-out bag from Beno's Pizzeria.

"Poor Doris and Eddy!—what a nightmare for *them*."

"Can you imagine? A son not simply missing, but suspected of being a drug dealer? The victim of a 'hit'?"

"I shouldn't say this, but—have any of you seen the kid?" Mickey Classen spoke in a lowered voice. He was a courteous bespectacled man rather like Terence Greene in appearance and manner, a well-to-do investment banker given to long pensive silences and sudden thoughtful, and jarring, remarks. " 'Studs' used to be a friend of our son David's, and, God, if anyone ever deserved to be shot and dumped, or whatever—!"

There followed then a wave of protestations, mainly from the women. Even Phyllis, who had been listening to the conversation with a strained expression, said, shocked, "Oh, Mickey—that's a terrible thing to say. The boy is *human*, after all."

" 'Is'?—or *'was'*?"

Terence took another swallow of his drink, which was tasting very cold.

His dream. His hideous dream. He hadn't had it since the night of Studs Schrieber's disappearance and he'd tried not to think of it since.

Ava-Rose Renfrew seemed to believe in dreams as "divinations," and so Terence had told her of his dream of killing a man (Terence had not wanted to identify the victim as a boy) who subsequently turned out to have disappeared *that very night.* "Was this person known to you?" Ava-Rose had asked, with a frowning professional air that Terence found touching, "—or unknown?" "Unknown," Terence said without hesitation. "Then," said Ava-Rose, settling the matter, "— he is only a *sign*, not an *entity*. Erase him from your memory."

Police officers had questioned a number of Queenston Day students, and teachers at the school had asked students to volunteer any information they might have; but, so far as Terence and Phyllis knew, Kim had not been any more involved than most of her friends. When news of the boy's disappearance first broke, Phyllis had said to Terence, alarmed, "Terry, it's him—'Studs'—do you remember? That boy who—" Terence broke in, evenly, "But Kim hasn't seen him, has she, in months?"

For days afterward, Terence observed his elder daughter with anxious eyes, but dared not speak to her of the missing boy. (Phyllis assured him, *she* had. There was "nothing to report.") Kim appeared excited, distracted, nervous; and then again subdued, preoccupied, and oddly sleepy. Her appetite, always finicky, grew more finicky still; she no longer wore earrings in her pierced ears; if the telephone rang, she did not rush to answer it. Then, at dinner one night, Cindy said, a bit crudely, "That Studs Schrieber, wow!—things they're saying about him, at school." She looked intently at Kim, who was not looking at her, and said, with a slight sneer, "Your old boyfriend, Kim. *Wow*."

Kim said, with mechanical quickness, licking her pale lips, "I never see Studs now. Not for a long time."

Cindy continued to peer at her sister, shaking her head as if in wonderment. Of course, she was being provoking— "*Wow.*"

"Cindy," said Phyllis sharply, "—that's enough."

But Kim remained subdued, her thoughts clearly elsewhere. She shifted her gaze about, not quite meeting anyone's eye, and said, so softly Terence had to lean forward to hear, "Not for a long time."

How lovely the girl was, even with shadowy dents beneath her eyes, and something swollen and pouty about her mouth! Terence felt his heart swell with love of her, and a fierce desire to protect her. Even from himself.

Yes, he must move out of the house at 7 Juniper Way. He belonged elsewhere now.

If they would have him elsewhere.

Cocktail conversation had meandered from "Eddy Jr." to more general subjects of crime. Those who had suffered the indignity of being crime victims—in each case, houses had been burglarized, and insurance companies had paid—proffered their stories. Hedy Montgomery told a breathless tale of having nearly been "accosted" in a parking garage in town—"I could see this little Hispanic man out of the corner of my eye, sort of sideways-skedaddling toward me! But someone else came along, in fact it was Marvin Bruns, so I was *saved.*" Phyllis startled Terence, who had not been following the thread of talk very closely, by telling their friends of how he'd been attacked and robbed in Florida, years ago on their honeymoon—"I never saw Terry looking so *fierce*! D'you know that expression, 'blood in his eye,' well I'm not exaggerating, that's just what he *had*. I drove him fast as I could to an emergency room, but I swear, he was so angry, I was afraid of *him.*"

Everyone laughed. Terence, who knew that the men were laughing, not at the evoked spectacle of Terence Greene in a fury, but Phyllis Greene's improbable memory of this fury, joined in the laughter as convincingly as he could.

Hettie's boy. Seeking justice, or is it revenge?

Erase him from your memory and so Terence did, or tried to do.

He waited for police to come by 7 Juniper Way to ask questions of him, yet no one came. They had not the imagination, evidently, to see how Timberlane Estates was contiguous with Fox Haven Estates, however self-contained each of the "planned residential communities" was. They had not the imagination to see that someone other than drug dealers might have wished to exact vengeance upon a vicious creature preying upon his daughter.

Still, as the days rapidly fell away, and Terence's dream faded, he became ever more convinced that it had been a dream, and not something else.

Hadn't he fallen asleep at his desk, and awakened at his desk?—in virtually the same position?

Hadn't Kim adamantly denied all knowledge of Studs Schrieber? Could Terence doubt his own daughter's word?

There was the mystery of the old rolled-up carpet from the family room, gone from behind the basement stairs. Maybe Phyllis had had the trash men haul it away? Terence thought this possible, plausible. But he had not wished to ask her.

He was not suspicious of Ava-Rose but the summer heat weighed upon his spirit, nor was he jealous of her because *Jealousy is the heart's first death* but he did not always believe those damned liars, Tamar or Holly Mae Loomis, when, on the telephone, they claimed not to know where Ava-Rose was or when she might be expected in. "Well, please ask her to call me when she can, will you?" Terence tried to keep his voice light, neither demanding nor pleading.

How long ago it now seemed, when Ava-Rose would return Terence's calls promptly, asking for him, at the Foundation, under childlike play-names—"Magnolia Pitts," "Rose-of-Sharon Wren," "Petunia Holly-Oak." Now, days passed and she was too busy to call at all.

One day, Terence showed up unexpected at the Chimney Point Shopping Center. He was wearing tinted glasses, the sepia-glittering urban-summer air so stung his eyes. As he entered Tamar's Bazaar & Emporium, the bell above the door clanged as if in alarm. Tamar, waiting on a customer, stared at Terence, blinking as if she did not quite trust her eyes. Dr. Greene? With no warning? He ignored her, and strode over to The Craft of Beauty, which was unattended—

no Ava-Rose Renfrew behind the counter. The merchandise looked less distinctive than it had the first time Terence had seen it, but the filmy, brightly dyed fabrics and the exotic jewelry excited his eye. A charmingly inexpert hand-lettered sign read YOUR FORTUNE TOLD!

But where was the fortune-teller?

When her customer left, Tamar came quickly over, to where Terence stood thoughtfully stroking and fingering a transparent black muslin dress or smock hanging from a rack. Unasked, Tamar said, "She isn't here, and I don't know when to expect her. Whyn't you try her home?" Terence glanced smilingly at the squat young woman in the absurd royal-blue sari and saw that she was nervous. He said, "Who is her lover now? Do they drive around in my Corvette?" His words, casually expressed, yet hung harshly in the air, like crude incense.

Tamar drew in her breath sharply. "Dr. Greene!"—as if chiding.

"He's a black man, is he?—a sheriff's deputy?"

Tamar, staring, did not reply. She was looking at something in Terence Greene's face he might not have known was there.

"Or one of the visitors up from West Virginia? I haven't met them yet, I haven't been invited to meet them yet, but I know they're there, at the house." Terence paused. He had been about to say, "at the house I help pay for," but that would have sounded too raw, self-pitying. *After all a man must have his pride.*

Tamar said in her flat, nasal, mean-sounding New Jersey accent, "Ava-Rose's private life is her own, mister. She goes her own way, you better believe it, and I go mine." There was a smug tone to this remark that grated against Terence's nerves.

Terence said, "Tell me, please: Was T. W. Binder Ava-Rose's lover?"

Tamar's small eyes narrowed. "Who?"

"You know perfectly well who T. W. Binder was. The

man who was tried for aggravated assault against Ava-Rose, and who was found guilty and sentenced to prison." Terence paused. He saw that crafty Tamar was planning to lie. "The man who died in prison."

"Died? Gee, when was that?" The young woman's feigned incredulity was an insult to Terence's intelligence.

"Don't you know when?"

Tamar shrugged, and giggled, hugging her hefty breasts in the thin silk costume; her midriff, so inappropriately bare, rippled in thin rolls of flesh pale as a chicken's skin. The red bead in her left nostril glinted, and her oversized gold earrings flashed as if with mirth. Terence had a sudden impulse to close his hands about her throat, so that she would take him seriously.

Fortunately, he made no threatening move, for Tamar surprised him by saying, negligently, "Well, yeah, I guess I heard T.W. did die—sort of. Last fall. Around Labor Day. Maybe it *was* Labor Day. I remember because—"

Labor Day? Hadn't Ava-Rose told Terence that T. W. Binder had died around New Year's?

" 'Because'—?"

"Ava-Rose had just got back from vacation, and she wanted to go visit T.W. at Rahway, her and me, she was feeling sorry for the poor guy I guess—Ava-Rose always feels sorry for them," Tamar laughed, "but that doesn't help *them,* much—then all of a sudden she tells me it's too late, T.W. is dead. Or something."

Terence swallowed. "What do you mean, 'or something'?"

Tamar shrugged again. It was unclear to Terence whether the mannish little woman meant to be flirtatious, or hostile. Her eyes gleamed as if with mischief. "Well, 'Dr. Greene,' it is stated in the *Guhyasamājantra,* 'To see appearance as an apparition, is to apprehend the apparitional body; to see apparition as 'open' (nothing in itself), is to realize The Radiant Light.' "

" 'The Radiant Light'—?"

Tamar laughed. "You sound like Darling the Parrot, 'Dr. Greene'! The Radiant Light is the core of all Being. It *is* Being. And we are but passing apparitions—'hungry ghosts.' "

"So, T. W. Binder did not die, exactly, but—?"

"Well, I guess you'd say his body died, but his inner Being passed on to another state. He—"

"Not another state as in 'New York' or 'Arizona' or 'West Virginia,' but another state of 'Being'?"

Terence's irony was lost on Tamar, who replied, thoughtfully, as if this were an abstruse epistemological problem to which she had given some time, "T.W.'s *body* was buried in the State of New Jersey, yeah! but his *Radiant Being* was helped on to another plane."

"But not a plane as in 'TWA' or 'USAir'—?"

Now Tamar did catch Terence's irony, and cut her eyes at him. She said, flatly, "No."

"And who 'helped' T.W. onto this new, radiant plane?"

Tamar shook her head. The scimitar-earrings jangled. "How the fuck would I know, mister?"

"A fellow inmate at Rahway? Somebody doing a favor for somebody else?"

Tamar shrugged. As if in caution, she took a small step backward.

"You knew Eldrick Gill, too, didn't you? Was he another lover of Ava-Rose's?"

Tamar said impatiently, "Look, mister: I told you, the woman's private life is her own. She came along one day, her and some fat bald guy asking would I rent her a little space in my shop for The Craft of Beauty, so I said yes. Her things are pretty nice, she makes them all herself, it's fine with me. But our relationship is mainly business. I'm sure as hell getting fed up with you guys coming in here all the time looking for her!"

Terence winced. "What guys?"

"She attracts you like a goddam *maggot*."

"Magnet, you mean."

"Magnet, you mean." Tamar laughed derisively. "Whatever you say, you're the professor, you're the big deal. From Queenston, eh!"

Terence winced again. The impulse to close his hands around the woman's throat, to erase that look of smug hostility from her face, rose in him like an urge to cough or sneeze; but he managed to speak in his usual affable voice, as if dealing with one or another obstreperous associate at the Foundation. "Tamar, you must have known Eldrick Gill? He was here one day last September. One day, at least. For the last time. Remember? You and Ava-Rose left the store, and he approached Ava-Rose—and you walked away, fast." Terence could see from the expression in the woman's bulldog face that she had known Gill, but that she would not admit it. "Was he a lover of Ava-Rose's, too?"

Tamar glanced over her shoulder uneasily. How empty the store must have seemed to her! The sign reading OPEN caught her eye, hanging on the door; at this time of day, it should have read CLOSED, which would mean that, to the outside, it read OPEN. But the significance of this reversal, if it contained any, was not immediately clear to her. She said, "I can't talk much longer, I'm busy, mister. You want to know about Ava-Rose Renfrew's private life, ask *her*."

She would have turned contemptuously away, but Terence seized her wrist. "Please, I'd just like to know: Was Eldrick Gill a lover of Ava-Rose's, too?"

Tamar pulled at her wrist, too startled to be frightened. "I said, ask *her*."

"Did you know—did she tell you—that Eldrick Gill is dead, too?"

Tamar blinked. The tiny red bead in her nostril looked like a tiny bead of blood. "Nah, Dickie's in New Mexico, they said. "He's—"

"Who said?"

"—relocated, doing business down there. Who said he's dead?"

Terence spoke with careful irony. "His inner Being

passed on to another plane, but his body disappeared. Back in September. A few days after T.W. passed on, too."

"Nah—I never heard *that*."

Tamar shook her head stubbornly, tugging at her wrist. Terence gripped her tight. "This 'Dickie'—who was he to you, and to Ava-Rose?"

"Nobody."

"What kind of business was he in?"

"I don't *know*."

"You really don't know that he's dead?"

Tamar shivered. Terence was standing very close to her, as in a clumsy dance; he could smell a scent as of musky perfume and perspiration lifting from her.

Tamar was a strong, wiry little woman, but she could not pull free from Terence's grip so long as he wished to hold her. She whispered, more angry than frightened, "Mister, let go! You got no right to touch *me*."

Terence hesitated. He did not want her to break free from him, to pull an alarm, or scream for help; but he did not want to hurt her—truly, he did not.

I must never kill again. Never.

Relenting, Terence could not resist a final question. "Tell me, at least—who was Ezra Wineapple?"

Now Tamar wrenched free of Terence, stumbling back against a counter. Defiantly she said, "Some old fool mad to marry Ava-Rose, who wound up in the river instead."

The precise date of T. W. Binder's death, Terence Greene learned, by way of several telephone calls to Rahway State Prison, was September 9 of the previous year; Eldrick Gill had died his secret death, and his body sunk in the Delaware River, on September 14.

T. W. Binder's murderer or murderers, presumably prison inmates, remained unidentified—he'd been found dead in a storage room of a kitchen, stabbed to the heart. Terence would have liked to ask if a man named Eldrick Gill had visited anyone at Rahway shortly before the murder, but did not dare.

What had Cap'n-Uncle Riff said—"A sucker is born every minute, and what are *you* going to do about it?"

"Ava-Rose ain't here, Dr. Greene, but, sure, stop by, y'know you're welcome any ol' time!"—Holly Mae Loomis's telephone voice boomed in Terence's ear.

So, after Tamar's Bazaar & Emporium, Terence drove to 33 Holyoak. Knowing of course that really he was *not* welcome.

He'd become, without his knowing it, a sort of tolerated old uncle, a kindly presence—"Dr. Greene."

The Renfrews' visitors had stayed so long, it seemed to Terence, that they had moved permanently into the house. At the same time, near as he could figure out from Ava-Rose's vague explanation, one of the twins had gone to live permanently with relatives in another part of the state. "Dara or Dana?" Terence had asked, concerned, a bit hurt, for he'd grown sentimentally fond of the girls and had assumed they were fond of him; and Ava-Rose mystified him by saying, with a pouty little frown, "Oh, they're so grown up now, they hate 'the twin thing'—as they call it. The girl you'll see, next time you come visit, is 'Donna.' "

"But—which girl is it? And won't I be seeing the other again?" Terence asked.

Ava-Rose said wistfully, "I'm sure you will, someday, Terence. Not that you'd recognize her, anyway—children grow up so quickly, in America!"

When Terence arrived, just before sunset, at 33 Holyoak, the girl, presumably Donna, was just leaving, climbing with a flash of bare legs into a gleaming black Sting Ray idling at the curb. Behind the wheel of the raffish sports car was a swarthy-skinned man in his thirties, with a thin black moustache and eyes hidden by mirror sunglasses; Terence despised him on sight, the more because he hadn't troubled to get out of his car to greet pretty Donna and open the passenger's door for her. How could the Renfrews allow a child that age to go out with a man so much older! (Though, in a tight-fitting summer-knit aqua shift that showed a good deal of her thighs, and her mouth so strikingly red, Donna did not much resemble a child.) Seeing Terence, the girl waved, and called out, laughing, what sounded like, "H'lo Dr. Applegreen!" Terence waved back, a bit frantically, "Donna?—just a—"

The Sting Ray moved off with a squealing protest of tires, gathering speed even as Terence stared after it. The air stank of exhaust.

Terence, standing in the street, stood for a moment, helpless.

'Donna'!—and now there is neither 'Dara,' nor 'Dana,' for me.

Terence saw that Ava-Rose's yellow Corvette was parked in the Renfrews' driveway. Which meant that, since she was out, she was out in someone else's car.

Jealousy is the heart's first death.

There were two unfamiliar cars in the driveway, with West Virginia license plates, the more battered with a HONK IF YOU LOVE JESUS! sticker on its rust-speckled rear bumper. Over in the tall grass, abandoned, was the old, unpainted van formerly used by Cap'n-Uncle Riff for his secondhand goods business. (Cap'n-Uncle was now the proud owner of a new model Ford van, which Ava-Rose had financed for him, ostensibly with her savings and credit, but in fact through Terence's generosity. Though somewhat pressed for money lately, Terence had thought it shameful that a man of Cap'n-Uncle's age and distinction should be forced to drive so rundown a vehicle.)

It was a soft, melancholy evening. Seeing the Renfrews' house, and the wild garden in the front, Terence felt, as always, that peculiar tug of emotion. *As if, somehow, many years ago, he too had lived here, among the Renfrews.*

Though Terence had spent a good deal of money on

the house since the previous September (the crumbling chimney had been shored up, the most damaged of the slates on the roof repaired, wooden trim repainted), it was hard to see much difference. The house was unmistakably ramshackle, and *old*. Straggly vines grew everywhere, even across windowpanes; the picket fence was about to collapse; the sagging veranda was more cluttered than ever with junk which, months ago, in the first flush of his romance with Ava-Rose, Terence himself had offered to clear away. (Ava-Rose had thanked him politely, but declined the offer.) And the garden was lushly overgrown—a colorful confusion of roses amid scrubby hollyhocks, briar-bushes, giant thistles, and every variety of weed. A gray wooden flamingo lay flat on the ground as if it had been shot down.

Of course, now the twins were gone, no one made the silly, charming ornaments any longer. An unsold stack lay rotting on the veranda.

As Terence approached the house, Buster, dozing in the driveway, looked up blinking. His tail thumped several times in a desultory manner as he sniffed, recognized Terence, and yawned.

Holly Mae Loomis, hoeing in the garden in her raggedy straw hat and coveralls, cried out, "Yoo-hoo, Dr. Greene! Over here! My lord, you did get here *fast.*" She seemed both amused and uncharacteristically edgy. "Like I told you, though—Ava-Rose ain't here, and I don't know when she'll be back."

Terence saw to his discomfort that Holly Mae was not alone: a younger woman, who resembled her, in features, skin tone, and even in her dyed coppery hair, was standing with crossed arms, sipping from a can of Rolling Rock beer. Introduced to Terence as "Lily Pancoke from Sheenville, West Virginia," the woman shot out her hand to shake Terence's, and grinned happily, showing an expanse of gum. "Real nice to meet *you*, Doctor." From the way the woman looked at Terence, he understood that she had been told tales of him.

Ava-Rose's besotted lover, a married man.

Ava-Rose's suitor who had killed, at least once, for her.

Or maybe she knew nothing of him—she was smiling at him in such a friendly, frank way, as if he were a neighbor who'd just ambled over to say hello.

Holly Mae was hoeing vigorously, her ruddy face gleaming with perspiration. Amid the festooning weeds and tall grasses there were cultivated beds of roses; their beauty leapt at the eye, like pain. Terence stared, and his vision misted over. He wanted only Ava-Rose, and Ava-Rose was not here —or was she? (Inside the house, through the opened windows, came the sound of a dog's high-pitched barking: But which dog was this?) It seemed to him that Holly Mae was somewhat stiff with him lately; on the phone, and in person. The lawsuit against the Trenton Transit Company was still pending after many delays, but lately, according to the team of lawyers, hopes for a multimillion-dollar settlement were "less certain." (For one thing, the treasury of the City of Trenton was nearly bankrupt.) It seemed to Terence unfair that Holly Mae should blame *him.*

Lily Pancoke asked pertly would Terence like a beer?— but Terence said no thank you, he would have to be leaving. Still, he did not leave. Lily Pancoke asked where he was from, he sure didn't sound like he was from Trenton, but Terence, distracted, did not hear. He was wondering if, under a pretext of using the bathroom—after all, he had paid to have that very bathroom improved—he might prowl about the house, maybe even slip upstairs and check out Ava-Rose's bedroom, to determine if Ava-Rose really was gone. (But what if, in her bedroom, he discovered her with another man— what then?)

"I'm not armed," he said, smiling, with a gesture as of turning his pockets inside-out, "—I'm not to be considered dangerous."

Lily Pancoke laughed heartily, not that Terence's joke was amusing, if indeed it was a joke. She was a busty woman of about forty-five with scrubbed-looking cheeks and close-set warm eyes. Her fingernails were long and curved and painted purplish-red. "Nah," she said, "—not *you*. A jury'd never convict."

Holly Mae did not join in her friend's, or relative's, good-natured banter with Terence Greene. She'd jammed her straw hat down farther on her head, and her breath was audible as she hoed, stooped to pull out weeds, or, cursing, picked insects off her roses. She cleared her throat and said again, "Huh!—like I said, Ava-Rose ain't here, and didn't say when she'd be back." She paused. Terence made no reply. "Could be," she added cautiously, "she won't be back till tomorrow."

Terence gave no sign of the emotion he felt at hearing this statement but continued to gaze at the roses, smiling, admiring, as if his visit were after all neighborly. He said, "Holly Mae, your roses are more beautiful than ever." A cheerful comment, but it came out sounding like a sob.

He reached out to touch a creamy-pink multifoliate rose, of the kind, so like a watercolor in its shading, he'd admired the previous summer. Possibly the blooms on the roses generally were less profuse than he remembered, and the bushes scrawnier, and—what was this?—an iridescent-glittering insect scuttled through his fingers; but these roses *were* beautiful, each subtly differing from the others, and giving off a faint, sweet scent. Terence stared, blinking moisture out of his eyes. What was the name of the hybrid tea-rose?— he knew, but could not remember.

Holly Mae said gruffly, "Pretty, yes, but, lord, are they *work*! Me with my bad back, and maybe whiplash-injury, an old woman toiling away for beauty, eh? And look here"— stooping with surprising dexterity to snatch up the insect, and squash it expertly between her fingers—"these damn ol' Jap'nese beetles!"

Lily Pancoke, eager to join in, said, with a smile at Terence, "*We're* so local, down in Sheenville, we don't even have any Jap'nese beetles."

There was a sudden hysterical yapping, and out through

the screened front door came a tiny henna-colored dog, a Pomeranian, with bedraggled red ribbons on his collar—literally through the screen, tearing a small rent into a hole. The door flew open, and a lanky bare-chested youth rushed after the dog, lunging to seize it, but missing, as the frantic little creature scrambled from the veranda and hit the ground already running on its stubby legs. The boy too leapt off the veranda, pursuing the dog around the garden, stumbling and swearing. He cried, with an angry laugh, "Fuck!" as the dog rushed through his legs, and would have fled to the street, except Buster, aroused and barking excitedly, was blocking its path. Another time the little creature reversed its direction, panting and yipping, and both the boy and Buster ran after it. Lily Pancoke shrieked with laughter—"Go, Randy Lee! Get 'im! Near-about your size, ain't he!"

Holly Mae had dropped her hoe in alarm, and was tugging the brim of her straw hat down as if to hide her head. "Jesus! Don't let that little bugger escape!"

At last the Pomeranian caught itself, flailing, in a climber rose bush, and the boy snatched it up in his arms in triumph—"Gotcha!" As soon as the dog realized it was pinned in the boy's ropy-muscled arms, it ceased struggling; the boy chortled, "Ain't you the one, Pip, eh!—fastest little fucker I ever seen!" The dog began to lick at the boy's face and the boy tried to lean his head away.

Lily Pancoke was choking with laughter, but Holly Mae, pressing a hand against her bosom, seemed to see nothing funny. She said, "Randy Lee, take Pip back inside, and lock him up somewhere. He gets away, you know Chick's gonna tear up the house."

"Nah, Auntie, he's okay now. He ain't going anywhere, are you, baby?" The boy held the dog against his pale, narrow chest with such tenderness, he might have been a young father holding his own infant.

Holly Mae introduced Terence to "Randy Lee Turcoe also of Sheenville, West Virginia"—a "kissing-cousin" of Ava-

Rose's and Chick's up in Trenton for the summer. Terence and Randy Lee mumbled greetings, each shyly, and made no effort to shake hands; the boy self-conscious in the presence of a stranger in a suit and tie, and Terence self-conscious, in fact uneasy, in the presence of a youth of his own gender so beautiful, and so seemingly careless in his beauty, his instinct was to look away.

Randy Lee Turcoe might have been anywhere from six-teen to twenty-six years old. Barefoot, he was an inch or so taller than Terence; his body was both slender and muscled, and oddly pale; there were curly dark hairs on his forearms, but his chest was nearly hairless, and his nipples were rosy-pink. Though he talked and laughed and carried himself without the slightest pretension, or awareness of his distinc-tive looks, his face reminded Terence of certain Renaissance paintings Terence had neither seen nor thought of in years —above all, the exotic, epicene St. John the Baptist of Leo-nardo da Vinci.

Don't look, maybe it's wiser. Just don't.

Yet it was difficult not to stare at Randy Lee, who, scarcely minding the Pomeranian's frantic licking of his face, seemed the most good-hearted of people. Like Leonardo's saint, Randy Lee had a perfect oval face, alabaster-smooth skin, luminous smoky eyes, and fine, thickly crimped hair to his shoulders; unlike the saint, he had tobacco-stained teeth with a pronounced gap between the two front teeth, and, on his right earlobe, one of those cruel-looking clamp earrings, gleaming gold. His low-slung raggedy jeans were snug across his small, muscled stomach and the fly front was missing a button. As he talked, and the women, especially Lily Pancoke, teased him, he wriggled his bare, bony-knuckled toes in the dirt.

Terence gathered from the chatter that the henna-colored Pomeranian Pip was the most recent of Chick's lost-pet discoveries—his predecessor having been Marcellus the Mystery Siamese. (Marcellus had been happily reunited with his desperate owner, a wealthy elderly woman eager to pay a $500 reward, no questions asked, some time ago.) He did not want to speculate how Chick acquired these pedigreed much-beloved creatures; as he had not wanted to think, virtually from the start, of much that went on at 33 Holyoak.

Nor of Terence Greene himself, lovesick as little Pip in his captor's arms, kissing his captor's face.

Terence saw that it was time to leave. He would not speak with Ava-Rose, and it was time to leave. They were hiding her from him and it was time to leave and he had nowhere to go. Yes, but he would go; he wouldn't stay. Even if Holly Mae relented, and begged him to stay for supper, he wouldn't, now. "Very nice to meet you, Lily, and—is it Randy Lee? Very nice." He rattled his car keys, which was a bright, expectant sound, and backed off, smiling, as Holly Mae Loomis and Lily Pancoke and smoky-eyed Randy Lee Turcoe watched him, and even Buster, lying now panting in the weedy zinnias, watched him, as if to see what he would do. But he too was good-natured as any Renfrew, resigned in defeat but cheerful enough to break into a whistle—except, impulsively, as if the thought only now entered his head, he said to Randy Lee, "*You* don't know where she is, do you?—your cousin Ava-Rose?" and the boy grinned without hesitation, and said, "Yessir Doctor, sure do—Ava's at that weird ol' church of hers, on Ed'son Street they call it, that ain't even any *Christian church* I guess!" He spoke with childlike vehemence, as if expecting Terence to share in his disapproval.

"Church?—oh, yes."

Terence's heart lurched in sickish triumph, but he managed to retain his smile, his easy, affable smile, calling back, "Why thank you, Randy Lee—that's kind of you. G'bye!" not letting on how he'd seen Holly Mae's ruddy face stiffen in alarm; and even Lily Pancoke, who could know very little of Terence Greene's history, winced.

As Terence drove off, he saw the three of them standing in the junglelike garden, staring after him. And Buster, in the driveway, stumpy tail wagging, but slowing, stared after him, too.

Terence located the church on Edison Street near the busy intersection with Eleventh, at the periphery of Trenton's seedy inner city. What a disappointment! He hadn't known quite what to expect, but, judging from Ava-Rose's remarks, he hadn't expected a "church" of such a kind, in such a neighborhood.

It was a low, squat, buff-brick building, narrow but long, with opaque glass bricks for its single front window, as in taverns of a certain era—in fact, the building looked unmistakably as if it had had a small bowling alley at one time. The brick was weatherworn and stained, and above the front entrance was a luridly bright marquee with red letters:

THE FIRST CHURCH OF THE HOLY APOCALYPSE,
TRENTON, N.J., USA
"PLANET EARTH"

Terence parked across the street from the church *wondering what he would do: what would be done to him.*

It seemed to him a very long time since he'd been in the house at 7 Juniper Way but in fact he'd been there that morning; he'd risen as usual, tasting the strangeness of his existence yet no longer questioning it. He and a woman named Phyllis Winston were the adults of the household, Kim and Cindy were the resident children, *their* children; they lived in such intimacy, what need was there to know one another? As he was leaving the house not long ago Terence happened to overhear Phyllis on the telephone, her voice lowered, as if with emotion, and he had not wanted to pause to listen but he'd done so, hearing, he thought, her voice catch as if she were sobbing, or trying to suppress a sob; he stood uncertain, not knowing what to do, or whether to do anything. *I must protect her,* he thought, *if*— But then, after a moment, Phyllis burst into laughter, and so he felt released: indeed, shoved out the door.

Ava-Rose, don't refuse me!

Ava-Rose, I have only you.

On the commuter train to New York that morning, Terence, taking his usual seat (beside Ted Bawden, an investment lawyer on Wall Street), had glanced about the car, smiling, seeing his fellow passengers, men, women, some of them known to him by name and most of them by appearance, and he'd thought, stunned by the recognition, *There are many of us, now.*

It was not an upsetting thought, still less was it a satisfying one. Rather, it was neutral, like a flash of lightning.

Only when Terence was in Ava-Rose's presence, or, as now, in pursuit of the young woman, was he fully awake, alive.

Alert.

"—but unarmed."

He sat in the Oldsmobile, shivering; he'd been sweating profusely, and the air conditioning was cold. He did not think of Holly Mae and the others, certainly he did not think of Tamar, it did no good to ponder others' motives for wishing to deceive him; for failing to wish him, as he'd always wished them, well.

Minutes passed, and it was 8:30 P.M., and the door of the Church of the Holy Apocalypse remained closed. Terence wondered what sort of "service" was in session. Several times he'd hinted that he would like to accompany Ava-Rose to church, but she'd been evasive; prettily, she'd deflected Terence's intention by teasing him—"Why, Ter-ence, you know you are an 'agnostic,' as you call yourself. A 'born agnostic,' isn't that your boast?"

(The word "boast" had been a bit of a taunt. Like the way Ava-Rose sometimes pinched Terence, in the soft flesh at his waist.)

He waited. He had no plan, but to wait. When he saw her, if he saw her, he would know what to do.

Staring mesmerized at the fresh-painted green door of

the building that had been a bowling alley and was now a church, a place of a distinctly American worship with a marquee boldly lit as that of X-RATED ADULT FILMS in the next block. *How has it come to this, Ter-ence? Poor old fella.* He wondered, What *is* religion? Why do men and women believe? Why do they want so passionately to believe? Ava-Rose's lovely eyes took on an opaque, dreamy look when she spoke of her faith—"All my life I have believed. In my heart. But it wasn't till three years ago when a friend took me to the Church of the Holy Apocalypse, and, oh my! my heart was turned *inside out.*" Terence had said, wryly, "It sounds like an evisceration." Ava-Rose had ignored this (perhaps she didn't know what "evisceration" meant?) and said, with an air of childlike conviction, "We have faith that, after the Apocalypse, divine justice will prevail. If there is no justice now, there will be, then. 'Only have faith, and do not be afraid, and the unspeakable shall be spoken.' "

Terence had asked when the Apocalypse might be, maybe he'd better prepare for it, and again Ava-Rose ignored his tone, and said, with a coldly dazzling smile, "Our Reverend Smithy Crystal says nobody knows, except for sure it's sometime between now and midnight of December 31, 1999."

Terence shivered now, remembering her certitude.

Years ago, as a child in Shaheen, New York, Terence had sometimes been taken by his Aunt Megan to a Methodist church in the country, he and his cousin Denton, if Denton didn't rebel. Once every six weeks, approximately—when the "spirit" moved Megan and the "dread of the Lord" was in her bones. (Aunt Megan's moods were unpredictable, except as they related to her husband's moods, which had to do with his drinking.) "If you don't anger God, He will not probably notice you," Megan told Terence, who might have been eleven years old at the time, "—at least, not to punish." Terence, who had seemed not to believe in God, much, even at that young age, thought this a pretty fair deal. But then his aunt went on to urge him to pray, on his knees, for his mother, and Terence became frightened, and asked, as if stubbornly, "But not my father?" and Aunt Megan's solid, stern face had tightened, and she'd said, "No. Not your father."

Terence recalled having tried to pray. Kneeling, and bowing his head, bumping his forehead against the back of the pew in front of him; clasping his fingers together in the way that others in the church did, as if something invisible was trying to wrench them apart. Yes, he'd tried to pray to God, but it was like speaking into his own cupped hands. The words were trapped and went nowhere.

It was nearly nine o'clock. Terence, still staring at the door of the Church of the Holy Apocalypse, had rolled down his car window, and a warm, sulphurous air eased in. That gritty urban smell of Trenton he'd halfway come to like *yes even to love.*

Then the church door opened, at last. People began to file out.

Quickly, Terence got out of his car, and crossed Edison Street; like a sleepwalker, or a drunk, so that car horns sounded, and a black man in a convertible yelled, "Hey man, you fucked? Get outta the street!" At the curb he stood uncertainly, self-consciously aware of himself as an intruder, an interloper: a tall, thin, rather pale, well-dressed if slightly disheveled man of youthful middle age, with intelligent features that looked as if they'd been pinched in a vise. His eyes snatched eagerly at the men and women who left the buff-brick building, some of whom glanced at him curiously—he was surprised to see how ordinary, how normal, they appeared. (And how did he appear to them? Unconsciously, he was standing with one hand thrust in the pocket of his seersucker coat, in the stance of a man gripping a pistol.) Surprising too that most of the church members were relatively young, in their thirties or twenties, Ava-Rose's age; most were whites, though here and there was a black face; there was an Asian-American couple, very American in their dress, in the cheaply stylish clothes bought at shopping malls. *And there was Ava-Rose Renfrew.*

Terence stood frozen on the sidewalk. The others, the strangers, melted around him, like ghosts. Ava-Rose, her arm through the arm of the handsome young light-skinned black man Terence had seen in the parking garage, had not seen him yet; she was laughing up into the young man's face with that sweetly playful expression with which, so many times, she'd looked up into Terence Greene's face.

The shock was such, Terence felt the breath knocked from him.

Even as he adjured himself—*Of course. I knew.*

Whatever the religious service of the Church of the Holy Apocalypse, it seemed to have left the worshippers, including Ava-Rose Renfrew and her sheriff's deputy friend, radiant, buoyant. Terence, standing on the pavement, alone, felt the keenness of loss, the insult of being excluded, the more sharply.

Amid that crowd of ordinary-seeming men and women, Ava-Rose certainly stood out. How did the others see *her*? She wore a turban of some silky orange fabric wound about her head, her crimped, fair-brown hair spilling out and cascading past her shoulders—Terence had never seen her in such apparel before. She wore countless necklaces, bracelets, and rings, as usual, and her delicate ears were nearly hidden by sunburst turquoise feather-earrings. How moistly crimson her lovely mouth, the lower lip fleshy as if swollen! A long, layered, uneven skirt of some gauzy red material drooped to her ankles; her feet in the narrow black ballerina slippers looked like a schoolgirl's.

Ava-Rose, how could you.

How, deceive me, who has killed for you, who has ransomed his life for you.

The black man, off-duty, out of uniform, yet had the air of a policeman; a certain swagger, a watchful manner. He wore khaki trousers, sharply creased, and a boxy checked poplin jacket of the kind made with wider than average shoulders, for men with "athletic builds." His eyes were both merrily sparkling and quick-darting—even before Terence stepped forward, he seemed to have noticed him.

How swiftly, then, things happened!—though it would require some time to absorb them.

In a hoarse, cracked voice he would scarcely have recognized in himself, Terence called, "Ava-Rose!" and Ava-Rose, seeing him, murmured, guiltily, "Oh—Dr. *Greene*," even as, in virtually the same instant, she gripped the sheriff's deputy's muscular arm and leaned forward to whisper something in his ear. At once, as if instinctively, the deputy moved to block Terence's way; Terence was advancing upon Ava-Rose, with a look of extreme urgency and hurt. "Ava-Rose?—please?—I must talk with you," Terence said, not so much pleading as demanding, and Ava-Rose cried, "Are you spying on me, is that it! I've told you *I will not be spied upon*."

"Just a minute, man, what's up, man, be cool, okay?"— the deputy expertly jammed the heel of his hand against Terence's chest, pushing him back.

But Terence too was belligerent, Terence too was strong, or so fueled by a sudden rush of adrenaline he appeared strong, pushing the deputy back, in his effort to get at Ava-Rose—to grasp her slender arm, to make her listen to him. By this time, a dozen people were watching, wide-eyed and expectant. Terence's face was slick with sweat and he was panting as if he'd run a great distance. "Ava-Rose, please, you know we must talk. You *know*—"

"Where is your pride, Ter-ence! I've told and *told* you! You're no better than the others, are you!"

Terence tried to push past the deputy, who was blocking his way.

"Ava-Rose, I—must talk to you—"

"Man, you better stay cool," the deputy said, "—don't be harassin this young lady, or somebody gonna get hurt!"

He was smiling, grinning: Ferocity and boyish elation shone in his face.

Terence said, as if reasonably, "Look, I only want to talk to Ava-Rose. Just for a——"

"Shit, man, the lady don't want to talk to *you*."

"I insist, God damn it——"

"Man, you watch that stuff! You gonna get hurt!"

Ava-Rose's face was flushed with alarm and indignation; she seemed about to burst into tears. She gathered up her skirt to dash back into the building, and Terence lunged around to grab her. Again the deputy struck Terence with the flat of his hand, hard enough to knock the breath out of him, but Terence insisted upon pressing forward, as if blinded, no longer knowing what he was doing, overcome with mute suicidal rage, and in that instant as in a film rapidly unwinding he saw how he would die—*the deputy would draw his Police Service revolver out of his coat, for of course, though off-duty, he was armed, as Terence was not; he would fire a single deafening shot, and Terence would fall down dead. And Terence Greene would lie on the filthy pavement outside the First Church of the Holy Apocalypse, Trenton, on Edison Street, blood gushing from a wound in his chest. Women would scream. Ava-Rose would scream—for of course she had some feeling for him, if only pity.*

"No."

Crouched, panting, Terence backed off. He held his hands out before him, fingers spread, to indicate that he was unarmed, and no threat; yet, still, in the grip of a furious momentum, the deputy drew his revolver, and, as women screamed, struck Terence several sharp, stunning, painful blows to the head and shoulders—"Get outa here, asshole! Go suck!"

Terence reeled, but did not fall. In a crouch, dripping blood from his nose, he ran across Edison, where again traffic lurched about him, and there was a sound of angry horns and screeching brakes.

He managed to get the heavy door of the Oldsmobile

open, and to collapse inside. At once, the cream-colored leather cover of the seat was slippery with blood. He could not see, there was blood in his eye, yet he jammed the key into the ignition, he managed to start the car, to drive away, not daring to look back suffused with shame and humiliation yet alive he drove away, he fled, he did not look back, he was free, he *was* alive.

He fled.

Vowing, *I will never see that treacherous woman again.*

Double Delight

*D*ays passed, and he did not call her. And she did not call him.

He rose early. He left the house early. Before taking the train to New York he swam in the pool of the Queenston Athletic Club, squinting against the cool, chlorine-smarting aqua water. His heart beat like an angry fist. His nose throbbed. If he had to blow his nose, after swimming, the watery mucus was likely to be threaded with blood.

He never thought of her who had betrayed him. *He thought of her constantly.* He had moments of fitful, surging strength. *He was wounded, sick, drowning.* He would never forgive her. *He would never forgive her.*

He rose early. He did not sleep. (In truth, Terence did sleep: But it was a thin, fleeting unsatisfying sleep, like strands of mist blown by a wayward wind, and he could not recall it afterward.) He did not dream.

He dreamt of her constantly but could not recall, afterward.

"Daddy?—why are you crying?"

Guiltily he glanced up, and there was his daughter Kim

staring at him. Her thin pretty face, large intelligent dark-lashed eyes—he had not looked at her in some time.

Quickly Daddy said, swiping at his face with his knuckles, "I'm not crying, honey—it's just my eyes." He laughed, to indicate that this remark, though true, was meant to be amusing.

What did he do? What did he do? A wild, reckless thing, he did: Precisely one month to the day after the disappearance of "Eddy Schrieber, Jr.," he telephoned Queenston Township police, to ask if there was any more news of him. He identified himself as a "friend of the family."

He was told his call would be transferred to one of the detectives assigned to the case, and so he was put on hold, and he waited. He'd begun to perspire. His head throbbed, and his nose. His eyes. Why did they water so frequently now, since the sheriff's deputy's blows? *Lucky to be alive, asshole. Lucky old fella.* He suspected that his call was being traced, or recorded, or both; but he did not hang up. He tried to remember the Schriebers' names—well, Edward was the father, of course; was the mother's name Diane? Doris? What would it mean to have "lost" a son? *Would he grieve for Aaron?—don't ask.*

The detective came on the line. Terence repeated his question. It was an innocent question, for he *was* a friend of the Schrieber family, all residents of affluent Queenston are friends, or friendly acquaintances, of one another. The detective did not sound friendly. He asked who was calling, and Terence mumbled a name, and the detective asked him to repeat it, and Terence repeated it—"Quincy Ryder."

Terence said quickly, "I knew the boy, and I know how his parents have been suffering, so I didn't want to ask them, but I wanted to know if—well, if there was any hopeful news, any 'leads' of any kind."

The detective paused. Terence was sure he heard a rapid clicking sound. But since the blows to his head, he often heard such sounds in his left ear and there wasn't the opportunity—in any case, he didn't feel he could risk it, even for a fraction of a second—to switch the receiver to his right ear, to ascertain whether the clicking sound was in his head, or in the connection

The suspicion of a drug-related abduction and killing of "Eddy Schrieber, Jr." had never been officially confirmed. It had been a rumor, in fact many rumors, as tributaries flow into a single solid stream, but, so far as Terence knew, it had never been officially confirmed. If the police were following "leads," they would not be likely to divulge them over the telephone, to a civilian. Wouldn't "Quincy Ryder" know that? Any adult male resident of Queenston is an intelligent man, *wouldn't he know that simple fact?*

"No, Mr. Ryder, sorry, there's not."

Terence had lost the thread of the conversation. " 'Not—'?"

"Not any more news. As of now."

"I see." Terence swallowed, not liking the taste in his mouth. He knew he should hang up, and quickly. But he lingered. (What *was* that clicking sound? Like the clatter of tiny tin millipedes' feet, a little army of them.) He said, apologetically, "I—guess your investigation can't proceed very well without a—body?" When the detective did not reply, he blundered on, stammering—"I guess you haven't found the boy's body, yet? I—" Terence felt as if he were on a high diving board, being urged toward the end, the edge. "—I mean I was thinking—all of us are hoping—Studs isn't dead, but—somewhere—*alive.*"

The detective said, "Yes, right, Mr. Ryder, that's right. Where did you say you live, in Queenston?"

"I didn't say I live 'in Queenston,' in fact I—I'm somewhere else."

Quickly, fumblingly, Terence hung up the receiver.

And walked quickly away from the pay phone booth in the Queenston train depot, and out onto the boarding platform, to mingle, tall and well-groomed and well-dressed as he was, and carrying a handsome Gucci attaché case, with some sixty or more men and women like himself.

"Quincy Ryder": Indeed, the former Poet Laureate of the United States *was* somewhere else.

In a cemetery in Charlottesville, Virginia, among numerous Ryders and blood kin.

The memorial service had been held in New York City, however, in the genteel-shabby headquarters of the Poetry Society of America on Gramercy Square. Terence Greene, though not a close friend of the deceased, had been invited to pay his public respects to him, along with a number of distinguished men and women of American letters. Most of the participants in the ceremony read poems of Ryder's, in addition to speaking of him; several of the poets read elegies written for him—or, perhaps, being poets, they had elegies on hand, written to honor other deceased friends and fellow poets, and these were appropriate to the occasion, and were duly read. Terence Greene made a striking, and sympathetic, impression upon the gathering: first, because he appeared to be so moved, even agitated, by the occasion ("Terence C. Greene," whom most of them knew solely by name and reputation, as custodian of the coveted Feinemann fellowships —a formidable person); second, because, not being a poet himself, he had searched for an elegy appropriate to the circumstances, and had discovered a really quite remarkably beautiful poem by Myra Tannenbaum, which, in a quavering but resolute voice, he'd read.

Get outa here, asshole! Go suck!

Bleeding from his nose and several cuts on his head, Terence Greene fled Edison Street, Trenton, managing to drive his car shakily but without mishap to northbound Route 1, and he stopped at a gas station near the Mercer Mall, and used the men's room to wash away the blood as best he could. The pony-tailed attendant looked at him, muttering, "Oh wow," but refrained from asking questions, nor did Terence offer any explanation. When he arrived home, luck was with him—Phyllis was out.

It was nine-forty in the evening, and Phyllis was out, at one or another of her meetings. Terence supposed.

Cindy saw him, however. She was coming downstairs, and she stood very still on the stairs. Abruptly, she began to cry.

Terence too stood very still. His nose began suddenly to bleed, when he believed it had stopped for the time being; there was a frantic search in his pockets for more tissues. (In fact, they were not tissues but wadded squares of toilet paper he'd taken from the rest room in the gas station.) A churning sensation inside his skull too gave Terence pause.

Here was the dilemma: He was in terror of collapsing in front of his youngest child, which might happen if he took a step; yet, he could not bear to allow the child to cry uncomforted.

"Cindy—hey? Honey? It's just—Daddy."

Startlingly, it seemed to Terence that Cindy was not his youngest child any longer. In the weeks, or months, he had not exactly looked at her, she'd gained height, lost weight, and though her healthy face was round as a baby moon, the cheeks were less pudgy, and there was a precocious maturity, an unmistakable *adult vexedness*, in her expression. Cindy was upset by Daddy's disheveled, bloodstained appearance, but she was angry, too.

"Cindy, don't cry, I—I'm perfectly fine. It was just a, an—"

Cindy cried, "It already happened like this! I was there! Everything happens *double*! I hate it! I'm so—scared, Daddy!"

"On Route 1, I—this other car—"

Cindy was backing upstairs, making a paddling gesture as if to push Daddy away, should he rush to her. Terence tried to explain further, but Cindy turned and ran, and, frankly, he didn't have the strength to run after her.

———

Never see that treacherous woman again but the days passed without incident, deep into summer, a muggy airless summer like water spilling placidly into water. He wondered how mankind had ever endured peace.

Ter-ence?—he looked up quickly, squinting, but of course there was no one there.

He was happy, though. He was at peace. No longer an adulterer. No longer unfaithful to his family. It was midsummer, and it had been midsummer for a long time. He rose early, and he went to bed early. He swam in the pool, coughing and choking as water splashed up his nose which felt to him swollen like a giant zucchini. Never did he dream *except continuously of Ava-Rose who had betrayed him.* Perhaps it was true, as Phyllis said worriedly, and accusingly, and as Mrs. Riddle suspected, that Terence slept poorly most nights but he rose from bed well rested and eager to begin the day *an empty cavity in his chest where his heart had been and that ashy-oily taste in his mouth.* His head ached where Ava-Rose's policeman lover had pistol-whipped him, but he understood he was damned lucky to be alive *unlike the others.* He drank vodka martinis to soothe his nerves. If Phyllis watched him, he drank vodka martinis where Phyllis could not watch him. In turn, if Phyllis drank (her drink of choice was good French wine, red: That brought out The Radiant Smile as little else could), Terence was too gentlemanly to watch. Or he was not present. He was elsewhere.

Unlike the others, he was alive. He hoped to remain so for as long as possible.

"But which police?"

Often, it seemed, that summer, he was leaning over the railing in the air-conditioned chill, and he woke to such a question. He did not always remember having ascended in the elevator, having stepped out. On the ninth floor. With his attaché case. He was the first to arrive at the Feinemann office, and the last to leave, because he had so much lost time to make up, and he meant to make it up. He meant to make up some of the money ("expenses") he had embezzled from the Foundation but it worried him that no one had seemed to notice *which was an incentive to further crime.*

The elevator spooked him. He shut his eyes, rapidly ascending. On the ninth floor, he swayed slightly as he stepped out, like a man who has been struck a blow to the head. He recalled how Quincy Ryder had died—swaying-drunk, and losing his balance at the railing, and falling. (Had the doomed man screamed? Terence Greene, shut away in his office, and, as he'd remarked to police, "very likely on the telephone at the time," had not heard.)

So he woke to find himself leaning over the gilt latticework railing, shivering in the refrigerated air. Far below, enticing, was the sparkling-white fountain. Sometimes he'd leaned so far over, blood ran into his head, not very pleasantly. His eyeballs throbbed. His nose began to bleed spontaneously. Like tears.

You must be punished for your wicked heart. If no one will punish you, you must punish yourself.

His mother had punished him when he'd deserved it. She'd loved him, he was "all she had," but she'd punished him, too. That was the way of such people in upstate New York, in the foothills of the Adirondacks.

When he cried, his mother had held him, and rocked him in her arms. Sometimes she'd cried with him. So he knew he was loved.

When his father punished him, he knew he'd been punished. No mistaking that. *Walloping* it was called. A man *walloped* his kid for the kid's own good, or to teach him a lesson. Rarely, with Terence's father, was it clear what the lesson was, what the two-year-old could have done to deserve such a *walloping*. Afterward, Terence's father did not hold him as he cried. But really Terence could not remember.

If no one will punish you, you must punish yourself: He accepted that.

Except—"Which police?"

He had his choice of the Trenton police, the Manhattan police, the Queenston police. Each department had its specific jurisdiction, of course, and could not intrude upon the others. With the passing of time it wasn't clear any longer exactly what Terence had done to merit confession and punishment but that was what the police were for, presumably.

Walloping which he deserved. If only not such a coward. And so highly regarded in the community. In his profession. A man of integrity, honor. A gentleman. *A nice man.* And his children—surely they did not deserve public shame, humiliation. And his wife.

"No, I can't. I simply can't. The children, Phyllis—I can't drag them into this."

Terence must have been leaning dangerously far over the railing, for blood rushed into his head, and he woke to his surroundings with a panicked start.

"No."

And the days passed. Weeks. And *he had never felt such grief* he exulted in his autonomy, his freedom from bondage. For what is erotic love but bondage?—the flesh contaminated by its greed.

Ava-Rose, how could you betray me!

How pleased with himself "Dr. Greene" was: never once giving in to the temptation to call either of the Trenton numbers his fingertips had long ago memorized.

If Ava-Rose called *him,* if she begged his forgiveness, making the first move toward a reconciliation—would Terence return to *her?*

"Yes."

No.

"I mean—*no.*"

Yes.

After all, a man must have his pride.

Where is your pride?—never would he forgive the woman,

for saying such a thing, in public. In the hearing of strangers.

Never again those lovely white arms, the softness of her breasts, voluptuous sleepy-playful kisses never see that treacherous woman again.

When he'd so extravagantly taken out the $500,000 insurance policy on his life, sole beneficiary Miss Ava-Rose Renfrew, he'd wanted to impress her (why not admit it?) and so he'd paid, with a cashier's check, the entire first-year premium. Which took him to May 1 of the next year. *Why?— because I adore you, I want to prove myself to you, how like a husband I might be.* A supremely foolish gesture, and yet Terence did not feel he could cancel out the policy and get some of his money back—what would Ava-Rose and the rest of the Renfrews think?

"And if something happened to me, at least they *would* be provided for."

One evening he sat with Mickey Classen on the train to Queenston. He heard himself say, with the blundering, eager air of a man with knowledge to impart, "Mickey, I've come to realize that the one thing that really matters is *family, home.* So little else is *real.*" Where one of their more exuberant, shallow-minded friends would have interrupted with grunts of affirmation, Mickey sat silent; perhaps a bit embarrassed, but attentive. Terence said, in a lowered voice, "A while back—it was years ago, actually—I nearly made a terrible mistake. I think of it often. As if, somehow, I'd been overcome by a sort of—impersonal madness. What is the fancy term— *crise.* My God, what a tragedy it would have been, for me! But I drew back in time. I managed to save myself, and my family." He was red-faced now and floundering, and he'd said more than he had wanted; the single vodka martini he'd had before getting on the train must have gone to his head. Yet Mickey seemed sympathetic, in his frowning silence, so Terence felt encouraged. "I don't suppose you, Mickey, have ever—? Come close to—? The same sort of—mistake?"

Never since moving to Queenston, New Jersey, and

claiming his place as a resident *not an interloper but one who belonged there by rights* had Terence, the least aggressive of men, risked so raw an appeal to another man; indeed, to any woman. (Including Phyllis.) It was not simply that Terence wasn't the type, which of course he was not: All Queenston men shun such intimate disclosures, out of an anxious presentiment that, if they accept them, they must then offer intimate disclosures of their own. Before his *crise*, Terence would have been appalled had any of their Queenston friends, including Mickey Classen, appealed to him in such a crude, clumsy fashion. He would have sat stiff in his seat, as Mickey was doing, gazing with a small frown at his ticket stub affixed to the rear of the seat in front of him; a boyish blush would have risen from his throat into his clean-shaven cheeks, and his necktie, impeccably knotted to the throat, would have begun to feel very tight. He would have cast his mind about, wondering how in God's name to reply.

Terence said, with a nervous, shamed laugh, "—Of course, it *was* years ago. I don't know why I bring the subject up now. I"—he floundered absurdly—"don't *know*."

Tactful Mickey Classen had always reminded Terence, in small ways, of himself: They were about the same age, and had the same ectomorph build; each man was shy, yet had learned to be warmly sociable; spoke with authority, yet quietly; was inclined to sobriety in repose, but quick to smile. In the presence of such "charismatic" personalities as Matt Montgomery, each man was likely to be overlooked.

Yet bore the bastard no grudge. Certainly!

Though Mickey Classen was wealthy, having made a fortune in the investment banking boom of the 1980s, neither he nor his wife Lulu seemed affected by money; Terence had long felt a keen sort of envy, that the Classens' son David, one of Aaron's high school friends, had grown into such a good, decent, hard-working kid—"And they'd started off, it almost seemed, like brothers," Phyllis herself had marveled.

Vaguely too Terence had envied Mickey Classen his marriage: not his sweet, rather placid and bland wife Lulu, exactly, but the ease, the stability, the sense of a match between equals, which was, both on the surface and intimately, the antithesis of Terence's own. Now the alarming thought struck him: What if Mickey told Lulu about this ridiculous conversation, and Lulu told Phyllis? The two women were not close friends yet, Terence knew, there is a sense in which, unlike men vis à vis men, all women are friends.

It might have been his breeding—Mickey Classen was the most tactful of men. He cleared his throat, and, reaching for his attaché case, at his feet beside Terence's, he said, gently, "Terry, I'd guess that we all come close to making 'tragic mistakes' sometimes—we wouldn't be fully human if we didn't. But"—here Mickey glanced at his companion, with a pinched sort of sidelong smile of the kind Terence sometimes gave himself in the mirror, a smile both embarrassed and forgiving—"as long as we don't make them, and don't talk about them, is it very important, really?"

The lush, tangled garden. Smelling of sun, heat. Bright flowers amid the weeds. Zinnias, roses. Those gorgeous creamy-pink roses. He reached out to touch a rose, and its petals, riddled with tiny holes like shot, scattered to the ground. An iridescent-shelled beetle flew up into his face, with an angry high-pitched clicking sound.
"No—help!"
"Dr. Greene—?"
Terence looked up, startled, to see Mrs. Riddle in the doorway. She must have knocked, and mistaken his outburst for an invitation to enter the office. He smiled at her as if nothing were wrong, and he hadn't just been having a waking dream, or a hallucination, at his desk. "Yes, Thelma?" His right hand was shut tight into a fist, the beetle trapped inside.

It was nearing the end of July. Soon, it would be August. And then Labor Day. In the fall, work at the Feinemann Foundation quadrupled as thousands of fellowship applications and grant proposals flooded in. *Terence could not bear to contemplate the future without Ava-Rose and the others* so in fact he'd astonished the chairman of the board who was his immediate superior, and the office staff, by informing them he would not be taking his customary three-week vacation in August. He had so much work to do, he intended to come into the office five days a week, even while his staff was away— "I've always found vacations deathly boring."

He hadn't yet told Phyllis and his children of these plans. He supposed they would object.

Mrs. Riddle, who revered Terence Greene excessively, certainly disapproved. He was touched by her solicitude, and made guilty by it; he knew he did not deserve it. For months, this good-hearted woman had deciphered Terence's haggard looks, his ghastly shadowed eyes and sickly grin as evidence of overwork. He was, indeed, "working himself to death." He assured her that he was, yes, seeing a doctor, in fact a neurologist (though not the one she'd recommended)—"Except, the problem isn't in my brain but in my mind." Terence had laughed to suggest that this was a joke, but Mrs. Riddle had not joined in.

"Excuse me, Dr. Greene—?"

"Oh yes, Thelma. Sorry." Somehow, he'd forgotten her. He was examining his opened right hand, the outstretched fingers, which trembled slightly. There was nothing in his hand, nor even the trace of a stain.

"I didn't mean to disturb you, but there's a young woman who insists upon seeing you. A 'Miss Renfrew.' 'Ava Renfrew,' she says. I advised her to make an appointment, but—"

Terence looked up squinting. His facial muscles twitched. "Who did you say, Thelma? *Who?*"

Mrs. Riddle consulted a pink slip in her fingers. " 'Ava Renfrew'—that's all the identification she gave. I explained how busy you are, and if she's an applicant for a fellowship it wouldn't do any good, anyhow, to see you in person."

Terence was on his feet, and running his hands swiftly through his hair. His heart was racing. "Show her in, Thelma. Please!"

"Right away, Dr. Greene?" Mrs. Riddle frowned doubt-fully.

"Right away, for God's sake yes!"

So she'd come to him after all. To him! to him! so he might forgive her! take her in his arms, and kiss her, tenderly! his blood gloating in sexual triumph!

"Ava-Rose, my darling—what has happened to you?"

It was one of the great shocks of Terence Greene's life: that, as he extended his hands to Ava-Rose Renfrew as she stepped into his office, he saw how severely she'd changed; how, within less than six weeks, she'd aged.

Her delicate beauty had faded, marred by a sallow, roughened skin and a deeply lined forehead. The lovely amber-green eyes seemed smaller, and had lost their lustre. Her hair, once so striking, was no longer springy and electric but a limp beige-brown, cut short, and brushed neatly behind her ears. The snubbed nose, the sensuous mouth, the high-held head—these were unchanged, yet had lost their vi-brancy. And how unimaginative her clothes: a dull-blue dress of some material so synthetic it had no texture, a single strand of bulbous, too-white pearls, the usual black ballerina flats, worn with no stockings. Her fingers, without rings, looked naked.

Terence was flooded with guilt and remorse. "My God, *you've* suffered, too!"

He would have embraced this young woman; but, with a deft movement, she shoved him back, using the heel of her hand. She was lithe and quick as a snake, and stronger than she appeared.

"Don't be ridiculous, 'Dr. Greene,' " she said, with a look of embarrassed disdain, "—I'm not 'Ava-*Rose*,' I'm 'Ava-*Grace*.' Didn't your secretary tell you?" Her voice was the hoarse, throaty, seductive one Terence adored, but her words were incomprehensible.

"What? *Who?*"

Terence stared at the young woman, astonished.

"I'm Ava-Grace Renfrew, *her* sister. I'm not surprised, she told you nothing about me." She put out her hand for Terence to shake: Her grip was cool, dry, and brusque. "May I have a seat?"

"You are—Ava-Rose's sister?"

"Her twin."

"Her *twin*—!" Terence stared, appalled.

"Don't look so shocked, this is *us*, *I* am us, and she is —God knows how she does it—something *else*." The woman laughed at Terence's distress. "May I have a seat, Doctor?— I won't stay long."

Terence mumbled yes of course, of course, and groped his way to his own chair, behind the gleaming expanse of his desk. He could feel the floor tilt beneath him. The thought came to him that it was an appropriate time for an earthquake; but an embarrassment, that Ava-Rose's sister should see Terence Greene so helpless.

Ava-Grace Renfrew had noticed no tilting floor, and sat straight-backed facing him, in the pert, prim posture of Ava-Rose, her chin uplifted. In Ava-Rose, the gesture was boldly flirtatious; in Ava-Grace, it was subtly belligerent. Ava-Rose's sweetly seductive smile had become, in Ava-Grace, an ironic, even angry smile. For Terence's reaction to her had not been flattering. "I suppose it *is* a shock, Doctor, seeing me," Ava-Grace said, not very sympathetically, "—when you were expecting to see *her*."

Terence managed to murmur, gallantly, that he hadn't been expecting to see Ava-Rose, really—"We've been out of contact since June." He saw that Ava-Grace was nodding impatiently, and so surmised that she knew about this. An unreasonable horror washed over him: Did the woman know *all*?

"Yes, I don't doubt it's a shock, for you"—Ava-Grace Renfrew made so airily contemptuous a gesture, Terence understood that *you* was generic, collective, referring to a vast horde of fools, "—to meet the identical twin sister of Ava-Rose Renfrew, and to have a hint of what she really *is*."

Terence tried to keep the disbelief from his voice. "You are, actually—*identical* twins?"

Ava-Grace laughed. Though without mirth. Her smile flashed like a blade. "In fact, Ava-Rose was born thirty-six minutes before me. And that was the last time, to my knowledge, Ava-Rose ever did anything more mature than I'd done." Her eyes narrowed meanly. "Thirty-seven years ago this past June."

"Thirty-seven—?"

"Thirty-seven years ago, we were born, in Sheenville, West Virginia. Our mother ran off with our father—who was not her husband, it's said—and the two of them lived up along the coast, in Maryland, and Delaware; he dumped her, and she came up to Trenton, and stayed." Ava-Grace recited these facts with a grim sort of relish. "*I* don't remember a thing, and neither does Ava-Rose, it was all so awful. I mean it was degrading, it wasn't 'romantic.' We had lots of 'Daddys' over the years." Terence listened, fascinated. He saw now how the beauty of the one sister had in a way congealed to the sallow, sullen attractiveness of the other; Ava-Grace *was* Ava-Rose, her features subtly altered. The husky, scratchy voice, so unexpectedly low, was identical, except Ava-Rose's typical speech rhythm was slower, more languid, than Ava-Grace's. Even the minute scars on Ava-Rose's face, so like dimples, or birds' prints in snow, were mimicked in nicks and blemishes on Ava-Grace's more coarsened skin. Her complexion had a harsh pewter sheen, as if scrubbed with steel wool.

"—heard about you from the twins, and, though I detest people who intrude in others' business, I always make it a policy to speak with Ava-Rose's 'man friends,' if I can get to them in time. Of course, I've severed all relations with my sister. And she with me. *I* had many times broken with them, and stayed away from them, before the final, absolute break." Ava-Grace paused, looking bemusedly at Terence. She was becoming, by degrees, more sympathetic; not friendly, and certainly not warm, as, virtually in an instant, with her quick dazzling smile, Ava-Rose was capable of exuding warmth; but less belligerent. There began to emerge, like a tiny moon at the horizon, a tone of *pity*.

"If you can get to them—'in time'?" Terence asked.

"Even so, it doesn't always do much good. Just like to-day, with you, I once made the trip, by bus, from Jersey City, where I've been living for the past six years, to this damned ol' city—I hate New York, I do!—to warn another of you, Mr. Bunsen was his name, y'know him?—'Randolph Bunsen'?— owned a jewelry store, and a real nice one?—well, anyway, I made the trip, expenses my own, and had a nice serious chat with the old fool, and a hell of a lot of good it did, in the end." Ava-Grace shook her head, laughing; she reached into her handbag, which was singularly ugly, made of scuffed black imitation leather, and pulled out a pack of cigarettes. "Y'mind?" she asked, even as, without waiting for Terence's reply, she extracted a cigarette and lit it with a tin-looking lighter that resembled (unless Terence was imagining it?) a snub-nosed revolver.

"What do you mean—'in the end'? What happened to him?"

Ava-Grace shrugged impatiently. Twin streams of smoke descended from her nostrils and curved away. Her tone was irascible and conversational, uncannily like Ava-Rose's in its rhythms—"Oh! and that even more pathetic case two or three years ago!—where, it turned out, his family was all beg-ging him to come back home, and he'd stolen money from his own father—'Wineapple.' " Ava-Grace curled her upper lip in a gesture of contempt. "You can't help feeling sorry for the family that's left behind, however it's hard to feel sorry for the blind ol' *fool*."

Terence asked quickly, " 'Ezra Wineapple'—? What happened to him?"

"Didn't you read about it in the Jersey papers, Doctor? Gosh-sake, isn't that where you live?"

Terence murmured apologetically that he read only *The New York Times.*

"And this 'Queenston' where the twins told me you live—isn't it close to Trenton?"

Terence assented, with some embarrassment.

He said, "In fact, I did intend to look up 'Wineapple' in back issues of the *Trenton Times*, but—for some reason—I never did. I—" His voice trailed off, feebly. Obviously he had not wanted to learn of Ezra Wineapple's fate. He had avoided learning of it for a year.

Ava-Grace Renfrew continued to speak in her chatty, vehement manner, as if she and Terence Greene were old acquaintances; intimates united in a campaign of some kind, with a powerful righteous undertone. Of Wineapple she said, relenting, "Well!—maybe I'm wrong, Doctor. It was a terrible scandalous thing and a tragedy for the Wineapple family but maybe, since it didn't go to trial, there wasn't all that much about it in the news."

Terence asked hesitantly, "I assume the man—died?"

"Now I recall," Ava-Grace said, musing, "—his picture in the paper. Front page of the *Trenton Times*. And the caption beneath—NUDE BODY OF COUNTY OFFICIAL PULLED FROM RIVER."

Terence shuddered. "I see."

"Just a regular-looking ol' fella, with glasses, fifty-three years old, had a pretty good job in the County Assessor's office; losing his hair, but not bad-looking; a sort of hopefulness in his eye—the way a man that age will look, taken unawares." Ava-Grace laughed, sighing. She'd been fouling the air with her cigarette and now made a desultory gesture of waving smoke away. "That *hopefulness*—that's the sad thing, I think. 'The kingdom of God is within' but the blind will not *see!*"

The transition to a religious perspective was too abrupt for Terence. He sensed, in this fierce twin of Ava-Rose's, a similar impulse toward dogma; he did not want the conversation to swerve away from poor Wineapple, floating nude in the Delaware River. "What exactly happened to Ezra Wine-apple?" he asked.

"Oh, Lord!—who knows? As much untangle a ball of string that's all snarled, as sort out what really happened, from what they claim happened, in anything the Renfrews do!" Ava-Grace said. Her amber-green eyes narrowed, with angry disapproval. "Seems this Mr. Wineapple met Ava-Rose somehow, I believe it was through some ol' lawsuit the family was trying out—this thing with Holly Mae, y'know, that you are helping them with, sure isn't the first of its kind—and shortly afterward the man is in love with her, he gives her presents, even a car; helps with the mortgage on the house. One day Ava-Rose tells him she's pregnant—*he's* the father, of course!—and she's too 'moral' to have an abortion but she does have a miscarriage, by accident—so there's lots of doctor bills, prescription bills—*he's* anxious to pay. (One of Ava-Rose's boyfriends is a doctor down in Camden, barred from practicing medicine but they'd cook things up together. You ever heard of 'Dr. Pyles'? No?) However it went, I don't know. It makes me sick to know such things. I'm proud, in fact, *I* don't know half of what goes on at 33 Holyoak."

Terence asked, grimly, "But just what happened to Mr. Wineapple, that he wound up nude in the river, dead?"

Ava-Grace ran a hand through her hair, and fingered a tendril at the nape of her neck. Terence was reminded, so keenly it made his heart ache, of the childlike yet seductive way Ava-Rose fussed, stroked, and plaited her own hair. "Exactly for sure, I don't know," Ava-Grace said, with the air of one making an admission, "—any more than the police did. They'd all gone swimming in the river one night, and *he*, poor ol' Wineapple, couldn't keep up, and drowned. He'd been drinking, too. Some sort of party, Fourth of July, I believe. Ava-Rose and Chick and Holly Mae (you'd be surprised, that woman can swim, sort of—float on her back and kick her feet like crazy) and Cap'n-Uncle Riff (*he* can swim as good as any man half his age), but also one of Ava-Rose's boyfriends, a mean ol' biker, that she'd been passing off, to Wineapple, as a cousin. All along the three of them went around together, and poor ol' Wineapple, such a fool, never guessed what was up. Why, he'd even lent the boyfriend money."

Terence murmured, almost inaudibly, "T. W. Binder!"

"So maybe they owed him too much money, or he was beginning to want too much in return, or, maybe, like they said, it *was* an accident—anyway, they all went swimming off the Point and Wineapple drowned, and the police arrested T. W. Binder (who they knew from plenty of other things he'd done and never got caught for) but there wasn't enough evidence for an indictment, and no trial. After all—who would the witnesses be, except the guilty parties?" Ava-Grace was smoking her cigarette furiously, yet with a measure of good humor. "In my line of work, Doctor—which I'd say is pretty different from yours: I'm a matron, and Sunday School teacher, at the Jersey City Women's and Juvenile Detention Facility—I know one thing, real well: It's easy to know who's evil, but damned hard to get a solid case against them. Damned hard!"

Terence was staring at Ava-Grace Renfrew with the look of a man who has been dealt a blow to the head. He felt, not pain, but its jarring aftermath.

"Excuse me, I—I don't quite understand. You seem to be saying—suggesting—that your sister was involved in a—murder?"

" 'A murder'—? Did I suggest only one?" Ava-Grace laughed, flicking ash onto Terence's desk.

"But—"

"Of course, to be fair to Ava-Rose, she never has been charged with anything, much; 'innocent till proven guilty.' "

Terence said, stiffly, "I should say so, yes. 'Innocent till proven—otherwise.' " The ghastly-white face of Eldrick Gill shimmered before him, submerged in the murky waters of the Delaware River.

ROSAMOND SMITH / 300

Ava-Grace said, "My little nieces told me, Doctor, that you were one of the jurors for T. W. Binder's trial, when he finally did get tried, for trying to kill Ava-Rose. So that's how you met my sister? Terrific!" And she laughed again, heartily.

"More or less." Terence felt as if he were sinking.

"*That*, they did get the poor bastard for, with Ava-Rose testifying against him. 'Aggravated assault,' eh?"

Terence protested, "But—surely Binder was guilty? We jurors weighed the evidence, we listened to witnesses, examined the hospital report on your sister's injuries—we voted unanimously for a verdict of 'guilty.' I refuse to believe that that man was *not* guilty."

Terence recalled with a pang of remorse how he'd coerced his fellow jurors into the "unanimous" verdict. But surely that too changed nothing, if the man was guilty?

Ava-Grace said, ironically, "Wouldn't *you* want to beat her up bad, if she'd gotten you to kill her old boyfriend, then kicked you out?—and kept all the money the old fool'd given her?"

"I—"

"*I* don't blame the Trenton police, nor any law enforcement agency that deals with these people however they can. I know what these people are—they're my people! The Trenton police wanted to get Binder, he's a small-time drug dealer and thief, probably has a hand in stolen goods fencing, like my 'uncle' Riff, so they hear what he did to Ava-Rose and make a deal with her, maybe to drop bench warrants against her, or other Renfrews, and she agrees, and gets on the witness stand, and tells a tale that, gosh-sake, *might even be true*, mostly—and it works. You guys found Binder guilty, and he goes to Rahway. Not a long sentence but at least he did get put away."

"And he died there, in Rahway. But you must know that."

Ava-Grace frowned. "Yes, I'd heard that. I didn't hear how, nor why. I mean, for sure, it was the Renfrews wanted him dead—scared what he'd do to them, when he got out.

But I never heard who did it, exactly. Who set it up. How money changed hands." With a look at Terence that reminded him of similar audacious-coquettish looks of Ava-Rose's, Ava-Grace suddenly winked. "*You* didn't do it, in any case, Doctor, eh! a gentleman like you"—glancing with naive admiration about Terence's office—"wouldn't know the first thing about arranging for a hit inside Rahway State Prison."

Terence drew breath to speak, but could not. His sensitive eyes were watering from this terrible woman's smoke; the sensation of sinking, as beneath the surface of murky waves, grew stronger. Yet, with feeble cunning, he thought to deflect the drift of the conversation. "Then the trial—*my* trial—in June of last year—was a sort of charade? A cynical manipulation of the judicial process, by the district attorney's office? A distortion of justice? And we jurors were unwitting collaborators?"

Ava-Grace was surprisingly off-hand, shrugging. "Oh, well! A guy who's guilty of murder, or, let's say, manslaughter, letting another man drown, is also guilty of 'aggravated assault,' eh? That's how the cops figure. God has His justice too—sometimes right here on earth."

Terence said, stammering, "But—T. W. Binder wasn't being tried for Wineapple's death—but for something else, entirely. We jurors were never informed. And even if Binder had helped drown Wineapple, he hadn't acted alone. Your sister—" He was unable to continue.

Ava-Grace said scornfully, "Yes, sir—but they couldn't get enough evidence for *that*; couldn't prove *that*, in court. If you can't get a jury to convict, forget about a trial. The wicked dwelling among us comprehend that real well, which is why most of them are *out*, not *in*, where they belong." Ava-Grace fingered the chunky imitation pearls around her neck. "At Jersey City, where I work, you'll find the women and kids who are *in* are mainly the dopes. Can't read, can't write, can't think. The smart ones, like Ava-Rose Renfrew, rarely get caught."

As Ava-Grace Renfrew spoke, reiterating earlier remarks, in her chatty, vehement way, Terence sat silent, rubbing his eyes. It seemed to him that his life *his life since Ava-Rose: since love* rushed past him, as in a mockingly accelerated film. Ava-Grace had brought him the truth Ava-Rose had obscured. And he had not known. *He had always known.* And now, he had no choice but to know.

"Hey—is my smoke bothering you?" Ava-Grace asked, innocently. She waved her hand about again, flicking ash. "You're looking kind of sick, Doctor."

Terence did not hear. Or, hearing, had not the strength to reply.

He was thinking. There was something important, urgent, of which he must think. He was losing it, and he did not want to lose it. Yes but his brain ached. And his eyes. Since those terrible blows to his head *just be grateful her new lover didn't shoot you dead, asshole* he had not felt quite himself.

Himself!—who was that?

Ava-Grace Renfrew was peering at him inquisitively; with a sort of bemused professional pity. Her cheap navy blue costume was a prison matron's uniform, the too-white pearls around her neck a mockery of feminine adornment. "Uh, Doctor—you *aren't* going to be sick, are you?"

Carefully, with the air of a man fighting nausea, Terence said, "I suppose I am a bit—sick, Miss Renfrew. Sickened. I *am* upset—of course. Miss Renfrew, you have—"

"Hey c'mon: 'Ava-Grace' is my name."

"—Ava-*Grace*—come into my office unexpected, without warning—I've no doubt, with a charitable motive—and you must understand that what you've told me is a shock, a profound—"

Ava-Grace made a snorting sound, as of disbelief. "Nah, you must've known—didn't you? Down deep inside?"

Terence shut his eyes, grasping the slender thread of his words as if it were a lifeline, keeping his head above water. "—shock. I have in fact ceased to see Ava-Rose. I believe she is in love with another man." *No in truth he could not believe:*

he knew she loved only him. "I would not force my attentions on any woman who did not want them, and I am willing to refrain from trying to see her again. And I am married, and happily married. And I will remain married. But, Miss Renfrew"—and here he nearly broke down, speaking suddenly in great anguish—"you've said such things! Such incredible things! Accusing your own sister of—of murder!— of conspiring to murder!—the woman with whom I was, or am, in love—"

Ava-Grace sucked her breath in, astonished. "What! 'In love'! Listen to *him!*" She briskly stubbed her cigarette out on an edge of Terence's desk, and dropped it into his wastebasket. "I see I've come to the wrong place, haven't I! And, gosh-sake, I hate this damn dirty ol' city, and that nasty Port Authority—"

Terence said, alarmed, "No, wait! I didn't mean—"

"—at my own expense, just to bring tidings of truth to deaf ears—'Greene'—'Bunsen'—'Wineapple'—God knows who all else." She was on her feet, swiping at her eyes. Terence was astounded by the immediate transformation. "Well, *I* am a Christian who knows her duty—unlike my family— and *she*—my heathen sister you are all in love with—*she's* a shameless devil worshipper, did you know that? Eh? Doctor?" Ava-Grace glared at Terence. Saliva glistened in the corners of her mouth. Terence tried to apologize, on his feet, too, but Ava-Grace interrupted. "Jesus sees, and He forgives, but He's pretty pissed off, too!"

Terence said quickly, "Miss Renfrew, I mean Ava-Grace—please don't leave yet. I didn't mean to insult you—"

"Insult me? How, insult me? No man can insult me—I do not 'cast my pearls before swine.' "

Terence hoped that the woman's outburst had not been overheard in the outer office. He was fairly wringing his hands, not knowing what to do. *Let her go. You don't want to hear more. She is a hard, cold, calculating woman. Erase her from your memory.* He said, "Please, won't you stay a little longer?

We have much to discuss. And—if it's a question of money —your bus fare from Jersey City—''

Ava-Grace refused to sit down again. She held her ugly, oversized handbag in front of her as if to keep Terence at a distance. But she seemed temporarily placated, and did not leave: Perhaps the offer of financial reimbursement had mollified her. ''Well! now we're speaking frankly, Doctor,'' she said, with a mean little twist of her mouth, of a kind Terence recalled having seen once or twice in Chickie, but never in Ava-Rose, ''—let me ask you: did Ava-Rose tell you, baldfaced, that those little girls are mine?—Dara and Dana, my girls?—that I abandoned?—yes?—did she?''

''Yes, she—''

''In fact, Doctor, Dara and Dana are *her* children, that she has so ill-treated, I am suing to get custody of them, through the state children's welfare bureau. So!—what d'you think of that?''

Terence, appalled, said, ''My God, what are you saying? Ava-*Rose* is the twins' mother? But I'd thought—''

Ava-Grace shook her finger rudely at Terence. ''And don't you finance any damn ol' lawyer to block my suit, or I'll expose you! *I'll* put your picture on the front page of the *Trenton Times*! You and her! The lot of you! The girls' own grandmother has betrayed them, and I despair!—Dana is hidden away somewhere, and I don't know where; and Dara is—starting to change. My darling little nieces, that always loved *me*.''

''Wait,'' Terence said, ''—let me get this straight: Ava-Rose is the girls' mother, not you; and Holly Mae is—your mother? Yours and Ava-Rose's?''

''That's what I'm saying, Doctor,'' Ava-Grace said fiercely. ''Don't tell me, deep in your heart, you didn't know.''

But Terence had not known. He simply had not known. Had he?

''—And Chick is Ava-Rose's son, too. That she had when she was sixteen, and ran away to Atlantic City with some gambler—who dumped her, nine months pregnant, and I had to go get her, by bus, and miss half my high school exams, and almost flunk out! Not that she cared, nor even thank me. Y'know what she said to me, Doctor?—'Why do you always poke your nose in my business, Ava-Grace!'—that's what the thankless girl said to me. I'll never forget!"

"Chick is Ava-Rose's *son?* But—"

"Oh, I devoted myself to him, too, when he was a little baby, and Ava-Rose would run off with men, and none of us knew where she was, or if she was alive, from one day to the next. That little boy loved me like I was his mother, yes and he loves me still, though he has long ago acquired his Renfrew ways, like a young snake growing into its markings. I pray for his soul, like for the twins, every day, Doctor, yes I do."

"Her *son*—?"

Terence saw the hulking blond boy in his mind's eye: the smirking smile, the "innocent" lift of the eyes, the handsome but blemished broad face. Ava-Rose Renfrew's son?

Like an avenging Fury, Ava-Grace paused to look at Terence with renewed scorn. " 'Why, Ava-Rose is too young to be that boy's mother'—that's what you're thinking, eh, Doctor? Same ol' crap you all say, right about now. You men!"

"Please, Ava-Grace, don't speak so loudly—"

"I will speak as loud as I please, Doctor, and 'he who has ears to hear, let him hear.' D'you want to know the truth, or not?"

"Yes, of course, I—"

"Well! Holly Mae Loomis, who is the biggest the most shameless liar of them all, *is* our mother, yessir: Ava-Rose's and mine. She'll deny it to this day, telling a bald-faced lie to her own girls, but we know. That's just some ol' tale she invented, that our real mother abandoned us; and she took us in. Now I'm not saying that the woman is pure evil—she's my mother, and there is good in her, I know. When Ava-Rose and I were in fifth grade, she did time up at Elizabeth, for bad checks, and there she found Jesus—then, afterward, backslid, as a certain percentage will; but once Jesus is in your heart, He's *in*." Ava-Grace paused. A steely look came into her eyes. "The cruelty of that woman is her favoring one child over the other, from the cradle onward. My twin sister and I started out this life equal, as all mankind is equal before God; then, a change came upon us, and Ava-Rose was favored. I believe it was because she acquired her Renfrew markings when we were still in grade school, and I never did. She was one of *them*, taking happiness from evil, and I never was. And I'm proud to say, *I never will be*."

Ava-Grace's forehead was deeply furrowed. Her sallow face appeared swollen. Terence sensed that, if he moved precipitously, she might haul off and strike him with the handbag.

"It's a fearsome thing, to have a twin," Ava-Grace said grimly. "To be a twin. Some primitive folks, y'know?—they kill twins soon's they're born. You ever hear that? Some other folks, it's said they used to make twins their rulers. (Maybe just boy twins?) I don't know any facts for sure, and all that stuff is heathen superstition, but it *is* scary, sometimes. I could never send any message to Ava-Rose with my thoughts, but she could send to me. I'd hear this sweet little singsong voice in my head, Ava-Rose's voice, 'Think you're too good for us, why don't you go swim in the river,' and I'd run to find her and tell her to stop and she'd just stare at me like butter wouldn't melt in her mouth, and say, 'Stop what, Ava-Grace?' but the voice would come back, the soft voice of the serpent it was, Satan in Ava-Rose's form as she herself is Satan in a comely human form, so I'd cry, and yank at my hair, and seeing her all innocent-like I'd rush at her and hit her with my fists, 'Ava-Rose you're driving me crazy, stop! stop or I'll kill you!' and she'd scream like she was being killed so somebody would come save her—somebody always came." Ava-Grace's voice dipped, with this last. She was breathing harshly. As if sensing she might have gone too far, she said, more evenly, "I don't doubt, Doctor, that Ava-Rose castigated me to you, and gave some ol' heathen-astrology reading that is false—not only in itself (for astrology is discredited by all enlightened people), but because she and I have the same sign exactly—not that I know what it is, I scorn such things, but my 'reading' is her 'reading,' and she knows it. We are the same person, *one of us gone wrong.*"

Terence, staring at Ava-Grace Renfrew, was overcome by the sense of vertigo he'd felt when she'd first entered his office. For there, inside the woman's faded, drawn Fury-face, gleaming out of her narrow vindictive eyes, was the other's face—the beautiful, radiant face, and those eyes shining like precious gems, of Ava-Rose.

"I suppose, Doctor, Ava-Rose boasted how she has cast me out of her heart, eh? Which is exactly what I have done with her."

Terence said quickly, "Why, no, Ava-Rose never said such a thing. I seem to recall her saying she loved you. But that you hadn't seen each other in—eleven years?"

"A bald-faced lie," Ava-Grace said, with satisfaction. "Not less than once a month I drop by that place of iniquity, hoping to see my little nieces; and sometimes I'm able to, and sometimes not. Holly Mae, my own natural mother, refuses to let me cross the threshold if she's home—what d'you think of that, Doctor?"

Terence tried to speak consolingly. "I'm very sorry to hear it, Ava-Grace."

"And all because of the trial—that damn ol' trial that turned them against me, and me against them, forever!"

"Trial?"

"Cap'n-Uncle Riff had to stand trial for mail fraud in a federal court in Trenton, and some of the family, including Ava-Rose and me, were subpoenaed by the prosecution to testify against him. *I* knew the old fox was guilty of all they'd charged him for, and—"

"Guilty? Mail fraud? Cap'n-Uncle Riff?" Terence spoke disbelievingly. In his mind's eye there rose the solemn patriarchal figure of the elderly white-haired and bearded man.

"Why of course, Doctor: 'mail fraud' was just one of his money-schemes, and he made a mistake to use the U.S. mail. What he did was run an ad in the classifieds in a whole lot of newspapers—'A call for ambitious men and women to earn $100,000 yearly in your own home! Send $11.95 cash and stamped self-addressed envelope for instructions!' And the silly fools would send money, hundreds and hundreds of them, to one or another P.O. Box (Cap'n-Uncle switched around), and he'd mail back as 'instructions' a little printed slip of paper like out of a Chinese fortune cookie—'Place my ad in newspapers.' " Ava-Grace laughed as if despite herself. "That old man *is* clever, you got to hand it to him. 'The Prince of Darkness' in disguise. But they arrested him, and he had to stand trial, and I took the stand, like I said, and spoke the truth of what I knew; and Ava-Rose took the stand right after me, and undid every word I uttered, by the telling of sheer lies. Swearing on the Holy Bible never meant the least thing to her!" Ava-Grace paused, her face suffused with blood. She was hugging her handbag ever more tightly against her chest. "And we looked more alike then than we do now. And out of deviltry Ava-Rose found out what I was going to wear to court, and wore something identical. Naturally, the fool jurors couldn't decide which of us to believe, and Cap'n-Uncle speechified so fine, from when he'd heard the Reverend Billy Graham preach once—they trooped back in with a verdict of 'not guilty.' " Ava-Grace paused, with a look of bitter resignation. "Only a single time I know of that man (who never was anybody's uncle, nor any sea-captain, nor even any Renfrew, probably) did get sent away to prison—manslaughter, down in Miami, seven years and he got out in three. But he'd been young then, the sinner, and hadn't his fancy white hair and beard."

"Manslaughter?—Cap'n-Uncle? Who did he kill?"

Ava-Grace said, in a voice heavy with sarcasm, "Who did he get caught for killing, is what you mean."

Before Ava-Grace Renfrew left, Terence insisted upon reimbursing her, with badly shaking fingers, for the bus trip from Jersey City. The price of the round-trip ticket was surprisingly low, and he wanted to give her twice the amount of money, but she staunchly refused—"Thank you, Doctor, but not *me.*"

She added, in parting, "I know it was a bad shock, but 'the truth shall make you free.' Bare your heart to your lawful wedded wife, and beg her forgiveness, in Jesus' name. Will you?"

Terence nodded gravely. "Oh yes."

"That sister of mine!—she's always attracted you men, no matter your age and sense, like maggots. *I* swear, I don't understand."

Terence, who had opened the door to the outer office for Ava-Grace to pass through, winced. He was aware, through a haze of pain, of how, in the outer office, under the guise of busying themselves with desk work, Mrs. Riddle and her assistants were listening avidly. He murmured, "Magnet, you mean. Not maggots."

Ava-Grace swung on out in her scruffy ballerina flats, with an airy, dismissive wave of her arm. "No, sir, Doctor," she said emphatically, "*—maggots* I said, and *maggots* I mean."

The floor did tilt beneath Terence Greene's feet. He scrambled to save himself, but fell heavily. His head struck a flat surface, and a sharp surface, and something opaque and durable with a polished sheen. He was unconscious; yet woke shivering convulsively. An agitated older woman and another, younger woman were looming over him, splashing water onto his face. From a steeply vertical distance they cried, in near-unison, "Dr. Greene! Oh, Dr. Greene!"

But he was too far away to console them.

Ending

*B*y the end of the summer, it would be known generally in Queenston, even among those not in the immediate social circle to which Phyllis and Terence Greene belonged, that the couple was separated; that they would soon be filing for divorce.

During the month of August, Phyllis Greene and her daughters were away, staying with Phyllis's mother at her summer place on Nantucket Island—"We're going up early, and Terry will be joining us a little later," Phyllis told friends. But it was observed by those Queenston friends who were not themselves away in August that, in fact, Terence remained alone in the large house at 7 Juniper Way, and continued to commute to New York during the week as if nothing had changed—except, of course, he was alone. And unreceptive to invitations. Negligent about returning telephone calls.

Then, at the very end of August, Terence moved abruptly out of the house and into a single-bedroom apartment near the railroad depot. He notified no friends, had no explanations except an embarrassed murmured "It's temporary" and "We think it's for the best right now"—as he told Burt Hendrie, unavoidably encountered in a Queenston liquor store one evening.

And then Phyllis and the girls, and, for a brief while, before leaving for college, twenty-year-old Aaron (who had been in Wyoming for most of the summer), returned to the house at 7 Juniper Way.

And it was clear that the family was split—but why?

And in the matter of the divorce—which of the Greenes wanted it?

It happened like this.

Late one July night, at the Mercer Mall, by Beno's Pizzeria, a gathering of area teenagers sighted Studs Schrieber on a motorcycle roaring across a corner of the parking lot to avoid red lights on Route 1—Studs Schrieber, or a wiry young man in black T-shirt, ragged jeans, crash helmet, and wraparound reflector sunglasses who so uncannily resembled Studs as to be a twin.

Of the eleven teenagers who saw the cyclist, eight were adamant, unshakable, that it had been Studs—"There's only one of him, man." But they were divided as to the motorcycle itself: whether it had been a black Harley Davidson, or a black Yamaha. Nor could they offer any plausible explanation why Studs, known to them all, would not have spoken with them; or, at least, waved in passing.

One girl believed that Studs had waved to her, sort of —"You'd have to know him real well, to've seen it."

Word of the sighting passed swiftly through the area as teenagers called friends, and these friends called others. It was eleven o'clock the following morning that Kim Greene picked up a ringing telephone, in her mother's presence: Phyllis heard the girl draw in her breath sharply as if she'd been struck, and cry, "Oh wow—that's great!" and then repeat, in a choked, failing voice, "That's—great," unable to continue as she burst into tears. The telephone receiver slipped from her fingers and slammed onto a kitchen counter.

Phyllis, astonished, was afterward to think that never in her life had she witnessed such a transformation; never had she seen anyone turn so waxy-pale, as if, within seconds, the blood had drained from Kim's face.

Phyllis asked, "Honey, what is it?" but Kim had turned aside, blundering gropingly through the dining room, murmuring, "No no no oh God no," and when Phyllis caught up to her she pushed away at first, on the verge of hysteria. But Phyllis would not let her daughter escape upstairs to her room; she embraced her, and held her tight, and comforted her, as, by degrees, Kim's resistance melted away, and at last she was hugging her mother in turn, hugging her hard, like a young, frightened child. "Mommy, it's Studs—he's come back," Kim sobbed, and Phyllis said, "Studs Schrieber?—he's back?—alive?" and Kim said, "Mommy, I thought he was dead, I thought he was gone, I'm so afraid of him, oh Mommy I'm so afraid," and Phyllis, holding the agitated girl, began to feel fear herself, sensing, with a mother's immediate instinct, what her young daughter would tell her, what she must hear—"Mommy, he made me do things, I didn't want to, he made me, with his friends, too, the other guys, oh Mommy he hurt me, he twisted my arms and punched me and laughed at me, I thought he was dead, I thought he was killed, I was so happy he was gone, I'm scared Mommy, he hurt me, he did nasty things, I was so happy he was dead and now he's back—"

And so, Phyllis Greene learned of one of the secrets of the household at 7 Juniper Way, Timberlane Estates, Queenston.

Later assuring Kim, now lying pale and exhausted atop her bed, as Phyllis stroked her burning forehead, that never never would anything like that ever happen to her again—"I promise."

Phyllis was herself pale, and exhausted, as if having lived through the ordeal of labor and childbirth another time. Her own daughter abused. Sexually exploited. By a young man whom at one time at least Phyllis had rather liked—hadn't, in any case, so strongly disliked as Terence had disliked him. (How accurate Terence's judgment had turned out to be!) Beautiful Kim, sensitive Kim, only fifteen years old, seemingly innocent, inexperienced, virginal. Certain of the details Kim had sobbed out, in Phyllis's arms, led Phyllis to suspect that there would be more to reveal, in time. If Kim was reluctant to tell her mother, perhaps she would tell a therapist.

"My God, what a horror!"

And who was to blame? Phyllis recalled, with self-disgust, how, as long ago as last winter, she'd happened to notice bruises on Kim's arms; but had been willing to believe, unquestioningly, that the bruises had been caused by Kim's newest passion—"gymnastics." Kim was always staying after school to participate in "gymnastics." And hadn't there been "practice sessions" even on Saturdays sometimes. And during Easter break.

And she recalled how, months ago, before Studs Schrieber had disappeared, the subject of Kim's bruised arms, yes and her bruised neck, had come up for some reason at dinner; and Kim had giggled nervously, then turned sullen, and changed the subject. And Phyllis noticed how Terence was staring at Kim—until, gradually, it become obvious that he wasn't seeing her at all. He was looking through her. He was thinking of something, or someone, else.

Not that the moment had made much of an impression on Phyllis. For she too had been thinking of something—someone—else.

"Jesus! How could we have been so selfish, and so blind!"

Phyllis sat beside Kim for a long time, until Kim drifted off to sleep. Stroking Kim's forehead, her long silky rippling hair. It was not a vow, nor even a promise, but a blunt statement of fact—"We will be changing our lives. All of us. Nothing like this will ever happen again."

She took Kim and Cindy on an impromptu outing—"It's been so long since we've done anything together, just the three of us!" She hoped the radiance of her smile deflected attention from the quaver in her voice.

No, it was no one's birthday. Nor an anniversary. It was not a holiday. Kim, subdued since the episode of the other day, perhaps understood that Mother had something to tell them. Cindy suspected nothing.

Phyllis drove them down into the Delaware Valley, westward from Queenston along a succession of curving, hilly, scenic hills. Through Mount Rose, through Hopewell, through Lambertville; across the high, narrow bridge above the Delaware River and into New Hope, Pennsylvania; then south along the river road to Washington's Crossing. To the old Inn at Washington's Crossing, where Phyllis had not been for years.

"Didn't we used to go here, Mom?—a long time ago?" Cindy asked.

"Yes," Phyllis said, "—a long time ago."

She remembered, but dimly; as if through a scrim. The Greenes—Terence and Phyllis and the children Aaron, Kim, little Cindy. *What a happy family, how attractive, how American.*

Gone where?

Phyllis was not a sentimental woman, but her eyes filled with tears.

In the Inn's foyer was a handsome, squawky parrot on display in a large brass cage. It was an Amazonian bird with bright feathers—red, yellow, emerald-green. "Hey, I remember this guy, sort of," Cindy said, peering up at the parrot. "Do you think it's the same parrot, then and now?"

Kim said, with that sudden flare of knowledge that, in a child, so impresses a parent, "Sure it is. Parrots live a long time—longer than *us.*"

Luncheon in the Inn's dim-lit, romantic old dining room was leisurely and very pleasant. It was very nice. It would be memorable for the three of them, and so Phyllis determined that it would be very nice. Her eyes filled repeatedly with tears (to her distress: for truly she *was* enjoying herself) which she brushed away, she hoped unobtrusively, with a corner of her napkin.

Cindy chattered happily throughout the meal. Kim, with little appetite at home, ate hungrily here. Phyllis regarded her daughters with love, wondering, Was I mad? maddened? to have neglected them so? my daughters whom I love? And my son—have I lost him? Is it too late?

Cindy knew nothing of Kim's revelation of the other day, and would know nothing. Kim was to begin seeing a woman therapist who specialized in adolescents the following week, and had asked Phyllis not to tell anyone—"Especially not Daddy." (Asked why "especially not Daddy," Kim had said, worriedly, "Because maybe he'd kill Studs?—if Studs really is alive, and comes back?") Phyllis had shared her emotion, which oscillated between rage at the young man who had abused her daughter and rage at herself for not having prevented it, with only one other person in Queenston. This person was not Terence Greene.

Near the end of the meal, Phyllis drew a deep, shaky breath, and smiled at her daughters, not one of her assured, radiant smiles but a faint, hopeful smile. "Kim honey, Cindy honey—I have something to tell you. It's about the family, and our future. It's—"

There was a burr in Phyllis's throat, and for a moment she could not speak. Kim, frightened, reached for her water glass and drank thirstily. Cindy arched her eyebrows and said in a brave, bright voice, "You and Daddy are getting a divorce?"

He knows. He must know. Does he know?
"Excuse me, Terry? May I come in?"
Terence glanced around quizzically, for Phyllis's pres-

ence in his study, at this late hour of the evening, was unusual. "Certainly," he said.

Phyllis had so rehearsed the crucial, irrevocable words she must say that, faced now with saying them, she could not. A flame passed up into her face. Her eyes flooded absurdly with tears.

She said, stammering, "I—wonder if you've heard? The Schrieber boy? There's a rumor he's back, after all these weeks."

Terence was sitting at the late Reverend Winston's massive desk, opening a stack of mail with the late Reverend Winston's ornate brass letter opener. The scrolled initials WSW—"Willard Symons Winston"—were prominent on the curved handle. As Phyllis spoke, Terence fumbled a bit with the knife, driving the sharp blade up inside the length of the envelope and tearing it unevenly. (How touching a sight it was, Terence Greene opening mail that held neither personal nor professional interest for him, in his usual methodical fashion! The gutted envelopes were discarded individually in a wastebasket, their contents arranged neatly before him.) Terence glanced up squinting, and asked Phyllis to repeat what she'd said—he hadn't quite heard.

"There's a rumor among the kids, evidently, that the Schrieber boy"—Phyllis, her jaw clenching, could not bring herself to call him by any other name—"is back. But the Schriebers themselves—"

" 'Back'? Where?"

This was an odd question, and Terence's squinting, incredulous expression was odd as well. But, in her preoccupied state, Phyllis scarcely noticed. "Back here. Somewhere in the area. One of Kim's friends—"

"He's back? But how? Back from—where?"

Terence's fingers twitched as if with a spasmodic nervous reflex. The brass letter opener fell clattering onto the desktop. Phyllis saw that her husband was greatly amazed by this news, yet that there was, too, an undercurrent of dread beneath: She wondered if somehow he'd known about Kim's experience with Studs Schrieber, and had spared *her*.

A bit rattled, she half-wondered if, without having told her she would do so, Kim had after all told Terence. Was that possible?

Phyllis's thoughts raced. She could not see how, given the brief amount of time Kim would have had, and the nature of their household, this was possible; nor why, after what Kim had so earnestly said, she would have changed her mind without telling Phyllis.

"Terry, how do I know? As I said, it's only a rumor among the kids. The Schriebers themselves know nothing about it. It was Suzi Ryan who called Kim, and I spoke with her mother, Marian, and *she* said she'd called Doris immediately—which is more than I would have done, I think—and Doris was terribly upset, because the family knows nothing about the boy except that he disappeared weeks ago, without a trace. Poor Doris!—she says they're waiting for a ransom note. They want so badly to believe he might be alive. And now this rumor—"

Terence's squint increased, as if Phyllis were standing in too much light. "He—'Studs'—is back? Back in Queenston?"

"Well, no one seems to know. Except—"

"But isn't he dead? Didn't he—die?"

So curious an expression had come over Terence's drawn, ashy-skinned face, Phyllis did not know what to make of it; except she recalled how, that first time Terence had ever set eyes upon Studs Schrieber, catching him and Kim in the family room, he'd reacted with extreme and uncharacteristic rage. But so far as Phyllis knew, and she was fairly certain, Terence had never seen Studs Schrieber since that day. When the subject of the boy's disappearance had come up conversationally, at home or elsewhere, Terence Greene's usual response had been none at all.

Phyllis, who had spent hours summoning her courage

to speak with Terence on another, far more urgent subject, now regretted having brought up this vexatious subject. Emotion welled in her voice; she so detested Studs Schrieber, she feared she was losing control. "I wish he *had* died, to tell the truth! At least, that he *was* gone. Safely away—somewhere."

Terence shook his head, as if to clear it. "He *is* dead. I mean—he was. Wasn't he?"

Phyllis said, "There never was any body found, and though the police claim to have questioned a lot of people involved in drugs around here and in Philadelphia, no one seems to know anything definite. If the Schriebers don't know, I doubt that he *is* back—it's probably just teenage fantasizing. Can we please change the subject?"

Terence had picked up the brass letter opener again, and was turning it distractedly in his fingers. "You say—someone called Kim? I'd better talk to her."

Phyllis was dismayed. "But why? Why talk to her? Call Marian Ryan if you want to, but leave Kim out of it. You'll just upset her—you know what girls that age are like."

"I'm not sure that I do. I'm not sure that I know what anyone is like any longer."

"Well, teenagers tend to be morbid about certain things. It's wisest not to indulge them."

Terence's face had grown warm; Phyllis could see oily beads of sweat at his hairline. If they were not having so tense a conversation *and if she still loved him* she would have wiped the sweat away with her fingertips.

Terence said abruptly, "Did *he* call her?—that's what I want to know."

"Who? What are you saying?"

"Did that—bastard, that—punk!—that *animal!*—call her? *That's what I want to know.*"

Terence's outburst was so sudden, the look of revulsion in his face so intense, Phyllis was almost frightened. She did not like the agitated way he was turning the letter opener in his fingers, gripping it by its sharp blade as well as its handle.

"Terry, I told you," she said, meaning to calm him, "—Suzi Ryan called her. And a few others from QDS. Certainly the —boy—himself has not called her. *No.*"

"She may have lied to you, Phyllis. She lies to us all the time. How do you know he hasn't called, if he's alive, and back?"

"Because Kim would have told me," Phyllis said. "I believe her. What do you mean by saying she 'lies to us all the time'? That's a terrible, cynical thing to say about your own—"

"Nevertheless it's true. Don't you know it's true?"

"Certainly not. I—love Kim. I love her very much. I—"

"She may love you too, and she may even love me, but that doesn't preclude lying to us. To whom would we care to lie, if not to our 'loved ones'?"

This bold admission was at once so blunt, and so subtle, Phyllis was taken aback.

"You're being ridiculous now. You're not making sense. I wanted to talk to you about—something. And—"

"Surely you *are* talking to me about something?"

"Something more—personal. Private. I've been putting it off for a long time, and now I—"

Terence hunched his shoulders, still seated at the desk. It was clear that he was extremely agitated; and that he was making an effort to contain himself. If only he would stop fussing with that damned letter opener!

Through the twenty years of their marriage, Phyllis had often been exasperated by her husband's quirky, half-conscious mannerisms; but this was the first time she felt a bit unnerved. Her wifely instinct was simply to reach over and remove the knife from his fingers, as one might do with a child, but a strange observation of her mother's, made at the time of Mrs. Winston's last visit, gave her pause. *Terence is a dangerous man. I'm afraid of him. I never want to be alone with him again.*

Fanny Winston had said this after a purported near-accident in Terence's car, when Terence was driving her home from the hairdresser's. Phyllis, who had not been present, and knew how her mother inclined toward hyperbole and melodrama, supposed she'd been exaggerating in describing the episode; Terence himself had said he'd skidded a bit, that the brakes on the Oldsmobile needed repair. But Phyllis's mother had persisted in thinking there was more to it than that, and, when she'd spoken most recently with Phyllis on the phone, she'd said she intended to revise her will —with the intention of leaving her son-in-law out.

Phyllis had been impatient with the older woman's complaints, which, she didn't doubt, sprang from wounded vanity, and not from any accurate perception of poor Terence. But now, uneasily watching Terence at his desk, turning the letter opener in his fingers, breathing audibly and sweating, she herself felt a stab of alarm. *Dangerous man. Afraid of him. Never want to be alone with him again.*

Phyllis said, hesitantly, "We haven't really talked together, Terry, in a very long time. I don't mean that it's your fault—it's both our faults equally. I've been so—busy. And you—at the Foundation, and—traveling—as much as you do. I— Oh God, this is so hard to say—"

Terence sighed, or was it a stifled sob? He flung the letter opener away from him, probably not intending so careless a gesture; The letter opener struck a squat ceramic vase filled with pens and pencils, and everything toppled off his desk and fell noisily to the floor.

Phyllis flinched. She hoped that Kim and Cindy were both asleep. She hoped that they would not mistake the noise for something it was not.

Terence said, with a melancholy little smile, "You don't have to tell me, Phyllis. I think I know. You're in love with another man, and you believe you want to divorce me, and marry him. Matt Montgomery—yes?"

Now Phyllis could not contain her emotion. Tears filled her eyes, and ran down her cheeks, more swiftly than she could prevent. She felt, in that instant, all her old, lost love for Terence Greene—an unspeakable sense of longing, embraced and then relinquished.

She said, in a choked voice, yet wifely and reproving even now, "Oh, Terry!—not Matt. *Mickey Classen.*"

For some months, since approximately September of the previous year, Phyllis Greene had suspected that her husband Terence was leading a double life. *He rarely makes love to me anymore* had been yet more grimly replaced by *He rarely looks at me anymore!* It was Phyllis's fixed idea, however, that Terence was having an affair—no doubt, he imagined himself "in love"—with one of his young woman assistants at the Foundation.

(Phyllis had no real reason to think this. But had not her own father, that figure of rectitude the Reverend Willard Winston, had, if not an actual affair, a "serious flirtation" with an attractive young secretary, when Phyllis was in high school?—hadn't the Winstons' seemingly unshakable marriage been cruelly shaken, with permanent results? Phyllis, never directly told anything, had inferred much, with the hurt, vengeful passion of an adolescent girl, and she had never forgotten.)

It would not have occurred to Phyllis to suspect anyone in Queenston, for she'd long had the sense that Terence was not at ease in Queenston.

Phyllis herself had, over the years, enjoyed romantic friendships with a number of Queenston men of her immediate social circle, and beyond. In so affluent and self-regarding a community, such "friendships"—shading sometimes, though not inevitably, into "affairs"—are not uncommon. Phyllis Greene was an attractive, ebullient, much-admired local personality; her husband was well liked, though considered, in some quarters, "too intellectual"— "too serious." It was natural that Phyllis emerge as the more popular of the Greenes, natural that she play tennis with the husbands of those friends who did not themselves play tennis, natural that she have lunch, and drinks, and occasionally even dinner, with male acquaintances who appealed to her sense of humor and "adventure." And Queenston Opportunities had brought her, surely not by design, numerous opportunities not restricted solely to business.

When Phyllis began seeing the husband of her friend Lulu Classen, in late December of the previous year, the theme of their relationship—such relationships, like adult education courses, always have "themes"—was the mutual wish for a simplicity of life, a "paring back to the essentials." Mickey felt most strongly, and Phyllis adamantly agreed, that the frantic nature of professional and social life in Queenston was depriving them of basic happiness—"What is money for, except to bring us peace of mind?" Mickey's complaint, surprisingly bitter in one who had always seemed resigned to his lot, was that his wife cared more for her "activities" than for *him*; Phyllis's complaint, which she knew to make wistful, not bitter, was that her husband cared more, far more, obsessively far more, for his work than for *her*. Mickey lent Phyllis an old, much-read hardback copy of Henry David Thoreau's *Walden*, the Bible of his life, to read; Phyllis, after some flurried searching amid cartons of books stored in a corner of the basement, discovered an aged and seemingly much-read paperback copy of *The Poems of Emily Dickinson*, which she lent Mickey to read—"The Bible of *my* life."

A subtheme of Phyllis's and Mickey's relationship, which evolved by quick degrees into a genuine affair, was that their spouses, both from "more modest backgrounds" than their own, placed too much of a premium upon social position, social reputation: They "worried too much" about how others perceived them. Conversely, Lulu was often slipshod in the quality of household help she hired, and allowed her hair to grow to an unbecoming length; she was overly indulgent with the children, out of moral weakness. And Terence!— well, Terence was impossible.

Phyllis told Mickey, sighing, laughing, "I doubt that that man could dress himself, even choose a decent necktie, except for *me*."

And, "He's so weak with Aaron, I think he fears our son *not liking* him."

It went discreetly unspoken between Phyllis Greene and Mickey Classen that each was extremely well-to-do. Divorce would not drain their resources in the slightest, and setting up a new household, in a "more rural" part of Queenston Township, would be an exhilaratingly exciting prospect. Phyllis had "always felt cramped, constrained" in the house at 7 Juniper Way, Mickey had "always wanted more acreage, real woods." A clay tennis court, an Olympic-sized swimming pool. Separate guest quarters. A studio for Phyllis. A kiln for Mickey, who had longings to be a potter, in which to "fire" his pots. Their spouses—the nervously sweet-smiling Lulu, the earnest, unfailingly courteous Terence—were perceived as selfish, restraining presences, like jailers, or bloated spiders inhabiting houses long outgrown. How hard, suddenly, to *breathe* in their company!

Unknown to Mickey, as it would be unknown to Terence, was the fact that, yes, Phyllis had been "involved" with Matt Montgomery—but the affair had scarcely lasted six weeks, and had ended with such unfeeling abruptness on Montgomery's part, Phyllis did not think it counted, really. She'd wept, a bit; she *had* been humiliated; yet, Matt Montgomery being the man he was, far and away the most sexually attractive of the Queenston men of his set, how could she resent him, for long? When now they met socially, Matt behaved as he'd always done; quite as if nothing had ever happened between them—no delirious kisses, no rapturous exchanges of pleasure. After her initial shock, Phyllis took her cue from Matt Montgomery, and learned to behave the same way.

In time, she didn't doubt, she would forget, entirely—for she'd never loved any man as she loved Mickey Classen.

"Not Matt, but Mickey!—my God, I would never have guessed."

Not once but several times, Terence Greene so exclaimed, staring at his wife as if he had never seen the woman before.

They wept in each other's arms. Talked, and wept; wept, and talked. Not in Terence's study but in the family room, in a farther wing of the house where it was less likely they would be overheard. Toward 2 A.M., Phyllis suggested they open a bottle of white wine—that good, expensive French wine the Classens themselves had brought over one evening last winter—to calm their nerves.

Then suddenly they were naked, naked as newlyweds, and weeping in each other's arms, and a frantic need overcame them to make love—not as they had been doing for years, but in the way of their early passion, their youth. "I love you," one whispered, and the other, "I love *you*." Terence, with tightly shut eyes, tried to summon back the image of his sensuous and provocative fiancée, the rich minister's daughter; Phyllis tried to summon back the image of her handsome, hungry young fiancé. Neither succeeded.

Yet wasn't there relief of a kind in this, their mutual failure? That their wine-soaked kisses were not after all enough to rekindle an old, outgrown passion? Not merely relief but forgiveness, even affection. Lying together a bit awkwardly on the nubby sofa in front of the cavernous, darkened fireplace, in each other's arms, and naked. For the final time.

After some time Phyllis asked if Terence was awake, and Terence indicated yes, and Phyllis said, gently, almost shyly, "You don't have to tell me, Terry, if you'd rather not. About your—" pausing, not knowing how tactfully to phrase it, your own friend? lover? secret life? until Terence helped her out by saying, "Phyllis, there is no one," and Phyllis said, as if rebuffed, "*No* one?" and Terence said, flatly, "No one," and Phyllis said, "But—wasn't there? Wasn't there someone?" and Terence said, "I really don't know, dear. Maybe, in fact, no."

Awkwardly drifting off to sleep as they did, neither slept well; toward morning, Phyllis quietly slipped away, to tiptoe upstairs to her own bed, and Terence, who had feigned sleep until Phyllis left, went away upstairs to his. There, groggy and faintly nauseated, he fell into sleep as into a deep lightless quarry.

I am a dead man, my life is over. My life is given me to begin.

And this was a coincidence of those turbulent hours: Terence woke abruptly from a dream of childhood in which both intense yearning and anxiety were commingled, to discover Phyllis, in a yellow terrycloth bathrobe, hair damp from the shower, calling his name. She smiled hesitantly, she was carrying a breakfast tray. Now there were no secrets between them, she said, she had something further to tell him. And, as she spoke, Terence realized that he'd been dreaming of his lost, dead mother Hettie Greene when Phyllis entered the room and wakened him.

Phyllis's secret was, strictly speaking, the elder Winstons'—they had extracted from her the reluctant promise, nearly twenty-five years ago, never to tell Terence. But now she would tell him. How, when Phyllis had fallen unexpectedly in love with Terence and decided, yes, she would marry him (a graduate student already in debt from college loans, a rawboned young man seemingly without any family), the Winstons had, outrageously, and without Phyllis's knowledge, hired a private detective to investigate their prospective son-in-law's background—"I was furious with them, checking up on you in such a way. As if you, the wonderful young man you seemed to be, weren't enough for Father and Mother!"

Terence Greene, the wonderful young man now middle aged, steeled himself to listen.

And so, within the space of a few minutes, on a warm July morning after the night in which his marriage dissolved, Terence Greene at last learned the rudiments of his lost life:

His mother had died "by her own hand"—hanged herself with a towel—in a jail cell in a county jail in upstate New York; she'd hanged herself two days into her trial for second-degree felony murder and as an accomplice to armed robbery.

Terence's father, who had in fact committed the crimes, shooting to death a bartender in a country tavern during a robbery, had not lived to stand trial—he'd been shot by police trying to escape.

Terence's mother's name was Hetitia Greene, born in Tintern Falls, New York, daughter of a farming family; she'd been twenty-three years old when she died. Terence's father's name was "something very ordinary, like Mack Smith, Mike Smith," and he too was from the Tintern Falls area, discharged from the Navy, served one or two prison sentences for car theft; he'd been in his mid-thirties when he died of multiple bullet wounds.

Terence, his young mother's only child, born "out of wedlock," had been two years old when his mother committed suicide.

Terence's father had died during a high-speed car chase. Hettie Greene and two-year-old Terence had been in the car with him.

When Smith was struck by police bullets his car had swerved off the road and overturned several times in a snowy field. Hettie Greene and her little boy, passengers in the rear seat, had been injured and hospitalized. Smith had died in the wreck.

It was Hettie Greene's claim that she'd been an unwilling accomplice to the robbery, the murder. She told police, and would later testify at her trial, that Smith, with whom she'd been living for several years, had often beaten her, and threatened to kill both her and their son if she didn't do everything he commanded.

There had been other thefts, armed robberies, committed by Smith, and Hettie Greene had been an "unwilling accomplice" to these, too. And she had a juvenile record—"runaway child." And there were "contradictions" in her various testimonies.

The tone of the trial—"I suppose the detective looked up newspaper accounts?"—was heavily against the defendant, when Hettie Greene took her life. Had she been convicted of both second-degree felony murder and as an accomplice to armed robbery, she might have been sentenced to as many as seventy years in prison.

After Hettie Greene's death, her son Terence was taken in by a succession of relatives, scattered through New York State. There were no further incidents of a "public nature" in his life.

Terence Greene did well in all the schools he attended, and eventually won a scholarship to the State University of New York at Binghamton. There, he excelled, and—"Which brought us up to the present time, when 'Terence Greene' met 'Phyllis Winston,' and they became engaged."

Phyllis, who had been speaking earnestly, yet a bit disjointedly, as if without having prepared beforehand much of what she intended to tell Terence, was clearly enjoying the drama, the *pathos*, of the moment. Terence's silence and the utter stillness of his posture, the rapt expression in his eyes, provided her with the ideal mood in which this old, near-forgotten secret might be revealed. Had it not been for Terence's hand shaking as he lifted his coffee cup, Phyllis might have supposed him unmoved; or, so fatally engaged by her words, he had no need to respond to them.

She said, with an air of girlish complaint, "Imagine—Father and Mother thought this report might make me reconsider marrying you! I remember Father, who in fact liked you, Terry, as a person, very much, taking me into his study and telling me in the gravest voice I'd ever heard, 'The sins of the fathers are visited on the heads of the sons'—then going on to talk about heredity, genetics, that sort of thing." Phyllis paused. Terence had now set down his coffee cup, was rubbing his eyes, was perhaps on the verge of tears; Phyllis alarmed herself that *she* might cry. "I told him, Terry, I remember I stood right up and banged my fist on his desk—that desk that's yours now—and said, 'Call yourself a minister of the Lord?—a Christian man? Saying such things about the man I love?' I told him and Mother that I was going to marry you with or without their blessing, and that was that. I was damned stubborn in those days!''

How like a heroine Phyllis Greene was emerging, so unexpectedly in her own eyes: she who, the previous night, had revealed herself as an adulterous and unrepentant woman!

Terence said, quietly, "You were brave."

He set down the coffee cup, and went to a window, to gaze out at the rear yard. Phyllis came quickly up behind him, and touched his shoulder. "Terry, are you all right? *Should* I have told you? Would you rather not have known?''

Terence did not reply; seemed not to have heard. Phyllis felt a clammy heat about his body. (He was in a cotton undershirt and shorts.) She went on, worriedly, "And such a shock, after last night. . . . You know, I'd always wondered, in a way, why you never made much of an effort to find out more about your past, as an adult. Going to court records, even hiring a private detective. If I'd been you, I would have wanted to know."

Terence did not move away from Phyllis's touch, but he did not seem to encourage it. He said, still looking out the window, at the massed evergreens and tall, leafy deciduous trees stretching to the rear of their property, "Maybe I already knew. I just didn't want to remember."

"We'll never tell the children—of course. Or"—and here Phyllis hesitated, delicately—"Mickey. I promise."

More briskly now, Terence said, "Well, we have many more practical things to discuss, than ancient history. I should move out, I suppose?—isn't that what's usually done? How soon do you want me gone?''

Phyllis shuddered. "Oh, Terry, that word 'gone'—it sounds so—final." She paused, tears welling in her eyes. In a gesture of wifely intimacy she pressed her forehead, and her damp eyes, against the back of Terence's cotton undershirt. "Maybe—by next Monday?''

The Summons

*S*trange *that it should have come to me by way of her, and not in memory, or a dream* though now, as if a trigger had been sprung deep in his soul, Terence was dreaming far more frequently than ever before in his life, and so vividly! In the melancholy-echoing house at 7 Juniper Way in which he lived alone for most of August, and, later, in his single-bedroom "luxury" apartment off Queenston Square.

Though sedated with drink as he was most nights, how strange that Terence Greene was capable of dreaming at all, or remembering, upon waking, that he had.

A young woman who is my mother, her frightened eyes. Squeezing me against her breasts. No no don't look! A man who is my father. His dark-stubbled jaws, blood-threaded angry eyes. Harsh hacking cough. And blood exploding out of his mouth as bullets tear into the back of his head.

Hettie Greene: only a girl, so young. Hanging herself in a county jail cell. The courtroom, the trial. The judge's high bench. The American flag behind the bench. The odors of wet wool, wet rubber boots. The sheriff's deputies, their impassive faces, eyes. Their holstered pistols. Everyone in the courtroom staring at the frightened young woman giving testimony. Condemning her beforehand—*guilty as charged.*

These sights, which I never saw. I was too young to have seen. I would not have been allowed to have seen. Yet—"So vivid, the nightmare, I *must* have been there."

Terence moved out of his house forever on August 29, well in advance of his family's return on September 7. (Labor Day came late this year.) Leaving the house with few possessions, yes with a backward glance of regret and, unexpectedly, a sharp pang of loss recalling the evening he'd carried poor Tuffi wrapped in an old beach towel for a winding sheet and buried him amid the evergreens, the soft earth fragrant with their needles.

That punk! that animal! with the gold ring through his nose had fallen there too, but Terence had not buried him there. Terence had not taken the trouble to bury him, at all.

Dreaming more frequently, and more luridly, now. Sprawled in his sweaty underwear across his bed. *Maggots I said, and maggots I mean. You men!* He woke, startled, to the sound of female laughter.

These were lengthy heat-stuporous days as summer waned, and even longer nights. *Never that woman. Treacherous woman. Again.* Even when sober and upright returning from the depot, attaché case in hand, walking to his apartment because it was only a matter of two blocks now, even then he seemed never to remember which doorway was *his*, that it was *that doorway* he must turn into, The Queenston Square Arms, a few steps from Qwik-Copy (photocopying, faxing services) to the right and Yogurt Delite to the left.

(Young teenagers patronized Yogurt Delite and hung about on the sidewalk. Terence Greene averted his eyes, not wanting to see his children, and be seen by them. But, of course, they were away—his daughters in Nantucket, his son in the West. Spared of being embarrassed by Daddy.)

Yes, he'd cooperated. He would instruct his lawyer to

cooperate with Phyllis's lawyer. He'd moved out of 7 Juniper Way well in advance of Phyllis's deadline, and surrendered all his keys. Terence Greene was a gentleman and would remain a gentleman until the unspeakable end.

And how considerate of Phyllis, after all: She'd changed her mind about kicking him out so abruptly, decided it would be a better idea if she, Kim, and Cindy went up early to Nantucket, to stay with her mother *I regret I didn't kill when I had the opportunity* for the rest of the summer. (Mickey had taken a house on Nantucket, too. An arrangement made months ago, without Lulu's knowledge.) This way, Phyllis said, Terence could remain at home to make his plans for the future under less pressure.

After the first flush of excitement, and personal triumph—how much the center of things Phyllis Greene had become!—Phyllis had taken on the less gratifying role of mediator, organizer. She professed an "agonizing concern" that the children not be "traumatized." She seemed to worry that Terence, in his very docility, or indifference, was making a bad impression.

Saying, in mild reprimand over the telephone, "This is damned hard on all of us, Terry. Not just *you*."

I want to confess to several crimes. I am uncertain how to go about it. One murder occurred in Trenton, last September: The victim's name was (is?) Eldrick Gill. A second murder occurred in Manhattan, in April of this year: The victim was the well-known poet Quincy Ryder, whose death in a ninth-floor fall was ruled "accidental." A third murder occurred in Queenston, New Jersey, in July: The victim was a young man named Studs Schrieber (Edward Schrieber, Jr.) whom police believe to be "missing." His body will be found, by now in a state of advanced putrefaction, in a rolled-up carpet in a ravine/landfill off Route 22 in rural Hunterdon County.

Each of these parties deserved death. I did not in fact intend to kill them. Nonetheless, I am the perpetrator. I wish to surrender myself immediately to the proper authorities. I forgo all legal counsel. I plead GUILTY. I will cooperate fully with police. I will not hang myself in the midst of my trial. This, you self-righteous bastards, I promise. So help me God.

Waking groggy and stubble-jawed, fallen across his bed. Was the telephone ringing? Was it his alarm clock? Terence sat up, wincing from the pain in his head, he'd drunk himself into a virtual coma the night before, but which morning was this?—Sunday, or a weekday?

He saw, amid the rumpled bedsheets, the handwritten letter he'd composed the night before. *I want to confess to several crimes. I am uncertain* . . . Appalled, he snatched up the sheet of paper and crumpled it in his fist.

Don't grieve, son. Your secret is safe with us.

At the Foundation, thank God no one knew (or did they?) of the breakup of Terence Greene's marriage. In time, he would have to tell Mrs. Riddle, and Marcia. But they were on their vacations now, until Labor Day. The single secretary in the office, seated at Mrs. Riddle's desk, was a relatively new employee. Smiling shyly, Good morning, Dr. Greene! but her eyes shrewdly watchful.

The young woman was black, not Haitian like Jamahl the security guard downstairs, yes but black-skinned. By now, the two had very likely become acquainted, *what had Jamahl told her of Terence Greene?*

Amid a stack of mail one morning in early September there was a perfumy mauve envelope, Terence's name and the address of the Foundation neatly printed in oversized block letters in bright purple ink, and on front and back were exclamatory warnings: PERSONAL PLEASE! and CONFIDENTIAL PLEASE!

Terence stared at this envelope, which was postmarked Trenton, N.J.

With the unthinking reflexes of a man protecting himself from a venomous snake he flicked it across his desk with the tip of a letter opener, no force on earth could make him open it, yet somehow he'd retrieved it and opened it, his

hands shaking so badly whatever it was she'd sent him—
petals?—rose petals?—fell to the floor, he squatted picking
them up, yes they were rose petals, fragrant dusky-pink petals
edged with ivory, and the ivory shading into cream, so exquisitely beautiful his eyes filled with tears even as he whispered, "No. No. *No.*"

There was nothing else in the envelope.

Even now when Phyllis called him, Terence was likely to
be vague, affable, polite, *off in a world of his own.* Thinking of
not thinking of her of her who had betrayed him, no force on
earth could make him see that woman again unless to demand from her a full explanation, an apology. And even then
he would never *he would never!* forgive her.

"Terry?" Phyllis's voice was shrill, as if she were in the
room with him. "Is something wrong? Didn't you hear me?
Is there—someone there with you?"

Terence absentmindedly glanced about the room (a living room, furnished by strangers) before replying. "Here?
Of course not."

And then, in the end, Terence Greene could not stay
away.

One warm, stagnantly humid afternoon, soon after Labor Day, he decided to drive to Trenton, without telephoning
Ava-Rose Renfrew. He told himself, *She will be there, and all
will be again as it was.*

Would she have summoned him to her, as she had,
otherwise?

The perfumed envelope, with the bruised and wilted
rose petals inside, he carried in his shirt pocket close against
his heart.

He thought perhaps it might have pleased Ava-Rose and
the other Renfrews, that he'd paid the mortgage on their
house even for those months when he hadn't seen Ava-Rose.
He had not cancelled his $500,000 life insurance policy.

"For of course I love her. I'm not going to give her up."

Terence was reluctant to drive to 33 Holyoak immediately. He recalled his last visit there, when, so clearly, his old friend Holly Mae Loomis had tried to deceive him. He recalled that young cousin of Ava-Rose's, the boy chasing the Pomeranian—there was something about him that had made Terence most uneasy.

Instead, he drove to the Chimney Point Shopping Center, to see if Ava-Rose was there.

But Tamar's Bazaar & Emporium was closed, with a look of having been closed for some time. "This can't be!"—Terence shaded his eyes and peered into the interior of the store, into a vague dreamy dimness that looked coated with dust. The CLOSED sign hung at a tilt inside the window and a faint embalmed odor of incense pricked his nostrils.

Terence tried the door, rattling it; but of course it was locked.

Recalling how, that day, a very long time ago it seemed, he'd surreptitiously turned the sign in the door from OPEN to CLOSED. *Had it never been turned back?*

"Excuse me, mister—you looking for somebody?"

It was a heavyset oily-skinned man of middle age, whom Terence had noticed as he'd approached Tamar's, lounging in the doorway of Howard's Discount Shoes next door, chewing on a toothpick. The rudeness of his stare and his drawling question put Terence on the offensive, but he was determined to be polite. "Isn't this store open any longer? Has something happened?"

The man shifted his toothpick about, peering at Terence. He took note in particular of Terence's shoes, which were of good quality, with rawhide laces, but badly worn. As his eyes traveled up to Terence's face Terence saw that they had a curious yellow tincture, as if stained. "You got any special reason for asking, mister?" The accent was nasal, New Jersey, very like Tamar's.

Terence smiled in what he hoped was a disarming way.

"I'm acquainted with the young women who work here, and I just wondered what—where they are. I—"

"You're not acquainted with them real well, or you'd know, eh?"

Terence felt his face burn. But he continued to smile. He supposed the man with the toothpick was the proprietor of Howard's Discount Shoes, and if anyone knew what had happened to Tamar's Bazaar & Emporium it would be "Howard."

Terence said, "I hope the store hasn't gone out of business?"

"Whosit wants to know?"

Terence's face flushed more deeply. "I'm just a—customer, I suppose. I bought several items here, from both Tamar and—the other young woman—some months ago—very striking, lovely things—and I—I'd hoped to buy more. That's all."

Brooding, the shoe store proprietor shifted the toothpick about in his mouth. "Is it."

" 'Is it'—what?"

"Is it all."

"Has something happened? Have they relocated their business?"

(The disagreeable thought had just occurred to Terence that another man might have financed The Craft of Beauty elsewhere, at a more affluent shopping center. What a fool he'd been, nursing his hurt pride these many weeks!)

The shoe store proprietor said, with a smirking sort of doggedness, "There's two of 'em, mister, or was. They wasn't sisters, hardly. Wasn't in the business together."

"What do you mean—'was'?"

"You looking for Tamar, or—?"

Terence said impatiently, "Yes, Tamar. I'm looking for Tamar."

"Why yes, mister, I'm sure you are," the man said, winking, as if Terence's lie was a sort of link between them,

"—except you're kinda outa luck then. That little gal from Asbury Park, 'The Bulldog' I usta call her, just in fun, she was a pretend-Indian, y'know, wearing them 'sorries' and some weird red seed in her nose, we got along okay even if she had a dirty mouth for a gal—she's dead."

Terence stared blankly.

"She's dead, that's why the store's closed. Permanently."

"Dead—?"

"Yeah! 'Tamar'—what she called herself: That wasn't never her name, for sure—was found dead in the back of the store, about two months ago. The other one, the hippie fortune-teller 'Ava-Rose,' found her next morning, after she'd been dead, like, fifteen hours. There was a wild scene around here, I'm telling you." The shoe store proprietor watched Terence closely, shifting the toothpick about in his mouth.

Terence said, stammering, "But—how did she die? Was she—?"

"Strangled."

"Strangled! My God." Terence heard his voice, hollow-sounding, as if from a distance. He felt sick. And the thought of poor Ava-Rose, discovering her friend's body, sickened him the more.

"The cops said they wasn't sure if it was robbery, or what. There was a little money left in the cash register but they didn't know if maybe that's all there was supposed to be, business being kinda slow in the summer." The man's white shirt strained across the compact bulk of his stomach; he sighed massively. "Yeah, it was one wild scene around here, everything cordoned off for hours. We got on local TV."

"Do the police have any idea who—?"

"Whadja think, this is Trenton."

"But—they must have some idea. Some suspicions. I can't believe—"

"This Chimney Point, usta be there wasn't much crime. Now the nigger crackheads are all over."

Terence winced, the man spoke with such loathing; his eyes fairly glared yellow. Terence asked, "Do police think it was a drug-related crime? From your description, it doesn't sound as if it was. If any money at all was left behind—"

There followed then a furious, spittle-flecked outburst. "Howard's Shoes has been at this location eighteen years, and I been a resident of Chimney Point since 1957 and I'll tell you, mister, I could afford it, I'd leave tomorrow. Chrissake I *would*." Harshly, doggedly, the man spoke for several minutes, cursing; the name "Chimney Point" was so repeatedly evoked, Terence could not resist inquiring, like one who had only now thought of it, "Excuse me—why 'Chimney Point'? What does it mean?" The angry man broke off his diatribe to say, "Hell, it's the old crematorium, farther out the point—it's named for that. Big ugly old brick place, on a hill, built in 1900 and shut down maybe forty years, now."

Chimney Point—a crematorium!

A mother with two fretting children who had been looking into the display window of Howard's Discount Shoes now entered the store; and the proprietor, alert, hurriedly wiped his face with a tissue and followed after. Calling back over his shoulder, fatly smirking—"Well! Hope your luck improves, mister!"

Terence stared after him.

He saw, contemplating the façade of Tamar's Bazaar & Emporium, what should have been obvious from the first—the store was empty. It had that bleak, dead look. The dust-coated CLOSED sign in the door meant exactly what it said. It hung at a tilt as if carelessly, or even contemptuously, set that way. Terence was certain that he hadn't been the one to have hung it like that—had he?

Forbidden territory. Expelled from the jury.
Except—who was to know?

As Terence drove westward on Holyoak Street, through working-class neighborhoods, through a no-man's-land of small factories, railroad yards, vacant lots, past the fire-damaged Methodist church and the grim-looking Chimney Point Youth Detention Home, he felt a rising sense of antic-ipation, and dread. He had not seen, nor even spoken with, Ava-Rose Renfrew since that humiliating episode at the Church of the Holy Apocalypse—how would she greet him, now? The rose petals in the perfumed envelope were a sign, *but of what, exactly?*

He drove through the intersection of small shops. He saw, flinching, the derelict old cemetery and, atop a wooded hill, an old, gaunt building of soiled buff-colored brick, with tall blackened chimneys—the crematorium.

He drove on.

His mild anxiety reminded him of the first time he'd driven into this part of Trenton. So daringly, in the midst of the trial. In flagrant, and uncharacteristic, violation of the judge's instructions to the jury. How worried Terence had been that he might be discovered, and expelled from the jury—"Publicly exposed." And how needless that worry, in retrospect. For of course no one knew. *Who was there, who is there, to know?*

Terence Greene had lately grown to see that we inhabit a world of ever-shifting façades, panels, mirrors, mirrors re-flecting mirrors, in which a violent man might be shot dead fleeing a crime he had in fact committed and in which a woman might hang herself in despair of a fate she did not deserve; it was a world in which a man might disappear, in-deed dissolve, into a river, and no one would know, or, perhaps, knowing, greatly care. Another man might plunge to his death in unspeakable terror and this plunge will sub-sequently be interpreted as the "inevitable trajectory of a po-etic destiny" (for so the consensus now seemed to be among the late Quincy Ryder's friends and admirers, that the poet had not only committed suicide but had prefigured the act in his poetry, from his first book onward); yet another victim might boast, *I do what I wanta do, man, just like you*—even as his skull is smashed (for hadn't the flashlight shattered into pieces in Terence's hand, in that hideous dream, later wrapped up in the carpet with the body and tossed, like trash, into a ravine).

A world in which a young woman might be strangled by disembodied hands, a strangler's hands, *belonging to no one.*

Yet it was a world in which a lover might be led onward, as one submerged in water over his head will be led by the wayward movement of a straw connecting him with the air above, by a fragrance of rose petals.

A world in which, in fact, a man might be happy. A man long in search of Justice, very happy.

Never realizing until now *I myself am Justice.*

How relieved Terence was to see that the Renfrews' old barn of a house had changed so little!—despite the money he'd given the family for repairs over the past year.

There were still Christmas lights, many of them broken, wound about the rotted posts. On the sagging veranda, the same sofa, chairs, cast-outs. Areas of fresh paint and new repair work jarred with older areas and were equally overgrown with wild rambler rose and raggedy vines. And Holly Mae Loomis's jungle-garden was spilling over onto the sidewalk, a tangle of color. Terence breathed in its rich, ripe smells.

Nothing more beautiful.

He'd parked in the rutted driveway behind the yellow Corvette (which was looking a bit worse for wear—the rear bumper was sharply dented and the tailpipe dangled loose); as he got out of his car, he saw, on the steep-pitched roof of the house, a partly-naked figure clambering about—the young man, Randy Lee Turcoe?—his slender torso bare, and deeply tanned, and his glistening black hair in swaths to his shoulders. He gaped down at Terence as Terence gaped up at him. Then, seeing who it was, he yelled in boyish welcome, "Hey! Hiya! It's you, eh, Doc?"

Terence waved a bit diffidently in return. "Hello, Randy Lee."

Randy Lee squatted against the slant of the roof, as something white and furry rushed past him; he lunged, and grabbed it, and held it up struggling for Terence to see—a large fluffy dazzling-white angora cat with a remarkable plume of a tail. He called down, "Damn li'l bitch is always climbing up here, but *I* got her! Pretty, ain't she, Doc?"

Terence craned his head back, shading his eyes. Yes, the angora cat was pretty.

And Randy Lee Turcoe, whom Terence had forgotten entirely, was the most beautiful young man Terence had ever seen in the flesh.

The screen door banged open, and there stood Holly Mae Loomis in baggy overalls, a T-shirt, and a kerchief around her head. "Lord, if it isn't Dr. Greene! This is a real nice surprise—just in time for our picnic!" Holly Mae was grinning with unfeigned pleasure. She looked no different than ever except her left arm was in a sling. With a boisterous enthusiasm that could not fail to flatter Terence, she called over her shoulder, "Ava-Rose honey, c'mere! Quick! Somebody to see you!"

Terence bounded up the rickety steps of the veranda, and shook Holly Mae's hand. How good it was to see her!—how good, despite her injury, she looked!—her brass-colored hair freshly dyed, her cheeks suffused with color. Terence asked what on earth had happened to her arm, and she sighed, and rolled her eyes, and said it had been an accident, sort of—"An escalator going up at Quaker Bridge Mall kinda *jumped* and *jerked*, I swear, and pitched me right down. Damn ol' nasty machinery folks my age can't *trust*."

Terence said, "Why, Holly Mae, that's terrible. Are you in pain?"

"Well—not every minute. But my heart's gotten all fluttery, the least little things sets it off."

"Were there any witnesses?"

"Hell, yes. But I didn't get any names."

There came up behind Holly Mae, with a quizzical smile, hefty blond Chick—who called excitedly into the interior of the house, "Hey Ava-Rose! It's *him*!" Chick then burst out onto the veranda, and put out his hand to shake Terence's, with a masculine directness that was impressive. "Real nice to see you again, Doctor!—it's been a long time, we thought something'd happened to you."

"Chick, it's real nice to see *you*."

Terence noted that the boy had grown. His voice was a deep baritone and his jaws were blond-stubbly. His hair was cut so short in a shaved-looking crewcut that his head appeared disproportionately small on his shoulders. "Yeah, man, we was worried, kinda—that something'd happened to you."

Terence said happily, "In fact, I'm fine."

Holly Mae said, "And you do look fine."

"A good deal has changed in my life, since I've spoken with you last. I'm certainly sorry if I upset Ava-Rose, or any of you. I—"

But then, rushing out of breath, her hand to her throat and her magnificent brown-glinting hair spilling down her back, was Ava-Rose.

"How could you stay away so long, Ter-ence!—you nearabout broke my heart."

"I—didn't know. I'd thought—"

"So finally Auntie says to me, one night I'm moping and feeling real sorry for myself, 'You got a fatal case of pride, that's your trouble, girl,' and my eyes opened and I saw it was so. In the Book of the Millennium it is written, 'Pride is ashes in the mouth,' yet I had not grasped the taste in my very mouth! So first thing next day, I picked a rose from Auntie's garden, and sent you—what I did. Oh, Ter-ence, I had nearforgotten how good it is, to be humbled, and purified, and brought low. Emptied of all pride that love may flow in."

"And do you really love me, Ava-Rose? This isn't a dream?"

Like a little girl Ava-Rose laughed, and hugged Terence tight, and covered his face with warm, damp, percussive kisses. "Could be it *is* a dream," she said in a husky whisper, "—except if it is we're in it together, all cuddly."

Ava-Rose my darling.
Ava-Rose have mercy!

When at last they left Ava-Rose's room to come downstairs, hours had passed, and it was dusk. Everyone was outside in the back yard, setting up picnic things. There was a happy bustle of activity; a ringing sound of voices and laughter; the sharp odor of grilling meat made Terence's mouth water. How drained and ravenous love-making with Ava-Rose had left him!

The air was still warm and rather stagnant. Though stirred now and then by a light, thin breeze from the river.

The family was celebrating Labor Day, Ava-Rose explained—"Only just a little late."

Ava-Rose had slipped on a flimsy wraparound smock that came only to her knees; the fabric was near-transparent, and inside it her pale breasts seemed to float. Her long legs were bare, and so were her feet. She had removed all her jewelry, except for her numerous rings, and had not put it back on; her hair cascaded in a damp tangle down her back. (She and Terence had quickly showered together upstairs.) Her arm linked tightly through his, Ava-Rose led her lover into the midst of the Renfrews. Whispering in his ear, "Now don't you be shy, Terence. Everyone here is your friend."

And so indeed, to Terence Greene's dazed delight, it seemed.

There came Lily Pancoke to greet him, and to introduce him to her grown daughter Flossie; there came pretty, long-haired Donna, a girl of perhaps sixteen in low-slung jeans and a tiny halter top, who greeted Terence with a wet, giggly peck of a kiss on his mouth; there came Cap'n-Uncle Riff, his beard trimmed, in a blood-smeared white apron and a tall chef's hat, a giant pronged fork in hand—"Glad to have you aboard again, son." And there was a face Terence had not seen, nor even thought of, in over a year—belonging to the neighbor woman Ronnie Reuben, who had given testimony against T. W. Binder! And there was Corky Reuben, Ronnie's spouse. And others, new faces and new names. "Real nice to meet ya, Doctor!" "Real honored, Doctor!" Terence's hand was shaken numerous times. Buster leapt up to kiss him, trailing his long floppy tongue against Terence's face. Holly Mac Loomis gave Terence an enormous catsup-leaking hamburger to eat, and Chick gave Terence a brimming glass of Cap'n-Uncle's Chimney Point Stout. Randy Lee, bare-chested still, and, like Ava-Rose and most of the younger people, barefoot, brought a paper plate heaped with potato salad, coleslaw, pickled beets, Waldorf salad. In the din of voices Randy Lee's was too soft for Terence to hear, so the two stepped off to the side, into the taller grass. Randy Lee said, blushing, "Just wanted to say it ain't no business of mine, for sure, but I'm real glad you're back with Ava-Rose, Doctor. Poor gal missed you."

Terence said warmly, "Well, I missed Ava-Rose. I missed all of you."

Hearing her name, Ava-Rose broke off chatting with Lily Pancoke's daughter, and came over to Terence and Randy Lee, slipping a proprietary arm around Terence's waist; and fondly, though a bit roughly, poked her handsome long-haired cousin in the belly button. "You, Randy Lee! Don't you be telling tales on *me*, or I'll tell a tale or two on *you*."

Darling the parrot made everyone duck for cover as, shrieking and flapping his clipped wings, he attacked the picnic table, coming away with some of the meat gripped in his talons.

Children Terence had never seen before ran and larked about, playing hide-and-seek.

A brilliant glowering moon rose above the highest peak of the old house. Terence blinked and smiled upward.

Never so happy. Never in my life.

He was not drunk but yes he was intoxicated, you could say
he was mildly intoxicated, Cap'n-Uncle's home-brewed stout
went quickly to his head, Ava-Rose's kisses left him giddy and
breathless, *I want to live I want to live forever please have mercy.*
One of the girls—was it Donna?—or someone else, slightly
plumper, with more developed breasts—ran over and tugged
at Terence's hand, there was dancing, loud rockabilly music
and laughing shrieking careening dancing, even Holly Mae
with her arm in a sling, stomping about in innocent abandon.
Chick, mischievous as a little boy, tossed a string of sparklers
high up into a willow tree, and the pinwheels of blazing light
and the *pop! pop! pop!* made everyone gape.

"Lord save us, I thought it was gunfire!"—Lily Pancoke
stood swaying, frightened, her hand pressed against her
breast.

The rockabilly music was deafening. Had Terence
Greene ever danced like this before in his life? He stumbled,
and righted himself; he kicked off his shoes, and danced in
his stocking feet; then pulled off his socks to dance barefoot,
like the young people. His heart leapt in his chest.

Ava-Rose was his partner now, breathless, giggling, her
lovely face glowing with exertion. Terence must have done
something comical and touching, for Ava-Rose stopped to
seize his face between her hands and kiss him full on the lips.
A talcumy-musky scent rose from her armpits.

Near by, comely Randy Lee Turcoe danced alone, wrig-
gling his shoulders, vigorously shaking his hips and pelvis.
He seemed not to mind that he was dancing alone, or was
he jealous of Terence Greene and his cousin?—eyeing them
through his long lashes, even as he spun indifferently away,
head flung back and long black hair flying.

The women were taking away dirtied paper plates, food
scraps. Buster was greedily devouring something that had
fallen underfoot, and the fluffy white angora cat pussyfooted
her way across the picnic table, her elegant plume of a tail
erect.

Cap'n-Uncle Riff, his chef's cap removed, stood tall and mock-somber beneath the bright moon. As all gathered around, he lifted a toast to Terence Greene and Ava-Rose; and all joined in.

"Children—a long and happy life! Blessings."

"Thank you, Cap'n-Uncle." Terence, deeply moved, raised his glass in turn to the old man, and drank thirstily. How the dark, tart, potent brew burned, going down! Ava-Rose snuggled in the crook of Terence's arm, and had a sip of the stout. Yes it was *strong*.

Darling the parrot, on a high perch of a nearby tree, flapped his clipped-looking wings and squawked—"Beeyyyt peeze! Beeeyyyt PEEZE!"

It was late. Though the night air was balmy and humid, with a metallic undertaste. The moon had shifted in the sky.

A midnight swim!—at once the cry was taken up by the younger Renfrews. *Yes, yes! A swim off the Point!*

It was a short breathless hike to the river. Terence did well to keep pace with the others, his arm around Ava-Rose's waist and Ava-Rose's arm around his waist. Stumbling a bit. Wincing. Damn!—the soles of his feet were so tender, it was hard for him to walk barefoot like the others in the rutted, pebbly lane.

The lane led downhill, at first gradually, then steeply. Through a tunnel of low-hanging branches and scrubby bushes, to the riverbank—and how wide the Delaware River, seen from this perspective, as Terence Greene had never seen it before, on foot, in fact barefoot, in a state of excitation bordering on euphoria. How wide, how beautiful!—how splendid by moonlight! Terence stared entranced.

Strange how, on the Pennsylvania shore, so few lights glittered. The land was curiously massed, dark. As if sparsely populated. Except for the rippling-swift current of the river, all was still.

A pewter-radiance fell over, or seemed to lift from, all surfaces. Except the massive old railroad bridge that spanned the river a quarter-mile to the left: The bridge was lightless, sheerly black, and its shadow floated and bobbed in the water sheerly black.

They were to swim as it seemed they frequently swam— all save Ava-Rose's friend Dr. Greene—from the straggly spit of land called the Point to the first concrete abutment beneath the bridge, where there was a ledge. Terence had a vague sense of the distance—"Hell, it's nothing. I swim three times that at the pool."

Except: hadn't so much happiness left him giddy, lightheaded.

Except: *Why am I here, who are these people, these strangers?*

Shy about stripping in front of the young people, shy about swimming naked, they laughed at him, fond and teasing-playful as children, as his own children years ago, Ava-Rose whispered in his ear she was embarrassed too, but— " 'Even shame shall be taken from you, at the last.' "

There was much hilarity. Terence's laughter rose with the others'. Chick, drunk or seeming-drunk, tore off his black T-shirt and waved it like a flag. "Whooee! Gonna beat y'all!"

Randy Lee had only jeans to strip—beneath, he was naked and pale as something prized out of its shell. The tender white of his buttocks contrasted sharply with his tanned back.

Bravely, laughing and biting her lower lip, Ava-Rose undid the sash of her flimsy shift, and removed the shift, and let it slip from her fingertips onto a rock. Terence, who was fumbling with the buttons of his shirt, could not bear to look at her, she was so beautiful.

And Randy Lee, with his perfectly proportioned body, his near-hairless chest, his chiseled-looking St. John the Baptist face—so beautiful.

Don't look.

Something hotly acidic rose in Terence's throat, he feared he might vomit. But he swallowed it quickly down.

Giggling wildly like children, Ava-Rose and Randy Lee competed helping Terence out of his clothes. Tugging off his trousers. His boxer shorts. So it was decided, yes he would swim with the rest.

The tip of Chimney Point had no beach, nor even sand. It was just rocks, large rocks, pocked and pitted rocks, rocks covered in slimy moss, and a scattering of pebbles. Styrofoam debris bobbed trapped against the rocks close to shore.

The waves were languid, and foamy. Except when choppy and urgent.

There was no wind. Except every fifth wave slapped against Terence's ankles hard enough to sting.

He smelled something faintly sulphurous. A near-imperceptible breeze, hardly more than a restless stirring of the air, touched his overheated face and body—his torso, stomach, pubic area, narrow muscular thighs. He shivered in anticipation and dread. *Yes but you can still turn back.*

Wondering where, off the Point, what remained of Eldrick Gill lay at the bottom of the river, undiscovered.

Wild-eyed Donna and another girl who'd been shyly shielding their breasts cried, "Oh hell—c'mon!" and waded out into the water splashing and squealing.

Chick, so big and fatty-muscled he seemed more naked than the others, had clambered out onto a jutting rock, showing off as, with a yodel, he dived into the river—surfacing some yards out, head slick as a seal's, swimming with wide flailing powerful strokes.

Ava-Rose gripped Terence's right hand, and Randy Lee gripped his left hand, urging him out. The slapping dark ill-smelling water rose to their knees, then to their thighs. Ava-Rose squealed, "Oh Lord!—it's *cold!*" and Randy Lee chided, "Nah, it's *warm*, ain't it, Doctor?"

Terence said, "It's—perfect."

The three of them pushed out and began to swim, at first keeping abreast of one another like coordinated swimmers. Then, Randy Lee began to swim away, and Ava-Rose with her slightly flurried butterfly stroke pulled away, and

Terence, despite his exertions, began to fall behind. The
river was surprisingly cold, in contrast to the muggy air; the
waves were rough, choppy and dense, as if made of a different substance from that of the chlorinated aqua-bright water
of the Queenston Athletic Club. Terence tasted panic, for his
body was somehow not his own; it was a stranger's clumsy
body, swimming poorly, with an uncharacteristic desperation,
fingers spread ineffectually so that water slipped through, yes
and this body was leaden, belly stuffed hideously with food
and bloated with liquid, shoulder muscles cramped as if he
hadn't exercised for months. *Yes, but you can still turn back: it
isn't too late, you can save yourself.* But Terence Greene could
not give up, could not bear to shame himself in the company
of the young Renfrews.

Nor even call after them, sputtering and gasping, begging—*Ava-Rose! Randy Lee! Wait!*

The others, five or six of them, or more, swam splashing
gaily ahead through rippling moonlight into the shadow of
the bridge. Terence, blinking water from his eyes, trying to
clear his clotted vision, could only vaguely make out the pale
bodies several yards ahead of him in the water, their bare
kicking feet, their swordlike muscular legs, swift-flashing
arms. If only he could be like them, if he could be one of
them! His lungs were strained nearly to bursting. His heart
pounded in desperation to send oxygen to his brain. *Swimming for my life, I will not turn back.* She'd left him once, abandoned him to an empty, jeering world, *Hettie's boy! Hettie's boy!*
many years ago when he'd been a small child and helpless
and lacking a voice and this time he would not surrender
her, he would clutch at her, keep her, oh God he loved her
so, loved her far more than his own life, for what was his life,
without her? And now it was too late to turn back and there
was a comfort, a relief, in that, in the knowledge that it was
too late to turn back, he'd come too far to turn back. The
oily waves slapped, nudged, mauled. How like human fists.
Swimming for my life through moonlight like broken pieces
of crockery, swallowing water, choking, unable to breathe ex-

cept through his mouth, his breath like torn strips of cloth, legs heavy and shoulder muscles cramping as if it was a stranger's body in which he was trapped, doomed. Yet his senses remained alert, sharpened. Seeing ahead the agile swimming figures in the treacherous water as they passed swiftly into the shadow of the bridge, their flashing white feet, legs easing from him—*Help me! Don't leave me! Wait!*

Then, somehow, it happened. Terence's desperation, his death-terror, pumped adrenaline to his heart, oxygen to his brain. For suddenly he began to swim with more efficiency and assurance; the frantic strokes of his arms, the thrashing of his legs, seemed to release strength. *Yes! like this! this!* He was stubborn, even in his exhaustion. He would not give up, sink. He would not drown. As the others reached the abutment about twenty feet ahead, Terence came up doggedly from behind, knocked about by the choppy water but swimming as he'd been taught, as his Uncle Frank had taught him, head erect, maintain your rhythm, don't breathe through your mouth, don't panic, look straight ahead and don't shut your eyes. Swallowing more of the dank poisonous water and choking at its vileness but—he would not give up!

Ava-Rose, her slender body streaming water, climbed laughing and breathless up onto the part-crumbled concrete ledge, assisted by Randy Lee; a call from Terence drew their attention, as if they'd forgotten him, and they turned to stare in a kind of perplexity at him, struggling in the water. And now all the Renfrews, lined up on the ledge below the bridge, were staring at Terence Greene there in the river. Their Renfrew faces glimmering pale in the deep shadow of the bridge.

Unbelievably, Terence had managed to swim to the very foot of the abutment, where rusted pipes like giant nails jutted out treacherously into the lapping water.

Terence choked, gasped—"Ava-Rose, give me a hand?"

Reaching up desperately, his entire arm trembling, toward the staring young woman. His breath came in shudders. His jaws were clenched in a smile. So very tired, so much more tired than ever he'd been in his life, yet at such a moment Terence was able to smile. He'd surprised these people, yes and he had more surprises for them, they would see.

"Ava-Rose, help me! I love you."

Across Ava-Rose's inscrutable face, sleek with river water, a quicksilver expression flitted. And Ava-Rose impetuously laughed, "Why, Ter-ence, what a good swimmer you are!"—extending her hand to his, helping the exhausted man to crawl up onto the ledge at her feet.

A NOTE ON THE TYPE ·

The typeface used in this book is a version of Baskerville, originally designed by John Baskerville (1706–1775) and considered to be one of the first "transitional" typefaces between the "old style" of the continental humanist printers and the "modern" style of the nineteenth century. With a determination bordering on the eccentric to produce the finest possible printing, Baskerville set out at age forty-five and with no previous experience to become a typefounder and printer (his first fourteen letters took him two years). Besides the letter forms, his innovations included an improved printing press, smoother paper, and better inks, all of which made Baskerville decidedly uncompetitive as a businessman. Franklin, Beaumarchais, and Bodoni were among his admirers, but his typeface had to wait for the twentieth century to achieve its due.